"I beg you to let me pass," Frances said desperately. "There is nothing to be said between us—nothing! Oh, pray believe me!"

"But there is," Crispin broke in gently. "Why are you afraid, Frances? Is it me you fear, or yourself?"

This struck too close to the heart of the matter; her ladyship took refuge in simulated anger.

"I tell you that I am not afraid of you! I know what you would say to me and I seek to spare you pain, for surely you can see how hopeless it is. Do you dare to speak to me of love—you, a pirate?"

In her haste and confusion the words were spoken before she realized what she was saying, and an ins̲t̲ ̲ ̲ ̲ter she would have given ̲ ̲ ̲ ̲ ̲ ̲ ̲have been able to r̲ ̲ ̲ ̲ ̲ ̲ ̲ ̲ ̲ ̲ ̲m-age was ̲ ̲ ̲ ̲

Fawcett Crest Books
by Sylvia Thorpe:

THE SWORD AND THE SHADOW

THE SCANDALOUS LADY ROBIN

CAPTAIN GALLANT

ROMANTIC LADY

THE RELUCTANT ADVENTURESS

TARRINGTON CHASE

THE SCARLET DOMINO

THE SCAPEGRACE

THE SILVER NIGHTINGALE

THE SWORD
and
THE SHADOW

A NOVEL BY

Sylvia Thorpe

A FAWCETT CREST BOOK

Fawcett Publications, Inc., Greenwich, Connecticut

THE SWORD AND THE SHADOW

THIS BOOK CONTAINS THE COMPLETE TEXT OF THE
ORIGINAL HARDCOVER EDITION.

A Fawcett Crest Book reprinted by arrangement with Hutchinson
Publishing Group, Ltd.

ISBN 0-449-22945-9

Printed in the United States of America

10 9 8 7 6 5 4 3 2

Book I

CHAPTER I

DESTINY AND CRISPIN BARBICAN

CAPTAIN CRISPIN BARBICAN—captain by virtue of the fact
that he had commanded a buccaneer craft under the great
Morgan—sat in a waterfront tavern in Bristol and tried to determine the future course of his life. He lounged on a high-
backed settle, booted legs outstretched and a pipe between his
lips, and stared reflectively into the fire blazing upon the open
hearth, indifferent alike to the babel of voices about him, and
the frankly admiring glances of the slatternly serving-wench
who passed to and fro among the tables.

Although it was a cold night in March, with a gusty wind
driving rain against the small and grimy windows, the seat by
the fire, of which Captain Barbican had taken possession
some time earlier, was not an unmixed blessing. At frequent
intervals the chimney belched forth an acrid cloud of smoke
which, trapped beneath the low ceiling, drifted slowly across
the room to mingle its choking reek with the odours of coarse
snuff, cheap wines and imported spices with which the atmosphere of the place was heavy. The patrons of the tavern were
for the most part sailors, lean, hard-bitten men bronzed by
tropic sun and bearing the scars of many a desperate fight, for
Bristol was the centre of the slave-trade and England's chief
trading port with those fabulous lands of blood and gold, the
West Indies. There was a sprinkling of women in stained and
tawdry finery, and here and there an apprentice or farm lad
listened open-mouthed to the wild tales which were bandied

5

to and fro, but though many covetous glances were cast towards the settle occupied by Captain Barbican, no one ventured to intrude upon his privacy until a party of sailors, some with women clinging to them, and all far gone in drink, burst noisily in from the street.

They were led by an ill-favoured fellow in a greasy velvet coat which accorded ill with his tarry breeches and great sea-boots. Although of no more than medium height, his massive shoulders suggested considerable strength, while his ranting voice and manner clearly bespoke the bully. There was a woman on his arm, a plump, black-haired girl, with moist red lips and a laugh which cut through the din like the scream of a parrot. She pulled off her cloak to shake the rain from it, revealing a green gown cut outrageously low, and complained stridently of the cold and wet.

Her cavalier peered through the murk in the direction of the fireplace, discovered the big settle occupied by a single figure, and led his party waveringly towards it. The Captain heeded their approach not at all. He sat very much at his ease, one hand supporting the long clay pipe, his elbow cupped in the palm of his other hand, his eyes fixed upon the flames. His coat of violet-coloured cloth was laced with silver; a broad black hat with a violet plume rested upon the settle beside him; there was a gleam of gold from the hilt of his long rapier. To the greasy ruffian lurching towards him this elegance suggested an easy prey, for he had never had the privilege of beholding Henry Morgan, in a finery of lace and velvet, leading his buccaneers upon a Spanish stronghold.

"Come to the fire, Moll," he said thickly. "Here's none to stay thee, an' if any tries, I'll break his scurvy neck, so I will." He halted by the settle and glared threateningly at its occupant. "Up, ye dawcock! Give room to your betters."

A burst of laughter from his companions applauded this witticism, and at neighbouring tables heads were turned towards the hearth. The Captain neither moved nor spoke; only from beneath his brows keen grey eyes cast one comprehensive glance at the group before returning to their contemplation of the fire.

The swaggering leader of the intruders was both surprised and annoyed by this indifference. For a moment he stared, then, growling an obscene oath, he dashed the pipe from the Captain's lips, to shatter it in a dozen pieces on the floor. The girl screamed with mirth and cried a lewdly-decked encouragement to her swain to carry out his threat.

6

Captain Barbican rose unhurriedly to his feet. In height he was some inches over six feet, so that his dark head brushed the smoke-blackened beams of the ceiling, while the width of the shoulders beneath the violet coat might have given the bully pause if he had had leisure to ponder them. He was not, however, given time for reflection. A lean, brown hand, on one finger of which a great emerald blazed, shot out and closed like a vice upon the nape of his neck, swinging him about, while another took an equally firm grip on the seat of his breeches. He was lifted bodily from the ground and hurled through the air to crash into the corner, smashing a rickety table to matchwood beneath him.

In the silence which followed, the Captain calmly resumed his seat and beckoned to the serving-girl, who was gaping blankly in the background. She came reluctantly.

"Fetch me another pipe, wench," he bade her, and tossed a gold coin into her ready palm. "There's to pay for any damage I may have caused."

She hurried away, and he became aware of the girl Moll standing at gaze before him, regardless of the fact that her companions were dragging the inert form of their leader towards the door, urged thereto by the landlord of the tavern, not all of whose patrons were as free with their gold as the taciturn stranger. Meeting the Captain's glance, Moll smiled invitingly and drew a pace nearer, but there was no response in the grim, dark face. The grey eyes regarded her bleakly.

"Your road lies yonder, mistress, with your friends." He jerked his head towards the door. "Best take it."

Moll was taken aback, and for a few seconds stared blankly upon him. The Captain resumed his study of the fire. Moll turned angrily on her heel and flounced out in the wake of her companions, followed by a burst of derisive laughter from those who had witnessed her discomfiture. Thereafter Captain Barbican was left severely alone.

He was, in fact, in no convivial mood that night. His had been a life of violent action, of hardship and danger, of riches quickly acquired and as quickly dissipated, a life which offered neither time nor desire for introspection, but tonight a mood of unwonted thoughtfulness had fallen upon him. He found himself reviewing that same life, from his childhood during the troubled years of the Civil War, through his narrow and restricted boyhood as the younger son of a country squire of Puritan sympathies, until, at the age of seventeen, he had set out in search of adventure beyond the dreary confines of Cromwell's England.

Adventure he had found in plenty. Shipping before the mast on a barque bound for Barbados, he stoically endured the discomfort, the bad food, and the floggings which were a daily occurrence, having always before his mind's eye the vision of the Indies, those lands of unimaginable wealth which he had made his goal. He was happily unaware of the fate awaiting him, as it awaited any penniless youth arriving in those fabled islands, of being sold as a bond-servant by the captain of the vessel to a master who regarded slaves as mere beasts of burden.

For five of the prescribed term of seven years Crispin Barbican laboured in the sugar-fields of Barbados before an opportunity of escape presented itself. Then, with a handful of his fellow-slaves, he broke free, stole a boat and provisions, and put to sea in an attempt to reach the pirate stronghold of Tortuga. Whether or not the mad scheme would have succeeded was never known, for the runaways were picked up by a galleon homeward bound for Spain, and short-handed as the result of an encounter with buccaneers.

They were forced to join her crew, with the prospect of the rack and fire of the Inquisition at the journey's end, but as Crispin had perceived nothing worth dying for in the religion in which he had been reared he promptly embraced the faith of his captors. His conversion was received with tears of joy and thankfulness by the Dominican friar who was chaplain of the vessel, but though Crispin had thus saved himself from the clutches of the Holy Office, he failed to purchase his freedom by the same means. Spain had suffered too much at the hands of the English sea-dogs to incline to mercy, and Crispin, because of his exceptional size and strength, was sent to the galleys.

There for a year he endured the miseries of the damned, in comparison with which his slavery in Barbados had been a mere pleasantry. Chained naked to the rowing-bench in conditions of indescribable filth, straining for hour after tormented hour at the tremendous oar, with the lash to spur him on if he showed signs of flagging, he prayed constantly for the death which was his only hope of release. His prayer remained unanswered, and at length he ceased to hope even for death, for if the galleys did not kill quickly they bred a strength equal to their terrible demands.

He broke free at last. After months of patient endeavour a weak link in the chain which held him gave way beneath his hands one night when they lay at anchor in a Spanish port, and he went over the side and swam ashore, leaving the rifled corpses of the bosun and a common seaman to mark his passing.

Even then he would have been recaptured had he not been befriended by a woman of the town, who concealed him in her own poor lodging until the hunt had died down, and he could, in reasonable safety, attempt to escape from Spain. He set out on foot for the French border, and many weeks later reached Bordeaux. He had no desire to return to England; the Indies were still his goal, as they had been six years before, and he had now the additional spur of a deep and abiding hatred of all things Spanish. He sought revenge, and he sought it among the pirates of the Caribbean.

After many difficulties he came at last to Port Royal in Jamaica, 'the wickedest city in the world.' Here he found no difficulty in joining the crew of a buccaneer craft, and having sworn the oath, on skull and dagger and torn black bunting, which made him one of the 'Brethren of the Coast', he set sail on his first filibustering cruise. Now at last fortune began to smile on him, and it was not long before he had made a place for himself in the lawless brotherhood, and was sailing in the fleet of the pirate Mansfelt, first admiral of the black.

Among the old pirate's followers was a young Welshman, Henry Morgan by name, whose exploits had already brought him some renown, and Crispin, perceiving that here was a leader worth following, joined his crew. His ability at both fighting and seamanship attracted the attention of the captain; he made him one of his lieutenants, and a friendship sprang up between them.

When Morgan succeeded Mansfelt as admiral of the black in 1667, England and Spain were, officially, at peace, but Jamaica's Governor, Sir Thomas Modyford, knew the Indies well enough to put little trust in a treaty signed upon the other side of the world. England would not send adequate forces to guard her Caribbean possessions, and Sir Thomas must look elsewhere for protection. He sent for Captain Morgan, and as a result of that interview the Welshman found himself with a Colonel's commission.

In the three years which followed Spain first broke truce with England and then signed another peace treaty, but the politics of the Old World had little or no effect upon the blazing career of Henry Morgan. Porto Bello, Puerto Principe, Maracaibo, Panama—one by one the cities of New Spain fell

9

into his greedy hands, yielded up their wealth, and perished by fire and sword. In those three short years the swaggering, heroic Welshman and his cut-throat followers broke the power of Spain in the New World and brought into Port Royal booty to the value of many thousands of pounds.

At length, however, the protests of the Spanish Ambassador at Whitehall grew too importunate to be ignored, and the lazy, sardonic Charles was obliged to make some sort of reparation. First Sir Thomas Modyford, and then Morgan himself, were summoned to England to answer for their offences against the Crown, but if the Castilian representative hoped to see his country's wrongs avenged he was doomed to disappointment. Modyford did indeed spend several years in the Tower, but he was eventually given the office of Chief Justice of Jamaica for his lifetime, while the 'terrible and tremendous' Morgan was not even imprisoned. His only trial, at which he was, of course, acquitted, was a private audience with the King, and he was later given a knighthood and the office of Lieutenant-Governor of Jamaica.

Before this happened, however, Captain Barbican had forsaken the Indies, though unlike his erstwhile leader he went of his own accord. He had had his fill for the time of Spanish blood and Spanish gold, and the whim took him to return to his native land and seek out the family he had not seen for so long. He was curious to discover how they fared in the gay and licentious England of the Restoration.

He came back one October day to the village among the rolling Cotswold hills whence he had set out fifteen years before to seek his fortune, but there was scant welcome for him at the grey stone house, half farm and half manor, where he had been born. His parents were dead, and the elder brother who ruled in their stead looked coldly upon the returning prodigal when at length Crispin succeeded in convincing him of his identity. He made him free of the house for duty's sake, but there was no affection in his heart for this gipsy-faced adventurer from beyond the seas. His only consolation lay in the reflection that the quiet of a country life would soon pall on one who for so long had lived by the sword.

This optimism was at length justified, for with the first hint of spring Crispin was away to Bristol in search of a ship westward-bound. His quest had not been immediately successful, and during the weeks that he tarried perforce in the port he began to ask himself why he was thus hastening back to the Caribbean. The question had occurred to him more and more frequently, and now he sat in that waterfront tavern and brooded with vague discontent over his adventurous past and uncertain future. He was still young, but there seemed to be no place for him anywhere in the world save among the Brethren of the Coast, and after nine years' buccaneering he was weary of roving. Life, Captain Barbican decided bitterly, was to him a very empty and useless possession.

At this point his melancholy reflections were interrupted for the second time. A burly, sandy-haired man who had just emerged from an inner room on his way to the street caught sight of the solitary figure, stood a moment at gaze, and then went towards him. Before anyone could utter advice or warning he clapped the Captain on the shoulder with an enormous hand and exclaimed jovially:

"Stap me if it an't Crispin Barbican! What make you in England, lad? Hast come to roister it in London wi' Welsh Harry?"

Contrary to everyone's expectation, the Captain took no exception to this greeting. He removed the pipe from his mouth, looked up at the newcomer, and replied with a smile:

"No, Tom Adams, I follow Harry Morgan into battle, not to Court. What would Sir Henry want with me? I am no courtier. But how fares it with you? I saw the *Jamaica Lass* in the harbour, but they told me you were not in Bristol."

"No, I've been away into Somerset." Captain Adams pushed to one side Crispin's plumed hat and sat down beside him on the settle. The other occupants of the room, realizing that there was to be no further violence, lost interest in the pair and returned to their own pursuit of pleasure. The hum of voices which had sunk to hopeful silence, broke out once more.

"I'm away again before the week's out," Adams continued. "I've seen enough o' England in the winter. Give me the Indies, where a man may take his ease without being frozen—or choked," he added, as a puff of smoke from the chimney set him coughing.

"You sail westward, then?" queried Crispin after a moment, but Adams shook his head.

"South first, to pick up a cargo. Then to Jamaica."

"You still trade in black ivory, then?"

The slaver chuckled.

"A man must live, Crispin, and the plantations must be worked." He glanced shrewdly at him. "D'ye seek a passage to Port Royal?"

Captain Barbican laughed shortly.

"Not by way of Africa, Tom, and not in that devil's craft of yours."

"My quarters are none so bad," said the slaver calmly. "Ye'll have known worse, no doubt."

"And better, Tom, and 'tis the better that I prefer. I'll wait for another ship. I am in no haste."

"As you please." Tom shrugged his broad shoulders. " 'Tis all one to me, but should you change your mind you'll find me aboard." He rose to his feet and looked down at Crispin. "We sail six days hence."

He nodded to the Captain and continued on his way to the door, which presently opened to let him out into the darkness, but Crispin sat on before the fire, the slaver's words lingering in his mind. He had followed Henry Morgan at some profit to himself—the emerald on his right hand had come out of Panama, and was a small part of his plunder—and for a little he toyed with the idea of going to London, where Morgan—Sir Henry, now—was living the life of a courtier, but the impulse died almost as soon as it was born. That prospect was no more enticing than any other.

He rose to his feet at last, cast his cloak about his shoulders, and made his way into the street. The rain had ceased, and the moon peered fitfully between ragged clouds. Captain Barbican clapped his broad-brimmed hat upon his head and set off at a brisk pace, with no suspicion that he went to meet his destiny.

The cry came to him faintly at first above the sound of the wind, but it brought him up short with a hand on his sword. He listened intently, and the cry came again, louder for an instant before it was swallowed by the next gust. A dozen strides carried him to the corner of the next street, where he beheld two men vigorously attacking a third, who, backed against a wall, defended himself as best he might. His hat had fallen off, and the moonlight gleamed silvery on cropped hair.

Captain Barbican's sword came out of its sheath with a vicious scrape as he bore down upon them, and one of the old man's attacker's swung round to face a swordsman famous among the Brethren of the Coast. The usual weapon of the buccaneers was the cutlass, but Crispin had ever preferred the delicate and deadly rapier, and in his years of roving he had acquired a formidable skill. The man who opposed him now was but an indifferent swordsman and delayed him scarcely a minute, but it was long enough for the second assassin to disarm his victim. The old man's sword clattered to the ground as Crispin ran his man neatly through the body, and his assailant felled him with a vicious thrust before taking to his heels.

Crispin let him go and turned his attention to the old man, who had slipped to the ground and was huddled against the wall. The Captain sheathed his sword and knelt beside him, searching with practised hands for the wound, which he presently discovered to be a deep thrust in the left side. He was staunching the flow of blood with his kerchief when the wounded man spoke.

"My thanks to you, sir, for your aid." The words came in a painful gasp. "I beg you—help me to my lodging. 'Tis but a step."

"Willingly, sir, but a surgeon is your most urgent need. If you will permit me—"

"No, no, a surgeon cannot aid me now. That murderer's sword did its work too well. My lodging, sir, I implore you. I am awaited there."

"So be it, then." Captain Barbican rose to his feet, lifting the injured man in his arms like a child. "Which way, sir?"

Following the faintly murmured directions he set off with his burden, leaving the body of the would-be assassin sprawled in the gutter. The brief fight had attracted no attention, for such occurrences were all too common in that seaport town, and Captain Barbican had lived too long by the sword to disturb himself over a mere killing. They came at length to a tall, narrow house in a poor street, and the Captain kicked vigorously at the door with a booted foot. After a little, shuffling steps sounded within, a bolt was drawn, the door opened an inch or two, and a querulous female voice demanded their business.

"Stand aside, woman, this gentleman is wounded," Crispin announced shortly, but instead of obeying the crone made as though to close the door. The Captain raised his foot again, thrust aside both the door and its guardian, and stepped into the house, ignoring the woman's indignant outcry.

He found himself in a narrow, grimy hall, dimly lit by a single, guttering candle which served only to emphasize the gloom and squalor of its surroundings. At the far end of the hall a flight of rickety stairs vanished into the upper darkness, and on the right a streak of light from a half-open door marked the room from which the crone had emerged.

She, seeing now for the first time the face of the man whom this impetuous visitor carried in his arms, lapsed from indignation into dismay, wringing her hands and sending up a veritable wail of grief. Crispin, realizing that he would get no help from this poor, half-witted creature, as he now perceived her to be, kicked the door shut behind him and advanced into the hall, raising his deep voice in a shout which echoed through the house.

As if in answer, light fell suddenly across the landing at the head of the stairs, and the next moment a young woman bearing a candle in her hand appeared at the top of the stairs and paused there, looking down into the hall. The candlelight fell softly over the grey gown and broad white collar of the Puritan, and beneath her close white cap showed a gleam of red-gold hair. This much Captain Barbican observed before she hurried down the stairs to peer distressfully into the face of the wounded man.

"Grandfather!" she exclaimed. "Oh, heaven! What has happened?"

"He was set upon by ruffians in the street, mistress," Crispin replied, for the old man seemed to have sunk into a swoon. "I fear he is sorely hurt. If you will show me the way—"

"Yes, yes, of course." She turned and mounted the stairs again, led him along a short corridor, and opened the door of a room, standing aside to let him enter. A lad of about twelve who had been standing by the hearth started forward with an exclamation, but she motioned him away and nodded towards a couch on the far side of the room.

"There, sir, if you please," she said quietly, and added to the boy: "Jonathan, fetch some pillows. Hasten!"

Crispin lowered his burden gently on the couch, and the boy vanished into an inner room. He was back in a trice with his arms full of pillows, and upon these they made the wounded man as comfortable as his condition allowed. He had recovered from the swoon, but his face was the colour of ashes and his eyes already glazed with approaching death. Crispin had seen that look too often to mistake it now, but the girl, it seemed, was less experienced. She stood for a moment with a hand to her cheek, looking down at her grandfather, and then she turned impulsively to Crispin.

"We must fetch a surgeon," she said quickly. "You have been so kind, sir! May I implore your aid in this also? My brother will go with you. Jonathan—"

She was turning to issue some instruction to the boy when

14

Crispin laid his hand on her arm. She broke off and looked up into his face, and he realized that she was little more than a child herself, seventeen or eighteen at most. He spoke gravely.

"If a surgeon could have saved him, mistress, I would have brought him to one ere this."

"No!" She jerked her arm free and stared up at him in horror. "I will not believe it. You are no doctor."

"No, mistress, but I have seen death too often not to recognize it now. If you doubt me, look well at his face."

Instead of following this advice she continued to stare up at him, frightened and resentful of this richly-dressed stranger who spoke so easily of death. Crispin, returning the regard, noted dispassionately that her face was of a fine, clear beauty, with delicate features, and very dark blue eyes beneath slim dark brows. He knew a sudden curiosity, roused by the contrast between that winsome countenance and the squalid gloom of its surroundings.

"He is right, my child," said the old man faintly from the couch. "This time they have made no mistake. So be it, then. A little longer, and nature would have accomplished their murderous work for them." He paused, fighting painfully for breath, and raised a shaking hand. "Come closer, my dears, where I can see you. Frances, set the candle here beside me."

She obeyed, and then bent over him, taking the feeble hand between her own.

"Grandfather, I beg of you! Let me at least tend the wound. It may not be as serious as you think."

"No, my dear, it is beyond your skill, and I have so little time. Hush now, and let me speak. Where is the stranger who bore me home?"

"He is here, Grandfather," she replied, and Captain Barbican, who had remained in the background, stepped forward and bent over the couch. He had removed his broad-brimmed hat, and the dying man looked intently into the dark face thus revealed, a strong, harsh-featured face somewhat grim about the mouth, but redeemed by fine grey eyes beneath level bows. Apparently he was satisfied by what he saw, for he nodded to himself.

"Sir," he said haltingly at length. "I know not who you are, or what led you to me tonight, but I believe that you came in answer to the prayer I made when I found myself beset by those murderous ruffians and knew myself sped. Therefore I dare to ask of you a favour which you have every right to refuse, and made as it is by one whose very name is unknown to you, and the danger of which you may judge by what has happened tonight."

A faint smile touched the Captain's lips.

"Danger, sir, has been my companion these many years," he replied, "and as for names—I am Captain Crispin Barbican, of Jamaica, at your service."

"And I, sir," said the dying man, "am Richard Crayle, second Marquis of Rotherdale. These are my grandchildren, Lady Frances Crayle and Lord Sherwin."

CHAPTER II

DEATH OF A NOBLEMAN

A LONG moment of silence followed his words. Captain Barbican straightened slowly to his full height and looked round the mean and shabby room. Though, unlike the hall and stairs, it was spotlessly clean, it was still a pitifully poor abode, the walls cracked and streaked with damp, and a broken pane in the window inadequately patched with a strip of cloth. Yet the boy and girl on the opposite side of the couch had a look of delicacy and breeding that their garb of worn homespun and coarse linen could not disguise, a proud carriage of the head which accorded ill with their present surroundings. Finally he looked again at the face of the wounded man, wasted by sickness and shadowed with the knowledge of approaching death, and something in those worn yet aristocratic features convinced him that he spoke the truth.

Crispin had learned long ago to betray nothing of his emotions, and none of the amazement he felt was visible in his face as, bowing slightly in acknowledgement of the words, he replied calmly:

"You were about to tell me, my lord, of some matter in which I might serve you."

A gleam of appreciation flickered in the eyes of the Marquis.

16

"I was, Captain Barbican," he replied, "but I appreciate that there is no reason why you should do so. We are nothing to you, and you, doubtless, have affairs of your own to consider. But enough of that! I have a story to tell, and my time grows short."

The story, as told by the Marquis, began nearly forty years earlier, before the differences between King and Parliament had flared into open warfare. The Crayles were bound to the throne by every tie of loyalty and tradition, but Richard, the heir, supported those who opposed the King, and for this his father cast him out and forbade him ever to return to Rotherdale. With his wife and little son, Richard went to London, and the only other occasion upon which he saw any member of his family was when, as an officer in the Parliamentary army, he encountered his only brother, Henry, serving beneath the Royal standard on the field of Marston Moor.

After the execution of the King, Lord Henry followed the younger Charles into exile, and Richard took possession of the title and estates to which he had succeeded on his father's death several years earlier. Fate, it seemed, had restored to him the birthright of which he had been deprived, and, with the Stuart tyrant literally begging his bread from Court to Court in Europe, there seemed to be no reason why he should not remain in possession of it. His son married, and in 1656 a daughter, Frances, was born.

Then came the time when England, wearying of the cheerless way of life forced upon her by her new masters, rebelled once more and invited her rightful ruler to return. Lord Rotherdale opposed the Restoration with every means in his power, and this coming to his brother's ears provided him with the weapon he was seeking.

Lord Henry Crayle by this time stood high in the Royal favour, and it was no difficult task for him to incense the King against Rotherdale to such an extent that Charles vowed to bring him to a traitor's death, and his son with him, and by thus lopping off the poisoned branch of an old and honoured family tree ensure that the title passed to one whose loyalty was unquestioned. This fate would undoubtedly have overtaken them had they not been warned of their danger by another exile Royalist, the Earl of Larchwood. This gentleman was the brother of the Marchioness, and though his sister was no longer living he felt it his duty to do what he could to save her husband and son from the peril threatening them.

17

Lord Rotherdale escaped with his family to Holland and settled in the town of Haarlem. Here a year later Jonathan was born, and here his parents died, within a week of each other, when he was only five years old.

The Marquis had discarded his title when he fled into exile, and for the next eight years he and his grandchildren lived tranquilly enough in the old Dutch town. There seemed no likelihood of a return to England, nor at first did Lord Rotherdale wish it. England under the lax rule of the pleasure-loving Charles, with the Court leading the way in every manner of excess, was not an environment which the Puritan Marquis would have chosen for his grandchildren.

But he was growing old, his health was failing, and he had no means of providing for Jonathan and Frances after his death. At last, knowing himself the victim of a disease which left him only a few months to live, he wrote to the Earl of Larchwood and begged him to use his influence on behalf of his young relatives. The Earl responded generously. In the event of their grandfather's death the children should become his wards, and meanwhile he would use every endeavour to oust Lord Henry from possession of Rotherdale. It might even be possible to arrange a marriage between Lady Frances and his own son and heir, Viscount Mountheath. Such a match would establish her position at Court and materially assist her brother in regaining his inheritance.

It was inevitable, however, that his endeavours to have the marquisate of Rotherdale restored to its rightful owner should come to Lord Henry's ears, and he took violent but effective means of countering them. More than one attempt was made on the lives of the Marquis and his grandchildren, until in desperation the old man braved the Royal vengeance and returned to England to place the children under Lord Larchwood's protection.

A series of unfortunate chances had so far prevented this. The Earl was not at his London house, and when they sought him at his country seat in Wiltshire they found that he had been summoned to London by the King and must have passed them upon the road. The Marquis left a letter for his kinsman at Larchwood Hall, as he had done at the mansion in Westminster, and then sought lodging in the nearby city of Bristol, thinking that in the busy seaport town their presence was less likely to be remarked than in a country village.

"But my brother's cut-throats followed closer than I knew," the faint voice concluded. "They lay in wait for me tonight, and 'tis probable that they know of our presence in this house." He struggled to raise himself from the pillows, but fell back with a groan. "When I am gone these children will be at the mercy of one who knows neither gentleness nor pity. Sir, I implore you! Do not let that knowledge follow me to the grave."

"What would you have me do, my lord?" Crispin asked quietly, breaking his long silence.

The Marquis did not reply at once. The sustained effort of telling his story had taxed his waning strength to the uttermost, and he lay now with closed eyes, while for a space the only sound in the room was his laboured breathing.

"Take my grandchildren hence," he gasped at length. "Think no more of me, for I am sped, but take them from this house before those murderous ruffians discover them. 'Tis their only chance of escape."

Upon the other side of the couch Lady Frances caught her breath in sudden dismay, and her eyes, which had been fixed upon her grandfather's face, lifted sharply to that of Captain Barbican. The light of the single candle flickered strangely over his dark features, lending them an expression which to the overwrought girl seemed almost satanic, and cast the shadow of his tall, cloaked figure grotesquely across wall and ceiling, so that it seemed to loom above her with indefinable menace. In sudden panic she cast herself on her knees beside the couch, catching one of the old man's hands between her own.

"No, Grandfather, no!" she exclaimed. "Do not send us away. We want to stay with you."

"My child," he answered her gently, "you must go. Your uncle will not be content with my life. He must destroy us all if he is to secure Rotherdale for himself and for his son." A sudden spasm of pain contorted his face, but when it had passed he continued, addressing Captain Barbican: "You do not speak, sir. Do you refuse the last wish of a dying man?"

Crispin hesitated no longer, for the very strangeness of the request appealed to him. The Puritan Marquis, dying in poverty in this mean room, struck down by a brother's hand, was bequeathing the charge of his grandchildren to a pirate captain who had become what he was through hatred of Puritan beliefs. There was a grim, ironic humour about the situation which pleased him.

"I am willing, my lord," he replied. "I can carry them

hence and conceal them somewhere until the coming of the Earl of Larchwood. But if the men who attacked you have knowledge of this place, we had best away at once. One escaped, and he will be upon us as soon as he can summon aid."

A nod from the Marquis approved his words, but the girl regarded him angrily.

"Are we then to fly, and leave my grandfather at the mercy of those ruffians? That would be brave indeed!" She looked beseechingly at the wounded man. "Sir, you have no right to ask so much of a stranger, and I will not go. If it be God's will that we perish tonight at the hands of my uncle's assassins why strive to escape?"

The Marquis moved his head restlessly on the pillows. His face was waxen now, and beads of moisture stood upon his brow, but by sheer force of will he continued to hold death at bay.

"You speak without thought, my child," he replied painfully. "If 'twere God's will that you share my fate, no protector would have been sent to aid you. 'Twas not chance which guided this gentleman to me tonight."

Unobserved by either, the Captain's brows lifted in sardonic amusement, for it was a novel experience for one of Morgan's comrades to be regarded as an instrument of Providence. This thought gave rise to another, and he addressed the Marquis abruptly.

"My lord, I am ready to protect your grandchildren to the best of my ability, but it is only right that you should know what manner of man I am. I have been a slave, and I have captained a pirate craft in the Caribbean. I am in Bristol now awaiting a ship to carry me back to Jamaica and my comrades of the black brotherhood."

He spoke with no trace of shame in face or voice, and it was this, as much as the facts he stated so calmly, which drew a gasp of dismay and anger from the girl. Lord Rotherdale, however, was regarding him curiously.

"Why do you tell me this?" he asked.

So faint had his voice become that Crispin was obliged to drop to one knee beside the couch to hear the words at all. From this short distance the keen grey eyes looked full into the fading blue.

"Because I would not deal falsely with a man who stands on the brink of eternity," he said simply. "If you bid me be-gone now I will go, but I tell you frankly that I shall wait below and do what I can to hinder any who come with intent to harm you."

A smile flickered for an instant in the eyes of the wounded man.

"I do not bid you go, young man," he murmured. "To one as close to death as am I it is given to tell the true from the false beyond all doubt or question, and all that is dearest to me in this world I place in your hands, assured that you are worthy of the trust."

In spite of himself Crispin was moved by the old man's words, for though he perceived that if Rotherdale wished to save his grandchildren he had no choice but to entrust them to him, he realized also the extent of that trust. Involuntarily his eyes sought the girl, and found her staring at him with undisguised dismay.

"Jonathan," the Marquis spoke painfully, fighting for breath, "bring the Bible to me." He waited until the boy placed a worn volume in his hands, and then looked once more at Crispin. "Captain Barbican, place your hand upon this holy Book and swear to me that you will guard my grandchildren from harm, nor part from them till they are safe in their kinsman's care."

Without hesitation Crispin swore the required oath, and his deep, quiet voice seemed to bring a measure of comfort to the dying man. Rotherdale lay very still now, and looked no more at those about him. Only by the painful struggle for breath could they tell that he still lived, and Crispin knew that the end was very near, though there was still, it seemed, one more task which he was determined to accomplish.

"Frances," he whispered, "you too . . . must swear . . . to obey Captain Barbican in whatever he may command . . . to ensure your safety . . . until you reach your cousin. This is . . . my last command to you. Swear it, my child . . . as he did . . . on the Bible."

The habit of obedience to him was strong in her, but as her fingers touched the Bible the implications of such a promise rose up to check her. She hesitated and would have withdrawn her hand, but Crispin read the intention in her eyes. His own hand rested still upon the leather-bound volume, and quick as thought the long fingers closed about her wrist, forcing her hand down upon the holy Book, while the grey eyes looked mockingly into hers.

"Frances . . . I command you," the faint voice repeated, and so perforce Lady Frances swore obedience to Crispin

Barbican. Almost before she had done, the Bible slipped from Rotherdale's failing hands and his head rolled sideways upon the pillow.

For a few seconds no one moved or spoke. Crispin and the girl knelt beside the couch, their hands still joined across it, and Jonathan stood close to his sister, his hand gripping her shoulder. In the silence a log on the hearth fell apart, and the wind thumped in the chimney with a sound like distant gunfire.

With his free hand Crispin gently closed the dead man's eyes, and then rose to his feet, drawing Frances up with him. Jonathan gave a stifled cry and, flinging himself face downward across the couch, burst into tears, but her ladyship stood dry-eyed and silent, staring up at the dark face of the buccaneer. Then, before either could speak, someone knocked loudly upon the door below.

Captain Barbican swung round on his heel and went quickly to the head of the stairs. The old crone had shuffled again from her room, but at Crispin's command not to open, delivered in authoritative tones, she halted and stood wringing her hands in dismayed indecision. The Captain left her thus and returned to the room he had just left.

"My lady," he said abruptly, "it is probable that those who knock come in search of you and your brother. Is there any way out of this house other than the door by which I entered?"

She shook her head and he cursed beneath his breath. The blows upon the street door had increased in violence, and Crispin, recalling its ramshackle condition, knew that it could not for long survive such usage. He picked up the candle and went quickly into the inner room. It was a bedchamber, and beyond it lay another which apparently belonged to the girl. The window of the farthest chamber opened on to a narrow and unsavoury alley, and Crispin, leaning out, could discern the roof of an outbuilding immediately below.

Here, then, was a way of escape. He returned to the outer room, where Jonathan lay weeping across the body of his grandfather, and Frances still stood in frozen immobility where he had left her. She seemed stunned by all that had passed, and when he spoke to her she looked at him without comprehension. Crispin stepped up to her and gripped her by the shoulders, his fingers digging with deliberate cruelty into the flesh.

"My lady," he said roughly, "you have seen your grandfather die by violence this night. Do you wish to see your brother suffer a like fate? The murderers are at your very door, and I cannot save you unless you bestir yourselves to aid me."

This time the words, or the tone in which they were uttered, roused her. She looked at him dazedly, like one awakened from sleep, and raised a hand to her head.

"I will try," she said slowly. "What must I do?"

"Gather together whatever money and valuables you possess, and any papers belonging to your grandfather. All else you must leave." A crash from below informed them that the door had given way. "Hasten, now! I will hold them as long as I can." He was half-way across the room as he spoke, whipping out his sword as he went.

He met the foremost intruder at the head of the stairs. The fellow checked and let out an oath when he saw the Captain's formidable figure looming above him, but perceiving him to be alone came on boldly and their blades rang together. On the narrow stairs only one of the three cut-throats could come at him at a time, but the lack of space restricted the movements of both combatants. Superb swordsman though he was Crispin could find no opening for a decisive thrust, and when the girl's voice called to him from the door of the room he was still engaged with his first adversary.

At length, however, he succeeded in dashing the fellow's sword from his hand, and almost at the same moment thrust him vigorously in the chest with his foot. The man lost his balance and fell backwards on top of his companions, and in the resulting confusion Crispin regained the room, slammed the door, and dragged a heavy wooden coffer across it before turning to face his charges, who were regarding him apprehensively. Frances had donned a hooded cloak and was clutching a leather wallet; Jonathan, his tears dried, was beginning to look a little excited.

"Into the farthest room with you, quickly!" Crispin commanded. He picked up the hat he had dropped and cast a swift glance round the room. A candle still burned beside the couch, and in its light the face of the dead man wore an expression of ineffable peace, but the door was shaking beneath a fusillade of blows. Crispin followed the boy and girl into the second chamber, barricading the door in the same fashion as the first, and so to the third, where he again piled furniture against the door to impede their pursuers.

"What are you going to do?" Jonathan asked eagerly. "There is no way out of this room."

"There is a window," retorted the Captain, crossing to it as he spoke, "and an outbuilding conveniently placed. That is our road. Here, lad, down with you, and see if yon roof is solid enough to bear our weight."

He helped the boy through the window and leaned far out to support him while he tested the roof of the outbuilding. The intruders had already entered the first room and, finding it tenanted only by the dead, were beating upon the barricaded door. Jonathan presently whispered assurance, and Crispin released him and turned to Frances.

"Give me the wallet, my lady," he said. "You will need both hands free for this ploy." He took it from her, dropped it into his pocket, and turned to the window. "I will go first and help you down."

He squeezed through the small aperture and dropped to the roof of the outbuilding with a lightness surprising in so big a man. Jonathan, active as a cat, had already slithered to the edge and jumped the few feet to the ground, but as Crispin lifted Frances over the sill the second barricade gave way with a crash. She had no time for fear, for he clipped an arm about her waist and swept her across the roof and down to her brother's side as though she weighed no more than a child. Dropping to the ground beside them, he spoke quickly to the boy:

"Follow me close, lad, as you value your life, and swiftly, for we must be away before they reach yon window. Come!"

He caught the girl's hand in his and they set off at a run. Where the alley opened upon the street he turned without hesitation to the right and led them on and on, twisting and doubling through the narrow streets until they reeled and stumbled on the verge of falling, gasping for breath. At last he paused before a house whose timbered gables overhung the street, a door hidden in the shadows below opened beneath his hand, and they stepped into musty darkness. Moving as one familiar with his surroundings, he led them up a flight of stairs and into a room where he bade them wait while he lit a candle.

The light revealed a big, low-roofed room panelled to the ceiling with black, worm-eaten oak. Tthe whole apartment, untidy and not over-clean, looked singularly cold and cheerless. That the Captain was aware of its shortcomings was obvious, for he looked about him with a frown, and kicked, without result, at a charred log on the hearth. Finally he turned to his companions.

" 'Tis no palace, my lady," he said, "but you will be safe enough here until I can take thought for the future. Will you not be seated?"

He made as though to lead her to a chair, but she recoiled sharply from his outstretched hand. For a moment he stared at her, and then he laughed.

"You have no cause to fear me, Lady Frances," he said shortly. "Do you forget that not an hour since I swore an oath to protect you from harm?"

"The word of a pirate!" she said scornfully. "Am I to trust to that?"

His lips tightened.

"Pirate or no, my lady," he replied, "it is not my custom lightly to break a promise. But since your mind runs so, it may reassure you to have the company of another woman." He went to a door on the far side of the room and flung it open. "Bess! Are you awake, lass?"

A drowsy voice answered him, and he went into the room, saying something else in a voice too low for them to hear. A minute passed, and then a tall, full-bosomed girl appeared in the doorway, pulling a cloak about her over a torn white shift and running the fingers of the other hand through her tousled flaxen hair. When she saw who stood there she stopped short with an expression of amazement on her face, and let out an oath which brought the colour to Frances's cheeks. Captain Barbican, towering shadowy in the darkness behind her, spoke mockingly.

"You will perceive, my lady, that had my intentions towards you been such as you suspect, I would not have brought you here." He came past the fair-haired girl into the room and looked from one to the other with sardonic amusement. "This lady remains here for the present, Bess. Look to her comfort."

"Does she, by God!" the girl exclaimed stridently. "And what of me? Am I to play tire-woman to any whey-faced doxy that pleases you? To the devil with her comfort."

The Captain's expression changed. Bess cried out as he caught her by the arm and jerked her towards him, looking down into her face.

"Do you take that tone with me, you slut?" he said harshly. "You will do as I bid you or it will be the worse for you."

He flung her contemptuously aside, and she staggered back against the table, sending a platter to the floor. Though she looked at him venomously she did not seem unduly disturbed

25

by this rough usage, but to Lady Frances it was the culmination of a night of horror, and the unnatural calm which she had maintained since her grandfather's death broke at last. A stifled cry escaped her, and casting herself into the nearest chair she began to weep hysterically. Captain Barbican swore roundly, and Bess's attitude underwent a sudden change.

"Now see what you have done!" she snapped. "Frightening the poor lass with your cursed ill-humour. Come with me, my girl, and pay no heed to his roistering, pirate ways."

She set a sturdy arm around Frances's shoulders and half-led, half-carried her into the inner room, shutting the door with a violence which made the windows rattle.

"A plague on all women!" said Captain Barbican fervently, and turned to confront the grave, considering gaze of the little Marquis. "Well, my lord, do you fear me also?"

The boy's chin went up. He was extraordinarily like his sister, with the same delicately-chiselled features, deep blue eyes and red-gold hair, but where in repose her ladyship's expression was withdrawn and a little severe, Jonathan's lips curved readily to laugher, and more than a hint of mischief danced in his eyes.

"No, sir, of course not," he said. "Frances is only a girl— you must not care for what she says. She is not usually so foolish."

"She has suffered enough tonight, poor child, to make any woman weep," said Crispin, half to himself, and then added more briskly: "Well, my lord, we have shaken off your pursuers for the present, but the sooner you are in Lord Larchwood's care, the better it will be. Tell me, do his estates lie far from Bristol?"

"About five or six leagues, I think. My—my grandfather took us to Larchwood Hall when we first came from London. It is near a village called Toddington. Are you going to take us there, sir?"

The Captain smiled.

"Eventually, no doubt, but first I must find out if any word concerning you has come from his lordship. You and your sister had best lie close here until he is ready to receive you. You will be safe enough. None saw you arrive."

Jonathan nodded, stifling a yawn, and Crispin's smile broadened.

"At present, an I am not mistaken," he said, "your most pressing desire is for sleep, though I fear that this couch is the best bed I can offer. Come, my lord, here is a cushion for

26

your head and a cloak to cover you. You may sleep without fear."

Jonathan obediently settled himself upon the couch, while Crispin went to a cupboard by the fireplace. He was fetching out writing materials when the boy spoke again.

"Captain Barbican."

"My lord?"

"Are you really a pirate?"

"I am, my lord. A buccaneer, if you prefer it."

There was a considerable pause. Jonathan yawned again, settled himself more comfortably, and finally remarked, in a voice heavy with sleep:

"I hope Lord Larchwood does not come back too soon. I should like to hear all about the buccaneers. Good-night, Captain Barbican."

"Good-night, my lord," Crispin returned gravely, hiding a smile. He had seated himself at the table, thrusting aside the litter to clear a space, and spread a sheet of paper before him. Now he picked up a quill, and sat for a while staring thoughtfully at the candle-flame.

At length he began to write, and for a time the only sounds in the room were the scratching of his pen and the regular breathing of the sleeping boy. At last the Captain finished his letter, folded and sealed it, and thrust it into his pocket. In doing so his fingers encountered the wallet he had taken from Lady Frances earlier that night, and drawing it out he turned it thoughtfully in his hands for a moment before opening it and tipping its contents on to the table.

There was a bulky packet of papers tied with a faded ribbon, a little pile of silver with a thin scattering of gold, and a massive gold ring set with a splendid intaglio sapphire bearing an armorial device. He had picked this up and was examining it closely when the door behind him opened and Bess came softly into the room.

"Your pretty Puritan has cried herself to sleep at last," she announced, and came to stand at his shoulder, staring at the money on the table and the ring in his hand. "God's light, Crispin, have you turned cut-purse?"

He shook his head.

"This ring, my dear, is the property of my lord the Marquis of Rotherdale, and bears, I believe, the crest of his house. His lordship is at present sleeping soundly upon your couch yonder."

Bess swung round to gape at Jonathan.

27

"That babe a Marquis?" she stammered incredulously. "Then—then the wench in there——"

"The lady," Crispin broke in coldly, "is his lordship's sister, Lady Frances Crayle. Their grandfather, their only protector, was murdered tonight, and before he died he entrusted them to me to convey to their kinsman, the Earl of Larchwood. Until they reach his care they go in danger of their lives."

In a few lucid sentences he sketched the outline of the story he had heard from the dying man, and explained how he had brought off the little Marquis and his sister. Bess was impressed, but inclined to wonder a little that he had chosen to burden himself in this manner.

"Unless," she added suspiciously, " 'tis the maid that's taken your fancy. She's a dainty piece, I own, but not for such as you. Her noble kinsfolk would have you hanged for it."

"What a fool you are, Bess," he said resignedly. "Her Puritan ladyship was not the reason I accepted the charge, save that I could not leave her to be murdered as her grandfather was murdered." He laughed softly at the recollection. "She was for staying to face the assassins, accounting them, I suppose, preferable to my protection, but the old Marquis made her swear obedience to me till we come to her noble kinsman. It vexed her mightily, as you may guess, but it was his dying wish and she dared not refuse."

"Small blame to her for misliking it," Bess replied sharply. "Obedience to you, forsooth! And she a lady born!"

A smile of genuine amusement flickered across his face, making it suddenly youthful.

"Would it surprise you, my dear, to know that I am a gentleman born, even though my coat-of-arms does not boast as many quarterings as my lady's? But had I the blood of kings in my veins she would not trust me, since she knows me for a pirate."

Bess stared.

"You told her that?"

"Why not? I am not ashamed of the trade I follow, though faith! I grow somewhat weary of it. And there, Bess, you have my reason for accepting this strange charge. The little lad yonder is a marquis and cousin to an earl, and if as a reward for my care of him and his sister I do not win a pardon—aye, and the chance to make something of a life which until tonight I accounted ruined—never trust me more."

"And this uncle who seeks to murder them?" Bess asked

28

gloomily. "If he learns of the part you have played in their escape it will go hard with you."

"There is no reason why he should discover it. His ruffians saw me for a short while only, and in a poor light to boot. None saw us come here, and none need know of their presence." He replaced the money and papers in the wallet and restored it to his pocket. "I ride now to Larchwood Hall, and if the Earl is there I may be rid of my responsibility at once. If he is not, I shall leave a letter for him and return here to await his commands. 'Tis simple enough."

She laughed derisively.

"You're mighty sure of yourself," she sneered, "but I'll wager the Earl won't see you. You'll not get past his lackeys."

"This ring shall be my guarantee," he replied, and slipped it on his finger. Then, rising to his feet, he set an arm about her and pulled her to him, putting the other hand beneath her chin. "Keep a still tongue, Bess, treat these children well, and you shall have your share of the reward. But if you play me false"—his hand moved until the fingers lightly encircled her throat—"Then, as God sees me, I'll choke the life out of you."

He smiled grimly into her suddenly fearful eyes, kissed her, and thrust her aside. Then, taking up his hat and cloak, he went out of the room, and presently she heard his footsteps die away along the empty street.

CHAPTER III

INTOLERANCE AND INGRATITUDE

LORD LARCHWOOD was not at his country seat. Captain Barbican, riding thither on a hired horse, was informed that his lordship was still in London, and had given no indication of quitting the capital in the near future. The Captain's assured bearing, backed by the Rotherdale ring, won for him a certain respect, and the Earl's steward himself came to inquire his business. In his hands Crispin left the letter, with instructions that it was to be handed to his lordship immediately he arrived, and in the event of a messenger for the Marquis of Rotherdale arriving at the Hall, word must be sent to the Queen's Head Tavern in Bristol. Crispin had no intention of divulging to anyone other than Larchwood the present whereabouts of the Marquis and his sister.

When he finally rode away from the Hall, Captain Barbican felt that he had done everything possible for the welfare of his charges, and being reasonably certain of their present safety resolved to spend that night at the inn at Toddington. There was nothing more to be done until the Earl arrived in Wiltshire, and in the meantime Lady Frances' attitude persuaded him that the less they saw of each other the better it would be.

In this he was not mistaken. His frankness in disclosing his lawless calling had not commended itself to her ladyship, and there was a profound contempt for him underlying her grief for her grandfather, and her very natural fears at being left wholly dependent upon a self-confessed pirate. Knowing nothing of the circumstances which had led him to follow the black flag, she was ready to condemn him unheard, and before they met again an incident occurred which transformed her contempt into active resentment.

When she woke on that first morning to find herself in an unfamiliar room, she could not immediately recollect how she came there. When remembrance of her loss swept over her she buried her face in the pillow and wept, but after a time, being a practical young woman, she dried her eyes and sat up to take stock of her surroundings.

Beside her Bess was sleeping, and in the cold, grey light of morning Frances could see that she was older than she had thought. The room, low-ceilinged and full of odd, shadowy corners, was not particularly clean and extremely untidy. Two gowns, one of tarnished brocade and the other of blue velvet, trailed from a chair, and on a chest by the wall a man's coat had been flung down. A baldrick stiff with silver bullion, supporting a silver-hilted sword, was looped over one bedpost.

Frances had grown up in Holland, that land of scrubbed and shining houses with their tiled courtyards and gleaming windows, and her nose wrinkled distastefully at the squalor of her present surroundings. She slipped quietly out of bed, resumed her shoes and stockings and prim, grey gown, and regarded herself wearily in the cracked mirror which stood on a table by the window. The face which looked back at her was white and drawn, with violet shadows beneath eyes swollen with weeping, but as she had been taught to disregard her own beauty, and was, in fact, scarcely aware of it, the sight occasioned her no concern. With a sigh she unpinned the heavy braids coiled round her head and shook her hair down over her shoulders. It fell all about her in a shining, red-gold cloak that even in the wintry morning light lent a sudden, vivid life to her face. A comb lay among the litter on the table, and after regarding it dubiously for a moment she took it up. With deft fingers she braided and pinned up her hair once more, finally quenching its glowing warmth beneath the severe white cap which had almost the look of a nun's coif.

Bess had not stirred. Frances tip-toed across to the door, opened it softly, and peered out. The outer room was occupied only by Jonathan, asleep on the couch, and she ventured to step out, wondering as she did so what had become of Captain Barbican. The condition of the room offended her as greatly as that of the bedchamber, and without delay she set to work, first mending the fire and then removing the soiled dishes from the table. Her brother awoke during this latter operation, and after staring about him in bewilderment sat up and announced that he was hungry.

"I fear you must remain so for the present," Frances informed him. "Mistress Barbican is still asleep, and we cannot help ourselves to a meal in her absence. Do you know what has become of the Captain?"

"I think he has gone to Larchwood Hall," Jonathan replied, clasping his arms about his knees. "Oh, Frances, is it not exciting? He really is a pirate—I asked him if it were so. Oh, how I wish he would take me to the Indies with him!"

"Jonathan!" Frances set down the platter she was holding and looked at him reproachfully. "How can you speak so, when Grandfather——" She broke off, biting her lip, unable to continue.

"Was it wrong to say that? Oh, Frances, don't cry." He scrambled up and came to set an arm around her shoulders. "He would not wish it."

"I know, I know, but to leave him like that! It seems so dreadful. Oh, Jonathan, what is to become of us?"

"Our kinsman will look after us," said Jonathan stoutly, "and perhaps the King will restore our lands. We have done nothing to harm him, after all, and for my part I should like to go to Court. When Grandfather decided that we should go to Lord Larchwood, he said that it was England we must seek to serve, and not the man who ruled her, were he King or commoner."

"Yes, Jonathan, I know, I know, and he was right, but we are not yet under Lord Larchwood's protection. The men who murdered our grandfather are searching for us, and we have neither friends nor money."

"We have Captain Barbican."

"Captain Barbican!" she repeated scornfully. "A chance-met stranger, a pirate self-confessed! Do you put your trust in him?"

"But, Frances, he swore an oath to protect us, swore it on the Bible." Jonathan's voice was shocked.

"What is an oath to such as he? I'll warrant he has sworn many a one before, and broken them too."

Unobserved by either, Bess had come into the room in time to hear the last remark, and now she spoke quietly.

"Set your mind at ease, my lady. What he has promised he will do, and you will come to no harm at his hands."

Frances swung round to face her in some embarrassment.

"I—I crave your pardon," she stammered. "I did not know . . . that is, I meant no disparagement of your husband but——"

"My husband!" Bess stared at her in blank astonishment. Then she flung back her head and laughed outright. "Saints preserve your innocence, my lady! Did you think we were wed?"

For an instant Frances stared back at her, her cheeks, which had been so pale, flaming scarlet. Then she turned abruptly and walked across to the window, and Bess looked after her in some amusement. There was a short and pregnant silence.

"Come, my lady," Bess said at length, "there is no need for this. If I offend you I am sorry, but I wish you no ill, and from what Crispin tells me you stand at present in sore need of friends."

"Yes," Frances turned slowly to face her, "I am in no position to choose what company I keep, and you have been very kind. I—I ask your pardon."

"Oh, to the devil with that!" said Bess good-naturedly. "I know your ladyship would not deign to notice me if matters were otherwise with you, but misfortune makes strange bedfellows. You and your brother are welcome here as long as you need shelter."

"Thank you," Frances tried to infuse some warmth into her voice, but without success. "I trust that we shall not be obliged to trespass long upon your kindness."

The strained atmosphere engendered by this incident persisted throughout that day and the next. Frances, it seemed, could not be still, and Bess, realizing that in the work she found a measure of relief, made no objection when her guest set about cleaning the room. She worked furiously in an attempt to keep at bay the thoughts and fears that tormented her, and by the time darkness fell upon the second day both rooms were sufficiently clean and tidy to satisfy even her exacting taste. Bess had gone out some time earlier, bidding them bar the door and open only to herself or Captain Barbican. Frances agreed half-heartedly, but when at last the latch lifted and then a knock fell upon the door, it brought her to her feet with quickened breath and thumping heart. Not until Crispin's voice spoke reassuringly from without did she sink back into her chair and bid Jonathan unbar the door.

The Captain came briskly into the room and stopped short to stare about him in surprise. A fire blazed merrily upon the hearth, and in its light and the light of the candles the room had an air of homely comfort.

" 'Sdeath, my lady," he said frankly, "you have wrought a miracle here. But such work is not for you."

"I have not been accustomed to idleness, sir," she replied coldly, "and while I work I have no time for thought. What news do you bring from Larchwood?"

"Little enough, I fear. His lordship is still in London. I have left word of your whereabouts, and for the present you will be safe enough here."

She frowned, but made no reply, and Crispin, coming to stand by the fire, looked down at her curiously. She sat gazing into the fire, her hands clasped in her lap, and the close white cap framing her face, and involuntarily he wondered what would become of her in the household of a friend of the King, as Larchwood was reputed to be. She would be obliged to cast off this icy Puritanism if she wished her brother to regain his inheritance, for nothing was more likely to antagonize Charles Stuart than a reminder of the faith which had brought about his father's death.

He held out his hand to the blaze, and the sapphire ring caught the light. He withdrew it from his finger and dropped it into Frances's lap, saying, as she cast him a startled upward glance:

"That bauble has served its purpose, my lady, in gaining me admittance to Larchwood Hall, and"—there was mockery in his voice and eyes—"I would not have you think I had stolen it. Here, too, is your wallet. You will need the money, no doubt, since you were obliged to leave everything when you fled, but do not venture out yourself. Bess will purchase anything that you require."

She thanked him coldly, and then, turning to her brother, spoke imperiously:

"Jonathan, I wish to speak privately to Captain Barbican. Go into the next room until I call you." She waited until the door had closed behind him and then rose to her feet and addressed Crispin in a low furious voice. "Captain Barbican, why do you seek to insult me? How dare you bring me here and lodge me with that—that woman!"

"With Bess?" he repeated in surprise. "Why, what has she done, my lady? Has she been uncivil to you?"

"No, she has been kind enough, poor creature! 'Tis not that which angers me, but the fact that you should dare expect me to share bed and board with a—a———"

"A harlot, my lady?" he said harshly as she hesitated. "Perhaps you would have preferred the lodging to which your uncle would have sent you—the grave?"

"Perhaps I would," she flashed. "That, at least, would have been no shame."

For a few seconds they faced each other in the firelight, and then Crispin turned away and spoke more lightly.

"Tell me, my lady, when you go to dwell in your kinsman's house, do you mean to go to Court?"

"I—I suppose so," she replied suspiciously, "but what is that to you?"

He turned again to face her, leaning his broad shoulders against the mantel and smiling into her puzzled face.

"Merely this, my lady. For every honest woman at Whitehall you will find two who are kin to Bess. You would do well to practise tolerance."

"Oh, infamous!" she exclaimed. "Merciful heaven, what have I done that I must endure such treatment?"

His smile broadened.

"Perchance 'tis a penance, my lady, for your besetting sins of pride and intolerance," he suggested. "That is why you have conceived so deep a hatred for poor Bess and me."

"Hate you?" she repeated. "No, not that. Her I can pity, and you I merely despise."

34

At that he laughed outright.

"In your opinion then, I am lower than Bess. I wonder why."

"Do you find it so strange? It is obvious that you are no common sailor, but a man of some education, and that such can find no better purpose in life than to rob and kill and torture is shameful indeed."

He was silent a moment, regarding her with eyes suddenly sombre.

"It is not always wise, my lady, to judge without knowledge of the circumstances," he said at length.

She laughed scornfully.

"Circumstances!" she repeated. "Is that your justification for all the shame and suffering you have inflicted upon innocent people in the plying of your pirate's trade?"

"You little fool!" Unexpectedly his anger flared again and taking a pace forward he caught her arm in a powerful grip, holding her face to face with him whether she would or no. "What do you know of shame and suffering? They are but words to you, and if you are wise you will pray that they remain so. Now let there be an end to these humours, and instead of censuring others consider whether you are yourself beyond reproach. There are virtues which you lack, my lady, and among them is gratitude. Gratitude to me, who saved your life two nights ago, and to Bess, who has given you shelter."

He let her go, and she stumbled to a chair and dropped into it, hiding her face in her hands. He stood for a moment looking down at her, and then crossed to the door of the bedchamber and opened it.

"My lord."

"Yes?" Jonathan's eager face appeared out of the shadows. "What is it, sir?"

"I am going forth again. Bar the door after me and do not open unless you are sure who is without."

He left the room without another glance at the girl huddled in the chair. Much later Bess returned alone, and informed her guests that the Captain had taken up his abode at the Queen's Head, and would remain there until word came from Lord Larchwood. Frances received this news in silence, but Jonathan was bitterly disappointed, and only partly mollified when Bess added that Crispin would visit him next day. He had conceived an admiration for the Captain which was rapidly becoming hero-worship.

The next three days passed uneventfully. Crispin visited them next afternoon as he had promised, and at Jonathan's insistence the visit was repeated on each successive day. In spite of his delicate looks, the little Marquis was a high-spirited lad with a healthy love of adventure, and his craving for stories of the buccaneers was insatiable. To amuse the boy, and beguile the tedium of his virtual imprisonment, Crispin related tale after tale, and Jonathan's eyes sparkled as he listened, but Lady Frances, quietly busy with some sewing in the chair beside the fire, gave no sign that she heard, and only acknowledged the Captain's presence when common courtesy demanded it.

But for all her outward indifference Frances listened almost in spite of herself to those wild stories, and if they sometimes drove the colour from her cheeks, at others her heart quickened with excitement. She came, after all, of a family long famed for courage and feats of arms, and not all the narrow bigotry of her upbringing could completely destroy that heritage of valour. These were stories to stir the most craven heart, of battles against overwhelming odds; of forced marches through the steaming jungles of the Isthmus, where hunger and weariness became the allies of Spain; of blazing cities and rich plunder in gold and gems. Out of consideration for his hearers Crispin omitted all reference to the orgies of rapine and torture with which the Brethren were wont to celebrate their victories, but even so, he reflected grimly, there was enough told of violence to turn her ladyship even more stubbornly against him.

But Frances, to her own secret surprise, felt no strengthening of her aversion towards the Captain. The adventures of which he spoke so calmly were dreadful enough in all conscience, but against that picture of violence and horror she found herself setting his behaviour towards herself and Jonathan in the past few days, and try as she would she could not reconcile the two. He had saved their lives, found them a secure haven, treated them kindly—was that the way of a pirate? She admitted to herself that he puzzled her, and studied him surreptitiously beneath her lashes, noting that his face was neither debased nor evil—was even attractive when his rare smile lit it—and that a humour not wholly mocking lurked in his grey eyes.

She had given much thought to his accusation that she was intolerant and ungrateful—she could not have forgotten the incident had she wished, for her arm was black and blue where he had gripped it—and she had come to the conclusion that the charge was not unfounded. He was under no obligation to aid her and Jonathan, any more than Bess was obliged to give them shelter, yet both had done so willingly, and in return she had scorned and reviled them. Intolerance and ingratitude! The accusation, to her shame, was well deserved.

She was too proud, however, to make the admission in so many words, and ask his pardon. She was still, after all, Lady Frances Crayle, and he a roving adventurer. But her attitude towards him underwent a subtle change, and when on that third afternoon the Captain came to the end of a story of the capture of Panama, and asked her ladyship's leave to smoke a pipe of tobacco, the permission was granted with unwonted graciousness. Faintly surprised, he filled his pipe and came to the fire to obtain a light for it, and Frances, her head bent over the inevitable sewing, continued:

"I fear, sir, that you find my brother's curiosity wearisome."

This was the first attempt that she had made at conversation. Crispin's surprise increased, but he answered in matter-of-fact tones:

"Not in the least, my lady, but I fear these tales are scarcely fit for a lady's ears. I trust that they have not too greatly offended."

"On the contrary, sir, I found them vastly interesting, and my brother, I know, dreams already of following in your footsteps."

Jonathan had come to stand beside her, and she put her arms around him, looking up at Crispin with the first smile that he had seen upon her lips. Bess, coming in just then with a market-basket on her arm, saw them grouped thus about the fire and set her burden down with a thump.

"What a pretty picture!" she said waspishly. "A pity I bring news to spoil it. Crispin, the house is being watched."

"What? Are you sure?"

"There's an ill-favoured fellow has been loitering in the street this hour past, and two more outside the wine-shop at the corner. I'll wager they're there for no honest purpose."

"So," said Crispin softly, "they have picked up the trail again. I feared that might happen." He went to the window and cast a cautious glance into the street. "Aye, 'tis the fellow I fought with on the stairs that night."

"What are we to do?" Frances had risen to her feet, her arms still about her brother. "They will bring others. You cannot fight them all."

"He'll fight no one if he remains in Bristol," snapped Bess. "Oh, you have yet to hear the worst, never fear! Those cowardly rogues have had their fill of Crispin's swordplay, and so they mean to be rid of him by other means."

"Other means?" Crispin swung round to face her. "What mean you?"

Bess leaned against the table and looked from one to the other, pushing her hair back from her brow with a hand which was not quite steady.

"The landlord of the Queen's Head sent a lad to warn you," she said. "I met him by chance on his way here. There are soldiers at the tavern with a warrant for your arrest."

CHAPTER IV

THE FUGITIVES

"For my arrest?" Crispin repeated slowly. "On what charge?"

Bess shrugged.

"Murder," she replied shortly. "You killed a man when you went to the aid of the old Marquis."

"But that was not murder." Frances's voice was horrified. "Those men were themselves assassins." She swung round to face Crispin. "Captain Barbican, they could not convict you, surely?"

"That is not their purpose, my lady," he replied gravely. "This is a plot to remove me so that they may finish their murderous work. For all they know I may have friends here to call upon at need, and a pitched battle they will avoid like the plague."

"But sooner or later the truth would become known," Frances pointed out, "even without the evidence of the letter you left at Larchwood for the Earl. They must realize that."

Crispin left the window and came slowly back to the hearth. He was frowning thoughtfully.

"I am not so certain of that," he said. "Bethink you, my lady! Even your grandfather had no real proof that his brother instigated the attacks upon you. There would be suspicion, certainly, but Lord Henry Crayle is a power at Court, and may be prepared to take that risk. 'Tis great, I own, but faith! so is the prize."

She sighed.

"Whether he stands or falls will matter little to us," she said. "Lord Larchwood may succeed in bringing my uncle to justice, but that will not restore us to life."

A fleeting smile touched Crispin's lips.

"Zounds, my lady, we are not dead yet!" he replied. "There is only one thing to be done for we dare wait no longer upon his lordship's coming. We must away to London in search of him."

Bess laughed derisively.

"What?" she sneered. "A hundred miles and more with a woman and child to hinder you, and soldiers in pursuit? Small chance you would have of winning through to London."

" 'Tis our only hope," he said abruptly. "My lady, are you willing to make the attempt?"

Frances shook her head.

"No, Captain Barbican," she said quietly. "Bess is right. We should but hinder you, my uncle's hirelings or the soldiers would overtake us, and you would have spent your life to no purpose. I beg you to save yourself while there is yet time. Those who watch this house will let you go unhindered, thinking that you are walking into the trap they have laid for you at the tavern, and you may make your escape before they discover their mistake. Let us be—you can do no more."

He stared at her, and it seemed that he paled a little beneath his tan.

"I know the poor opinion you have of me, Lady Frances," he said in a low voice, "but I swore an oath to bring you safe to your kinsman, and that oath I mean to keep. But even without that, and in spite of all that you may believe to the contrary, it is not my custom to abandon those who look to me for protection."

"I do not doubt your courage," Frances was pacing the room, clasping and unclasping her hands, "but what need for three to die when one might be saved? You cannot hope to

39

bring us to Lord Larchwood now, and without his protection there is no safety for us anywhere in England."

"God's light!" Crispin took a pace forward, sudden hope in his voice. "You have hit upon a resolution, my lady. No safety in England, you say? No, but why stay in England? We are not trapped as long as we have the sea at our backs, and there are ships in the harbour."

They stared at him in amazement, and for a moment no one spoke. Bess was the first to break the silence.

" 'Tis a chance," she said slowly, "but how can you go seeking a ship? Those villains below will be upon us as soon as you leave the house, and for all we know the ships may have been warned."

"No need to seek far," he replied. "The *Jamaica Lass* sails with the morning tide, and her captain has already offered me a passage to Jamaica. I know Tom Adams, and he is not the man to refuse help to a friend in danger of arrest."

Bess looked at him sharply.

"The *Jamaica Lass?*" she repeated. "But she is——" she caught his eye, hesitated, and concluded lamely, "she is ready to sail."

"Is that not what we need?" Crispin retorted. "Bess, you must go to Tom Adams with a message from me. I'll give you nothing in writing in case you are stopped. Tell him that I accept his offer of a passage, that I bring two companions with me, and also that I stand in danger of arrest. Take care that you are not followed—carry the basket again as though you go to buy food."

"Captain Barbican, this is madness!" Frances, hitherto held speechless by surprise, suddenly found her voice. "Surely you do not imagine that we shall accompany you to Jamaica?"

"Why not?"

"Why not?" she repeated, and made a helpless gesture with her hands. "How could such a course avail us? To leave England and travel to an unknown land, a land peopled by pirates and savages—oh, 'tis unthinkable!"

"My lady," he said quietly, "you have no choice! 'Tis England and certain death, or the Indies and a chance of life. When we reach Jamaica I will take you to the Governor, and you will be safe enough until the Earl, your kinsman, sends to fetch you home. Believe me, it is the only way." He paused, but when she made no reply he turned to the other girl. "Away with you, Bess! Tell Tom that we shall come aboard just before he sails."

"Be easy, I'm going," Bess picked up her basket, which she had already emptied, "though I'm damned if I know how you think to reach the ship with three cut-throats lying in wait for you in the street. And what if the soldiers grow weary of waiting at the tavern and come in search of you?"

"No fear of that," he replied confidently. "My lord's noble uncle will not wish my arrest to be connected in any way with what his hired assassins think to do here. As long as I remain in this house neither they nor our military friends will make any move."

Bess turned towards the door, making no further comment, and after a moment's hesitation, while he looked consideringly at her ladyship, Crispin followed her. Frances and Jonathan looked at him in some dismay and he shook his head.

"I shall return in a moment," he said reassuringly. "Now, Bess, one other thing——" the door closed behind him, and the rest of the sentence was lost.

From the window they watched Bess stroll down the street, basket on arm, as though bent upon nothing of more moment than marketing. The man lounging against the house-front opposite watched her out of sight but made no move to follow her, and Crispin, who had returned to the room, nodded his satisfaction.

"They do not suspect her," he remarked. "Now, my lady, another letter for my Lord Larchwood, informing him of your destination. It would be best, I think, if you wrote it yourself, else he may think that I have carried you off against your will."

"I am not sure that he would be wrong," said Frances resignedly, sitting down at the table. "In sooth, I fear we are both mad to embark upon such a scheme."

He smiled, but made no reply as he set paper and ink before her. In spite of the fact that he had already acquainted the Earl with the situation, Lady Frances found it somewhat difficult to explain to her future guardian the exact circumstances which had led her to agree to a voyage to the New World in company with a pirate captain. Stated baldly in black and white the situation seemed preposterous, and the difficulties of composition were so great that for a time she had no opportunity to dwell upon their present danger.

Bess returned at last, after an absence so prolonged that even Crispin was beginning to show signs of uneasiness, with the tidings that Tom Adams was more than willing to carry Captain Barbican out of danger, though he had been somewhat curious concerning the identity of the two mysterious companions.

"What did you tell him?" Crispin demanded, and she looked at him scornfully.

"Do you take me for a fool? I told him that it was no concern of mine, and that his curiosity must wait until you went aboard. After that I went to the Queen's Head and arranged to have your gear taken secretly aboard the *Jamaica Lass*—that is what delayed me." She nodded towards the basket, which stood on the table with a cloth hiding its contents. "There are the clothes you bade me obtain."

"Good!" He turned to Frances. "My lady, for your own safety I must ask you to assume a disguise. Bess has brought the necessary attire, and you will oblige me by changing into it at once."

Her ladyship frowned.

"A disguise?" she repeated. "Is that necessary?"

"It is, my lady." He took a bundle of clothing from the basket and put it into her hands. "I must ask you to hasten. We have not overmuch time."

Frances looked at the garments in her hands and then cast them on the nearest chair, her face flaming.

"Men's clothes!" she exclaimed, in tones of the utmost horror. "Do you dare suggest that I dress myself so? I would die rather."

"That, my lady, is precisely the choice before you," he retorted drily, and Bess added:

"Why, what ails your ladyship? Believe me, you'll be a deal safer aboard that craft if you pass yourself off as a boy."

"I will not!" Frances cried angrily. "If that is the only way to safety I will not take it! I——"

"God's death, girl!" Crispin brought his fist down upon the table with a crash that smote her into startled silence. "Can you think of no one but yourself? Will you sacrifice even your brother's life to your accursed modesty?" He leaned forward and spoke more quietly, but with no less emphasis. "Hearken to me, Lady Frances! You are going aboard the *Jamaica Lass* tonight and you are going as a boy. Whether or not you don those clothes of your own free will is for you to choose, but as God sees me, my lady, don them you shall!"

For a long moment they faced each other in the firelight, he at his grimmest, and she with flushed cheeks and stormy eyes. There was no sign of yielding in his face, and at length her gaze faltered and she turned away to pick up the despised garments from the chair where she had flung them. Bess followed her into the bedchamber, making a comical grimace at Crispin over her shoulder.

Time passed, and the Captain was beginning to cast impatient glances at the clock when Bess came back into the room, her hands full of red-gold hair. For an instant Crispin was startled, for he had forgotten that if Frances was to masquerade as a boy she would be obliged to sacrifice her tresses. Bess held out the shining mass regretfully.

"Faith, 'twas a shame to cut it," she said, "but needs must when the devil drives, and she makes a vastly pretty boy." She looked mockingly at the Captain. "The good, red gold! A favourite colour with the pirates, eh, Crispin? Take a lock of it now, to bring you good fortune." She paused a moment, watching him shrewdly, and then laughed. "You fool! Do you think I am blind?"

"Cast it into the fire," said Crispin indifferently. "Is her ladyship not yet ready? It grows late, and we have yet to win out of the house."

Bess chuckled.

"She is ready, but reluctant to come forth," she replied. "Only fear of you persuaded her to don the disguise at all." She went back to the door of the bedchamber. "Come, my lady! Time grows short."

In response to the summons Frances came slowly into the doorway and hesitated there, with burning cheeks and downcast eyes. The clothes she wore closely resembled her brother's, and now that her hair was no longer concealed, but, like his, framed her face in bright waves which barely reached her shoulders, the likeness between them was startling. They were much of a height, and, since Jonathan was slightly built, might well have passed for twins.

"They're wondrous like," said Bess admiringly, "and when her ladyship learns to hide her blushes and swagger a little in boyish fashion, they'll pass for brothers any day."

"It is fortunate that they will," Crispin replied, "since aboard the *Jamaica Lass* I intend to pass them off as my half-brothers, who, our father being lately dead, are now in my care. Remember that, if you please. Henceforth you are Francis and Jonathan Barbican."

Finding this accepted in silence, he went on to outline his plan for their escape, speaking in swift, decisive sentences which permitted of no argument. To Bess he gave the letter for Lord Larchwood and a purse containing gold, bidding her make her way to Toddington and wait there at the inn until the Earl returned to Larchwood Hall, when she would give him the letter and answer any questions he might put to her concerning the Marquis and his sister. She was to leave the house first, since it was obvious that no move would be made to prevent her, and they would give her time to make good her escape before venturing forth themselves.

"Go now, lass," he concluded. "It grows late, and Tom Adams will not delay his sailing on my account. Go forth openly, and let that rogue below see your face, so that he knows 'tis not my lady making her escape, as he may suspect."

"Bess!" Frances fumbled at her breast and brought forth the Rotherdale ring, which she had hung on a ribbon about her neck. "This will open your way to Lord Larchwood. Give it to him to keep for Jonathan until we return."

Bess looked strangely at the ring on her brown palm, and raised her eyes to Frances's face.

"Can you trust me with such a jewel, my lady?"

"What is a jewel, when these five days past you have had our lives in your keeping?" Frances took the elder girl's hand and closed the fingers over the ring. "Heaven knows how little I, at least, merited your loyalty, but if ever we come to possession of Rotherdale you shall see that I am not as ungrateful as I may have seemed."

"That you shall," said Jonathan stoutly, and planted a hearty kiss on her cheek. "I wish you were coming with us, Bess."

Bess looked from one to the other with eyes which were suddenly very bright.

"Oh, the devil!" she exclaimed. "I'm near to weeping. God bless you both, I'll not fail you. Look after them, Crispin."

A moment later she was gone. They heard the outer door close behind her, and her footsteps in the street below fading uninterrupted into the distance, and knew that she, at least, had walked unhurt from the trap. Ten, fifteen minutes crawled past before Crispin rose to his feet.

"Our turn now," he said briefly. "You know what to do."

Jonathan assented eagerly, all agog for the adventure to begin, but Frances looked wistfully about the firelit room, for the despised lodging of a few days ago seemed now a veritable haven of security and comfort. Tears pricked her eyes, but, catching the Captain's sardonic glance, she blinked them away and tilted her chin defiantly.

"We know, sir," she said haughtily. "Come, Jonathan."

In the end it was absurdly simple. Crispin walked alone from the house, leaving Jonathan and Frances concealed in a lower room, and as soon as he was out of sight two of the watchers flitted quietly across the shadowy street and into the house, leaving the third to guard the door. The fellow never remarked Crispin's swift and stealthy return until it was too late, and while his companions were forcing an entry into the locked inner room above Captain Barbican and his young friends fled silently towards the harbour and the sanctuary of the *Jamaica Lass*.

They came safely aboard a scant half-hour before she weighed anchor, and were conducted to the main cabin, where Captain Adams presently joined them. He greeted Crispin jovially, with a humorous reference to his narrow escape from justice, and then turned a surprised and questioning eye upon his young companions.

"These, Tom," said Crispin calmly, in answer to that look, "are my half-brothers, Francis and Jonathan—the cause of my presence in England. Our father died recently, and since their mother has been dead these many years, the care of them has fallen to me."

The slaver set his hands on his hips, looked from Crispin's harsh, dark face and towering frame to the fair grace of his companions, and spat in token of his profound astonishment.

"Your brothers?" he repeated. "These copper-headed whelps?"

"Half-brothers, Tom," Captain Barbican replied carelessly. "They favour their mother, a frail, pretty creature as I remember her, but sickly. Pay no heed to them—they are but children."

Fortunately Captain Adams had more pressing matters to engage his attention just then, and he chose to take Captain Barbican at his word. Crispin showed his supposed relatives to the cabin they were to share, bade them stay there until they were well away from Bristol, and then went to join Tom Adams on deck. Frances stowed away their few scanty belongings and then lay down fully dressed on her narrow bed, bidding Jonathan do the same, for she was not yet sure that they were no longer in danger of pursuit. She had extinguished the lantern which was the only source of illumination, and lay there tensely in the darkness, straining her ears for any sound on the deck above and fully convinced that she would lie thus wakeful for the rest of the night.

In this she was quite mistaken. When with the dawn the slave-ship *Jamaica Lass* slipped quietly out of Bristol on her long voyage to Africa and the Indies, Lady Frances Crayle and her brother the Marquis slept soundly in one of her cabins, while on the deck above the buccaneer captain who was now their only friend leaned upon the bulwarks and watched the lights of England fade into the distance.

It was not until the following evening that her ladyship discovered what manner of craft it was in which she travelled. They sat about the table in the main cabin—Frances and Jonathan, Captain Barbican, Tom Adams and Lee, the mate—over the remains of a meal. The three men smoked and talked, Frances wondered how soon she might retire to her own cabin without drawing unwelcome attention upon herself, and Jonathan listened enthralled to every word uttered by his elders. Her ladyship was paying little heed to the conversation until a chance remark by Captain Adams caught her attention.

"Cheated me, they did!" he said indignantly. "Three-score full-grown Negroes they had of me, that would have fetched eight pounds apiece in Port Royal or Bridgetown, and what did I get for 'em? Barely enough food and water to reach an English port, and the threat o' the Holy Office when I tried to protest. I tell you, Crispin, that's the last time I trade wi' the Dons, curse 'em! Henceforth I sell my cargoes in the English colonies."

Captain Barbican removed his pipe from his mouth and was about to make some appropriate reply when he was forestalled by Frances. She had started to her feet, her cheeks flushed and her blue eyes bright with anger, righteous indignation quivering in every line of her body.

"The slave-trade!" She almost spat the word at the startled Captain Adams. "You are engaged in that accursed traffic of selling your fellow-creatures into bondage! You drag them from their homes to slavery and torture, trade in human beings as though they were cattle——"

"Francis!" Crispin spoke sharply on a note of mingled reproof and warning, but instead of stemming the torrent it merely turned it upon himself.

"You knew!" she cried accusingly. "You knew upon what devil's work this ship was engaged before you brought us aboard her. Do you think I would not rather have faced

46

my——" The rush of words ended in a strangled cry as Captain Barbican struck her across the mouth.

It was not a heavy blow, but it had the desired effect. Her angry words ceased as abruptly as though cut off with a knife, and she dropped back into her chair, pressing the back of one hand against her lips and looking at him incredulously.

"You insolent puppy!" he said softly. "Who gave you leave to question my actions, or those of my friends?" He glanced at Adams. "I cry pardon, Tom. This brat was ever my father's favourite, and being a sickly lad has been indulged far more than was good for him. Well, the time for indulgence is past. He shall learn discipline, and learn it now." Rising, he gripped Frances's arm and jerked her to her feet. "Get you to your cabin, you whelp!"

He thrust her before him out of the cabin, and as the door closed behind them Captain Adams chuckled deep in his throat.

"The boy has more spirit than I thought," he observed, "but it will go hard with him if he beards Crispin Barbican in that fashion." He glanced at Jonathan, who sat white-faced and silent, staring down at the table, and added kindly: "Look not so woebegone, my lad. A thrashing will do your brother no harm."

The Marquis smiled perfunctorily but made no reply. He did not think that the Captain would beat Frances, but he guessed that only the utmost necessity would have compelled him to strike her at all, and he was for once quite out of sympathy with her. To Jonathan a voyage to the Indies, even on a slave-ship, was the most delightful thing imaginable, and he saw no reason why his sister should not agree with this opinion.

Frances, however, facing Crispin across the narrow confines of her cabin, did not share her brother's confidence in her immunity from violence. The buccaneer's face was at its most forbidding, and there was an expression in his eyes that frightened her, though not for the world would she have let him see her fear.

"Will you never learn caution?" he said at length, and though his voice was quiet it struck like a lash. "Now listen to me, Lady Frances! I have borne with your whims and humours this week past because it seemed that there was sufficient excuse for them, and because when I undertook to protect you I expected that it would be only for a short time. Now we shall be forced into each other's company for many weeks, and I will have you know who is master. Had your brother behaved as you did in the cabin yonder I would have taken a whip to his back."

"I nothing doubt it," she replied scornfully, "and I marvel that you do not do so to me—pirate!"

He smiled unpleasantly.

"I have never yet whipped a woman, Frances, though God knows I am sorely tempted now. But it will suffice, I think, to make clear to you what will follow should your secret become known, as it so nearly did tonight. This is a slave-ship, and the men who engage in the slave-trade are no better than the pirates you so despise. If you betray yourself it is doubtful whether I can protect you from the consequences of your folly." He paused, regarding her sardonically. "Do I make myself clear, madam, or must I use franker terms?"

Frances shook her head. She had turned pale, and all her fine indignation had faded.

"I understand," she murmured. "I did not know. . . . I thought——"

"You thought that in forcing you to assume that disguise I sought only to shame you," he broke in contemptuously. "You were mistaken. You wear it for your own protection. Remember that, my lady, and remember also that you swore to obey me implicitly while you are in my care. What I do is in the best interests of us all, and not for you to question. Your obedience I must and will have, and if you disregard what I have said tonight I must find other means of ensuring it."

CHAPTER V

FATHER AND SON

LORD HENRY CRAYLE sat before a roaring fire in his bed-chamber and stared wrathfully at the leaping flames. A bed-gown of richly-hued brocade wrapped him about, and his periwig being laid aside, a silk night-cap covered his sparse white hair, while the fingers of one hand toyed idly with a glass which steamed on a table beside him, but in spite of these aids to comfort his lordship was in no placid frame of mind. He had that day completed the last stage of a wearisome journey from Bristol to London, and the cold and damp of a protracted winter had entered into his bones, to set old scars throbbing and make movement difficult. Yet the discomfort which irked him was mental rather than physical, and the scowl which rested on his brow not caused entirely by bodily pain. From his black thoughts he was presently roused by the opening of the door, and looking round irritably he discovered the newcomer to be his heir and only child, Gideon, whom he had not seen for more than two months.

Nature had blessed Gideon Crayle with a face of surpassing beauty, and cursed him with a deformity which no modish finery could disguise. He was, in fact, a hunchback, and the effect of that pale and perfect face, framed in glossy black curls, atop his mis-shapen body was at times indescribably evil. Though he was in fact twenty-seven, his age might have been anything between twenty and fifty, for his countenance had a peculiar agelessness which was at once fascinating and repellent. Only his eyes, large, dark and brilliant, hinted at a restless and ambitious spirit, and they were commonly veiled by heavy lids. He came slowly forward to stand before the fire, and his coat of crimson velvet glowed in the light of the leaping flames.

"So you have returned at last," he said, and his voice was low and wonderfully expressive, a voice which, once heard, would ring forever in the memory. "I had begun to despair of you."

"The roads are like quagmires," said his father sourly, "and I have been engaged upon affairs of moment."

"So have I, my dear sir, so have I," Gideon replied gently. "We are devoted, are we not, to the interests of our youthful cousins?"

Lord Henry made a strangled sound but seemed for the moment incapable of speech. Gideon regarded him for an instant and then continued pensively:

"During your absence I have applied myself to the task of persuading the King of the impropriety of bestowing these children in the care of the Earl of Larchwood, who is, after all, a comparatively distant connection, when we who are bound so closely to them by ties of blood are eager to receive them. I pointed out that Larchwood is at present fully occupied with the vagaries of his own son. But I forget—you will have heard nothing of that! I must tell you that young Mountheath—an engaging youth, but callow—is greatly enamoured of a certain lady of the theatre, and has been rash enough to offer her marriage. A quite unnecessary proceeding, since he could have enjoyed her favours, as others have done, without that. Needless to say, however, the wench, though surprised, was quick to perceive the advantages of such a match, and now Larchwood finds himself faced with the prospect of receiving into his family one of the most notorious strumpets in London. One cannot but sympathize with him, and it is not to be thought upon that at such a time he will welcome the additional responsibility of a half-grown boy and girl, as I pointed out to the King." He sighed. "Dear Charles! Such a reasonable man! He agreed that it was only right that the children should come to their natural protector —yourself."

"You might have spared yourself the trouble," his lordship retorted irritably. "The brats have vanished quite away. They——"

"I know!" Gideon checked him with upraised hand, on one of whose preternaturally long fingers glowed an antique ring set with a huge opal. "Thanks to you, they have. Damned, blundering fool!"

The last three words were spoken in the same gentle pensive tone as the rest, but they had a curious effect upon the elder man. Instead of resenting such epithets from one who should have shown him respect, he paled and shifted uneasily in his chair, nervously moistening lips that were suddenly dry.

"I thought 'twas for the best," he defended himself. "But for a stroke of ill-fortune, the advent of a chance stranger, a ruffling, roistering dog of a pirate——"

"Captain Crispin Barbican, of Port Royal in Jamaica," Gideon broke in thoughtfully. "For some years a slave, since then a pirate. Lately one of Morgan's chief lieutenants. He was in Bristol seeking a ship for the Indies when he went to the aid of your brother, whom your hired assassins were attacking. Go on!"

Lord Henry was staring at him with mingled admiration and dismay.

"My God, do you know everything?" he demanded. "In the fiend's name, how?"

"I am well served," his son replied enigmatically. "Go on with your story."

"Why? You know it as well as I, no doubt."

Gideon smiled.

"Naturally, my dear sir, but I wish to hear it from your own lips. Continue, I beg of you."

"There's little to tell," said his lordship shortly. "My accursed brother is dead, but this Captain Barbican escaped with the children. I found out where they were hid, and arranged to have the fellow arrested, but somehow he had warning and now they have all three vanished—devil knows where!"

"I know," said Gideon calmly. He ignored his father's sudden, eager movement and continued coldly: "But if they had not escaped, if your ruffians had butchered them as they butchered your brother, how do you imagine that you would have benefited? Larchwood would have seen to it that you did not go free. We are the only people who stand to gain by their deaths, and he would surely have laid the crime upon us."

"Something had to be done," Lord Henry retorted sullenly. "Larchwood had almost succeeded in persuading the King to restore Rotherdale to the boy. You would not care to be left penniless."

"I should not be left penniless, even without Rotherdale," Gideon pointed out pleasantly. "You forget the plantation in Jamaica which I inherited from my uncle, and since my visit to it four years ago I assure you that it is not my only interest in the Indies. I have a share in another, and more lucrative, trade than the cultivation of sugar. No, I should not starve, but neither should I wield the power which would be mine were I Marquis of Rotherdale—as I intend to be."

"I have the same intention," said his father. "Therefore something had to be done."

"Something was being done, you fool! I told you that I had arranged for the children to be bestowed in our care. Do you forget that you are Jonathan's heir? He is barely thirteen and years must pass before his marriage; time enough for some accident to befall him when the world had seen how we doted upon him." He took a pace forward, leaning his hand upon the table and looking down at his father with eyes that glittered in his pale, handsome face. "For years I had planned it! Five years ago I set a man to discover the whereabouts of my uncle and his family, and since then I could have put my hand upon them at any time. But there was no need for haste! The old man could not live for ever, and one day the children would come into my hands. That day was almost here, and you, with your accursed blundering, have destroyed all my work, so that I must begin to plan anew. Why could you not leave matters to me, who have the wit so to order things that we gain all and risk nothing?"

"You are so secretive, Gideon," Lord Henry complained. "At all events, what use in quarrelling over it now? The children have vanished."

"Oh, not vanished, sir! They have merely eluded me for a time. I know where they are, never fear." He lowered himself into a chair facing his father and stretched one white hand towards the fire. The opal on his finger glowed evilly. "Let me tell you what happened that night in Bristol. Barbican took our young relatives aboard a slave-ship, the *Jamaica Lass,* bound for Africa and thence for Port Royal. He had disguised Frances as a boy and passed them off as his half-brothers. The woman with whom they had been lodged until then, a common harlot who had been Barbican's mistress, was sent to Toddington with a letter for Larchwood. He arrived in Somerset two days later, saw the woman, and learned all that she had to tell. So you see, my dear father, he knows very well how your brother Richard met his death."

Lord Henry stared at him for a moment, his features twitching, then he raised his glass and took a long pull at it. His hand was unsteady, and some of the liquid trickled down his chin.

"Whence had you this story?" he stammered at length.

"From the woman herself when she returned to Bristol. My men were waiting for her at her lodging. I gather that she was at first reluctant to speak, but eventually"—he smiled—"she was persuaded."

"Then not only Larchwood knows, but this woman, who may blab the truth in every tavern in Bristol. My God, Gideon, you speak of my blundering——"

"I am neither careless nor a fool, and I choose my men carefully," Gideon broke in, and there was that in his voice which laid an icy hand on Lord Henry's heart. "The woman is dead."

"Dead!" repeated his father, and raised a trembling hand to his mouth. "That was—that was wise, Gideon. You are shrewd, my son, shrewd." His voice was tremulous and eagerly ingratiating. "You will help me out out this coil, will you not? You will know how to allay Larchwood's suspicions, and if you know what has become of your cousins there is no great harm done. We can fetch them home again—if you have the King's sanction Larchwood is helpless. We——"

"Not 'we'," said Gideon softly, "I. Henceforth our paths run not together." He raised a hand to check his father's protest. "The choice was yours. When you went blundering about your cut-throat schemes you made impossible any partnership between us. Tomorrow I leave this house."

"No, Gideon, no!" Panic rang now in Lord Henry's voice. "Larchwood knows how I plotted against Richard. If you desert me now, what will become of me?"

"That, sir," said the son, getting to his feet, "is a matter of supreme indifference to me. Though if it is any comfort to you, I think it unlikely that he will move against you until he has Frances and Jonathan safe under his hand. It is their evidence, and that of Crispin Barbican, which will convict you, and they are all three far away."

"But if he accuses me!" quavered his father. "I do not lack enemies. No man does who stands close to the throne. You cannot stand aside and see me fall. My disgrace would be yours also."

"You perceive the obvious." Gideon paused in the act of turning away and stood, a sinister, crook-backed figure, silhouetted against the firelight. "Look you, Father, I swore long ago that one day I would be Marquis of Rotherdale, but I mean to succeed to the title in a manner which will disarm suspicion. Little Jonathan shall suffer no violence at my hands, and if it is to become known that you caused the death of his grandfather, I want no shadow of suspicion to fall upon me. Therefore, I go."

"You devil!" Rage and fear strove for mastery in Lord Henry's voice. "You unnatural monster! Do you care nothing for what may become of me?"

"No," said Gideon pleasantly. "I do not, but I care a great deal for what may become of me. Good-night, Father."

It soon became known, in the fashionable circles about the Court, that Gideon Crayle had left his father's house after a violent disagreement, and since the hunchback had ever disguised his true nature beneath a charm which made most people forget his uncanny appearance, it was readily agreed that the fault must have been Lord Henry's. Speculation concerning the exact nature of the quarrel ran high, but Gideon consistently refused to make any comment upon the subject, and Lord Henry was equally reticent.

Presently, however, ugly rumours, whose origin no one could discover, began to circulate concerning the violent death of the exiled Marquis of Rotherdale and the disappearance of his grandchildren. Some said that the unfortunate brother and sister had been murdered, others that they had been sold into bondage in the Indies, while yet a third story ran that they had fled thither in company with a stranger who had befriended them. Only upon one point did these conflicting tales agree—the man responsible for the crimes was Lord Henry Crayle. Gideon neither confirmed nor denied the rumours, but when he announced his imminent departure for Jamaica his friends nodded wisely, and dismissed the notion that the little Marquis and his sister were dead. Their cousin, obviously, was going in search of them.

In this conviction they were quite correct, but they would have been surprised and shocked to learn the plans he was weaving concerning the future of his young relatives. Gideon was, in fact, well pleased with the turn events had taken, for had it been given to him to choose a setting for the tragedy he was planning he would have selected the Caribbean. His mother's brother had owned a plantation not far from Port Royal, and being a bachelor entirely without heirs, he had willed it to the son of his only sister. Upon the planter's death four years before, Gideon had visited his inheritance, and found much to please him in the white plantation house, with its well-stocked byres and stables and slave-quarters, with the fields of sugar-cane stretching beyond.

He went down into Port Royal itself, then at the zenith of its evil prosperity, when Henry Morgan was pouring into it the plunder of the Spanish Main. In its taverns and brothels he saw the followers of the black flag, in blood-stained rags or stolen finery, with priceless jewels blazing on grimy fingers, squandering gold as freely as they squandered lives. He drank and talked with them, and gradually a scheme took shape in his mind. Their chief lack, he found, was shipping. They would put to sea in small boats, canoes even, and trust to fortune to send them a larger craft, which they would take by the process of boarding, a method of fighting at which they were unsurpassed. Observing the results obtained by these means, Gideon wondered what could be accomplished by a picked crew in a really fine vessel, and recalled, perhaps, that in the early days of the century more than one English nobleman had maintained a pirate ship for his own personal gain. Gold was power, and to Gideon Crayle power was the very breath of life. He determined to revive the custom.

Among the buccaneers whose acquaintance he had made was a man named Randolph Sarne, frequently referred to among the Brethren of the Coast as the 'Torturer'. He had learned his cut-throat trade under the flag of the infamous L'Ollonais, cruellest of all the pirates, and in the years that he had prowled the tropic seas had proved himself a worthy pupil of the monster he had once served. In appearance he was an odd-looking creature, tall and thin and lantern-jawed, with a face the colour of parchment and a habit of dressing always in rusty black and frayed linen reminiscent of a country parson. Never was an appearance more deceptive. Beneath that mean and inoffensive exterior was concealed a shrewd, imaginative mind and a ruthless cruelty, and he knew the Caribbean as he knew the streets of Port Royal. In Sarne, Gideon decided, he had found the ideal partner for the venture he was contemplating.

The pirate was fully alive to the advantages of such an association. Crayle was a member of a family powerful in England, and his protection would stand the buccaneers in good stead should they fall foul of English justice, while a ship such as Gideon meant to supply was a rare prize indeed. To disarm suspicion the vessel was built in Tortuga, and though many wondered whence Randolph Sarne obtained the money to purchase a forty-gun frigate, no one suspected that it came from the pleasant-mannered young hunchback who was a virtual newcomer to the island. They might have found a clue, however, in the macabre humour which named the vessel the *Vampire*, and which was in no way characteristic of Captain Sarne. That it was characteristic of Gideon Crayle Port Royal had yet to learn.

Since then the *Vampire* had become notorious in the Indies. Sarne was a bold leader and his men carefully chosen, while the speeed and armament of his ship brought him many a rich prize. With Morgan gone, and the fleet of which he had been admiral broken up, Sarne became one of the most famous captains in the black brotherhood and might have commanded a fleet of his own had he so wished, but he preferred to hunt alone, committing excesses which at length began to cause dismay even in the lawless Caribbean. The more sober-minded English planters began to talk of placing him under arrest, but, secure in the knowledge of a powerful protector, the Torturer laughed these ominous signs to scorn and continued on his sanguinary way.

Gideon, for his part, had never regretted his venture into piracy, and now he was positively thankful for it, since it might well prove the means of removing the last obstacle between him and possession of Rotherdale. For reasons of his own he chose to set sail from Bristol, but he was delayed there for some days for lack of a suitable ship. At length he obtained a passage to Barbados, where it would be easy enough to find a vessel to carry him to Jamaica, but on the day that he was due to sail—he was, in fact, already aboard—a weary and travel-stained messenger arrived from London in search of him. Lord Henry Crayle was suddenly dead.

His son received the news in the great cabin, standing in that favourite attitude of his leaning forward with one hand upon a table, which seemed to make his hunched shoulders and forward-thrust head look a little less unnatural. His companions, the captain and a planter and his wife homeward-bound for Barbados, regarded him sympathetically, for the charm which he could assume at will had already wrought upon them.

"It is a judgement," said Gideon solemnly at length, and his beautiful voice was charged with emotion. "He had sinned grievously, but—he was my father. God rest him!"

There was a pause. The gentlemen bowed their heads; the planter's lady dabbed her eyes with a lace handkerchief; the messenger let a decent interval elapse before he ventured to inquire respectfully whether Mr. Crayle would now postpone his voyage.

"Postpone it?" Gideon slowly raised his head. "No, my friend, that I cannot do. My father is dead, but somewhere out yonder"—he gestured towards the west—"are two helpless children, my cousins, who suffered great wrongs at his hands. I go to seek them, for it is the only reparation I can make, a duty to them, and to myself."

With that he turned abruptly and left them, and they, respecting his grief and the unselfishness of that decision, let him go. The captain and his two remaining passengers wondered a little at the meaning of his cryptic words, but the messenger took his leave and returned to London, to spread the news that rumour had not lied in blaming Lord Henry Crayle for the murder of the previous Marquis of Rotherdale and the disappearance of his heir. His lordship's son had tacitly admitted his father's guilt, now that his unexpected death had placed him beyond the reach of justice.

But to one person at least Lord Henry's death came as no surprise. Gideon Crayle was nothing if not thorough.

CHAPTER VI

THE BLACK FRIGATE

The Marquis of Rotherdale sat cross-legged on the deck of the *Jamaica Lass,* his red-gold head bent over the stick which he was whittling with a fearsome-looking knife, and whistled between his teeth a tune he had heard the mariners sing. He had essayed the words himself, but had been so sharply called to account by his sister that in her presence at least he confined himself to whistling.

Frances was seated on a coil of rope in a nearby patch of shadow, and at that moment she was paying no heed to her brother. Instead, she leaned back against the bulwarks and gazed dreamily up at the sails swelling against the cobalt sky, her bright hair blowing about a face which had lost its pallor and much of its uncompromising severity. She was not precisely happy—there was too much aboard the slave-ship to revolt and sadden her—but there was a dream-like unreality about her present situation which did much to lessen both her fears and her sorrow. She had learned to ignore the moans and cries of the slaves imprisoned in the noisome hold, and the brutalities which were part of the daily life of the ship, and was thankful to find herself ignored by both captain and crew. She guessed vaguely that she owed this in some way to Crispin Barbican, though she did not realize how constantly he shielded her, or the horrors she might have witnessed had he not placed himself between.

They had been many weeks at sea, for the *Jamaica Lass* was neither a new nor a swift vessel, but now they were within reasonable distance of their goal. Frances viewed their approach to Jamaica with mixed feelings, for though she would be glad to set foot on dry land once more she knew that it must mean the end of this strange interlude; Francis Barbican would give place once more to Lady Frances Crayle, and in her heart of hearts she would be sorry to see him go.

Presently Jonathan put away his knife, tossed the stick overboard and wandered off in search of other amusement, but Frances remained where she was until Captain Barbican came up the companion from the waist. He paused beside her, a hand on the ratlines, and looked down quizzically.

"The voyage grows tedious," he said, between statement and question, "but 'tis almost over. A week at most, and we shall reach Port Royal."

"And then?"

"Then?" he repeated, faintly surprised. "Why, I shall take you to Spanish Town, to the Lieutenant-Governor, Sir Thomas Lynch, who rules, as I have told you, in Modyford's absence. Unless, of course, your cousin the Earl is awaiting you in Jamaica."

Frances looked up sharply.

"Is that possible?"

"It is, unless Bess failed us, for we sailed first to Africa, and delayed there while Tom took in his cargo. Sailing direct from England to Jamaica, his lordship may well have reached Port Royal some time ago."

There was a pause, and then Frances said slowly:

"Are you sure, Crispin, that there is no danger for a—a pirate in an English port?"

"Not when the port is Port Royal," he said. "It is the pirates' haven, a golden hell. Some say 'tis the wickedest city in the world, but one thing at least is certain. No man of Welsh Harry's is in danger there."

"But Sir Henry Morgan is in England."

"Aye, roistering it there like a courtier born, boon companion to such nobles as the Duke of Albermarle and my Lord Carlisle, but his name is potent still in Port Royal. Have no fear! You will not be left friendless there by my arrest."

She bit her lip and turned to look out across the sea.

" 'Twas your danger that concerned me, not my own," she said in a low voice. "Why must you always think so badly of me?"

There was a moment's silence; then he laughed oddly.

"Think badly of you?" he repeated. "I? Child, you are easily deceived."

Something in his voice brought the colour to her face, and she looked up at him half-shyly, half-eagerly. For a long moment the grey eyes held the blue, and then from aloft the hoarse voice of a seaman came floating down to shatter the brief enchantment.

"Sail on the starboard bow!"

At the words a ripple of excitement and concern ran through the ship, for in these waters such a cry might well be the herald of battle, capture and death. Men swarmed into the rigging to catch a glimpse of the stranger-craft, and Captain Adams came stumping up the companion to join Crispin and Frances, his shirt open to the waist and a blue kerchief swathed about his cropped head.

"God send they be not Spaniards!" he said shortly. "I am in no case to lose another cargo, and disease has wrought havoc enough without Spanish guns to aid it."

Without waiting for an answer he turned away to bawl an order; Frances rose to her feet and looked in some alarm at Crispin.

"There will be a fight?"

"Perhaps. We shall know more certainly when we see what flag she flies. If 'tis that of Spain we may have no choice, but she may well be a friendly craft."

Presently from the lower level of the deck the masts and sails of the distant ship became visible, and it became evident that she was overtaking them with some rapidity. When at last she was full in view Captain Adams clapped a telescope to his eye and studied her in silence for fully five minutes.

"Yonder is no Spaniard," he announced at length, but his voice betrayed none of the satisfaction the discovery warranted. "What think you, Crispin?"

Captain Barbican, who had been lounging against the bulwarks with Frances and Jonathan beside him, took the proffered glass and trained it upon the other vessel. After a minute he returned it to its owner and said indifferently:

" 'Tis the *Vampire*."

Captain Adams swore.

"Sarne's black hell-ship! I hoped I was mistaken. Oh, what cursed ill-luck to chance upon him now, with the voyage almost done!"

"Why, what's here?" Captain Barbican was faintly surprised. "The Brethren of the Coast do not prey upon English ships. What have you to fear from Randolph Sarne?"

"Enough and to spare," said the slaver savagely. "I fell foul o'him in Port Royal when last I was there, and that sallow-faced devil knows no laws. He's not the man to let slip a chance o' vengeance. We must fight or run!"

"You are mad, Tom," said Crispin bluntly. "Yonder is the *Vampire,* and this hulk of yours can neither out-sail nor out-fight her. You know that as well as I do."

Tom Adams stared at him, his mouth twitching.

"One or the other we must do," he said. "I'll not yield me tamely to Sarne's torturers." His gaze shifted to the pirate ship, now appreciably nearer. " 'Tis no use to run—she's too swift for us—but if we fight we may disable her with a lucky shot and so make our escape."

"Don't be a fool!" Crispin spoke angrily. "Her guns are so far superior to yours that she will lie out of range and batter you to pieces at her leisure. You will sacrifice a ship, a cargo, and the lives of us all, and gain nothing by it."

But the slaver's fear of what might befall him at the hands of the notorious pirate outweighed all other considerations. In vain Captain Barbican and Lee, the mate, argued with him, pointing out the impossibility of defeating a vessel of the *Vampire*'s size and armament, and the havoc which would be wrought among his human cargo by the great guns of the pirate ship. In the grip of an overmastering panic Adams turned a deaf ear to all their reasoning, and while they argued the menacing shape of the black frigate crept closer and closer over the sparkling water. The crew of the *Jamaica Lass* were making the usual preparations for battle, but slowly and with many reluctant glances in the direction of the quarter-deck. They had taken the measure of the foe, and had no heart for the coming conflict.

At length, realizing that their efforts were useless, the mate turned aside with a gesture of helpless resignation. Crispin paused a moment longer, and then with a curt command to Jonathan and Frances to remain where they were he went briskly below. When he returned a short time later his sword was at his side and he carried also a pair of finely-mounted pistols, after the fashion of the buccaneers, at the ends of a leathern stole about his neck. As he set foot upon the quarter-deck a small cloud of smoke blossomed from the black hull of the *Vampire,* and to the boom of a gun a shot whistled across the bows of the *Jamaica Lass* and plunged into the sea a short way off.

It was the recognized signal to heave-to. The eyes of every man aboard the vessel turned towards her captain, hoping against hope for the order which did not come. The *Jamaica Lass* held steadily upon her course, and after a little a second gun boomed and this time the shot screamed warningly through her rigging. A growl of protest came from the assembled sailors.

Standing yet at the head of the companion, Captain Barbican looked down into the waist of the ship where many of her crew were gathered, and realized that they were on the verge of mutiny. His eyes, wintry grey in the shadow of his broad-brimmed hat, shifted to Tom Adams, who stared straight ahead with his mouth set in stubborn lines and his face a pasty white beneath its tan. From the depths of the ship came faintly the shrieks of the despairing slaves, roused to panic by the roar of the pirate guns, but neither to these nor to the increasingly angry mutterings of the crew did the slaver pay the slightest heed. Last of all Crispin looked at Frances, and the fear in her white face spurred him to action.

"Tom, for the last time, will you not listen to reason?" Captain Barbican's deep voice was clearly audible to the men below. "We rush upon our doom. In a moment she will loose a whole broadside and pound us to matchwood. For God's sake give the order to heave-to!"

"I am captain of this ship, Barbican." Adams spoke without looking at Crispin. "I give the orders here, and if any seek to gainsay me I'll clap 'em in irons."

"Is that your last word, Tom?" Crispin's hands were resting on the butts of his pistols.

"Aye," growled the slaver. "It is and be damned to ye."

"As you will," said Captain Barbican softly. "Your last word in truth, you mad fool!"

His right hand lifted, and a pistol spoke sharply with a spurt of yellow flame. Adams's head jerked back, he stiffened for an instant and then crumpled to the deck, and without a second glance at him Captain Barbican turned to give the order so long delayed.

It was greeted with a cheer, and in a commendably short space of time the *Jamaica Lass* lay with idly flapping sails, and a boat was putting off from the pirate ship towards them. Crispin went across to where Jonathan stood beside his sister, who leaned against the bulwarks with her face hidden in her hands. The little Marquis was rather white about the mouth, but he faced the captain gallantly and summoned up a smile.

"Are we not going to fight now, sir?"

"No, not now." Crispin set a hand on the girl's shoulder

61

and said meaningly, "Frances, this weakness is womanish."
She looked up then, and in answer to the horror in her eyes he
added: "I had to do it. There was no other way."

"You could have stunned and bound him," she whispered.
"My God, you did not have to kill him!"

Crispin frowned, and shot a quick glance to right and left,
but they were for the moment unheeded, all interest being
centred on the approaching boat. He spoke again, very
gravely.

"There was no time to consider ways and means, and if he
had made an enemy of the captain of that ship he is better
dead. Yonder is Randolph Sarne, whom men call the Torturer." Then, conceiving that this might merely add to her
fears, he added reassuringly: "But Sarne has no quarrel with
us, though it is more than ever important that you play your
part convincingly. But have no fear! I will bring you safe to
Jamaica yet, if you will but trust me."

With a visible effort she tore her gaze from the slaver's huddled body and looked up at him.

"I do trust you, Crispin, with all my heart," she said, and
laid her hand on his as it rested upon her shoulder. "But they
are pirates, and oh! I am afraid."

"No need for fear." He drew his hand away and spoke
curtly, almost bitterly. "You forget that I am myself a pirate.
Dog does not eat dog! Come with me."

They followed him obediently to the waist of the ship, and
the sailors drew aside for them to pass, tacitly acknowledging
the leadership of Captain Barbican. There they waited until
the boat drew alongside, and up the ladder came the emissary
of Captain Sarne of the *Vampire*.

He was a slight, wiry young man, dark-haired and olive-
skinned, with flashing dark eyes, and full lips below a small
moustache. He was dressed with raffish gaiety, his laced coat
girt with a broad sash of crimson satin, and gold ear-rings
gleaming through his greasy curls, and he paused for a moment on the bulwarks, steadying himself with a hand on the
shrouds and scanning the faces of the men before him. From
the forefront of the throng Captain Barbican returned the
look sardonically, and, making an extravagant gesture of surprise with his free hand, the young man addressed himself to
him.

"*C'est bien toi*, Crispin? By all the saints, what do you
aboard this pestilent hulk? Where is Captain Adams?"

"I travel in her, Jean-Pierre—to Jamaica, until you chose to interrupt our voyage," Crispin replied drily. "As for Tom Adams, he lies yonder with a bullet in his brain."

"*Mon Dieu!*" Jean-Pierre jumped lightly to the deck and advanced towards him. "It will not please my captain, that! He had a score to settle with Captain Adams, and I was sent to fetch him aboard the *Vampire*, but he will have small use for a corpse."

"I doubt it not," Crispin retorted calmly, "but the fool meant to engage you, and I took the only course to prevent it. What does Sarne intend by the rest of the crew?"

"He has no quarrel with them." Jean-Pierre raised his voice so that it was audible to the assembled sailors. "This vessel will accompany us to Port Royal, whither we are bound, and there she and her cargo will be sold and the profits divided among her crew according to custom. Here," he gestured towards a burly, one-eyed individual who had followed him from the boat, "is one to take the place of your captain until we reach Jamaica."

He paused inquiringly, but none questioned this arrangement. It was fair enough, and in any event there were the guns of the black frigate to enforce it should the need arise. All things considered, the crew of the *Jamaica Lass* felt that they had come off very well.

"*Bien!*" said the Frenchman at length. "It is agreed, *n'est-ce pas?* Now, Crispin, we go aboard the *Vampire*."

"We?" Captain Barbican was taken aback. "You want me to come with you?"

"But yes." Jean-Pierre set his hands on his hips, and his white teeth flashed in a smile which seemed friendly enough. "It is not possible that I take Captain Adams, and of a certainty I must not return empty-handed. I take you instead."

Crispin shrugged. There was no more to be said.

"As you will," he agreed indifferently, "but these lads come with me."

"These?" Jean-Pierre eyed Frances and Jonathan with some surprise. "They are your property?"

"My half-brothers. I am taking them to Jamaica. Do you permit us to collect our belongings?"

"But of course, my friend, of course," Jean-Pierre agreed amiably. "You come as guests, not as prisoners. Collect your gear by all means."

At a sign from Crispin, Frances and Jonathan made their way below, and he followed them a few minutes later, leaving Jean-Pierre on deck. He was profoundly disturbed at the prospect of transferring his charges to the pirate ship, for he knew that Randolph Sarne, deprived of one victim, was capable of meting out the intended punishment to the man who had baulked him of his revenge, and if any accident befell him it would go hard with Frances and Jonathan.

Crispin did not seek to deceive himself. He knew that the extreme action which he had taken to prevent a battle had not been prompted by concern for the crew of the slave-ship, the wretched Negroes crowding her hold, or even for his own life, but simply to ensure the safety of the girl whom, in those past few months, he had come to love. He had depended upon his own high reputation among the buccaneers to carry matters through, and it had never occurred to him that he might be obliged to go aboard the frigate, much less take Frances there.

Suppose her masquerade were discovered? It had been easy enough to deceive Adams and his crew, and even the devil-may-care Jean-Pierre, but Sarne was a different proposition. He wondered whether he dared leave her aboard the *Jamaica Lass,* and for a few minutes paced the narrow confines of his cabin in an agony of indecision, but at length he decided against it. Discovery might come at any time, and if come it must, at least she should have what protection his sword could give her. It may be, after all, that he was starting at shadows, for the danger he feared at Sarne's hands might never materialize.

Thus he made his decision, in the mistaken opinion that he knew the full extent of the danger which his lady might encounter aboard the pirate ship. A little time was yet to pass before the mis-shapen shadow of Gideon Crayle fell across their lives.

CHAPTER VII

STRANGE ENCOUNTER

CAPTAIN SARNE was waiting for them when they came aboard the *Vampire*, Jean-Pierre leading the way up the tall black side of the frigate, with Crispin immediately behind him and Frances and Jonathan bringing up the rear. By the time they were all on the deck the Frenchman was explaining the situation, with a wealth of gesture and many lapses into his native tongue, and Sarne listened patiently, his long, lugubrious countenance void of all expression.

Frances studied him in amazement, scarcely able to credit that this was the pirate who had inspired in Tom Adams such fear that he had been prepared to risk his ship and the lives of every being aboard her in an effort to escape him. She had pictured a ranting, swaggering bully, bearded and bloodstained and armed to the teeth, and this gaunt, grey-haired man, with his almost Puritan attire and air of profound gloom, filled her at first with a mixture of contempt and relief. Then, while she still stared, his melancholy glance was turned full upon her for the first time, and the terror of Captain Adams was suddenly understandable. The pirate's eyes were of a blue so light as to be almost colourless, cold and flat as the eyes of a snake, and yet so penetrating that instinctively she withdrew a little into the shelter of Captain Barbican's tall figure.

Jean-Pierre's lively narrative came to an end, and Crispin braced himself for whatever might follow, but it seemed that for once Captain Sarne was disposed to be lenient. He was returning to Jamaica after a singularly profitable cruise with the *Vampire* laden with plunder, while a captured galleon, also richly laden, had already been sent back to Port Royal. The capture and torture of Captain Adams would have been an enjoyable incident with which to round off this successful voyage, but it was a matter of no real importance. The fellow was dead, and would therefore annoy his betters no more, and Captain Barbican was too good a fighter to be wasted in that fashion. The *Vampire's* prizes had not been won without some loss of life, and her captain felt that Morgan's friend and erstwhile lieutenant would be a valuable addition to her crew. Crispin was therefore made welcome, and quarters assigned to him and to his young companions.

Jonathan was delighted beyond measure at finding himself aboard a pirate ship, though he was disappointed in his sister's reaction to this unexpected privilege. Frances's only source of satisfaction appeared to be the reflection that the black frigate would carry them to Port Royal more swiftly than the slave-ship could have done.

This sudden eagerness to reach Jamaica was not inspired by fear, for she soon discovered that her presence provoked no more attention than it had done aboard the *Jamaica Lass,* but she was impatient now to have done with this life of violence and bloodshed. The murder of Captain Adams had rudely shattered her growing contentment, and earnest self-examination revealed the disturbing fact that it was the identity of the slayer, rather than the actual deed, which had shaken the very foundations of her world.

The discovery did nothing to calm her. Why should it matter so greatly that a pirate behaved after the fashion of his kind? The motive for the deed had been selfless enough, and his attitude towards her and her brother remained unchanged even now that he was among his old comrades again, so why should it hurt her to see him upon such friendly terms with the infamous Captain Sarne and his cut-throat followers?

Why indeed? Her ladyship found herself on the brink of a discovery even more unpalatable, and drew back in alarm. She told herself sternly that her association with Crispin Barbican was but a transient interlude in her life, that she was confusing gratitude with some deeper emotion, and that once she was safely in her guardian's care she would soon forget these odd fancies. Finally she reminded herself that she was all but betrothed to her cousin, Viscount Mountheath, and though her heart grew unaccountably heavy at the thought, she found in it a sort of sanctuary.

Crispin, unaware of her ladyship's mental conflict, attributed her obvious uneasiness to the surroundings in which she found herself. He was himself deeply preoccupied, for his relief at their reception aboard the *Vampire* was of short duration, and was, in fact, dispelled on their first night aboard the frigate.

He was alone with Sarne in the great cabin, a fantastic apartment eloquent of the pirate's strangely-contrasted nature. Randolph Sarne had two overmastering passions in life—the greed for gold and a love of beauty. This queer twist of character had led him to turn his ship into a floating treasure-house, and to hoard for his own personal gratification any object which took his fancy, whether it were worthless or a priceless work of art, and all these treasures were crowded into the spacious cabin of his ship.

The bulkheads were hung with pictures and tapestries of great beauty and value, and the furniture, magnificently carved and with a coat-of-arms emblazoned upon it, had been filched from the palace of a Spanish nobleman. Every available space was crammed with the fruits of many filibustering raids, and since Sarne had no knowledge of the things he collected, splendid altar-pieces and sacred vessels from Christian churches rubbed shoulders with trinkets of gold wrought by Indian hands. In the midst of all this stolen splendour the pirate captain sat like a gaunt black vulture, drinking rum out of a crystal goblet, and taking coarse snuff from a box of solid gold.

He had invited Captain Barbican to take the place of one of his officers lost in a recent fight, but Crispin showed himself reluctant to accept this offer, Captain Sarne waxed persuasive.

"Look you, Barbican, 'tis no small thing I am offering you. Now that Morgan is gone there are many eager to sail with me. For every man I take I could have a score, had I the space to carry them. The *Vampire's* a lucky craft. What say you, now?"

Crispin smiled and shook his head.

"My thanks to you, but I've no mind to return to the trade yet awhile. For one thing, there are these lads of mine to be considered. They are over-young yet for such a life."

Sarne made an impatient movement.

"We shall remain at Port Royal long enough for you to find a place to bestow them. That is no reason for refusing my offer. 'Tis but an evasion, and I could make a shrewd guess at the cause. You've no fancy to sail under my command when you've been accustomed to commanding a ship of your own."

67

"I don't deny that I prefer it," Crispin admitted levelly, "but, as I say, I had no thought of returning to the trade at present."

"Not even with the command of a thirty-gun ship to be had for the asking, and the chance of an enterprise such as the Brethren have not known since Harry Morgan burned Panama?"

Crispin looked up quickly.

"What ship, and who offers her?"

"I offer her, the *Santo Rosario* out of Cadiz. We took her not long since and sent her ahead of us to Port Royal. She's a sound craft, and with a few trifling alterations to add to her speed would be a fit companion for this vessel. I'll be plain with you, Barbican! I've a venture in mind too great for the *Vampire* to attempt alone, strong as she is, but with the *Rosario* also we might well make the attempt. I need a man to command her on whom I can rely, and you sailed long enough with Morgan to have learned his methods. 'Tis wit of that kind I'll be needing, and it's a captain's share I offer you."

"It is the custom of the Brethren," Crispin pointed out mildly, "to appoint their captains by vote."

Sarne shook his head.

"Not in any ship o' mine," he said. "My officers are the men most fitted for the task, and not those who know how to sway the feelings of a mob. That is why I am successful."

"Aye, you're a shrewd leader, I grant you that. What enterprise is it that you are so set upon?"

A smile which closely resembled the grin of a wolf dispelled the pirate's customary gloom.

"That, my friend, you learn when you accept the command of the *Santo Rosario*, or not at all," he replied. "There is no need for haste. Your decision can wait until we reach Port Royal."

"I'll think on it," Crispin promised him, "but I doubt not that the great days of piracy passed with Modyford and Morgan. Lynch rules now in Jamaica, and, like the greasy merchant he is, favours the Assiento, and would trade with the Dons rather than plunder their cities. You'll not be thinking of following in Welsh Harry's footsteps, and ending your days with a knighthood?"

Captain Sarne refilled his glass and tossed off the raw spirit as though it were water.

"Perhaps," he replied enigmatically. "Morgan achieved it without the advantage of influence at Court."

Crispin raised derisive brows.

"You have such influence, I suppose?"

Again the wolf-grin revealed yellowish teeth.

"Aye," Sarne agreed equably, "I have. How think you I came to by this frigate?"

"I have often wondered," said Crispin frankly, "but now I begin to perceive a possible answer."

The pirate nodded.

"Your eyes are then keener than most, Crispin Barbican. I've a mind to tell you the whole, but first, your promise that whether you join me or no, this matter shall remain a secret between us."

Crispin gave the required promise readily enough, more out of curiosity than anything else, for he knew too much of Randolph Sarne to desire any close assiciation with him, though it seemed that others were less squeamish. Sarne regaled himself with yet another tot of rum, and then thrust the delicate goblet aside and leaned his folded arms on the table.

"Sir Thomas Modyford was not the only English gentleman to see the value of piracy," he said, "though not all were in a position to grant a commission, as Modyford did to Morgan. But these matters may be arranged as well, better even, privately. The man who caused the *Vampire* to be built, and who set me in command of her, has been repaid many times over in Spanish gold, and if we stand in any danger from the law he has influence enough—and wit enough, I'll warrant—to turn it aside. You'll have heard that even justice has its price in England today."

"You have proof, then, of his power?"

"I know his name, and no other proof is needful. He is his father's son, and all the world knows how close to the throne stands Lord Henry Crayle."

Captain Barbican was in the act of filling his pipe. For an instant the long fingers were stilled, and keen grey eyes shot a glance of level inquiry at Sarne. The pirate grinned and nodded.

"Aye, ye may well be surprised!" he resumed smugly. "Ye'll not know, perhaps, that Gideon Crayle owns a plantation not far from Port Royal? He was in Jamaica four years ago and 'twas then I made his acquaintance. The rest followed easily enough."

"I heard some talk in England of Lord Henry Crayle," said Crispin casually. "Is he not kin to the Marquis of Rotherdale?"

"A brother," Captain Sarne agreed. "The old Marquis is in exile, and Lord Henry controls the lands and the fortune. Let that be proof of his son's power to protect us."

"What like is he, this Gideon Crayle?" Crispin asked, still deliberately casual.

Sarne grinned.

"A devil," he replied succinctly. "A hunchback with a voice that would charm Satan out of hell. Pleasant enough to outward-seeming—he was mighty popular with the gentry around Port Royal—but that's the face he shows to the world. His father is Marquis of Rotherdale in all but name, but I'd stake my life that Gideon will have the title, too, before all's done, no matter what obstacles stand in his way. I tell you, Barbican, if there's a living man I fear, 'tis Gideon Crayle."

The entry of Jean-Pierre at this point set a term to the conversation, but Crispin had heard more than enough. He perceived that he had led his young charges into a trap, and that their only chance of escape lay in keeping secret the true identity of Jonathan and Francis Barbican. He knew nothing of Gideon Crayle, but the fact that he was Lord Henry's son was damning enough, and Sarne's description of him was in no way reassuring. If the hunchback could inspire fear in the Torturer he must be extraordinarily adept in the ways of evil.

His oath of silence, so thoughtlessly given, prevented him from telling Frances and Jonathan of their cousin's association with Captain Sarne, but as he imagined that Gideon Crayle was far away in England this did not unduly trouble him. He did indeed warn them once again of the vital necessity of maintaining their disguise, but the next day an incident occurred which drove the matter temporarily from his mind.

In the forenoon the look-out sighted a drifting object which was presently identified as a ship's longboat, and the *Vampire* altered course a trifle to come up with it. As she drew nearer a man raised himself in the boat and waved a feeble arm, the weakness of the gesture suggesting that he had been drifting thus for some time.

When at length the black frigate drew close to the little craft those on her decks saw that there were four men in it, though only one showed any sign of life. The others lay huddled in the bottom of the boat, and did not stir even when a ropeladder was cast over the *Vampire*'s side and two sturdy ruffians swarmed down it to their aid. They made fast the boat and then, while one examined the three motionless figures, his fellow brought the still-conscious man up to the deck of the frigate.

He was a copper-skinned half-breed, lean and wiry but now on the verge of collapse, his face haggard and livid beneath its bronze, the lips cracked and swollen. Thy laid him on the deck in a patch of shadow, and someone held a pannikin of water to his lips. He drank greedily until at a word from Sarne the mug was removed.

The water seemed to revive the half-breed a little. His eyes focussed themselves more clearly, and after two or three vain attempts he achieved a cracked whisper.

"In the boat . . . his lordship . . . help him."

There was a murmur of surprise, and Sarne's cold eyes quickened.

"His lordship, is it?" he said. "Jean-Pierre!" He jerked his head in the direction of the boat.

The young Frenchman was over the side in a flash, shouting an order to the man below as he went. A noble prisoner was always welcome, and a ransom would go to swell the common loot.

The man who was presently laid upon the deck was young and well-favoured. A golden periwig, now sadly out of curl, framed an attractive, boyish face, and his long, slim person was arrayed in what had once been a finery of gold-laced satin, now stained with sea-water and faded by the tropic sun.

"This will be the milor', my captain. The others are mere seamen," Jean-Pierre announced, and added reassuringly: "He still lives."

"Take him below. Let him have every care." Captain Sarne turned to Crispin. "Here, Barbican, those lads of yours can look to him. 'Tis time they made themselves useful."

"As you wish," said Crispin indifferently. "Francis, Jonathan, come with me."

He bent, lifted the young nobleman to his broad shoulder, and strode off with Frances and Jonathan at his heels, and Captain Sarne turned his attention once more to the half-breed. Crispin carried the young man to his own cabin and laid him upon the bed, sending Jonathan for water.

"I had best return to Sarne before he grows suspicious," he told Frances. "Unless you need my help with his lordship here."

"Thank you," she replied with dignity, "but I have nursed a

71

sick man before now, and I fancy I am tolerably capable. Jonathan can give me any aid that I require."

"I will go, then." Crispin turned towards the door. "Send word to Sarne when the boy regains his senses."

He went out, and Frances bent over the motionless figure on the bed, pushing the lank strands of the periwig back from his brow, and wondering as she did so who he was and how he came to be in his present plight.

When Jonathan returned with the water they bathed the unknown's face and hands and forced some of the liquid between the cracked lips. Frances was holding a wet cloth to his brow when her brother, standing beside her with the basin, gave a gasp and clutched her shoulder.

"Frances!" he exclaimed, his voice shaking. "His right hand! Look at his right hand!"

Frances looked. The cloth dropped suddenly to the floor, and she stared with quickened breath and dilating eyes at the limp hand protruding from the torn lace ruffles. On the third finger was a great gold ring set with an intaglio sapphire bearing an armorial device. The signet of Rotherdale.

CHAPTER VIII

BY RIGHT OF CONQUEST

FOR the space of a minute Frances and Jonathan remained silent and motionless, frozen into stillness by the sight of the familiar ring on the hand of this young stranger. At last the girl reached out and lifted the inanimate hand to examine the jewel more closely. Her own fingers were shaking and her heart thumping painfully, for the strangeness of this meeting in a far clime with one who wore the signet of her family made her suddenly, unreasonably afraid.

"It is the ring," she said slowly. "Jonathan, fetch Crispin, quickly."

The boy came out of his daze of surprise with a start and

ran to do her bidding. Frances remained where she was, bending over the bed with the stranger's hand still in hers; and then he opened his eyes.

For an instant startled blue eyes gazed into puzzled brown and then his lids drooped again. Frances recovered herself, and slipping her arm beneath his shoulders held the pannikin of water to his lips. When he had drunk he opened his eyes again and looked up at the fair face so near his own.

"Am I dreaming still?" he murmured. "Sweet lady, I pray you——"

Frances's hand came down gently across his lips. She whispered urgently:

"For the love of God, sir, be silent! You will betray me else."

She rose to her feet, went to the door and opened it softly, but to her relief no one was within sight. She turned to find the young man regarding her in some bewilderment and, suddenly conscious of her attire, she coloured furiously.

"I pass for a boy, sir," she said quietly, returning to his side. "This is a pirate ship. Later I will explain, but first"—she paused, half afraid to put the question foremost in her mind—"tell me, I pray you, how you came by the ring you wear."

He stared up at her beneath knitted brows.

"I had it from my father," he replied with an effort, "the Earl of Larchwood. I am Mountheath."

Her eyes widened.

"Mountheath?" she whispered. "Then we are cousins. I am Frances Crayle."

They were still staring at each other in blank surprise when Captain Barbican entered the cabin. Frances turned to him impulsively, with outstretched hand.

"Crispin, what think you? The strangest chance! 'Tis my cousin, Viscount Mountheath."

"Softly, child, softly!" Crispin came to stand beside her, while Jonathan, wide-eyed and curious, stared in silence at his new-found kinsman. "Your danger is not yet past." He looked down at the Viscount. "So 'tis my Lord Larchwood's son? Do you come seeking your cousins, my lord?"

"I do, sir. You are Captain Barbican?"

Crispin bowed slightly.

"At your lordship's service," he said formally. He saw that the Viscount was about to speak again, and raised a hand to check him. "All that is for later, my lord, when you are

73

stronger," he said authoritatively. "For the present it matters only that your cousins pass here for my half-brothers. To forget that is to betray us all. The rest can wait."

Wait it did, until the following day, by which time his lordship had more or less recovered from his ordeal, and those aboard the *Vampire* had already learned the outline of this adventure from his companions. The ship in which his lordship was travelling had been set upon by Spaniards, and only succeeded in driving them off after a fight which left the English ship in a sadly battered condition. While in this plight a storm had overtaken them, which they had been unable to weather. The ship sank, and only the Viscount and his three companions had succeeded in reaching the longboat, where they remained at the mercy of the elements until the storm abated. They found themselves without food or water, or any means of propelling their frail craft, and had drifted for three days before sighting the *Vampire*.

Captain Sarne, when he came to question his prisoner, learned only his name and rank, and the fact that if he were conveyed to safety to Port Royal his lordship would be more than willing to reward his rescuers. He was, he said, acquainted with the Lieutenant-Governor of Jamaica, and Sir Thomas Lynch would undoubtedly vouch for him. Captain Sarne retired, well-pleased.

To Captain Barbican, Frances and Jonathan the tale was told in more detail. They heard how the Earl had arrived at Larchwood Hall only two days after their flight from England, and learned the whole story of his kinsman's murder from the letters awaiting him, supplemented by such information as Bess could give him. He had returned post-haste to London to lay the proof of Lord Henry's villainy before the King, but experiencing some difficulty in convincing Charles of his favourite's guilt, he had at length despatched his son to the Indies in search of the little Marquis and his sister.

The Viscount did not feel called upon to mention his parent's real reason for setting him a task which would take him far from England—namely his entanglement with a play-actress. Already Lady Frances's delicate beauty had completely eclipsed the memory of Madam Sarah's opulent charms, and he found himself recalling with pleasure his father's wish that he should marry his cousin. A desire which, before leaving England, he had declared he would die sooner than fulfil.

"Then our uncle will be punished for having caused Grandfather's death?" said Jonathan when the story was done, but Mountheath shook his head.

"He is beyond the reach of justice now, and you have no more fear from him," he said. "He died suddenly before I left England. An apoplexy, it was said. He was a choleric man. So you may return to England in perfect safety."

"Lord Henry had a son, did he not?" Crispin asked quietly.

"Yes, Gideon," Mountheath replied pensively. "They had quarrelled violently, and some said 'twas because of Lord Henry's crimes against his brother. At all events, Gideon had set out in search of his cousins before I left England, and not even the news of his father's death could stay him."

"Do you mean, then, that we have nothing to fear from our cousin?" Frances asked doubtfully.

"Faith, no!" exclaimed his lordship. "Gideon's a pleasant enough fellow, in spite of his looks. He is a hunchback, you know, poor devil! But he is popular. Everyone likes him."

Crispin held his peace, but remembering Captain Sarne's comments upon that same popular gentleman, he was more than a little uneasy. Sarne, after all, was in a better position to judge the true nature of Gideon Crayle than was Lord Mountheath, and it seemed likely to Crispin that the hunchback would prove to be an enemy a hundred times more subtle and dangerous than Lord Henry. Only his promise to Sarne prevented him from telling his companions of Crayle's connection with the pirates, for to Crispin Barbican a promise was sacred, even when made to one who had little regard for a given word. It was not long, however, before he had cause to regret his reticence.

By the second day after his rescue Lord Mountheath found himself fully recovered, and ventured forth from his cabin. He was treated with great civility, and being an amiable and easy-mannered young man he was soon quite at ease with his rescuers. It was remarked that his lordship had taken an obvious like to Captain Barbican's young half-brothers, and was observed on the poop with Francis, absorbed in an earnest conversation which lasted for more than an hour—until, in fact, it was interrupted by Captain Barbican himself.

Ostensibly he came to warn them of the danger of drawing attention of any sort upon her ladyship, but he knew in his heart that this was merely an excuse. He cursed himself for a fool that the young Viscount's possessive attitude towards

Frances should fill him with jealous fury, and was only partly consoled by the promptness with which she took heed of his warning. She announced her intention of going below and Crispin found a malicious pleasure in engaging Mountheath in a conversation which prevented him from following her.

They were presently joined by Captain Sarne, and the talk turned upon West Indian matters. Sir Henry Morgan, the Viscount informed them, had lately been appointed Lieutenant-General of the Jamaican forces, but there was at present no indication that he would be returning to the Caribbean to take up his various appointments there. He was still, after two years, a prominent figure in London society, a favourite with the King and close friend of many gentlemen of rank and fortune. He had travelled far, this son of a Welsh farmer, since the days when he had led an uprising of his fellow-slaves in Barbados, and broken out of bondage to follow the black flag.

Strangely enough, however, Captain Barbican displayed little interest in the career of his erstwhile friend, and after a while made his way below, leaving Mountheath with Sarne and Jonathan on the poop. His anxiety had become so great that he had finally determined to disregard his promise to Sarne and tell Frances the truth concerning Gideon Crayle, but it presently transpired that he had delayed too long.

While he had been talking to the Viscount, Jean-Pierre had chanced to saunter into the great cabin. He entered with no set purpose, but the sight of a flask of wine on the table invited him to linger, and a few moments later, savouring its excellence—for it had come out of the captured galleon—he leaned against a nearby chair and looked benevolently at the only other occupant of the cabin.

This was Francis Barbican, who was dozing on the cushioned locker below the square windows astern. Apparently Master Barbican was feeling the effect of the tropic heat, for he had cast aside coat and waistcoat and his white shirt was open at the throat. Jean-Pierre took another mouthful of wine, and wondered lazily how it happened that the formidable Captain Barbican had so frail and timid a half-brother. The little Jonathan was sturdy enough, but this Francis— *mordieu!* the lad was as delicate as a woman.

With the thought there occurred to Jean-Pierre a suspicion so startling and yet so obvious that for a moment it held him spellbound. Then he set down his glass to move, silent as a cat, across the cabin to halt beside the locker. His dark eyes travelled unhurriedly over the slim, unconscious figure before

76

him, and as slowly a smile dawned upon his face. He laughed softly.

The sound, or perhaps some instinct of danger, woke Frances. For one breathless instant she stared up at Jean-Pierre, and knew by his eyes that her masquerade was discovered. She started up and made one desperate effort to escape, but he was too quick for her, and an arm which seemed to have the strength of steel caught her about the waist, clipping one arm to her side. She screamed, and struck wildly at his face with her free hand, but he dodged the blows, laughing still, and the thin cambric shirt ripped beneath his brutal fingers.

"So!" he exclaimed exultantly. "The good Crispin has deceived us, mademoiselle——" He got no further, for the door flew open with a crash and Captain Barbican himself was in the cabin.

Jeane-Pierre swung round with a curse, his hand flashing instinctively to his side, but he had no time to possess himself of a weapon. Crispin's first blow sent him staggering back against a bulkhead, and before he could recover Barbican's hands were about his throat. He broke free with a cunning twist and snatched a dagger from his belt, aiming a vicious blow at his assailant. Frances cried out again, but Crispin caught the murderous hand about the wrist as it descended and for a moment they swayed to and fro, each struggling for possession of the knife. A chair went over with a crash.

"God's death, what's here?" Randolph Sarne loomed in the doorway, a pistol in his hand, a curious throng at his heels. "Have done! Have done, I say, or I'll pistol the pair of you!" The gun barked, and a ball buried itself in the woodwork just above their heads.

"That's for a warning," Sarne continued through the drifting smoke. "Another time I'll show less patience. What the devil's amiss here?"

Jeane-Pierre leaned against the table and wiped a trickle of blood from his mouth with the back of his hand. He was breathing quickly, but he contrived to laugh.

"As you see, my captain, our comrade has been deceiving us, and resents discovery." A graceful gesture indicated Frances, who was backed against the wall with one hand clutching the torn shirt across her breast. Sarne's cold eyes turned thither, widened for an instant, and then narrowed.

"God's death!" he said again, more softly. "So that's the way of it!"

He took a pace toward the cowering girl, and with a sob she started away from him and cast herself into Captain Barbican's arms.

"Crispin!" she gasped. "Save me, for the love of God! Don't let them touch me!"

"Softly, my heart! You shall come to no harm." Crispin's voice was gentle, but as his eyes rested upon Captain Sarne they were cold and uncompromising. He set a hand on the hilt of his sword, and the pirate grinned unpleasantly.

"No need for that, Barbican," he sneered. "You cannot fight us all, and a sword is of small use against pistols. If you choose to bring your doxy aboard my ship she must be prepared to share her favours."

"It was, of course, given to me to choose," said Crispin ironically, and as he spoke he was thinking swiftly. The betrayal was not yet complete, for Sarne had no clue to the girl's real identity, and if the present danger could be averted, all might yet be well. If it could be averted!

"It is so, my captain," said Jean-Pierre unexpectedly. "He did not choose to bring Mademoiselle aboard the *Vampire*. I forced him to accompany me, and of a certainty he could not leave her alone aboard the *Jamaica Lass*."

Sarne eyed his lieutenant incredulously.

"What's to do now?" he demanded, while Crispin shot a suspicious glance at his unlooked-for ally. "D'ye dare defy me, ye dawcock?"

"My captain!" Jean Pierre lifted his shoulders and spread his hands in a gesture of mingled mockery and reproach. "I do but remind you that the *Jamaica Lass* was ours by right of conquest, and any prize which came out of her would join the rest of the loot which is to be divided among us. Is it not so? His hot gaze turned once more towards Frances, and he repeated slowly, "Any prize."

"Ecod, ye're right!" Sarne spoke triumphantly. "You ever had a shrewd head on your shoulders, my lad, the more so where a wench was concerned. By right of conquest, eh? 'Twas well thought on."

"So you see, my friend," Jean-Pierre said softly to Crispin, "this so unreasonable attitude is quite misplaced. Whatever prize the Brethren capture belongs not to one, but to all, as you should know. What say you to that, *mon brave!*"

He was advancing towards them as he spoke, and from the buccaneers grouped about the door came a lewd jest to spur him on. Captain Barbican's lips thinned ominously. He put Frances gently behind him, and his rapier whipped out of its sheath with a high, wicked note of glee.

"I say this," he replied grimly. "While I live not one of you shall lay a hand upon her."

"But then, my friend," said Jean-Pierre apologetically, "you may not live very long."

Ribald mirth from those about the door greeted this pleasantry, and Sarne added:

"Put up your sword, Barbican. You are too lusty a fighter to fling your life away for a wench. I've no wish to pistol you, but unless you stand away from the doxy, as God sees me, I'll do it."

"Crispin!" Frances spoke pitifully, and clasped both hands about his sword-arm. " 'Tis no use—they will murder you. If you have any kindness for me, turn your sword against my heart."

"Wait!" A voice spoke sharply from the doorway, and the young Viscount elbowed his way through the crowd. "Captain Sarne, I warn you! Lay one finger on that lady and it will go hard with you, for she is no common wench to become the plaything of a pirate ship. She is a lady of high degree, and my own cousin." Crispin made an urgent gesture of warning, but it went unheeded. The Viscount swept on, "That is Lady Frances Crayle, and you touch her at your peril!"

Jean-Pierre laughed derisively, but Sarne raised a hand to check him. He was watching Mountheath with narrowed eyes.

"If that be so, my lord, how comes she to be wandering the world in that guise, and in such company? Strange doings those, for a lady o' quality."

The Viscount drew himself up to his full, slender height, and in spite of lank periwig and bedraggled finery he was at that moment very much the great gentleman.

"Her ladyship," he replied austerely, "was in danger of her life as long as she remained in England, as was also her brother, the Marquis of Rotherdale." A nod indicated Jonathan at his side. "There was one who stood to gain by their deaths, and when their grandfather was murdered Captain Barbican befriended them and fled with them from the country to escape their pursuers. I followed to bring them home to the care of their guardian, my father."

Sarne pursed his lips.

"It can be proved?"

"Of course."

"There is in Jamaica, not far from Port Royal," continued the pirate, "a plantation belonging to one Gideon Crayle." He looked questioningly at the Viscount.

"You know him?" Mountheath exclaimed. "But that is excellent. He also is kin to her ladyship, and had already set forth for Jamaica when I left England. He should be there by now. You have only to go to him for whatever proof you need."

For a long moment of silence Sarne stared at him thoughtfully, and slowly understanding dawned in his face.

"I doubt it not," he said smoothly, and turned to Frances, who still cowered in the shelter of Crispin's arm. "My lady, I ask your pardon. Have no further uneasiness, for no harm shall come to you aboard this ship." His glance shifted to include Jean-Pierre and such of the crew as were within sight. "You hear, ye dogs? Any who offers insult to her ladyship by word or deed, dies." He paused, and his eyes met those of Captain Barbican. He grinned unpleasantly. "You're a secretive devil, an't you, Barbican? But I have your measure now, thanks to his lordship here, and I've a notion that Mr. Crayle will be mighty pleased to learn that his search is at an end, and his noble cousins safe aboard the *Vampire*."

CHAPTER IX

THE LADY AND THE PIRATE

HE took Jean-Pierre firmly by the arm and led him out of the cabin, dispersing the group about the door with one terse command. Lord Mountheath looked across at Captain Barbican, and the faintest of frowns wrinkled his aristocratic brow. It was right and proper, of course, for the fellow to be prepared to defend Lady Frances, but was it equally proper, now that the danger was past, that he should continue to hold her in his arms? Or, for that matter, that she should be content to stay there, as presumably she was? It seemed regrettably evident that her ladyship was in danger of losing all sense of decorum, and equally evident that it was his duty to point this out to her. He cleared his throat.

"A satisfactory ending to a most disturbing incident," he remarked somewhat pompously. "It is fortunate for you, my dear cousin, that Captain Barbican arrived so opportunely."

It was not exactly what he had meant to say, but it had the desired effect. Frances started, and moved away from Crispin to drop into a chair by the table. Heartened by his success, the Viscount made another attempt, this time addressing Barbican himself.

"As her ladyship's kinsman, sir, permit me to thank you for your gallant, though foolhardy, attempt to save her." This pleased him better, for he felt it marked the gulf between them, and he continued a trifle maliciously: "I fear, however, that it would have gone hard with you but for my intervention. You might, of course, have revealed my cousin's identity yourself, but no doubt you considered your sword a more potent weapon."

This speech had little apparent effect upon the Captain. He was still watching Frances, and now he came forward to the table, poured a glass of wine and set it before her.

"Drink that, child," he said gently, and waited to see her raise it to her lips before he answered the Viscount. When at last he deigned to notice his lordship his manner had undergone a surprising change.

"I did so consider it, my lord," he said grimly. "I had a good reason for my silence. Do you imagine 'twas her ladyship's rank, or your presence, which shielded her?" He laughed shortly. "This is a pirate ship, as your lordship seems to be in danger of forgetting, and aboard such it matters little whether a woman be a lady of quality or a drab from the streets, so that she be young and comely."

The Viscount glared at him.

"You grow offensive, I think," he said haughtily. "That we stand talking here now gives the lie to your words. I repeat, sir, the lie."

"God's light, boy, do not seek to pick a quarrel with me!" Crispin replied impatiently. "Believe me, the danger is by no means past, and Lady Frances may need both our swords before this venture is done. D'ye know to whom this ship belongs?"

Mountheath raised his brows.

"To Captain Sarne, I presume, but I fail to see how it concerns us."

"But when you do know you will perhaps perceive the reason for my silence. The man whose gold purchased the *Vampire*, and into whose pocket flows a large part of her plunder, is Gideon Crayle."

There was a stunned silence. With shaking fingers Frances set down her glass and said unsteadily:

"Our cousin? Is it possible?"

"I fear so, my lady. Sarne told me of their partnership the first night we spent aboard. He invited me to join it."

" 'Tis a thing not unknown," announced the Viscount, recovering himself. "I do not say that I condone it, but since the King does not hesitate to profit by the activities of the buccaneers and even confers a knighthood on the boldest of them, why should his subjects not follow his example? I perceive in that no reason to conceal my cousin's identity, but rather an added incentive to reveal it."

Captain Barbican looked him straight in the eye.

"Lord Henry Crayle," he said deliberately, "did not hesitate to murder his own brother in order to possess himself of the wealth and title of Rotherdale. It is not impossible that his son cherishes a similar amibition."

"Sir, you go too far!" Mountheath exclaimed indignantly. "I'd stake my life that Gideon has no such villainous intention. My lady, I beg that you will pay no heed to these unworthy accusations."

"And I, my lady, entreat you not to trust this man Crayle. 'Like father, like son' is an old adage, and a true one."

Frances sighed, and looked from one to the other in some distress.

"There is sound sense in what you say, Crispin," she admitted, "and yet 'tis but speculation, after all. My lord knows Gideon Crayle, and we do not." Her voice quivered, and she raised a hand to her head. "I do not know what to believe. I think I will go to my cabin."

"Of course, my dear." At once Mountheath was all solicitude. "I vow we are brutes to plague you so. Permit me to offer you my arm."

"Thank you." She rose to her feet and laid her hand on the proffered arm, but paused to look up at Captain Barbican. "I am very grateful, Crispin," she said quietly.

The Viscount escorted her in silence from the great cabin.

Reaching the door of her own apartment she would have parted from with a word of thanks, but he detained her.

"You have endured a great deal, my lady," he said, "but the ordeal is almost over. Have courage a little longer and you shall be free of these pirates." He hesitated for an instant, and then added meaningly, "All of them."

She regarded him curiously.

"Do you number Crispin Barbican among them, my lord?" she asked quietly, and he raised his brows.

"Is it not where he belongs? He has served you faithfully and well, but now that I have found you your need of him is past." He took her hand and raised it to his lips. "If you have forgotten the plans which were made for our future, my dear, I have not."

Early upon the following day the *Vampire* came safely into Port Royal, firing a salute as she glided past the fort at the harbour mouth. It was answered by the guns of a tall yellow galleon which Sarne pointed out to Captain Barbican as the captured *Santo Rosario,* and by a rattle of musket-fire from two other buccaneer craft which lay at anchor in the haven. The noise roused the inhabitants of the evil city, and by the time that the black frigate dropped anchor a fleet of small boats was clustering about her like cygnets about a swan, and a cheering crowd had gathered on the mole to welcome the victorious pirates.

The buccaneers swarmed joyfully ashore to squander the fruits of their voyage in their usual unholy fashion, leaving only a handful of men to guard the prisoners. For prisoners they undoubtedly were, although they had the freedom of the ship and were treated with all civility. Captain Sarne was one of the first ashore, shortly informing Crispin that he would return when he had seen Gideon Crayle, and that they were to remain aboard the *Vampire* meanwhile.

From the information which Mountheath had let fall, and his own knowledge of Crayle's character, the pirate had formed a fair notion of the situation between Gideon and his young relatives, and looked for an ample reward from the hunchback when he delivered the prisoners into his hands. If he was mistaken, and Crayle meant no harm to the little Marquis and his sister, he must ransom them from the pirates according to custom. Whichever attitude Gideon chose to adopt, Sarne and his men would profit.

After the pirates had left the ship, Crispin stood with Jonathan on the poop and answered the lad's eager questions somewhat absently. He was profoundly uneasy, distrusting both Sarne and the unknown Gideon Crayle, and apprehensive of the danger into which the high-handed behaviour of Lord Mountheath might carry Frances and Jonathan. That the Viscount resented his influence over them was obvious, and Crispin guessed that he would spare no pains to turn them, and the girl in particular, against him.

He had not seen Lady Frances since the previous day, and now he suddenly became aware that the Viscount also was absent. He turned to Jonathan, and, interrupting him without ceremony, inquired the whereabouts of his lordly cousin.

"Oh, he is in the great cabin with Frances," the Marquis replied cheerfully. "They were talking about our cousin Gideon."

Crispin grunted, and resumed his frowning study of the distant town, Jonathan leaned his arms on the bulwarks and watched the boats bobbing on the water between the frigate and the quayside; from time to time he sighed heavily, but without effect. Captain Barbican was absorbed in his own thoughts, and the grimness of his dark face suggested that they were not particularly pleasant.

Some time elapsed, and then up the companion to join them came my lord himself. He halted at Crispin's elbow and addressed him peevishly:

"In the fiend's name, Captain Barbican, how much longer must we kick our heels here? Why do we not go ashore?"

Crispin took his arms from the bulwarks, straightened himself lazily, and looked sardonically down at the Viscount, for tall though Mountheath was the buccaneer topped him by an inch or two.

"We await the return of Captain Sarne," he explained.

Mountheath's frown deepened.

"Is that necessary?"

Captain Barbican's glance went past him to the group of buccaneers who were casting dice in the waist of the ship.

"There is half a score of stout rascals yonder," he remarked meditatively. "We might account for them all between us, my lord, but I take leave to doubt it."

The Viscount swung round to stare at that group of sturdy ruffians, and then looked incredulously at Crispin.

"Do I understand you to say that we are prisoners?"

The Captain bowed.

"But—but that is ridiculous!" stammered his lordship. "Stap me, sir, this is an English port! They cannot hold us

84

against our will! Can we not attract the attention of someone ashore, or in one of those boats?"

"My dear sir, this is Port Royal, not London river," said Crispin impatiently. "It appears that you in England know little of the Caribbean. Jonathan here is more knowledgeable. Perhaps he will instruct you."

He turned on his heel and descended the companion, and as he went he heard Jonathan's clear voice explaining the evil reputation of Port Royal to the indignant Viscount. A fleeting smile touched his lips, and he made his way to the great cabin.

Frances was seated on the locker beneath the open stern windows, looking out across the harbour. She glanced round with a smile as Crispin entered, and he went to stand beside her, but for a little neither spoke.

"Port Royal!" she said softly at last. "The end of the journey—and of Francis Barbican." She turned to look up at him, and put out her hand. "I have no words to thank you, Crispin, for all that you have done for us. 'Tis a debt which can never be repaid."

Crispin took the proffered hand between his own.

"If you wish to repay me, my lady," he said gravely, "pay less heed to the words of my Lord Mountheath where Gideon Crayle is concerned."

She frowned at that, but more in distress than anger.

"Why are you so sure that he is not to be trusted? Hal"— she paused, colouring a little—"I mean Lord Mountheath, knows him well, and he assures me that he is very well liked. Everyone in London, he says, knew that Gideon became estranged from his father because of Lord Henry's crimes against us, and would they have quarrelled if Gideon, too, had wished us ill?"

He answered the question with another, which seemed to her irrelevant.

"Are you of the opinion, my lady, that Randolph Sarne is a man easily intimidated?"

"Captain Sarne?" she repeated, bewildered. "I should say that he fears neither God nor man."

"Exactly, and yet he admitted to me that he fears your cousin, and Sarne is, I trust, more experienced in the ways of evil than is his lordship."

"Perhaps," she suggested, "it is because Captain Sarne is evil that he imagines evil in others."

"Imagines——!" He broke off, staring down at her in exasperation. "Oh, you are bewitched! This pretty Viscount has cast a spell upon you!"

She flushed scarlet at that, and snatched her hand away.

"You forget, I think, that the masquerade is over. I am no longer your half-brother, to be bullied or sneered at at your pleasure. Why must you be so unreasonable? Hal knows Gideon Crayle, and you do not, and yet you will pay no heed to him. You have decided that Gideon is not to be trusted simply because of his father's crimes."

"My lady," he broke in abruptly, "do you seek to convince me, or yourself?" She stared at him, momentarily bereft of words, and he continued: "I ask only that you will use caution. The Viscount tells you what he believes to be true, assures you in all honesty that you may trust your cousin, but what does he know of a man such as Gideon Crayle?"

"What do you know of him?" she retorted. "Hal, at least, does not condemn him unheard. You have no right to make these groundless accusations."

"Groundless?" he repeated. "Groundless? God's light, girl, the man is hand-in-glove with Randolph Sarne!"

"And if he is," she countered swiftly, "is it for you to censure him? Are you above reproach?"

He paled a little at that, but answered calmly:

"I have never pretended to be other than what I am, my lady. When your grandfather lay dying I told him what my life had been, and yet he chose to entrust you to me. Have I ever betrayed that trust?"

She bit her lip, and turned to look out of the window.

"No," she admitted in a low voice. "No, you have not."

"Then trust me a little further. Let me take you to Spanish Town as we had planned. I will contrive it somehow, and once you are in the care of the Lieutenant-Governor no-one will dare to harm you."

She made an impatient movement.

"But we are in no danger. I am persuaded that our cousin Gideon means us no harm, and even if he did, what could he do now that Hal is with us? In truth, Crispin, I do not know what ails you! You were not wont to start at shadows."

"Do you not know indeed?" he said slowly. "Do you not realize that I fear for you every instant that you are out of my sight? That if we are parted but for a moment I know no peace until I am assured of your safety? Frances——"

"No!" She spoke sharply, almost fearfully. "You must not go on! I cannot—I will not listen!" She rose to her feet with the intention of leaving him, but found her path barred by his outstretched arm. "Crispin, this is madness! Let me pass."

He shook his head, smiling a little.

"Hear me first," he suggested. "Why are you afraid?"

"Afraid?" she repeated. "Of you, Crispin?"

"Not of me," he replied, "but of what I would say to you. For you know well enough what it is."

Frances twisted her hands together and frantically searched her mind for some way of escape. She knew indeed, and though three days ago she might have listened, much had happened in the interval. For one thing, she had made the acquaintance of Lord Mountheath, and was secretly a little dazzled by his open admiration, and his air of the great world to which, as he constantly reminded her, she also belonged. He appeared to take their eventual marriage so much for granted, to regard their betrothal almost as an accomplished fact, that it was not easy to protest, nor was she sure that she desired to do so. Duty, and obedience to the wishes of her dead grandfather, urged her to accept the situation, and now inclination was beginning to add a more potent voice to theirs.

Where Crispin was concerned her emotions were even more difficult to determine. The thought of him recurred in her mind with disturbing constancy, but the pictures it presented were so sharply contrasted that she became ever more hopelessly confused. The memory of him standing, sword in hand, between her and the pirates was followed an instant later by the thought of the cold-blooded murder of Tom Adams; to see him accepted as a comrade by Sarne and Jean-Pierre poisoned the recollection of the long weeks of growing friendship aboard the *Jamaica Lass*.

She did not realize that her increasingly critical attitude towards Crispin was due to the influence of Lord Mountheath, for his lordship had perceived at once that openly to disparage the buccaneer would harm only himself. Instead he praised him, but in words which served only to mark the immeasurable gulf which yawned between a pirate captain and the sister of the Marquis of Rotherdale. He stressed the necessity for keeping secret this strange adventure, and for maintaining a proper reserve where Captain Barbican was concerned. She was, he hinted delicately, a trifle too free in her behaviour towards him.

Recalling this latter advice, Frances felt guiltily that perhaps she was in part to blame for the present situation, and this did nothing to soothe a state of mind already chaotic. Beneath her dismay and anger, and often feelings proper to the occasion, she was conscious of an insane desire to make no further protest, and this evidence of weakness in herself merely increased her anxiety to escape.

"Crispin," she said desperately, "I beg you to let me pass. There is nothing to be said between us—nothing! Oh, pray believe me!"

"But there is," he broke in gently. "Why are you afraid, Frances? Is it me you fear, or yourself?"

This struck too close to the heart of the matter; her ladyship took refuge in simulated anger.

"I tell you that I am not afraid! I know what you would say to me and I seek to spare you pain, for surely you can see how hopeless it is. Do you dare to speak to me of love—you, a pirate?"

In her haste and confusion the words were spoken before she realized what she was saying, and an instant later she would have given the earth to be able to recall them. Crispin went white to the lips, and his eyes hardened.

"I thank your ladyship for your frankness," he said bitterly. "Permit me to observe, however, that though you are so immeasurably above me it has not prevented you from depending upon me for protection and sustenance these four months past."

"Oh, abominable!" There was nothing feigned about her anger now. "Was that through any fault of mine? Did you not force me aboard that horrible ship?"

"I had an oath to fulfil, my lady, a promise to bring you safe to your kinsman. Well, I have done so! You find yourself with a surfeit of kinsmen. One is a Court libertine, the other the son of a man who sought to murder you, but since they are of noble blood no doubt they are above suspicion or reproach. I give you joy of them."

"So!" she exclaimed scornfully. "Now we come to the root of the matter. My cousins come too early upon the scene, do they not? They set all your fine plans awry?"

"My plans?" He was genuinely surprised. "What the devil do you mean by that?"

She turned an angry shoulder and looked out across the harbour. She scarcely knew herself, for she had spoken wildly in a furious desire to wound him, and the same desire prompted her next words.

"Do I know what is in your mind?" she flung at him. "Am I

to hazard a guess at what might have awaited me at your hands in this—what was it?—this pirates' haven, this golden hell?"

He did not reply at once. She would not look at him, but there was something frightening about that prolonged silence so that when at length he spoke she was glad of it, in spite of the cold fury in his voice.

"Runs your mind so?" he said between his teeth. "Has your noble cousin so quickly poisoned it against me? By God, my lady, you deserve that I should teach you a lesson!"

He moved suddenly, and before she realized what he was about had caught her in his arms, imprisoning both her hands in one of his. She struggled furiously, but she was as helpless as a child in his grasp, and he laughed on a note of savage mockery.

"What ails you, my lady? You rested there quietly enough but yesterday."

"Oh!" It was a cry of loathing; she was too angry now even to struggle. "That is brave! That is noble! To taunt me with that, when you know that I was nigh distracted then!"

"Aye," he agreed harshly, "half mad with fear of the pirates from whom I sought to save you. But who is to save you now?"

"You will learn soon enough if I choose to call," she replied venomously. "I am not obliged to look to you for protection now, God be thanked!"

"Call, then," he said mockingly. "Let the little Viscount dash to your rescue. He is like to meet death instead."

"Yes, you would murder him, would you not?" Her rage was so consuming that it left no room for fear. "You would welcome an excuse to butcher him as you butchered Captain Adams. The taking of life is nothing to you if it helps you to attain your evil ends."

"But then, I am a pirate," he said, and there was pain as well as anger in his voice. "And yet you do not fear me as you feared Jean-Pierre. Can it be that in your heart you trust me still? I must teach you differently, it seems."

He set a hand beneath her chin and kissed her with brutal violence. She, finding her hands free, tried vainly to thrust him away, and for the first time he saw fear in her eyes. He laughed softly on a note which did nothing to reassure her.

"Not long since, my dear, you spoke of a debt. I am minded to make you pay it."

89

"You fiend!" There was a distinct break in her voice. "You cowardly beast! But I'll not call Hal to be murdered by you, do what you will."

They were brave words, but her face was ashen, the blue eyes dark with fear, for there was no sign of mercy in the grimly-smiling face above her. She thought he looked a devil. Terror swept over her suddenly, and her eyes filled with tears.

"Crispin, have pity, for the love of Heaven!"

The mockery in his face deepened.

"Faith, here's a change of tune!" he taunted her. "Calm you, my lady. I am no ravisher, pirate though I be." He kissed her again, almost contemptuously, and released her so abruptly that she stumbled back against the bulkhead and leaned there, shaken and trembling. His eyes mocked her. "Hereafter, madam, when Lady Frances Crayle bethinks her how high she stands above the common herd, let her remember also how once she was humbled by a pirate."

CHAPTER X

GIDEON CRAYLE

MIDWAY through the afternoon Randolph Sarne returned to Port Royal. He was rowed out to the *Vampire* and, coming aboard, found a handful of his men lounging on the forecastle and Captain Barbican leaning upon the poop-rail in moody abstraction. Of the three other prisoners there was no sign. Captain Sarne mounted the companion to Crispin's side and addressed him in tones of profound perplexity.

"There's something here I don't understand," he announced. "When his lordship told me yesterday who the wench and her brother were, and said that in England their lives were in danger, I thought I could see how matters stood. 'There was one who stood to gain by their death,' he said. That would be Lord Henry Crayle, who must be the little lad's heir, and from what I know of Gideon Crayle he would have a hand in a matter of that sort. And Gideon, his lordship tells me, is in Port Royal. It seemed simple enough!"

He paused and waited for question or comment, but neither was forthcoming. Sarne glanced curiously at the strong profile presented to him and resumed the account of his grievances.

"He is here, right enough, but when I went to him with the tale of the prize I had captured, expecting to be told to carry it off again and make away with it, he behaved as though I had done him the greatest service imaginable. Spoke of his poor young cousins, and how thankful he was that they were found, so that he could atone in part for his father's sins against them, and the end of it was that he sent his own coach to carry them to the plantation. May I perish if I can understand it! He could be rid of them both with no trouble at all. He has only to lift a finger to make himself Marquis o' Rotherdale, and instead he is busy preparing a welcome for them, and for the Viscount too."

"Then in God's name take them to him, and have done," said Crispin, breaking his long silence. "You will be doing me a service thereby."

Sarne raised his brows.

"Sets the wind so?" he remarked. " 'Twas a different attitude you were yesterday. What ails you, lad? Has the dainty piece spurned you in your turn now that she is among her own folk again?"

"Have done, I say!" Captain Barbican turned on him with something of a snarl. "My task was to bring her and her brother safe to their kinsfolk, and it was never to my taste. What, am I the man to play nursemaid to a pair of children? But their grandfather was dying and begged me to protect them. Now, thanks be to God, the task is done, and I may be about my own affairs again."

"With no thought of reward?" the pirate prompted slyly, with a sidelong glance at his companion, and Crispin laughed shortly.

"Reward enough to be delivered of that vixen," he replied. "My lady has too exalted an opinion of herself. You may take her to your friend Crayle with my compliments."

Sarne grinned.

"You'll take her yourself," he said. "Crayle is eager to see you." He anticipated the Captain's protest with uplifted hand.

"No use to argue, Barbican. He wishes to see you, and I have the means to force you if you refuse to go willingly. Use sense, man! He may have it in his mind to reward you."

This Crispin was disposed to doubt, for he was still unconvinced of Gideon Crayle's honesty. As Sarne had said, Crayle had but to lift a finger to succeed to a marquisate, and to Captain Barbican at least his protests of good faith rang false, but these doubts no longer troubled him. In his present black mood the fate of the little Marquis and his troublesome sister was a matter of complete indifference to him.

He accompanied them perforce to the plantation, for he knew that if he refused he would be carried thither in bonds, an humiliating experience which he had every intention of avoiding. He was relieved to discover that he and Frances were not to be forced into each other's company on the journey, for though Lord Mountheath rode with his cousins in the great, gilded coach, saddle-horses had been provided for himself and Captain Sarne.

Night was falling when they came at last to their destination, that pillared, white-walled house set in the midst of fragrant gardens. The heavy coach lumbered to a standstill before the door, the two captains swung out of their saddles, and Negro slaves came running to take charge of the horses and conduct the guests into the house.

The main door gave on to a spacious and well-lit hall, and as they entered it another door at the far end opened and Gideon Crayle, splendid in purple satin laced with gold, emerged and came towards them. Frances felt a momentary revulsion at the sight of that shambling, mis-shapen figure, but distaste was supplanted by pity as her gaze rested upon the wistful beauty of the pale face between the flowing black curls. He halted before her, and a hand as white and slender as a woman's, smothered in a foam of lace, came out to take hers and carry it to his lips.

"Lady Frances! My dear cousin, how happy I am to bid you welcome at last to my house. Your brother also, safe after so many dangers." A welcoming smile was bestowed upon Jonathan, and then this amiable, soft-voiced gentleman was turning with outstretched hand to the Viscount. "Hal, my friend, well met! I little thought to have the pleasure of seeing you again so soon. Captain Sarne has told me how you came aboard his ship. My dear boy, it was a miracle, no less."

On this flood of gentle eloquence he swept them across the hall and into the room he had just left. Here he led Frances to a chair, waved the Viscount to another, addressed some order to a liveried Negro who was busy with bottles and glasses at a side-table, and then turned for the first time to the tall and silent figure in the background.

"This, of course, will be Captain Barbican." He extended his hand, shaking back the cloud of lace. "Sir, words cannot express the gratitude I feel towards you, the protector of these innocent children through so many dangers. Some small mark of my esteem I may hope to give you, but not all the wealth of the Indies would be sufficient to repay the debt."

Crispin took the delicate hand in his own strong fingers and looked down curiously at that handsome, ageless face. The hunchback was studying him narrowly, his head twisted sideways in a tortuous movement necessitated by the Captain's great height, and for an instant Crispin met the full brilliance of his dark, unfathomable eyes. He knew then that Sarne's description was apt; the man was a devil, with a soul as warped and twisted as his deformed body, and a driving ambition which would be merciless to those who stood in its way. And Frances accounted herself safe in the hands of this monster.

"You exaggerate, Mr. Crayle," he replied calmly. "I was drawn into the affair by chance, and I accepted the charge of your cousins merely out of compassion for a dying man."

"Nevertheless, Captain Barbican, it is due to you that Lady Frances and her brother are safe here tonight, and I am able to make some reparation for the sins of my unhappy parent." He turned away from Crispin and smiled sadly into Frances's startled countenance. "Yes, my lady, I know only too well who was responsible for the murder of your grandfather, and since my father is dead—an event which I can only regard as a judgement for the horrible sin of fratricide—I do not hesitate to admit it. But enough of that! The danger is past, and it is my profound hope that you will soon return with me to England, to take your rightful place in the world into which you were born, and which will inevitably be graced by your presence."

Frances, quite overcome by this courtly speech, murmured something indistinguishable and looked helplessly at the Viscount. The coloured servant took advantage of the pause in the conversation to ply them with wine and sweetmeats, and in the small diversion thus created the necessity for an answer passed. When they had drunk, Gideon addressed himself once more to her ladyship.

"It occurs to me, my dear cousin, that after so many weeks

of travelling you will not wish to embark at once upon the tedious journey to England. May I suggest that you reside here for a few months, to recover from the hardships which you must undoubtedly have endured? I have interests here which require my attention, and though I shall, of course, be guided by your wishes in the matter, as your guardian——"

"What's that?" Mountheath broke in. "Begad, Gideon, you go too fast! His Majesty appointed my father guardian of Frances and Jonathan. That is why he sent me in search of them."

Crayle turned to look at him, and a smile which for all its sweetness held something of malice curved his lips.

"Is it, Hal?" he asked gently. "I thought that there was another reason. However, my dear boy, you should have informed yourself more particularly of the situation before you left England. His Majesty did indeed bestow them first in the care of your father, but upon reflection he decided that it was more fitting that their guardian should be one of their own name and blood—in short, myself. He was good enough," he added pensively, "to give me a document to that effect, to prevent any confusion such as arises now."

Into the sudden silence which this announcement provoked Frances said breathlessly:

"Do you mean, sir, that we are not, after all, to reside in the household of Lord Larchwood?"

The gentle smile was turned upon her, and he shook his head.

"I mean, my dear, that you will reside at Rotherdale, as befits the Marquis and his sister. The administration of the estate and fortune, which has for several years been my responsibility, will remain so until Jonathan comes of age." He paused, studying her face, and his own saddened. "You look doubtfully, Lady Frances. Can it be that you distrust me because I am my father's son?"

Her ladyship crimsoned, and bit her lip.

"I—I have no desire to offend you, sir," she stammered, "but I did not know—it was my grandfather's wish that Lord Larchwood——"

"But the King's wishes must override all others," he reminded her gently. "The situation, after all, is a delicate one. Your grandfather opposed His Majesty—and the late sainted King, God rest him—by every means in his power, and it says

94

much for His Majesty's forebearance that he is prepared to restore so large and wealthy an estate to one who has been reared in an atmosphere antagonistic to the Stuarts. However, your brother is very young, and His Majesty believes that there is yet time to undo the teachings of your excellent but misguided grandfather, and to show our little Jonathan where his true loyalty lies. This task he has seen fit to entrust to me, and I accepted it joyfully, seeing in it an opportunity to expiate the sins of my unhappy parent."

He paused, and in the background Captain Barbican smiled grimly to himself. He was clever, this Gideon Crayle, and ruthless, for all his outward charm. My lady would be no match for him, and she might yet have occasion to regret the pirate she had scorned, for Mountheath would be no more able to protect her than would Jonathan, so convinced was he of Crayle's honesty.

The hunchback was speaking again:

"How can I convince you, Lady Frances? Useless to protest my innocence, though Hal will tell you that as soon as I learned of my father's guilt I left his house, and never saw him more. Useless to tell you that I have had all made ready to receive you—apartments prepared, women found to wait upon you. Will it at all avail me to say that here you may command as you would at Rotherdale itself? Make any request of me you choose. I shall welcome it gladly."

Frances had been sitting lost in thought, a frown wrinkling her brow, but at that she looked up sharply.

"Any request, sir?"

He bowed.

"Whatever you choose, my lady, and if it be in my power I will grant it gladly."

"Then, sir, will you be good enough to lend me, at once, five hundred pounds?"

There was a startled pause; even Gideon looked faintly surprised, but he replied without hesitation.

"Of course, madam. Pray excuse me an instant. I will not keep you long."

He went out of the room, and Captain Sarne remarked with a laugh:

"A poor test, my lady! Gold is easily come by in Port Royal, and no proof of honesty. Ecod, 'tis the honest here, if there be any such, who are the only poor."

She ignored him, and no-one else ventured to voice their

perplexity. Five minutes passed, and then Crayle came back in the room, bearing a weighty bag which gave forth an encouraging chink as he set it on the table before her.

"Five hundred pounds, my lady," he said. "Have you no other command?"

"I thank you, cousin. You are very kind, and I am loath to trouble you, but I find myself with a creditor who grows importunate." She looked up at Crispin, and the contempt in her eyes was like a blow across the face. One small hand thrust the heavy bag along the table towards him. "You spoke of a debt, Captain Barbican. I am minded to pay it."

"Frances!" The cry of protest came from Jonathan. There was dismay amounting almost to horror in his voice. "You cannot! 'Tis an insult!"

"Be quiet, Jonathan!" A note in her voice, which he had never heard before, silenced the boy. She was still looking at Crispin. "Why do you hesitate, Captain Barbican? My grandfather employed you to conduct us to our guardian, and that you have done. I am not disposed to retain you in my service. Take your wages, and go."

A silence at once tense and curious followed the words. Lord Mountheath and Randolph Sarne stared open-mouthed; Jonathan, almost in tears, stood gripping the back of his sister's chair; and Gideon Crayle looked from the white-faced girl to the tall buccaneer and thoughtfully fingered a curl of his periwig, a smile of malicious amusement glittering in his eyes beneath the heavy lids.

For the space of a dozen heartbeats Crispin stood motionless, staring at Frances, then, without a second glance at the bag of gold, he turned upon his heel and left them. His receding footsteps rang on the polished hardwood floor of the hall, and then the outer door closed behind him with a crash that echoed through the lofty rooms. Lady Frances, outwardly composed, but with a desolate sense of protection withdrawn, rose to her feet and addressed herself to Gideon:

"You spoke, cousin, of apartments prepared for me. By your leave I will retire to them. I am very tired."

He was at once all concern for her. A soft-footed slave was summoned to conduct her ladyship to her apartments, and to perform a like office for Lord Mountheath and the little Marquis. When all three had withdrawn Gideon picked up the bag of gold and looked across at Captain Sarne.

"A proud man, this Crispin Barbican," he observed, "but he shall not go unrewarded for the service he has rendered me, and I have in mind a gift which may be welcome to him now that my fair cousin has so summarily dismissed him. Seek him out for me, Sarne, and let me know where he is to be found."

It was upon the following evening that Gideon Crayle again spoke with Captain Barbican. Crispin was sitting in one of the many disreputable taverns in the worst quarter of Port Royal, a glass of rum in his hand and black hell in his heart. All about him surged a motley throng; true buccaneers in blood stained shirts and rawhide breeches; raffish ruffians in laced coats; women as brilliantly clad and as strident of voice as the parrots which screeched on a perch in the corner. The rattle of bottles and dice, and the chink of coins, mingled with laughter and oaths and raucous singing. Captain Barbican sat alone, staring morosely before him and seeing only the searing contempt in a pair of blue eyes, hearing nothing but a clear, scornful voice bidding him take his payment and be-gone.

A sudden hush fell upon the noisy room. Laughter and talk died away, and a woman cried out hysterically. Roused by the unexpected silence, Crispin raised his head and saw the hunchback standing like an evil spirit upon the threshold, his gloved hands crossed on the knob of a tall, ebony cane. A black cloak, lined with scarlet, hung almost to his heels over a black coat heavy with gold lace, a ruby glowed balefully in the creamy Mechlin at his throat, and in the shadow of a broad black hat with sweeping scarlet plumes his dark glitter-ing eyes swept the room and came to rest at length upon Cap-tain Barbican. He advanced slowly, and that ruffianly crowd drew back to let him pass, one or two of them crossing them-selves in superstitious fear.

"Good-evening, Captain Barbican," he greeted him. "By your leave I will join you awhile."

He drew up a stool and sat down, regarding the Captain thoughtfully across the rough, stained table. The buccaneer was unshaven, his long dark hair dishevelled and his cravat untied, while the faint flush on his bronzed cheeks and the un-natural brightness of his eyes suggested that he had been drinking heavily. Clearly the fellow had been stricken hard by Lady Frances's abrupt dismissal; Gideon's heavy lids drooped lower to hide the satisfaction in his eyes.

"I have been seeking you, Captain Barbican," he informed him pleasantly, "for I do not wish you to imagine that we are all as ungrateful to you as Lady Frances showed herself to be. I fear that you must have offended her in some way—no, do not tell me how. It is a matter of complete indifference to me. But you have rendered a very great service to my family, sir, and I cannot permit you to go unrewarded."

Crispin's lips twisted in a mirthless smile, and he stretched out a slightly unsteady hand towards the bottle before him.

"I wonder, now, what price you set upon that service," he said bitterly. "Her ladyship valued it at five hundred pounds."

Gideon made a gesture of scornful dismissal.

"Five hundred pounds," he repeated. "My dear sir, a bagatelle." He crossed his hands once more on the gold knob of his cane, and rested his chin upon them. "I have learned a good deal about you, Captain Barbican, since I arrived in Port Royal. You have something of a reputation, and Sir Henry Morgan thought highly of you. If you had a ship, you might take your pick of the pirates who infest this amusing city, and be off to harry the Dons again, and fill your pockets with Spanish gold."

Crispin laughed shortly.

"A ship is not so easy to come by, Mr. Crayle."

"No?" Gideon spoke pensively. "There is in the harbour a galleon of thirty guns, the *Santo Rosario,* which Captain Sarne captured during his recent voyage. I make you a present of her, Captain Barbican, well-found in food and ammunition and ready to put to sea. Is that a reward more to your taste?"

The buccaneer put down his glass and stared in amazement at the gently-smiling face of the hunchback. It was a princely gift, and one which would give him immediate employment to rid his mind of these tormenting memories. But there were obstacles.

"What of Sarne and his men?" he said slowly. "They'll not stand aside and see their prize delivered to me."

"They shall have her full value to divide among them," Gideon replied smoothly. "In fact, I have already purchased the vessel from Captain Sarne. I trust that you will accept her, sir. It is but a small reward for the service that you have rendered me."

Crispin had now no doubt that this was so. This ill formed, sweetly-smiling fiend had some deep and subtle plot to possess himself of the marquisate, a scheme which his father's blundering had seriously imperilled, and he was not exaggerating his gratitude to the man who had now delivered his victims safely into his hands. Here in lawless Port Royal, with Sarne

and his cut-throats at Crayle's command, their only hope of
escape lay in the man who had protected them so far; and
Frances had shown very clearly that she needed him no
longer. He had loved her greatly, but with the memory of her
proud and cruel dismissal branded for ever on his heart and
mind that love was transformed into a hatred of equal intensi-
ty. Perhaps when her ladyship discovered the true nature of
her courtly cousin she would look again for aid to Captain
Barbican, but in his present pain and anger he vowed that she
should look in vain.

"You are generous, Mr. Crayle," he said at length, "and I'll
be taking advantage of your generosity. The *Santo Rosario*
shall sail as soon as I can muster a crew."

Sail she did, five days later, spreading her sails to the trade
winds and bearing away the only man who might have saved
the girl who dwelt in false security in the white plantation
house among the Jamaican hills.

Book II

CHAPTER XI

THE CROOKED SHADOW

INTO the broad harbour of Port Royal, past the massive fort which guarded its entrance, a tall yellow galleon was moving slowly. Idlers on the mole, with keen eyesight and good memories, presently identified her as the *Santo Rosario*—the Holy Rosary—a Spanish prize which had sailed thence seven months before under the command of Morgan's redoubtable lieutenant, Crispin Barbican. These same experienced spectators also gave it as their opinion that she returned none too soon, for she had obviously suffered by storm and battle and was in no case to remain much longer at sea. Whether or not she had found a golden unguent for her wounds would not be known until her crew came ashore.

Upon the high poop of the vessel her captain paced to and fro, a tall, virile figure in a suit of lilac and silver which made the most of his splendid proportions. Delicate lace foamed at throat and wrist, his boots were of fine Spanish leather, and he carried a pair of fringed gauntlets in one hand. A broad, plumed hat, set slightly a-cock on his dark hair, shadowed a face at once eager and troubled, for he had no means of knowing what news awaited him in Port Royal. Were the little Marquis and his sister still in Jamaica, or had their sinister guardian carried them off to England? Or—and this was a possibility which Crispin could not bring himself to face—had Crayle's subtle and wicked mind found some means of disposing of his wards and making himself Marquis of Roth-erdale?

The wound dealt him by Lady Frances had been long in healing, but gradually the bitter resentment which he had cherished against her gave way to remorse. No matter how cruelly she had treated him, he had sworn a solemn oath to protect her, and that oath he had deliberately broken when he left her in the power of Gideon Crayle. There was Jonathan also to be considered, who had harmed him not at all and whose danger was even greater than his sister's. What right had he to abandon the boy merely because a wilful slip of a girl looked coldly upon him?

It was this sense of dishonour which brought him back to Port Royal, but when the mountains of Jamaica appeared like a dusky blue cloud on the horizon, he made the final surrender of his pride and admitted to himself that he could no more put Frances Crayle out of his heart than he could cut the heart itself from his body. Despise him she might, hate him, even, but he would love her as long as he drew breath, and would give his life to serve her.

The *Santo Rosario* came to her anchorage at last, and after an interval which seemed to him an eternity he was free to go ashore. He wasted no time in Port Royal itself but, procuring a horse, set out at once for the plantation. What he would find there he did not know, any more than he knew what he would say to Frances if they met, but of one thing he was certain. If any harm had come to her of Gideon Crayle's contriving, the hunchback was a doomed man. He would have his life in payment of that monstrous debt, if he had to follow him half across the world and strike him down at the foot of the throne itself.

When he drew rein, however, before the white stone house with its tiers of arched verandahs, none of this inward turmoil was visible in his face. Calm and self-possessed, he surrendered his horse to a groom and passed, in the wake of a Negro slave, into the house. Mr. Crayle, he was informed, was still in residence there, and would be apprised of his presence.

He was left to wait in a cool, shadowy room where an illusion of great space was created by the fine tapestries and the few pieces of heavily-carved furniture. There were long windows opening on to the shady verandah, and beyond that the garden flamed in a riot of colour in the strong, brilliant sunshine. The house was not excessively large, but it was solid and satisfying, a house such as he had once hoped to own, before fate and the Spanish galleys had made him what he was today.

The arrival of his host put an end to his reverie. The hunchback came slowly into the room, smiling an amiable welcome.

"Captain Barbican, this is indeed a pleasure! I did not know that you had returned to Jamaica. You have had a successful voyage, I trust?"

"Successful enough, sir, I thank you, though we suffered a pretty mauling at the hands of a Spanish man-o'-war a week since. However, we brought the *Rosario* safely into harbour this morning, and she carried that in her hold to make our labours worth while."

"Excellent, excellent!" Gideon's voice expressed only warm congratulation. "A glass of wine with me, Captain?" He turned aside to pull the bell-rope. "This morning, you say? And you come at once to visit me? I am honoured, Captain Barbican, deeply honoured."

Was there a hint of mockery in the fellow's voice? Crispin's eyes hardened, but he replied pleasantly enough:

"Do you find in that a cause for surprise, Mr. Crayle? It is only thanks to you, after all, that the voyage was made. I come to express my gratitude, and to assure myself of your well-being, and, of course, of the well-being of your cousins."

"The debt, sir, was mine, wholly mine." A slave came into the room bearing wine and glasses on a silver tray, and Gideon paused to fill the goblets before he continued. "The well-being of my cousins, you say, Captain Barbican?" He sighed. "I wish with all my heart that I could give you that assurance." He picked up both glasses and handed one to Crispin. "Your health, sir."

The buccaneer accepted it with a word of thanks and made an appropriate reply, though only he knew what it cost him to maintain that outward calm. When they had drunk he said:

"I apprehend, sir, that all is not well with Lord Rotherdale and his sister?"

Gideon sighed again, and slowly shook his head.

"The boy is ill, Captain Barbican," he said. "A mysterious malady attacked him three—no, four—months ago. We cannot discover what it is that ails him, though I fear—yes, I very much fear—that he has passed beyond mortal aid." He set down his glass and moved away to the windows, the embodiment of helpless anxiety. "I have installed a physician in the house so that he may have constant attention, but all to no avail. He grows steadily weaker."

"And—her ladyship?" Crispin's voice was level, but his hands were clenched tight upon the back of the chair on which he leaned.

"Ah, that sweet saint!" Crayle turned once more to face him, and at his words a cold hand seemed to close about Crispin's heart. The hunchback never knew how close he was to death in that instant before his next words brought reassurance to the man before him.

"She is well, sir. As well as one can be who spends all her days nursing a sick child, and who is racked by the anxiety which troubles us all. She is with her brother now—indeed, she hardly leaves his side. The boy seems to find comfort in her presence."

"That I can well understand." Crispin spoke at random to cover his overwhelming relief. "I had remarked a devotion between them stronger even than that which customarily binds brother and sister. I am deeply grieved, sir, to learn of his lordship's illness. Is there nothing to be done?"

Gideon spread his hands outward in a helpless gesture.

"What can we do, my friend, when we know not what ails him? I have thought that mayhap 'tis the climate of this place which has bred a little-known malady of the tropics, and for that reason I wished to carry him back to England, but the doctor forbade it. Jonathan is too weak to survive the journey."

Crispin nodded in assumed agreement, and was silent for a space. He put no trust in what Crayle told him, for if the lad was ill it was more than likely that his guardian knew the cause well enough. There were subtle poisons, in the New World and the Old, which would bring about a lingering death. He knew that somehow he must obtain more definite knowledge, and the thought of Lord Mountheath occurred to him. After a brief pause he inquired whether the Viscount had returned to England.

"No, he is in Jamaica still," Gideon replied, readily enough. "He spent some weeks here, and then removed to the house of Sir Thomas Lynch at Spanish Town. Sir Thomas is, I believe, an acquaintance of his father's. Mountheath comes here at intervals to see Lady Frances, and inquire after Jonathan, and he will not, I imagine, leave the Indies until the boy's illness is over."

"No," said Crispin slowly. "No, I suppose not. Well, Mr.

Crayle, I will trespass no longer upon your hospitality. This is not a time when you will wish to be entertaining uninvited guests." He ignored the other man's hasty disclaimer and added, looking down at the glass in his hand, "But if it were possible, if her ladyship would receive me, I should like, before I return to Port Royal, to express my sympathy and my readiness to serve her should the need arise."

He made the request with little hope of it being granted, but to his surprise Gideon replied with a smile:

"You are a brave man, Captain Barbican, or else you have forgotten the manner of your parting with her ladyship." He saw the flash of anger in Crispin's eyes and added hastily: "No, no, I did but jest! She has, I think, realized how unmerited that insult was. Poor child, this sorrow has all but broken her spirit, and I fear that you will find her greatly changed. Pray excuse me, sir, and I will tell her of your request."

He went out, and the Captain was left alone. He set down his empty glass and went slowly across to the window, looking with unseeing eyes across the garden. Something was amiss here, but to define it was like trying to grasp a shadow. The sick boy, the devoted sister, the anxious guardian—all ordinary enough on the surface, but what lay beneath that commonplace exterior? This sense of danger, of impending tragedy, might be a figment of his own imagination, born of anxiety for the woman he loved and his certainty that Gideon Crayle was evil, but he was not a man given to wild fancies. Some peril threatened, and not knowing what form it would take he was powerless to prevent it.

Someone came softly into the room, and he swung round to face Lady Frances. She had closed the door and was leaning against it, gowned in blue silk, silver-embroidered, the sleeves and bodice fastened with rose-coloured ribbons. There were ribbons of rose and blue in the shining curls that framed her face, and against the dark panels of the door her white shoulders were like ivory above the low, lace-trimmed bodice. She was beautiful, with a tragic, haunting loveliness that caught at his heart, her face pale, and thinner than he remembered it, the blue eyes made enormous by the shadows about them.

"My lady." He bowed low, and his deep voice was level and calm. He had himself well in hand. "This is a privilege I scarcely dared to hope for. Mr. Crayle told me how greatly your time is occupied, and by what sad duties."

She came farther into the room, not looking at him, her hands clasped nervously upon a fan of brilliantly-coloured feathers.

"It was good of you to come," she said expressionlessly. "I told Jonathan that you were here, and he sent you a message. 'Ask him,' he said, 'if he will not take me with him when he sails again.' He wanted to see you, but I fear that it is out of the question. The doctor will permit him to see no-one save myself and our cousin."

"Poor little lad!" Crispin spoke quietly. "My lady, if there is aught I can do for him, or for you, you have but to command me."

"Thank you, there is nothing. Jonathan has every attention; we can but wait, and pray." She was seated now in one of the high-backed chairs, but still she would not meet his eyes. It occurred to him, as he listened to the soft, colourless voice, that she spoke as though she had learned the words by heart. "I am glad that you have come, Captain Barbican, and that I have an opportunity to ask your pardon for that which I said to you in this house seven months ago. It was unforgivable when you had risked so much to help us, but I have hoped that you could find it in your heart to forgive me."

"Forgive you?" He took a pace forward. "Aye, willingly! I stand in need of forgiveness, too, my lady."

"It is freely given," she replied, and a trace of feeling crept into her voice. "Oh, that I had the power to erase that whole day from my memory! To blot it out of my heart and mind for ever!"

She dropped the fan and pressed her hands against her eyes for a moment; when she withdrew them her fingers were wet. She rose to her feet and looked past him to the garden beyond the open windows, and her face was like a mask, beautiful and expressionless again.

"I must tell you, Captain Barbican," she said in a low voice, "that I am shortly to be married to my cousin."

Had she been looking at him she must have seen how great a shock to him her words were. He paled, and it was a moment before he could trust himself to speak.

"I see," he said quietly at length. "Lord Mountheath is to be congratulated."

"Mountheath?" Her startled gaze flew up to meet his for the first time. "You mistake me, sir. It is Gideon Crayle to whom I am betrothed."

"Frances!" Even Crispin's iron self-control was not proof

105

against the horror which swept over him at that. "God's light, child, you cannot mean it! You to wed Gideon Crayle?"

She drew herself up.

"You are impertinent, sir, I think. I was not aware that I had given you the right to criticize my choice of a husband." She turned towards the door. "I will bid you good-day, Captain Barbican."

In silence and with anguished eyes he watched her cross the room. To the young Viscount he would have yielded her, if not willingly, at least with resignation, but not to that mis-shapen monster. The mere thought of such a marriage overwhelmed him with anger and loathing until his mind seemed to hover on the brink of madness.

Frances had reached the door now. An instant she paused, her hand on the latch, and then as though impelled by something stronger than her will she turned, with trembling lips and outstretched hands, and faced him across the width of the room.

"Crispin!" There was fear and entreaty in the cry, and something more that made his heart leap wildly, but before either could move or speak again a crooked shadow fell across the floor, and Gideon's voice spoke softly from the verandah.

"Frances, my dear, we must not detain the Captain, and Jonathan is asking for you."

The girl gave a gasp of dismay, and as the hunchback came to her side it seemed to Crispin that she shrank from him. Crayle took her hand, raised it to his lips, and then drew it through the crook of his arm and held it there. He smiled at the buccaneer.

"Frances will have told you of our betrothal, Captain Barbican," he continued gently. "Our wedding takes place in three days' time, and we shall look for you then, shall we not, my love?"

She was staring at him as though fascinated, and though she tried to reply no words emerged from her trembling lips. Crispin had the curious fancy that the announcement of that imminent wedding-day was as great a shock to her as it was to him, and yet she made no attempt to deny it. He looked at her searchingly, but she stood with averted face and would not meet his eyes.

"Your brother," said Gideon again, "is in need of you, my dear. Take your leave of Captain Barbican and go to him."

In silence she held out her hand, and Crispin had no alternative but to take it. The slight fingers were lifeless and cold as ice, but as he bent his head to kiss them they tightened and clung to his, and when, startled, he looked up at her, he encountered a look of terror and despair such as he had rarely seen. With the watchful eyes of Gideon Crayle upon him he could make no response to that mute appeal, and though it cut him to the heart to withhold the reassurance of which she seemed in such desperate need, he forced himself to maintain the cool formality which the occasion demanded.

"Lady Frances, your servant," he said civilly. "Mr. Crayle." He bowed, and stepped past them to the door. They heard him cross the hall and call for his horse, and Gideon smiled pensively into the tragic face of his bride.

"Thus we rid ourselves of the gallant Captain," he said softly. "You had best go to your brother. Remember, it is only your devotion which is keeping him alive."

Captain Barbican was frowning as he rode away from the house, and when he reached the road he drew rein in the shade of a great tree and sat for a while lost in thought. Then, with sudden decision, he turned his horse's head in the direction of Spanish Town, the inland capital of the island.

Arriving at Sir Thomas Lynch's house, he had his name sent in to Lord Mountheath, and after a brief interval was ushered into that gentleman's presence. The Viscount greeted him courteously, though with some surprise, and inquired if there was any way in which he could serve him.

"Yes, my lord, I think there is," Crispin replied, and added by way of explanation: "I have just come from the Crayle plantation."

"Oh!" Mountheath rose to his feet and took a turn about the room. "You will have seen Lady Frances, perhaps."

"Yes, I saw her." Crispin was watching him narrowly. "I understand that she is to be married in three days' time."

"Three days?" The Viscount swung round to face him, his face white. "You are not serious?"

"Mr. Crayle himself informed me of the fact, and expressed a hope that I would be present at the ceremony. Did you know nothing of it?"

"That they were to be married, yes, but not that it was to be so soon. I was there a week ago and no mention was made of it then." He went to a sideboard, and filled a glass with a hand that was not quite steady. "Forgive me, Captain Barbican. This matter touches me closely."

A somewhat bitter smile touched the buccaneer's lips, but when he spoke it was merely to ask:

"How long have they been betrothed?"

"How long?" Mountheath considered the point. " 'Twould be three months and more, for it was announced only a few days after Jonathan fell ill."

Captain Barbican raised his brows.

"A strange time, surely, to be thinking of betrothals," he remarked. "What ails the boy, my lord?"

"I do not know, sir," Hal replied in some surprise. "Even the doctor is at a loss."

"But what is the nature of the malady? A fever, a wasting sickness——?"

"I do not know," Hal said again. "I have not seen him."

Crispin frowned.

"Not at all? Not even when he first fell ill?"

The Viscount shook his head.

"No-one has seen him save her ladyship, Gideon, the doctor and an old Negro who waits upon him."

Crispin rose to his feet and paced the length of the room and back, his hands clasped behind him and his chin sunk into the lace of his cravat. At length he halted beside Mountheath and addressed him abruptly.

"My lord, has it never occurred to you that Crayle may be forcing her ladyship to marry him against her will?"

Hal looked startled.

"It did cross my mind, I admit, when first I heard of the betrothal, but it cannot be so. She would need but to appeal to me for help, and she has not done so."

"Has she had any opportunity, my lord?"

"We have been alone together more than once when I have visited the plantation. She has been withdrawn and unhappy, it is true, but Jonathan's illness might account for that."

Crispin shook his head.

"Anxiety for her brother is not all that ails her. I tell you, my lord, I have seen her face death and worse, and seen the fear of it in her eyes, but never such terror as I saw there today. She had the look of one standing on the brink of hell."

The force of his words seemed to convince the Viscount; he moved his hands helplessly.

"But suppose you are right, what can we do? We cannot

even obtain sure knowledge that she is being constrained to marry him."

"We must obtain it. You say that you have spoken with her alone, but if it was at the plantation you may be sure that Crayle was not far away, or that he had set spies upon her. Somehow we must have speech with her without his knowledge."

Hal laughed shortly.

"Easier said than done, my friend. She rarely leaves the plantation. If she does, her woman sits beside her in the coach, and Gideon's men are on the box. Even when she rides out, two of his grooms attend her."

"Nevertheless, it must be contrived, and that at once, for if we are to aid her at all we must do so without delay." He paused, and looked Mountheath straight in the eyes. "My lord, we have no great kindness for each other, but I think that I may safely say that to both of us the well-being of Lady Frances is of paramount importance. Shall we agree to forget our differences for the present and unite our efforts to save her from this hellish travesty of marriage?"

Hal hesitated only for a moment, then he nodded.

"With all my heart," he replied eagerly. "There is nothing that I would not do to prevent it. How we are to accomplish it I do not know, but you may depend upon me—to the death."

"We will hope," said the Captain, with a rather grim smile, "that so much will not be demanded of you. Are you willing, my lord, to leave the ordering of this venture to me?"

"Certainly, sir," Hal agreed, "for I have no notion how we are to proceed. Tell me what I am to do to assist you, and it shall be done."

"Come to Port Royal tomorrow." Crispin picked up his hat and prepared to leave. "Meanwhile I will find some way of learning what hold it is that Crayle has over her ladyship, for until we know that we can plan nothing."

"You are confident, sir," said Hal with a smile, "and yet I have an odd fancy that you will accomplish even that." He held out his hand. "Until we meet in Port Royal, Captain Barbican, and good fortune go with you."

CHAPTER XII

MIDNIGHT MEETING

On the second night after his conversation with the Viscount, Captain Barbican stood in Gideon Crayle's garden and looked up at the unlighted windows of the house. In the time which had elapsed he had not been idle, for a reluctant slave had furnished him with certain information concerning the interior of the house, and was now a prisoner aboard the *Santo Rosario*. Lord Mountheath was installed at an inn in Port Royal, holding himself in readiness for whatever might follow this midnight visit.

Crispin moved cautiously forward in the shadows until he stood close to the building, immediately beneath the windows of her ladyship's apartments. A flowering creeper gave him a foothold, and he went up easily, with a silent blessing upon colonial architecture with its pillars and balconies. In a few moments he was astride the balustrade, clearly outlined by the moonlight against the white stone, and then he swung his other leg over and melted silently into the shadows of the verandah.

The long windows were closed and curtained, but without hesitation he rapped softly upon the glass, repeating the summons at intervals until he heard a movement within the room, and a gleam of light showed through a crack between the curtains. He drew back then, flattening himself against the wall beside the windows. A streak of light fell across the balcony as the curtains were drawn aside, and then the casement was opened and Lady Frances emerged, the light of the candle she carried gleaming on her bright, unbound hair. As she stepped forward to the balustrade Crispin moved swiftly, one hand closing gently over her mouth, the other upon the hand that held the candle.

"Have no fear, my lady," he said softly. " 'Tis I, Crispin Barbican."

He swept her back into the room again, released her, and drew the curtains close before turning to face her. She had set down the candle and was staring at him with dilated eyes, one hand holding together at the throat her robe of green-striped satin.

"Have no fear, my lady," he repeated. "I have come because I feared that all was not well with you, but if you have no need of me I will depart as I came. Or you have but to pull yonder bell-rope to bring your servants upon me."

"No need of you?" she whispered, and with the words cast herself into his arms. "Oh, Crispin, I have prayed that you would return!"

Captain Barbican stood very still, scarcely believing, even now, the miracle which had come to pass. Frances was weeping, with her face hidden against his breast, and he touched her hair gently with one hand.

"Frances," he said tenderly. "My dear, there is no need for tears."

"I have been so frightened," she said piteously, "and I did not dare to hope that you would return after what I had said to you." She looked up at him, blinking away her tears. "Oh, Crispin, you should not have come! The danger is so great——"

"There is no danger," he interrupted gently, "and if there were, do you think it would keep me from you when you stand in need of help?"

"There is no help for me," she said hopelessly, and turned away from him to sink down on a near-by couch. "I am caught fast in a trap from which no-one can free me, and I cannot take even the one sure road of escape—death." She buried her face in her hands.

"Frances!" He came to kneel before her, drawing those hands down from her face. "Dear my lady, tell me what manner of snare it is that holds you, and, God aiding me, I will break the bars."

"Yes, you are strong," she murmured, and smiled a little through her tears, "but he—Crispin, he has the cunning of Satan himself! He smiles, and speaks you gently, but he is cruel, cruel!" She shuddered. "And I must marry him!"

"No!" He still spoke softly, but there was a new note in his voice. "That you shall never do—I swear it before Heaven! If all else fails I will kill him myself."

"Ah no, they would hang you for it, and I am not worthy of such sacrifice. This web is of my own weaving, and I will not drag you into it." She touched his cheek lightly with her fingers. "Dear Crispin, you have brought me comfort, but you cannot show me a way of escape."

He caught the small hand to his lips.

"I will find a way," he promised her. "It would be simple enough to carry you away. I could bear you off now and none the wiser, if 'twere not for your brother's illness."

"But, Crispin, do you not see? That is how Gideon holds me. Jonathan is not ill, save that he grows pale from long imprisonment, but if I were to escape he would surely die."

For a moment he regarded her, frowning, and then he moved to sit beside her on the couch.

"I begin to understand," he said. "Tell me exactly what has happened here in my absence, and then we may arrive at some plan for your escape."

" 'Tis soon told," she replied slowly. "When first we came here Gideon was kindness itself. He said that we would remain here for a few months and then return to England. Hal was staying here then, but after a while he removed to Spanish Town. I never knew what caused him to leave, though I realize now that Gideon must have planned it so, for it was then that his attitude towards me underwent a change. He began to pay court to me, and though I did all I could to discourage him he persisted, and finally asked me to be his wife." She paused, biting her lip. "I refused him, but next morning he told me that Jonathan had been taken ill."

"But he had not?" Crispin prompted quietly, and Frances shook her head.

"No, 'twas merely an excuse to keep him prisoner. Gideon took me to Jonathan's room, and told me that his life was in my hands, and that only as long as I was obedient to his wishes would no harm come to my brother. He announced our betrothal two days later, but Jonathan is to be kept prisoner until after our marriage. If I make the smallest attempt to escape, Gideon will have him killed. He is never left alone for a moment. The doctor is a creature of Gideon's, and either he or the Negro slave is with him night and day, and they have instructions to kill him if I attempt to escape, or tell anyone of my plight."

"And with the boy supposedly on his death-bed these three months, no suspicion would be aroused by his death," Crispin added thoughtfully. "But after your marriage, my lady? What then?"

"Jonathan will be allowed to 'recover'," she replied bitterly. "That is to be the reward of my obedience."

Crispin shook his head.

"I take leave to doubt it," he said. "If I read Gideon Crayle aright, he has not set the stage thus carefully merely for the purpose of forcing you to become his wife. Everyone believes Jonathan to be dying of some obscure disease, and if he does die Gideon becomes Marquis of Rotherdale, and that, my lady, has been his object from the first."

"Oh, no!" She looked up at him despairingly. "He would not dare."

"He would not hesitate an instant," said Crispin quietly. "What would he have to fear? You would be safe wedded to him, and as for those others, the slave and the doctor"—he shrugged—"'tis none so difficult to dispose of such in Port Royal. You see, my lady, you would have sacrificed yourself to no purpose."

"But what am I to do? I cannot refuse, and see my brother murdered."

"When does the marriage take place?"

"On the day after tomorrow," she replied, and shuddered. "He has made no mention of it until you returned to Jamaica. I think he fears you."

"He has good cause," said Crispin drily. "We have, then, a day and a night in which to contrive your escape."

He fell silent, and this time Frances did not speak of the hopelessness of her plight, for his quiet confidence was infectious. She remembered that twice before when hope seemed dead, and death itself yawning to engulf them, this man had brought them safely out of danger.

"Where is the boy imprisoned?" he asked at length.

"In his own room on the other side of the house. It is a chamber very like this, with a balcony overlooking the garden."

"He is guarded, you say?"

"Yes, by the doctor or the slave during the day, and at night the Negro sleeps in his room, which is kept locked, Gideon having one key and the guard the other. I may visit him whenever I choose, but we are never left alone."

"Then you could not talk to him without being overheard?"

Frances considered the point, frowning a little.

"I could contrive it, I think. They grow careless after so long, and the Negro often sleeps when he should be watching

113

over us. If anything is to be done it should be attempted when he is on guard."

"He is there always at night?"

"Yes, from the time we sup. A meal is carried to him there."

"Could you contrive to be there when the meal is brought?"

She nodded, regarding him with some surprise. He proceeded to explain.

"If I furnish you with a drug to put into the fellow's food or drink, Jonathan can possess himself of the key while he sleeps. I will enter the house as I did tonight, and we can make our escape through Jonathan's room. If we have horses waiting we can be in Port Royal before they learn of your escape." He looked at her searchingly. "Can you do it, my lady? Much will depend upon you."

"I will do anything if it means escape," she replied fervently, "but why to Port Royal? Should we not go to the Lieutenant-Governor at Spanish Town?"

He shook his head.

"Crayle is your guardian," he said, "and I, after all, but a pirate captain. Lynch, unlike Modyford, has little kindness for the Brethren, and if Crayle set his wits to work you might well find yourselves in his hands again, and I, as like as not, on my way to Gallows Point. No, my lady, we will away to Barbados, or some other island where you may find a ship to bear you back to England."

"You know best, Crispin," she said submissively. "What of the drug? Will you bring it to me yourself?"

"No, I had best not venture here openly again," he replied. "Lord Mountheath will bring it to you. Did I not say that he is with me in this venture?"

To his surprise she made no comment upon the Viscount's part in the affair, and after a little he rose to his feet.

"I must away now," he said, "for there is much to be done. Be ready tomorrow night, my lady, at an hour after midnight, and bid Jonathan have a care. The success or failure of this attempt depends upon him and upon you."

"We'll not fail you." She stood up, drawing her robe about her. "You enable me to hope again, and hope is a potent draught."

With his hand on the curtain he turned to smile at her.

"Have a care it be not too potent," he warned her, half seriously. "Put out the light, my lady. We want no gleam of it to betray us now."

She did as he asked, and soft darkness enveloped them for a moment until the lifting of the curtain revealed the moonlit world without. He stepped out on to the balcony, and turned to find her at his side. The temptation to take her in his arms again was great, but he stifled it resolutely, for he would not take advantage of her utter dependence upon him. Time enough to speak of love when they were safely away from Jamaica and out of the reach of Gideon Crayle.

"Until tomorrow night, my lady," he said, taking her hand. "God keep you, my dear."

He kissed her fingers, and was gone before she could speak again. She leaned over the balustrade to watch him descend and breathed a sigh of relief as he came safely to the ground. He raised his hand in farewell, and then the shadows of the garden swallowed him up, but Frances remained on the balcony, straining her ears for any sound which might indicate that his presence had been discovered. None came, but at last, and faint with distance, receding hoofbeats told her that he had won safely away. Then only did she return to her room, which no longer seemed the prison it had become three months before.

Captain Barbican reached Port Royal in the dawn, and, deciding that it was too early to rouse Lord Mountheath, went instead aboard the *Santo Rosario*. Here he found the mate, Matt Briarly, an old henchman of his who had sailed with him under Morgan. Matt came yawning into the great cabin, summoned by his captain's shout.

"Pox on it, lad, do you never sleep?" he growled. "We've been two days in port, and in that time you must have ridden over the best part o' the island."

"Never mind that," Crispin broke in, tossing his hat and gloves on to the table. "What of the prisoner?"

"Safe and snug, lad, according to orders. What, is Matt Briarly the man to let a prisoner slip through his fingers? Though what you want wi' a greasy slave is more'n I can tell."

"Well, keep him fast, or we are undone." Crispin unbuckled his sword and laid it beside his hat and gloves. "You will have to bestir yourself today, old friend. We must sail with the morning tide tomorrow."

"Sail?" Matt repeated incredulously. "Tomorrow? Crispin, is it crazy you are?"

"I hope not." He flung himself down in the great chair at the table's head and looked up humorously at Matt's indignant face. It occurred to Briarly that his captain looked ten years younger than when they had first put in to Port Royal, and he wondered in passing what had wrought this miracle. Crispin was speaking again.

"You have four-and-twenty hours, Matt, to take in food and water and get the men aboard."

"You are mad!" said Matt with conviction. "Stark, staring mad! This ship's in no condition to put to sea, and you know it. If we meet foul weather she'll sink like a stone."

"Nevertheless, we sail tomorrow." He raised his hand to check the other's protest. "I am still captain, Matt. That is an order."

Briarly regarded him exasperatedly.

"Captain you may be," he said shortly, "but you'll not get the men aboard for all your ordering. They've been a scant two days ashore after months o' sailing, and they know the *Rosario* is barely seaworthy. I tell you, Crispin, they'll not do it."

"Then find another crew. God's death, man, there are more mariners in Port Royal than those who sailed with us! I care not who they are or where you find them, but find them you must. Enough men to handle the ship is all we need—two score should serve."

Matt opened his mouth to make some comment, but thought better of it and closed it again. He took a turn about the cabin to soothe his ruffled spirits, and finally asked:

"Whither do we sail?"

Captain Barbican had been gazing thoughtfully into space, a half-smile playing about his lips, but at his companion's words he transferred his glance to him.

"You may tell them," he said, "that we shall set a course for Barbados. In reality our destination is Antigua, but I want no-one to know that until we are at sea."

Matt eyed him suspicously.

"What devilment are you planning, Crispin?" he demanded. "I've never before known you wanting in sense, but now you are behaving like a madman. Sail this hulk out o' Port Royal wi' only forty men to man her, saying that you are bound for one place and setting course for another, when there's no hope of plunder in either! You're either crazed or drunk."

"I am neither." Crispin leaned forward and emphasized his words with a long forefinger. "Look you, Matt, there are two good friends of mine ashore yonder who are in grave danger, and who look to me for aid. I must have them away by to-morrow's dawn and carry them to some place where they can take ship for England. Now do you understand?"

"No," said Matt bluntly, "but I'll do what I can. 'Tis a mad scheme, but when all's said, a man can die but once."

On this cheerful note they parted, and Crispin presently went ashore. For a while he was busy about the town, and then he made his way to the inn where Lord Mountheath was lodged, walking in upon that young gentleman while he was at breakfast. He accepted his invitation to join him, and over the meal acquainted him with all that had passed, and the plans made for that night. At the end of the recital he took from his pocket a tiny glass phial and placed it on the table before the Viscount.

"There, my lord," he concluded, "is the drug which you must carry to her ladyship. 'Tis a sleeping-potion powerful enough to make the fellow slumber for many hours, but otherwise harmless. I would not place the burden of murder upon those children."

Hal picked up the phial and turned it between his fingers. His comely, boyish face was troubled.

" 'Tis a dreadful risk," he said. "If they are discovered there is no knowing what vengeance Gideon will exact."

"It is the only way," Crispin replied firmly. "They are both quick-witted, and 'tis only a slave with whom they have to deal, not Crayle himself. Believe me, my lord, Lady Frances would take greater risks than this to escape from what threatens her."

The Viscount did not reply at once, but sat fingering the phial, a heavy frown disfiguring his face. It was, of course, of paramount importance to rescue Frances and Jonathan from their present plight, but he was by no means happy concerning the method by which this was to be accomplished.

It was now three months since her ladyship's betrothal to Gideon Crayle, and to one familiar with the true story of her flight from England such an announcement, following hard upon her brother's sudden illness, should have appeared suspicious in the extreme. He had received the news with surprise and dismay, but though the thought had crossed his mind that compulsion of some sort had been used upon her, he had dismissed the idea as absurd. Now, knowing the truth, he realized what mental anguish she must have endured during those months, while he, who had intended to protect her, had remained idle.

Then Crispin Barbican had returned to Jamaica, and within two days he had discovered the truth and formed a plan of escape. Would it be altogether surprising, Hal asked himself, if Frances looked with more than kindness upon the man who had saved her from an unthinkable marriage, and her brother from death? The Viscount realized that compared with Captain Barbican he made a sorry figure, and the jealousy which had troubled him in the early days of their acquaintance, and which anxiety for Frances had temporarily stifled, leapt to life again full-armed to prompt his next words.

"If this attempt is successful, Captain Barbican, I shall be eternally in your debt. You must have guessed what my feelings are where Lady Frances is concerned, and I have reason to believe that she is not wholly indifferent to me." He hesitated, and then added with a sudden show of candour, "In fact, sir, we love each other, and she had promised to become my wife even before I left her cousin's house."

For a moment Crispin stared at him in silence, and Hal, not daring to meet those disturbingly keen grey eyes, looked down at the phial in his hand.

"Then, my lord," said the buccaneer quietly, at length, "I marvel that you received the news of her betrothal to Crayle so calmly, nor sought to discover the reason for it."

His lordship scowled. Curse the fellow's shrewdness! Did nothing escape him?

"I told you," he replied impatiently, "that I was at first suspicious, but when I had seen Frances, and she had behaved as though no words of love had passed between us, I concluded that she had been deceiving me. I realize now how bitterly I wronged her, but, thanks be to God, it is not yet too late."

"You possess a truly remarkable modesty, my lord," said Crispin in a hard voice, "if you imagine that any woman would wed Gideon Crayle in preference to yourself. That, however, is no affair of mine, and once her ladyship's safety is assured you may adjust your differences with her as best you may. Meanwhile I have much to do, and so I will leave you now. You will find me aboard the *Santo Rosario* when you return from the plantation."

On that he left him, and Mountheath congratulated himself on the success of his stratagem. Of course the fellow loved Frances—that was scarcely to be wondered at—but since he appeared to possess a remarkable sense of honour for one of his lawless calling the belief that she was already promised in marriage should set an effective barrier between them. Well pleased, his lordship finished his breakfast and set out for the Crayle plantation.

Crispin made his way to the waterfront and, summoning a boat, was rowed out to his ship. As he came aboard Matt Briarly met him with a query concerning their imminent departure, but after one glance at his captain's white, set face he thought better of it and withdrew with his question unasked. What new devilry was afoot, he wondered, to give Crispin Barbican the expression of a man in hell?

Crispin went to his own cabin and, laying aside hat and sword, flung himself fully dressed on the bed. What a fool he had been, what a blind, complacent fool, to imagine even for a moment that Frances loved him! In her present desperate plight she turned instinctively to the man who had saved her a year ago, but her heart and hand she had pledged to a Court wastrel who had not lifted a finger to aid or comfort her in the past three months of torment. It was a bitter discovery to make, the more so when his hopes had risen so high, and his intensely proud spirit rebelled at the thought that he must put her out of his life once more. All that was worst in his nature rose uppermost, and ugly lines deepened about his mouth as he reflected that within twenty-four hours, if his plan were successful, both Lady Frances and her betrothed would be with him on the high seas, aboard a ship where he was absolute master.

For a time he dwelt with grim satisfaction on that thought, until with a sudden revulsion of feeling he realized that he loved Frances too greatly to make her his against her will. She had suffered enough since her grandfather's death, and if her happiness lay in the hands of Lord Mountheath then he must use every endeavour to bring them both safely back to England.

It was not an easy decision to make for one who for years had known no law save his own will. It carried him back to a point in his life reached a year ago, when the future had seemed unimaginably empty, and he had not cared whether he lived or died. That same black loneliness yawned before him now, increased a hundredfold by the glimpse vouchsafed him of all that life might have held, and he knew with bitter certainty that the battle was by no means over. It would have to be fought again and again as long as Frances was within his reach.

He fell at last into a troubled sleep, and dreamed of her helpless in the power of Gideon Crayle, while he stood by, powerless to intervene. He saw the hunchback's beautiful, evil face, heard Frances's voice calling to him for help, and started awake with the sweat damp on his brow. After that he slept no more, but went on deck to discover how the victualling of the ship was progressing, and whether Matt had yet succeeded in finding a crew.

Hal's return, just before sunset, afforded him some relief, for the Viscount was able to tell him that he had been able to give her ladyship the drug without arousing suspicion, but as this was the least hazardous part of the plan the relief was short-lived. They dined together aboard the *Santo Rosario*, whither Hal had already transferred his effects, and an hour or two later set out on their desperate venture.

They rode at an easy pace, each leading a spare horse. The animals had been hired in Port Royal, and Crispin had chosen them with care, for their lives might depend upon the speed of their mounts before the night was done. They came at last to the grove of trees where he had left his horse during his previous visit and, having tethered the beasts in this concealment, continued their way on foot. The Captain had carried at his saddle-bow what Hal had thought to be a coil of rope, but which upon closer examination proved to be a ropeladder, light but extremely strong, and this he slung now over his shoulder.

The garden was surrounded by a stone wall seven or eight feet in height, and upon the outside of this, where a tree growing within cast a black shadow, Crispon told the Viscount to wait. This was not much to his lordship's taste, but he had agreed that Captain Barbican should have the ordering of the affair, and he had sense enough to waste no time in argument. He watched his companion mount the wall, pause to scan the garden and such of the house as was within sight, and then disappear from view.

Crispin made his way without hindrance to the balcony giving on to her ladyship's apartments, and as he climbed the balustrade Frances herself emerged from the room, dressed in a riding-habit of dove-grey. The broad, plumed hat left her face in shadow, but when he took her hand he found that she was trembling.

"All is well, my lady?" he asked anxiously, and she nodded.

"Yes, we were successful. Jonathan distracted the man's attention while I put the potion into his drink, and he swallowed it all without question."

"Then he should be sleeping soundly by now, and we need delay no longer, for the sooner we are out of this house the better. Lord Mountheath awaits us beyond the garden."

"Come, then." She led the way into the room, adding as she did so: "We had best not risk a light. There is moonlight enough, and I know the way only too well." She opened a door and looked out. "All is quiet. Give me your hand, Crispin."

He put his left hand into hers, and his right dropped to the hilt of the dagger at his belt, for if they encountered anyone he must act swiftly and silently before the rest of the house could be roused. She led him along a corridor, and in the silence of that sleeping house it seemed that their footsteps must be heard, although they moved slowly and with infinite caution. At last, however, Frances paused and scratched softly upon the panels of a door: a moment of breathless suspense followed, and then a key turned, the door opened softly, and Jonathan's eager face looked out.

Her ladyship drew a long breath of relief, and Crispin thrust the dagger back into its sheath. They entered the room, where the Negro sprawled, breathing stertorously, in a chair, and he turned the key in the lock once more. Jonathan was beside him, gripping one of his hands in both his own.

"Crispin!" he whispered joyfully. "Oh, 'tis good to see you again!"

"And to see you, lad; but we must waste no time. We are not out of danger yet."

They followed him out on to the balcony and watched him uncoil the ladder and make it fast to the balustrade. He turned to Jonathan.

"Down with you, my lord, so that you may steady the ladder for your sister. As quietly as you can, now, and do not stir from the foot of it until I join you."

The boy nodded, already astride the balustrade. The ladder swayed wildly as he went down it, but he accomplished the descent in safety and raised his hand to signal them as he reached the ground.

"Your turn now, my lady," said Crispin, and without ceremony lifted her in his arms. "Have no fear. The ladder is stout enough."

He lowered her over the balustrade, and after a moment she found the ladder beneath her feet. The rope sagged a little under her weight and she knew a moment's panic, but his arm was about her still, supporting her until she found a firmer foothold. She went down steadily enough then, and was on the ground almost before she realized it.

Once assured of her safety, Crispin unfastened the ladder and let it fall to the ground. They would need it again to scale the wall, and he could descend by the same means as he had used to reach Frances's balcony. When he reached the ground Jonathan had already coiled the ladder and slung it over his shoulder, and they moved off across the garden without further delay.

The outer wall presented little difficulty. One end of the ladder being tossed over to the Viscount, Jonathan climbed up and sat astride the wall to help his sister over, and within a few minutes they were all safely outside the garden. Hal turned to her ladyship and took both her hands in his.

"Frances!" he said earnestly. "Thank God you have escaped from that devil." He kissed her hands. "My dear."

"We are not yet out of danger." Crispin spoke in a hard voice, his eyes intent upon the rope-ladder which he was coiling again. "There's no time to be lost."

Thus reminded of their peril, they followed him to the grove where the horses were tethered, and a few minutes later were galloping along the road to Port Royal. Light was brightening in the east by the time they reached the town, and Crispin was frowning as they dismounted in the courtyard of the inn from which the horses had been hired, for he had hoped to have his companions aboard the *Santo Rosario* before dawn broke.

With her ladyship on his arm, and Hal and Jonathan following, he led the way at a brisk pace towards the harbour, a hand on his sword and his eyes watchful as they passed taverns and wine-shops where lights still burned and raucous voices were raised in song. So intent was he upon these possible sources of danger that when they turned a corner and found the harbour before them he did not immediately look towards the sea. It was Frances who stopped short, one hand tightening upon his arm and the other pointing tremblingly across the harbour.

"Crispin!" she gasped. "That ship! Is it not——" She broke off, looking up at him in fearful inquiry.

Crispin's gaze followed the direction of her pointing finger and his tall figure stiffened. At no great distance from the battered *Santo Rosario* a great frigate rode at anchor, her masts a delicate tracery against the brightening sky and her black hull casting an ominous shadow across the faintly glimmering water.

"Yes, my lady," said Captain Barbican slowly, "it is the *Vampire.*"

CHAPTER XIII

BARBICAN'S LUCK

DISMAY held them motionless for a moment. Hal said:

"Sarne's ship! What cursed ill luck! What are we to do?"

"The boat will be waiting," Crispin replied. "There is a chance that we may get aboard without being seen."

He moved forward again at a quickened pace, and they were within sight of the waiting boat when a man reeled laughing from a tavern and cannoned into Frances. He recovered his balance with difficulty, swept off his hat and bowed.

"A thousan' pardons, madame," he said thickly, and, straightening, showed them the face of Jean-Pierre. He swayed on his feet and stared with drunken gravity at the Captain. "Crispin!" he discovered pleasedly. "Come an' have a drink?"

"Stand aside, you drunken fool, we are in haste," said Crispin impatiently, but Jean-Pierre was not as far gone in drink as he appeared to be. His dark eyes took in the little group— the white-faced girl clinging to Crispin's arm, Hal and Jonathan in the background—and understanding came into them. He chuckled knowingly.

"Carryin' off Lady Frances," he decided, and shook his head. "Can't 'low that, Crispin. Gideon Crayle won't like it."

He turned his head slightly and opened his mouth to call

123

over his shoulder to those within the tavern, but before the cry could take shape Crispin struck hard and true to the Frenchman's jaw. Jean-Pierre dropped in his tracks without a sound, and Crispin swept his companions past his recumbent figure to the waiting boat. No sound of pursuit came to them as they were rowed out to the galleon; the encounter with Sarne's lieutenant had passed unnoticed.

Aboard the *Santo Rosario*, near the head of the ladder, Matt Briarly awaited his captain. He had succeeded in scraping together sufficient men to handle the ship, but they were the very dregs of the pirate stronghold, and between that fact and the condition of the ship his mind was far from easy. There was mutinous material in that cut-throat crew, and had he not had experience of Crispin Barbican's ability to handle such men he would have refused point-blank to accompany him. As it was, he looked longingly across at the black frigate which had so lately come to anchor and wished that they might sail in her instead of in the battered Spanish prize.

He heard the boat arrive alongside, and presently, up the ladder came Captain Barbican, who, stepping down on to the deck, turned to offer his hand to the person following him. Matt saw red-gold curls beneath a plumed hat, a trailing habit of dove-grey, and swore beneath his breath.

"A petticoat!" he muttered to himself. "So that's the cause of all the trouble! I might ha' guessed it!"

He slouched forward to greet his captain, casting a jaundiced eye over his three companions, for Hal and Jonathan had followed her ladyship aboard. Crispin turned to the girl.

"My lady, this is Matt Briarly, mate of the *Santo Rosario*. Matt, Lady Frances Crayle and her brother, the Marquis of Rotherdale, whom we are carrying to Barbados." He took a pace closer and added in a lower tone: "Weigh anchor with all speed, my friend. I have reason to believe that we may have the *Vampire* on our trail ere long."

He did not wait for a reply, but led his guests away in the direction of the great cabin. Matt looked after him and spat disgustedly.

"So we're to have that black devil on our heels, are we?" he remarked, addressing his absent captain. "And you must needs carry off a lady and a couple o' noblemen. Pox on it, my lad, you're meddling in matters too high for you. We'll all dance on Gallows Point before you're done."

This gloomy prophecy, however, showed no immediate

prospect of being fulfilled. The *Santo Rosario* slipped out of Port Royal almost unnoticed, and sailed eastward before a fresh breeze. A sharp watch was kept, but the blue mountains of Jamaica faded into the distance, and still no pursuing sail could be seen. The escape it seemed, was complete.

Upon the advice of Captain Barbican the three passengers retired to their cabins to rest, but Crispin himself had much to do. With Matt, he inspected his ship and his crew, and neither the one nor the other impressed him very favourably. He suspected that his difficulties, which his friends accounted already over, were only just beginning. The *Santo Rosario* was in no case to fight even if they encountered a possible prize, and without plunder the ruffians he commanded might easily get out of hand. Later that day he confided his suspicions to Briarly.

"Aye, they're a mangy lot," Matt agreed disparagingly, "but I could do no better. Though if I'd ha' known you meant to bring a woman aboard there's more than one I'd ha' refused, even if it meant sailing shorthanded. Ye'd best keep a close guard on the lass, Crispin. 'Tis a dainty armful, when all's said."

Crispin frowned, leaning his arms on the poop-rail. The old buccaneer had put into words the anxiety which had been troubling him since first they came aboard. Had he rescued Frances from one peril only to thrust her into another?

"But there was so little time, and what else could I do?" he said aloud, answering that unspoken doubt. He caught Matt's questioning glance and added, "Had I left her in Jamaica she would have been married by now to her cousin, a crook-backed devil who is the power behind Sarne and his men."

In a few crisp sentences he related the story of Frances and Jonathan, knowing that he could trust Briarly to the death, and wishing to correct any false impression Matt might entertain concerning her ladyship's presence aboard the galleon. From Antigua, he explained, she and her brother would proceed, in the care of their cousin, Lord Mountheath, to England, where their place at Court was assured. Matt heard the tale out, and then grunted contemptuously.

"D'ye mean ye'll let her go?"

Crispin frowned, and when he spoke his voice was curt.

"What the devil do you mean by that?"

"I mean that you didn't go to all this trouble, and put to sea in an undermanned, half-rotten hulk, for the sake of the little

Marquis. 'Tis her ladyship's blue eyes that have made you behave like a madman, and now you're for letting that young coxcomb carry her off to England."

Crispin laughed shortly on a note of bitterness.

"Some time ago her ladyship made very plain to me how far apart are our stations in life. She is the sister of a marquis, I a pirate. Moreover, she is promised in marriage to Lord Mountheath."

Matt made a guttural noise eloquent of profound disgust.

"What's that to do with it?" he demanded. "You could break that pretty popinjay wi' your bare hands. You'll not let a trifle like that stand in the way if you've a fancy for the lass?"

Crispin shook his head.

"Pirate's ways, Matt. They would not commend me to her ladyship." He paused, and the bitterness deepened in his dark face. "Besides, what have I to offer her? Neither home nor honour, only a tainted name and hands stained with innocent blood." Matt made a protesting noise, and he repeated: "Yes, innocent blood, Spanish though it was. Do you forget the screaming nuns we forced before us up the scaling-ladders at Porto Bello, or the way we slew and tortured at Panama? No, I could not ask her to be my wife. She must go back to England, and one day she will marry Mountheath, and perhaps think kindly sometimes of a man who would have died to serve her, pirate though he was." He took his elbows from the rail and stood upright. "Faugh! I am talking like a lovesick schoolboy. 'Tis fortunate that no one but you can hear me."

"Aye," Matt agreed drily, "if the men hear such talk from you 'twill go hard with all of us. 'Tis an iron hand you'll need there, lad! They're treacherous as snakes and as dangerous, and meantime there's mischief of another sort brewing yonder."

He nodded towards a great bank of cloud, purple and slate-blue and black, which was piling up in the north. The breeze which had served them so well had died altogether and there was a hot, sullen stillness in the air, the horizon veiled by a thick haze. The *Santo Rosario* lay becalmed, heaving gently to the oily swell of a violet-tinted sea.

The mate was not the only man to observe these ominous portents, and the crew began to mutter among themselves, their sullenness matching the sultry menace of the weather. There was not a man aboard, with the possible exception of the young Viscount, who was not aware of the peril in which they stood.

The weight of that danger was heavy on Crispin's heart when he went below to sup with his passengers, though for their sake he contrived to dissemble his anxiety. By nightfall, however, even their inexperienced eyes could see the peril clearly enough, for the calm had given way to a storm so violent that it seemed no ship could survive it. Stripped of every rag of canvas, lashed by torrential rains and with great seas breaking over her, the *Santo Rosario* was driven steadily before a gale which bore her far out of her course.

For hours Captain Barbican and his men fought desperately to keep afloat the straining, shuddering vessel that staggered like a wounded beast in the grip of the tempest, while below in the great cabin Frances, Hal and Jonathan sat together, white-faced and apprehensive. Only once in that long night did they see Crispin, when he came to the cabin to give them what assurance he could. He was coatless; water dripped from his hair, and the sodden cambric shirt clung to his wide shoulders. The grim weariness of his face confirmed their worst fears.

"Well?" inquired Hal, with a feeble attempt at lightness, "have you come to tell us that we must abandon ship?"

Crispin shook his head.

"At present we are still afloat," he replied. "I can say no more than that." His eyes sought Frances's. "While we live there is still hope."

She rose to her feet and came to his side, raising her eyes to his.

"Is there hope, Crispin?" she asked quietly. "Tell me the truth—I am not afraid."

"I have told it, my lady," he said. "There is a hope, no more." A spasm of pain crossed his face. "I cannot forgive myself for exposing you to such danger."

A lurch of the storm-tossed vessel unbalanced her, and he put out an arm to steady her. For an instant she leaned against him, and her voice came softly to his ears, too low for the others to hear.

"There was only one peril that I feared, and you saved me from that. Come now what may, I am content."

The memory of those words, and the steadfast courage in her eyes, went with him when he returned to the deck. The *Santo Rosario* was in a desperate plight. Much of her rigging had been carried away, the pounding of the huge waves had reduced two of her boats to matchwood, and when they came to tell him that she had sprung a leak it seemed that all was lost. With an unmoved countenance he gave the order in which lay their only hope of salvation—to jettison the guns. One by one the heavy cannon were thrust overboard, and, thus lightened, the galleon remained afloat.

She was still afloat when with the dawn the last of the hurricane swept by, and left her wallowing between the long, smooth rollers which seeemed almost black, but how long she would remain so was another question. The pumps were working furiously in an effort to counteract the leak, and this, together with the damage she had suffered above-decks, made it seem probable that she had weathered the storm only to founder of the wounds it had dealt her.

As the light increased Crispin sent a man aloft to scan the horizon in the hope of sighting another ship, but for a long while the heaving waste of water remained blank and empty. He was pacing the poop, his face haggard with anxiety, when the look-out's voice floated down to him:

"Land on the starboard quarter!"

The news sent a ripple of excitement and hope through the ship. Men who had gone about their duties with sullen or despairing faces flung themselves with renewed zest into their tasks, or crowded to the bulwarks to peer eagerly at the horizon. The land might belong to friend or foe, it might be swarming with Spaniards or hostile Indians, but it was land, the most welcome sight of all.

It became visible at last, a blue-grey smudge like a cloud on the horizon, resolving itself slowly into a low, wooded island. With this clearer view the pirates were transported with glee, for they recognized that providential scrap of land. It was a favourite rendezvous of the dread Brethren, and one of the finest natural harbours in the Caribbean. clearly a kindly fate was watching over them. Someone remembered a phrase familiar among the followers of Morgan in the great days of the Welshman's career—'Barbican's luck'. It had been a byword among the buccaneers, and the spell was powerful still. A rousing cheer went up for the captain whom, a short while ago, they would readily have murdered.

The day was still young, clear and sparkling after the storm, when they reached the island. Crispin, still standing on the poop, saw Frances emerge from the cabin and pick her way through the tangle of wreckage to the companion. She came to stand beside him at the poop-rail, and looked with eager eyes at the land which now loomed so close.

"How beautiful it is," she said. "Where are we, Crispin?"

"Many miles out of our course, I fear," he replied. "This is known among the Brethren of the Coast as Pirates' Island, since it is a favourite place to careen their vessels. It is the mercy of Providence which brought us here, my lady, for we could not have stayed afloat through another night."

"God is good," said Frances softly, and looked from the wooded shore to the man beside her. "A safe harbour after storm and peril—what more could we ask?"

A short while later the *Santo Rosario*, defenceless, shattered, all but foundering, staggered through the channel between reef and headland and into the broad lagoon of Pirates' Island. There she dropped anchor, and while the most skilled of her crew set about the task of stemming the leak until a more lasting repair could be effected the rest went ashore in the remaining boats to prepare an encampment.

In the first boat went Captain Barbican and his three passengers, all somewhat weary but in reasonably good spirits. The lagoon was rimmed by a wide beach of silvery sand, where turtles scattered in panic before the invaders, and beyond that the forest rose in a solid wall of green, broken at one point by a sizable stream of fresh water.

Jonathan was the first ashore, jumping out as the boat's keel grated on the sand and splashing knee-deep through the wavelets to the beach. The sturdy ruffians who had manned the oars followed him and dragged the boat farther up the gently-sloping beach, looking insolent appraisal of the girl who sat in the stern. The presence of their captain prevented any open expression of admiration, but Frances was conscious of their glances and rendered uneasy thereby.

Crispin carried her ashore and set her on her feet on the yielding sand, and she looked about her appreciatively. The island lay quiet in the morning sunlight, and the spicy scent of the forest was borne to them on a warm breeze. After the long months of grief and fear, and the storm-racked hours through which they had recently passed, it seemed like another world where the twisted shadow of Gideon Crayle did not fall.

Under Crispin's command the buccaneers went briskly to work, with an efficiency born of long experience. Stores were landed from the galleon, and at one tip of the crescent-shaped strip of sand tents of sail-cloth were erected to house her crew. At the other end of the beach trees were felled at the edge of the jungle, and in the clearing thus made there arose with incredible rapidity a cabin of logs roofed with palm-fronds. A curtain of sail-cloth masked the doorway, and the interior was made habitable with furniture brought from the ship. This was for my lady, and at no great distance, that she might be well guarded, tents were erected to house her brother and cousin and Captain Barbican. A Negro slave, who had filled the office of steward aboard the galleon, was detailed to cook for the little party.

The pirates worked with a will, relief at their narrow escape from death engendering in them an unwonted industry. Seeing them thus at work, hearing them roar a raucous ditty, it was hard to believe that each one of them carried the burden of heinous crimes; they might have been honest mariners going about their lawful tasks.

Towards sunset Captain Barbican came slowly along the beach from the buccaneer encampment to that other among the trees. The Negro was preparing supper over an open fire, and on the opposite side of the clearing Lady Frances sat beneath a great tree, where a rug from the cabin of the galleon had been spread upon the turf. At her invitation he seated himself beside her and leaned back against the bole of the tree.

"Hal and Jonathan have climbed the bluff yonder," she said, nodding towards the low headland. "They said that they would bring back some fruit for supper."

"It will be welcome." Crispin spoke absently, making a mental note to point out to the Viscount that it was unwise to leave her ladyship entirely alone, with the pirate crew encamped less than a quarter of a mile away. Mountheath must watch over her, for Crispin knew that his only hope of abiding by the decision he had made lay in avoiding Frances as much as possible. Every pair of hands would be needed if the *Santo Rosario* was to be made seaworthy again, and he would make that his excuse to spend most of the time among his men.

"How quickly your men work." The girl's voice broke in upon his thoughts. "I would not have believed it possible to

130

build such a cabin in so short a time. When I went into the tent yonder to rest this morning they were felling the trees, and when I woke the cabin was finished."

"They have had much practice," he replied, with a smile, "though I fear 'tis but a rough place at best. But you could not remain aboard the *Rosario* since we intend to careen her."

"Careen her?" she repeated, and her voice was puzzled.

"When we have lightened her," he explained, "we shall drag her up on to the beach, high and dry, so that we may the more easily come at her keel. When it is repaired, the foulness burnt off, and she is seaworthy again, we refloat her. After that the damage above-decks must be repaired."

She regarded him with a mixture of incredulity and admiration.

"You will do all that, with so few men?"

He laughed.

"The buccaneers, my lady, are accustomed to such work, though I fear it will take a considerable time. Unless another ship puts in here for water or careening, we are like to be on the island these three months."

There was a pause. After a little she said in a low voice:

"I do not mind. I am in no haste to reach England."

"It is perhaps better so." Crispin was pursuing his own train of thought. "When it becomes known that you fled from Jamaica in the *Santa Rosario* the hunt will be up, but they will not seek you on Pirates' Island. It may even be supposed that we did not survive the storm. 'Tis something of a miracle that we did."

His voice was hoarse with fatigue, and she realized suddenly that he had barely slept at all in the past three days. She looked at him and saw with a stab of remorse the lines of weariness in his face. He had powers of endurance beyond the ordinary, but the strain was telling upon him at last.

"You are tired, Crispin," she said gently. "Surely you may rest now?"

He raised his head with an effort and looked along the beach. The crew of the *Santo Rosario* had finished their day's work and were taking their ease, some clustering in groups before the tents, gambling with cards or dice, while others penetrated the fringe of the forest to gather fruit or straggled along the shore in search of turtles' eggs. It was upon these last that his tired gaze rested, and he shook his head.

131

"Not until Lord Mountheath returns," he said. "These rogues of mine are not over-nice in their manners, and I would not have them frighten you."

"Then rest you here," she said. "I promise not to stir from this spot until Hal and Jonathan return, and if anyone draws near I will wake you."

He hesitated, but his overwhelming weariness could be held at bay no longer, and with a gesture of resignation he stretched himself full-length beside her. He was almost immediately asleep, and for a space the little camp was very still, for the Negro had gone to the stream for water.

Presently Frances moved, and taking the embroidered cushion against which she had been leaning she slipped it beneath Crispin's head. A moment she paused, looking down at this man who twice had rescued her from deadly peril, and whom she had once scorned as a pirate, then, stooping lower, she kissed him gently on the lips.

CHAPTER XIV

RETURN OF A HERO

THE flight of the Marquis of Rotherdale and his sister from their guardian's house was discovered by the physician in Gideon's pay. According to his usual custom, the man went to his lordship's room early on the morning of what should have been Lady Frances's wedding-day, but when his repeated knocks evoked no response he hastened in some anxiety to his master.

Gideon was still abed, but on hearing these ominous tidings he paused only to don his periwig and a bed-gown of flowered brocade before hurrying to investigate. The door of Jonathan's room being opened, they discovered the Negro guard snoring in his chair, but of the little Marquis no trace at all. When all attempts to rouse the slave failed, the doctor came to the rather obvious conclusion that he had been drugged, but when he imparted this information to Gideon the hunchback turned on his heel and hurried from the room, cursing beneath his breath.

With mingled curiosity and apprehension his henchman followed him to her ladyship's bedchamber, where a similar scene awaited them. The bed was smooth and unruffled, the sumptuous bridal gown trailed from a tall, carved press, but Lady Frances, like her brother, had vanished without trace. Gideon stood in the middle of the deserted room and cursed with a savage fluency before which the doctor maintained a respectful silence.

"But how in the fiend's name," he ventured at last, when the torrent had abated somewhat, "did they contrive it? Who could have helped them?"

"Barbican!" The thwarted bridegroom spat out the name with the venom of an oath. "He is the only friend they have in this accursed island. As to the 'how' of it . . ." He went out on to the balcony and looked over the balustrade. A broken spray of creeper hung trailing, its blossoms already withering.

"This would be no difficult climb for an active man—and he must have come here twice at least, curse his impudence!" He came back into the room and cast himself down on the couch, gnawing at his lip. "I underrated the fellow! I should have turned dogs loose in the garden, and set a duenna to watch over that little slut. Her pirate lover could not have come at her then."

He broke off, and for a space brooded evilly over what had passed in a silence which the doctor did not dare to break. At last Gideon got up and went towards the door.

"Summon my coach," he said abruptly. "We will see if anything more is to be learned in Port Royal."

An hour or so later he sat in the great, swaying vehicle as it made its ponderous way along the road to the coast. He had recovered his usual outward calm, but beneath that unruffled exterior lay an icy rage which was akin to madness. Once the first shock of discovery had passed he wasted no time in profitless ranting but set out to repair the harm that had been done. As he had said earlier, he had underrated Crispin Barbican. He had dismissed him as a mere adventurer who had kept Frances and Jonathan safe in the hope of rich reward, and having presented him with the captured galleon had deemed the matter at an end. By the time that the buccaneer returned to Jamaica, if he ever did return, brother and sister would be fast caught in the web which for years he had been spinning with such loving care.

Captain Barbican had returned, and the bonds were broken, but not for long. Gideon swore that if it were within human power to recapture his errant bride and her brother he would do so, and break the man who had carried them off. Crispin Barbican should learn the power of Gideon Crayle as Frances and Jonathan had learned it. Learn it and fear it.

His musings were interrupted by a sudden shout, and the coach lurched to a standstill. Gideon thrust his head out of the window as a horseman drew rein beside the vehicle. It was Randolph Sarne.

"I was seeking you," the pirate announced without preamble, "but it seems that you know what news I bring."

Crayle looked at him a moment, his eyes narrowed. Then he opened the door of the coach.

"Get in, Sarne," he said briefly. "We may talk here without being overheard."

Sarne dismounted and surrendered his horse to one of Gideon's servants, and for the first time the hunchback noticed that he was not alone. A frightened Negro bestrode another horse a few yards away, and at the pirate's command tumbled hastily out of the saddle and approached, cringing.

"Here is one who also has news for you," Sarne remarked grimly, "so by your leave we'll have him into the coach, too."

He thrust the trembling black into the vehicle, climbed in after him and shut the door. As the coach lumbered forward again he asked abruptly, "How much do you know?"

"Lady Frances and her brother have fled from my house with Captain Barbican, probably to Port Royal. What more can you add to that?"

Sarne leaned back in his seat and folded his arms, regarding his confederate sardonically.

"They fled farther than that, my friend. His ship sailed with the tide, bound, so we are told, for Barbados. Lord Mountheath was with them."

"Mountheath?" Gideon spoke sharply. "So that was it! He visited her yesterday." He looked at Sarne. "You are sure of that?"

"Jean-Pierre saw them on the wharf this morning. Barbican struck him down before he could give the alarm, and by the time he regained his senses the *Santo Rosario* had sailed. He has a heavy hand, this Crispin Barbican."

"He will learn that mine is heavier," said Gideon softly. "But wait! Why did you not follow him? Your ship was in the harbour."

Sarne laughed shortly.

"And her crew ashore. Could I sail the *Vampire* single-handed? But calm your fears! He's not out of reach." He leaned forward, elbows on knees. "I've learned a deal about the *Rosario* this morning. She came into port only three days since, badly mauled by a Spanish ship-o'-war, and in no case to put to sea again without refitting. Her crew knew that, and they'd have no part in this new venture. Somehow Barbican contrived to scrape together enough men to handle her, but they're a cowardly pack and a glimpse o' the *Vampire's* guns will make 'em see reason. You've naught to fear."

"You think we can overtake them?"

"The *Vampire* can outsail any ship in Port Royal."

"And they are bound for Barbados?"

The pirate grinned.

"So 'tis said."

"You fool!" Gideon spoke contemptuously. "Do you think that Captain Barbican would blazon his destination to the world when he has been at such pains to keep his movements secret? Depend upon it, this talk of Barbados is but a trick to throw us off the scent."

"To be sure it is," Sarne agreed equably, and jerked his head towards the silent Negro. "Do you recognize this fellow? 'Tis one of your house-slaves."

For the first time Crayle looked closely at the third occupant of the coach, and recognition dawned in his face. Recognition, and something else which made the slave shrink back into the corner, whimpering with terror.

"It is indeed," he said gently. "Well, you black swine, what part do you play in this?"

"He has been a prisoner aboard the *Santo Rosario*," Sarne explained, seeing that the Negro was incapable of answering. "He escaped just before they sailed."

"So!" Gideon said softly. "I wondered how Barbican contrived to find her ladyship without rousing the household. You treacherous cur, I'll have the flesh cut from your bones for this."

"Mercy, master, mercy!" The slave found his voice in the face of that monstrous threat. "He say he kill me if I not tell. He say he mean no harm to Lady Frances. I no traitor, master!" He slipped to his knees on the floor of the coach, stretching out imploring hands. "I serve you well, master. They go to Antigua, not Barbados—I hear them talk. You not flog me, master——"

"Silence, animal!" Gideon struck him across the face with the back of his hand, and the opal ring laid open the slave's cheek. "Do you think to save your miserable hide so easily? Without your help the rogue could never have entered the house. You would have been wiser to have remained his prisoner." He leaned back, crossing his hands on the knob of his cane. "Sarne, you have a pistol. In God's name rid me of this vermin. 'Tis of no further use to me."

The pirate grinned wolfishly, and with unhurried movements drew and cocked his pistol. With a despairing shriek the Negro flung open the door of the coach, leapt out, and fell sprawling in the dust. He struggled to hands and knees, but before he could rise farther the pistol barked once and he pitched forward on his face. Sarne reached out and caught the wildly-swinging door, slamming it shut.

"So they are bound for Antigua," Gideon remarked softly, as though there had been only a trifling interruption. "A damaged ship, a treacherous crew, and Barbican and Mountheath both mad for the girl. Upon my soul, Sarne, 'tis a situation fraught with possibilities."

He laughed softly, and Sarne regarded him uneasily. Evil he was himself; he had robbed and slain and tortured, and, like the pirate Rogers, might well have wondered whether he could swim farther in the wine he had drunk or the blood he had shed, but even he knew fear in the presence of Gideon Crayle. There was something sinister and unholy about the hunchback, with his wistful face and mellifluous voice which was at its sweetest when he was planning some monstrous villainy. Violence Sarne understood, the plundered ships, the sacked and blazing cities, but not this slow, secret plotting, this weaving of webs and waiting, spider-like, for the victims to become entangled in the meshes.

Gideon interrupted his thoughts to ask abruptly:

"How soon can we sail in pursuit?"

The pirate pursed his lips.

"The men will not take kindly to the notion," he said. "They've gold in their pockets and they're eager for the pleasures it will buy in Port Royal. They'll not be willing to sail again so soon."

"They will be if they are well rewarded," Crayle replied impatiently. "Offer them my share of this latest cargo to be divided among them, and the share that would come to me of any prizes we take on this voyage. That should content them."

Content them it did, and it was agreed that the *Vampire*

should sail in pursuit of the *Santo Rosario* on the following day. By the time dawn broke, however, Captain Sarne entertained grave doubts concerning the fate of Barbican's ship, for the fringe of the storm which carried the galleon so far out of her course swept Port Royal also, and caused the pirate to give thanks that his own vessel still lay safely within the harbour. Knowing the condition of the *Santo Rosario* he would have abandoned the idea of pursuit, but Gideon was insistent. Luck might have favoured the fugitives, and he intended to take no chances; accordingly the black frigate set out to track them down.

Barely a fortnight after her departure another privateer dropped anchor in Port Royal harbour, commanded by the old pirate Thomas Rogers, and carrying no less a person than the new Lieutenant-Governor of Jamaica and Lieutenant-General of the Jamaican forces, Sir Henry Morgan. The Welshman had crossed the Atlantic aboard the *Jamaica Merchant,* but for reasons which no-one—unless perhaps Morgan himself—fully understood, the vessel had been wrecked on the Isle of Cows, that rendezvous of pirates, where Rogers had found his one-time crony.

'The wickedest city in the world' went wild with joy at the return of its greatest hero, but Morgan spent only a comparatively short time receiving its acclamations. He had won his race across the Atlantic against Lord Vaughan, the newly-appointed Governor, and was in haste to establish his own position before the arrival of his sour and unlikeable superior. By the time Vaughan did appear on the scene, just one week later, Sir Henry was firmly established as uncrowned king of that city of outlaws, a position from which his lordship never succeeded in dislodging him. So matters stood some six weeks later, when the Earl of Larchwood arrived in Jamaica.

His lordship had been entrusted with a special and somewhat delicate mission, but of that he chose at first to say nothing. Ostensibly he came to visit his young kinsman, the Marquis of Rotherdale, and to make the acquaintance of the lady whose charms had kept his own son and heir in the tropics for so many months. At first, however, he could discover nothing, for the great house on the Crayle plantation was closed, and neither its owner nor his two wards, nor Viscount Mountheath, to be found on the island. Sir Thomas Lynch, with whom the Viscount had been staying, could tell him little beyond the fact that Mountheath had taken leave of him some two months earlier, and advised him to seek news of his son in Port Royal. Sir Thomas was still too greatly put out by the worldly successes and high-handed actions of his old enemy, Morgan, to devote much time to other matters.

So back to Port Royal his lordship went, greatly perplexed and more than a little uneasy, and both these emotions were soon to be increased tenfold. There was no lack of information in Port Royal, but there were so many conflicting stories abroad that Larchwood was no nearer the truth at the end of his inquiries than he had been in the beginning. The little Marquis was dead, said some, of the mysterious malady which had attacked him months before, and his sister, on the eve of her marriage to Gideon Crayle, had eloped with Captain Barbican. No, said others, the buccaneer had carried off both brother and sister by force. A third story had it that it was Lord Mountheath with whom Lady Frances had fled; Barbican had merely supplied the means of escape. Gideon Crayle had given chase in the *Vampire*, bribing the pirates with an enormous sum because theirs was the swiftest ship in Port Royal. The more questions his lordship asked, the more vague the answers became. No-one in Port Royal really knew the truth of the affair, but they were suspicious of this courtier from beyond the seas, and the graceless city knew how to protect its own. In despair, the Earl did at last what he would have been wiser to have done in the beginning. He carried his doubts and fears to Sir Henry Morgan.

They had already met in London, where both had been friends of the witty, cynical Lord Carlisle, and Morgan was willing enough to be of help. The secrets of Port Royal were yielded readily to the hero admiral, and, within two days the truth—or as much of it as was commonly known—was in his hands. My Lords Mountheath and Rotherdale, and Lady Frances, had left Jamaica aboard Crispin Barbican's ship, and two days later Gideon Crayle had followed in Randolph Sarne's *Vampire*. The black frigate had since been sighted off the coast of Porto Rico, but of the *Santo Rosario* nothing had been heard since the great storm of the night following her departure, and it was taken for granted that she had foundered.

The Earl received these tidings in stricken silence, for Hal was his only son, but after a little he composed himself and announced his intention of using every endeavour to track down the man who was the cause of the tragedy—Gideon Crayle, now presumably Marquis of Rotherdale. He could not even guess what story lay behind that desperate flight, but clearly something was very much amiss, and Crayle and his pirate friends should pay for it.

Sir Henry listened thoughtfully to this denunciation. He had his own plans for the future of those buccaneers whom he knew he could trust, but Randolph Sarne was not among them. Moreover, it had been suggested to him before he left England that one of his first actions in the Caribbean should be to rid the seas of the pirate who had become as great a plague to his own countrymen as he was to the Dons, and as there was no love lost between Morgan and Sarne the suggestion accorded well with Sir Henry's own inclinations.

He begged Lord Larchwood to be seated again, told him of his intention to put an end to the sanguinary career of Captain Sarne, and suggested that it might be possible to arrive at some arrangement of benefit to them both. After only the briefest hesitation the Earl confided to Sir Henry the real reason for his visit to Jamaica, and a discussion ensued which lasted for the best part of an hour and satisfied both gentlemen completely. It was noticeable, however, that though Morgan was now in possession of Lord Larchwood's secret, his lordship knew nothing whatsoever of Sir Henry's somewhat unorthodox plans for the future. The sometime admiral of the black frigate knew how to keep his own counsel.

CHAPTER XV

INTERLUDE ON AN ISLAND

On the broad, silvery beach of Pirates' Island the *Santo Rosario* lay careened, one entire side of her yellow hull exposed to view as she lay over on the other. The work upon her had progressed but slowly during the three months since her arrival at the island, for the men were lazy and resentful and Crispin dared not drive them too hard. At any time resentment might flare into open mutiny, and his little party was outnumbered by more than ten to one, for of all the crew he knew that only upon Matt Briarly could he rely.

In the clearing at the other end of the beach, where chairs and a table had been set beneath a tree, sat Lady Frances and Lord Mountheath, while on the headland, mercifully screened from his sister's view by the intervening branches, the Marquis of Rotherdale was scrambling about the face of the cliff in search of nests of the sea-birds which dwelt there. Of all those who had sailed in the *Santo Rosario*, only Jonathan was completely satisfied with his present situation.

Her ladyship sat silent, her hands idle in her lap, and gazed abstractedly across the lagoon to the line of foam that marked the reef; the Viscount was silent also, and with his elbow on the arm of his chair, and his chin upon his hand, looked intently at her ladyship. She made a picture worthy of study, with her delicate profile outlined against the dark foliage and the breeze stirring the tendrils of red-gold hair at her temples, but there was wistfulness in her eyes and in the curve of her lips.

Presently her gaze shifted, and she looked along the beach to the distant bulk of the careened galleon, about which the buccaneers were moving sluggishly. Crispin was there, working among his men, as he had been almost every day since their arrival at the island, returning to the encampment only to sleep. Though he said little concerning the progress of the work on the *Santo Rosario*, the very silence, and the added grimness of his dark face, told them that all was not well, though even then they did not suspect the true gravity of their position. Frances's heart ached when she saw the lines of anxiety in his face, and she longed to comfort him, but since their coming to the island an intangible barrier seemed to have risen between them. He used towards her now the distant courtesy of a stranger, and she asked herself whether his tenderness on the night they planned the escape had been a figment of her imagination, born of her own desire.

It was at this inauspicious moment that the Viscount deemed the time ripe for a declaration of his own feelings for her ladyship. Although he had been paying assiduous court to her until her unexpected betrothal to Gideon Crayle, and since her escape had resumed the attitude of gentle possessiveness which had so offended Captain Barbican in the past, he had never, in so many words, offered her marriage. He now determined to repair the omission.

He coughed gently to attract her attention, but the attempt was a failure. Frances continued to look wistfully along the beach, and a gentleman of greater perception than the Viscount might have hesitated to broach such a delicate subject when the lady was so preoccupied. Mountheath, however, blundered on.

"Frances," he said, and then, when she paid no heed, repeated more loudly, "Frances."

"I beg your pardon, Hal." She came to herself with a start. "Did you speak?"

This was scarcely a promising beginning. His lordship looked hurt, but continued resolutely.

"You grow weary of the island," he remarked, giving her no time to deny the statement, "but it cannot now be long before the ship is seaworthy again, and by this time the search for us, if search there was, will have been abandoned. Once we win away from here we shall have little to fear. We shall find a ship homeward bound, and then you will be able to bid farewell for ever to this accursed land of pirates and hurricanes."

Frances's lip trembled. The prospect did not appear to afford her proper gratification, but the Viscount, approaching the climax of his speech, did not perceive this.

"Then," he added, "then, dear cousin, I shall claim fulfilment of the promise that binds you to me, and ask your hand in marriage."

This time there was no doubt that he had captured her attention. The colour fled from her cheeks and she stared at him in wide-eyed dismay.

"There was no promise," she exclaimed faintly.

"There was no formal betrothal," he agreed a trifle impatiently, "but you know full well that it was what our respective families desired. I myself saw the letters which passed between them, and you could have raised no objection then, for I am persuaded that your grandfather would not have obliged you to enter into any contract disagreeable to you."

She made a little, helpless gesture.

"I was but a child," she said. " 'Tis so long ago."

"So long?" He stared at her. " 'Tis less than two years."

"Upon occasion, Hal," she replied slowly, "time cannot be measured in years and days. When this matter was first mentioned I was a very babe. I knew nothing of the world or of men, and I was content for my grandfather to arrange a marriage for me. I would have wedded you then in obedience to his wishes, but now all that is changed."

"Changed indeed," he agreed readily. "Then we were strangers; the marriage was a matter of convenience, of duty. Now we know each other, and I love you."

"Oh, Hal, please!" She turned her head away sharply and her voice trembled. "Let us not speak of it, for I—I cannot care for you in that way, greatly though I value your friendship."

"But, Frances——" he was beginning, when she cut him short.

"Hal, I beg of you! This subject is painful to me. Forgive me if I hurt you, my dear, but I cannot discuss it further."

For a second or two he regarded her, very crestfallen, and then he perceived what he thought to be the cause of her agitation.

"What a clumsy fool I am, to be plaguing you with talk of marriage!" he exclaimed. "It follows too close, does it not, upon that travesty of a betrothal into which Crayle forced you? I should have realized it."

Frances opened her lips to correct his mistake, but after a moment's reflection closed them again without speaking. It seemed the simplest way of putting an end to the conversation, or at least of postponing it indefinitely. Somehow she seemed incapable of thinking beyond their departure from the island.

There the matter was left, but thereafter the Viscount, who had accounted his lady already won until her very positive refusal had given him pause, was zealous in his efforts to please her. He perceived the wistfulness in her manner, mistook it for boredom, and cast about in his mind for some means of diverting her, and one of his suggestions was that they should stroll along the beach to see for themselves how the work on the galleon was progressing. Crispin had told him that the vessel was almost ready to be refloated, and Hal thought that the sight of so great a stride towards their liberation would be enheartening to her ladyship.

She agreed at once, glad of any excuse to seek out Crispin, but when they reached the *Santo Rosario* neither he nor Matt Briarly were to be seen. The buccaneers had watched with every indication of interest the approach of Lady Frances and her companion, and by the time that the couple halted close to the towering bulk of the beached galleon all pretence at work had come to an end.

Although her ladyship's once elegant habit of brocaded silk was shabby now, and frayed about the hem, she still made a charming picture with her bright curls and winsome face shadowed by the broad grey hat with its plume of blue, and the men made no attempt to conceal their admiration. She became aware of sly winks and grins, and looked uneasily for Captain Barbican. Not seeing him, she turned to the Viscount.

"Hal," she whispered, "pray let us go back. I fear we should not have come, and Crispin will be displeased to find us here."

The reference to the Captain was a mistake. His lordship frowned.

"To the devil with his displeasure!" he said arrogantly. "Gad'slife, Frances, you permit the fellow too much freedom. What right has he to tell us where we may or may not go?"

Before she could reply a bearded ruffian who stood nearby tossed aside the tool he was holding and lounged forward, his eyes flickering over her in a glance which was in itself an insult. She drew back as he approached, and he grinned.

"What ails you, lass," he demanded, "that you keep so close? 'Tis scarce a glimpse we've had o' you in all these weeks. Ecod, it's unfriendly, so it is!"

"Confound your impudence, fellow!" Hal placed himself ostentatiously in the pirate's path. "D'ye dare address her ladyship?"

The buccaneer barely glanced at him, but with a sweep of his muscular arm thrust the Viscount aside so ungently that, staggering back, he tripped over a piece of timber and measured his length on the sand, to the accompaniment of ribald laughter from the watching pirates. Frances had lost colour, but she stood her ground and looked up at her tormentor.

"I am seeking Captain Barbican," she said steadily, "and I warn you that you had best tell me at once where he may be found."

His grin broadened.

"To hell wi' Barbican!" he said. " 'Tis a cursed jealous dog to ha' kept you so long to himself. No need to fear him, fondling. In the Brotherhood all men are equal."

"Are they so?" a deep voice broke in unexpectedly, and Captain Barbican himself thrust between the watching men to confront him. Like the rest, he was barelegged and stripped to the waist, revealing bronzed shoulders scarred in ghastly fashion by the mark of the lash, and his attitude was distinctly menacing.

"Are they so?" he repeated, and dealt the fellow a blow that sent him sprawling. Crispin picked up a length of rope which lay nearby. "You scurvy dog," he said softly. "I'll teach you who is captain here."

Using the rope like a whip, he lashed the fallen man mercilessly about the head and shoulders, so that he did not dare to rise, but crouched on the sand with his arms raised to protect his face. Finally Crispin tossed the rope aside and in a tense silence his glance swept challengingly over the rest of the crew. It was a moment fraught with danger, for he knew that if one of them had the courage to take up that unspoken challenge the rest would follow like a pack of wolves, and he and his little party be swept away on a red tide of mutiny.

But 'Barbican's luck' held. The men of the *Santo Rosario* were hardy enough individually, but they lacked leadership, and though they glanced sidelong at each other and muttered among themselves, no-one ventured open defiance.

"Get back to your work," Crispin said curtly at length, and turning his back contemptuously upon them went to where Frances stood with Hal at her side. The Viscount was still brushing sand from his clothes, but in spite of this his glance travelled scornfully over the buccaneer's half-clad figure.

"Upon my soul, Captain Barbican," he exclaimed, "your men are cursedly disrespectful, stap me if they are not! Have you no authority as their commander?"

"They are pirates, my lord," Crispin replied shortly, "and as such acknowledge no superior save when in action. It is a fact which you would do well to remember."

His manner did nothing to soothe the feelings of the Viscount, who, knowing that he had been made to appear ridiculous before Frances, was in an exceedingly bad temper. He looked past Crispin at the man he had thrashed, who had dragged himself to his feet and was limping painfully away. There was blood on his naked shoulders.

"It would appear, however, that you have established your position by brute force. Violence, no doubt, is the only language understood by the ruffians who follow the black flag." His tone coupled Captain Barbican insultingly with the rest.

Crispin's lips tightened.

" 'Tis a language, my lord, which I learned in a hard school," he said grimly, and looked away from him to meet Frances's eyes. She was regarding him with an expression he could not read, but which he thought to echo the contempt and disgust of which Mountheath's voice was eloquent, and

144

for that reason he spoke harshly, a bitter, mirthless smile on his lips.

"Aye, my lord," he said, "in the galleys of Spain, where the fortunate die, and those who survive sink lower than beasts. I escaped from the galleys, but until my dying day I shall carry their brand upon my body and upon my soul. Now take her ladyship hence before her delicacy is further offended. The black brotherhood is no fit company for her."

Hal gaped at him, speechless before this sudden gust of passion, but Frances did not wait for her escort. Jerking her hand from his arm she turned and walked rapidly in the direction of their own encampment, stumbling in her haste on the yielding sand. Crispin took a pace nearer to the Viscount and spoke in a voice none the less angry because it was subdued.

"You young fool, how dare you bring her here? Why do you suppose that I have kept her almost a prisoner all these weeks past? I have difficulty enough in maintaining mastery over this scum, without you reminding them what prize awaits them in yonder cabin if they choose to take it. Aye, take it, my lord! We are three swords at most—could we prevail against half a hundred? Now get you hence, and if any harm comes to her as a result of this folly, by God, you shall pay dearly for it!"

For a moment Hal faced him truculently, his face darkly flushed and an angry retort trembling on his lips, but something in the buccaneer's face daunted him. He turned on his heel and strode after her ladyship, catching up with her half-way along the beach. Neither spoke until the camp was reached, for Hal was still smarting from the lash of Crispin's words. All his old hatred of the Captain, which had slumbered of late, sprang up again, aggravated by the knowledge that the rebuke was not undeserved, and when they arrived at the deserted encampment his malice found an outlet in words.

"So!" he exclaimed contemptuously. "We see the gallant Captain in his true colours at last. A galley-slave has been concealed beneath his gentlemanly manner, just as his scars have been hidden by silk and fine linen."

He ran on in this strain for some time, while Frances stood with bowed head, her hands gripping the back of a chair. At length, however, with the air of one goaded beyond endurance, she turned upon him, and he saw to his amazement that her cheeks were wet with tears.

"Hal," she exclaimed, "I will not let you speak so! Why

should you look down upon him because he has been a slave? Rather should you feel pity and admiration for one who could endure so much." Her voice broke, and she dashed a hand across her eyes. "Dear God, how he must have suffered!"

His lordship was taken aback, but recovered himself in a moment.

"It is natural, I suppose," he conceded, "for one as gentle as yourself to feel compassion for the sufferings of any fellow-creature, but do not forget what his life has been since he escaped from slavery. He is a pirate, steeped in all the evil that name implies. Do you suppose that your grandfather would have entrusted you to him if he had known what manner of man he is?"

"He did know," she retorted. "Crispin told him before he would accept the charge, and yet Grandfather chose to trust him. Do you dare to say that that trust was misplaced?"

Her ardent championship of the buccaneer merely fanned the flames of his lordship's wrath, for he was already labouring under a sense of injury. His mouth twisted unpleasantly.

"I am hardly in a position to judge of that, madam," he sneered. "If at any time the fellow has made free with you it seems unlikely, from your present attitude, that you would complain to me of it."

She gasped, and was about to deny the unworthy imputation when remembrance of that day in the great cabin of the *Vampire* flashed upon her. Colour flamed into her face, occasioned as much by the vividness of that memory as by the realization that there was some truth in his lordship's words. Hal read the betraying blush aright, and jealousy came to increase his wrath.

"Do we come at the truth at last, my lady?" he demanded, and clapped a hand to his sword. "By God, if he has dared——"

"Oh, have done!" She broke in upon his heroics, angrily contemptuous. "I have not yet given you the right to take that tone with me—no, nor ever will!"

"There are rights, Frances, which are not yours to bestow. You forget that I am your kinsman, your natural protector."

"My protector!" She laughed shortly, and the scorn in her voice made him flinch. "Had it been left to you I should have been married these three months to Gideon Crayle. No, there is but one man in all the world to whom I may look for protection, and that is Crispin Barbican." She raised her hand to check his protest. "Do not seek to belittle him in my eyes,

Hal, for by doing so you harm only yourself. I listened to you once, to my sorrow, when I should have believed the promptings of my own heart."

An incredible suspicion was borne in upon his lordship. He could scarcely credit it, and yet her words could mean but one thing, unbelievable though it was. After a dumbfounded pause he gave it strangled utterance.

"Is it possible . . . can it be that, in spite of all, you have conceived an affection for this—this pirate?"

Frances hesitated, for she had not meant to betray so much. Then with a gesture of resignation she dropped into a chair and met his gaze frankly, though with heightened colour.

"Yes," she said simply, "I love him. Do you find that so hard to believe?"

Apparently he did, for he gaped at her wordlessly for some seconds before recovering the power of speech. He had not expected to meet with such frankness, and at first surprise overwhelmed every other emotion. Then jealousy stirred in him once more, and a determination to win this tantalizing creature for his own in spite of all. It should not be difficult, he reflected, once they had left this uncomfortable world of violence and bloodshed, where only swashbucklers like Captain Barbican showed to advantage, and a courtier was quite out of place. In that other world across the sea matters would be very different, and Lady Frances, dazzled by its glitter, would turn readily enough to one who so obviously belonged in that splendid setting.

In the meantime it was obviously his duty to protect her from herself, and to see that her infatuation for the Captain —he would not permit himself to think that it was anything more—did not lead her into behaving foolishly. He had perceived that Crispin was deliberately avoiding her ladyship, and congratulated himself on his forethought in telling the buccaneer that Frances was already betrothed. Captain Barbican spent so little time at the encampment, and when he was there maintained such a forbidding silence, that at length the Viscount decided that he had little to fear.

It was in his reaction from his recent anxiety that he agreed, a few days later, to accompany Jonathan on an exploring expedition along the coast in the opposite direction from the pirate camp. He was moved to this decision by Frances's anxiety that the boy should not go alone, for he was eager to please her, and as Crispin was at the other camp and

Frances proposing to rest awhile in her cabin he saw no reason why he should not indulge her.

She watched their departure with some relief, for her insistence that the Viscount should accompany Jonathan was not wholly disinterested. She was heartily tired of his lordship's company and assiduous attentions, and welcomed the prospect of an hour or two of solitude. As soon as they were out of sight she emerged from the hut and strolled into the forest, following a path that she had trodden often before, though never alone. It was pleasant to be able to devote oneself entirely to one's thoughts, even if they were not entirely happy, without the necessity of maintaining a conversation with a gentleman of whose society one had had a surfeit.

At the camp, the coloured servant observed her departure with pleased surprise, and, finding himself alone, set off at a rapid trot for the buccaneer encampment, where he would find the company he craved. The pirates were taking their ease, deeming it impossible to work in the blistering heat of mid-afternoon. Captain Barbican, restored to his customary elegance, sat in the shade of the rough shelter erected by his men, conferring with Matt Briarly over a drink compounded of rum and limes and sugar, but when he caught sight of the Negro he broke off and beckoned imperatively. The slave obeyed the summons reluctantly.

"What are you doing here?" Crispin asked sharply. "Is anything amiss at the camp?"

On being informed that the two young gentlemen had set off along the coast, and the lady, having watched them out of sight, disappeared into the forest in a quite different direction, he swore under his breath and dismissed the black with a gesture.

"What devil possesses young Mountheath these days?" he demanded of Matt. "First he brings her here, and now he needs must go off with the boy and leave her to wander alone in the forest. Does he not realize the danger in which she stands?" He thrust back his chair and rose to his feet. "I must go seek her, and when next I see that young fool I'll read him a lesson in caution that he'll not forget in haste."

He strode off along the beach without waiting for an answer, and Matt looked after him and shook his head. There would be steel drawn there before long, if he was any judge of the matter, and though he felt that the Viscount could well be spared, he feared that such an occurrence would do nothing to ease a situation which was fast becoming intolerable. He cursed all women, and, refilling his glass, drank a silent and solitary toast to his own freedom from the madness which afflicted his captain.

Crispin hesitated only a moment at the smaller encampment before plunging into the forest, for there was only one path that Frances was likely to have followed. He came upon her at last in a small clearing, where, alarmed by the sound of his approach, she had halted and was looking somewhat anxiously to see who came. When she caught sight of him the apprehension faded from her face and she smiled.

"Why, Crispin," she greeted him, "I did not think 'twas you who came. What brings you here in such haste?"

"You, my lady," he replied shortly, relief at finding her rendering his voice abrupt. "I should have thought that by now you are sufficiently well acquainted with the ways of pirates to realize the folly of walking thus alone. Lord Mountheath should know better than to leave you unprotected."

"Do not blame Hal," she said quickly. "He would not have gone had he known I meant to leave the camp. I sent him away."

"You sent him away?" he repeated, staring. "In the fiend's name, why?"

She made an impatient movement.

"Because I am weary of his society," she replied. "We have been so long and so constantly in each other's company that now we sit mumchance, staring at each other. Even solitude is preferable to that."

He raised his brows at that, but made no comment. Instead he said:

"In your present situation, my lady, there is danger for you in solitude. His lordship knows that, which is why he guards you so closely."

Frances hesitated, and stretched out her hand to touch a great scarlet blossom which grew nearby. With her eyes intent on the flower she said softly:

"Is there no-one else to guard me, Crispin?"

"We all seek to do so, my lady," he replied matter-of-factly, "but Matt and I are better employed among the men. If they are left to their own devices they may well plot mutiny. Moreover, there is work to be done. The sooner the ship is afloat again the sooner will you be delivered from the tedium of your present situation."

She bit her lip, and in real or simulated vexation turned her back upon him.

149

"Then, sir, I pray you, do not let me keep you from these pressing duties. I am very well here."

In proof of this statement she sat down on a nearby log and became engrossed in earnest contemplation of the foliage on the opposite side of the clearing. Captain Barbican regarded her for a moment, then, making no comment, leaned his shoulders against a tree, folded his arms, and prepared to wait. There was a lengthy pause.

The silence was broken at last by her ladyship, who, after fidgeting uneasily beneath his gaze, looked over her shoulder to inquire pettishly how long he intended to stand there.

"Until it pleases your ladyship to return to the camp," he replied equably. "Observe my forbearance, for I could, if I wished, carry you thither whether you would or no. But I remember your dislike of such rough, pirate ways."

For a second or two she regarded him speculatively, tempted, perhaps, to provoke him into making good that threat. Then, suddenly abandoning all attempts at coquetry, she asked simply:

"Crispin, why do you so persistently avoid me?"

"Avoid you, my lady?" he repeated, but she broke in impatiently:

"Do not put yourself to the trouble of denying it, for it is obvious to anyone who is not wholly blind. But what have I done? How have I offended you?"

"You have done nothing, my lady," he said repressively. "Your safety and well-being are my foremost consideration, and for that reason I leave you as much as possible in the company of your brother and your cousin, who are the only fit companions for you on the island. In the cramped quarters of the ship we have little choice, but while we are ashore there is no reason for you to be constantly afflicted with the presence of a pirate."

"So that is it!" she exclaimed. "It rankles still that once, in scorn, I named you thus. I thought that you had forgiven me. You said that you had."

"I told you truth, my lady. It is myself that I cannot forgive, for having earned the name. For earned it I have, make no mistake about that."

She stared at him, frankly puzzled.

"What if you have? Is that any reason to avoid me as you have done since we arrived at the island?"

"No, it is only half the truth." He took his shoulders from the tree-trunk and stood upright; his face was pale now, and his voice shook with suppressed passion. "If I avoid you it is for my own peace of mind. God's death! Do you think that I am made of stone? That I can bear to be near you day after day, to see you with Mountheath, and keep my hands from his throat? Oh, I know that he has the right! That you are promised to him, and that were we not cast away here you would have been wed ere now, but it is hard. Dear God, it is hard! Love you he may, but were his love increased tenfold it could not equal mine."

"Crispin!" She had risen to her feet and faced him now across the little glade, her breathing hurried, a hand at her breast. "Who told you that I was betrothed to Hal?"

"Mountheath himself," he replied slowly, "on the day before we fled from Jamaica. He said that while he dwelt at your cousin's house you had promised to wed him, but that when your betrothal to Crayle was announced he thought that you had deceived him."

"He lied," she said in a low voice. "He paid court to me, yes, but not until a week ago did he ask me to become his wife."

A week ago! Crispin's heart seemed to stand still. Had he, through the Viscount's treachery, lost her by so narrow a margin? Scarcely aware of what he did, he went to her and gripped her by the shoulders.

"Frances," he said, "what answer did you give him?"

The lovely colour swept into her face, and she trembled beneath his touch and the ardent gaze of his grey eyes. Her own were lowered in sudden shyness.

"I refused him," she whispered, "for I will not marry where I do not love, though I go unwed to my grave."

She looked up at him then, and there was an end to all pretence between them. With an inarticulate exclamation he caught her in his arms, and this time she surrendered her lips willingly to his. With his love in his arms at last it was small wonder that the Captain forgot for a while the barrier which stood between them, the barrier of his own past life and deeds. When at length a measure of sanity returned to him she was cradled still against his heart, her face, with closed eyes and softly tremulous lips, upturned to his.

"Frances," he said huskily, "this is madness."

She smiled a little, without opening her eyes.

"Sweet madness," she murmured, "but why?"

He did not reply at once, for the words were not easy to find, and remorse for the pain he must cause her stabbed him like a sword. Hard though a parting would have been before, it would be a thousand times harder now. A stifled groan broke from his lips, and his arms tightened about her even as he spoke the words of renunciation.

"Because I am what I am, my heart, and no fit mate for you."

The long lashes lifted at that and she looked up at him in hurt bewilderment. In answer to the sudden, frightened question in her eyes he continued quietly:

"There is a gulf between us which can never be bridged, for we belong to different worlds. In the years that I have followed the black flag I have committed crimes which you, in your innocence, cannot even imagine, but some shreds of honour I still retain, enough to prevent me from taking my own happiness at the price of yours."

She shook her head.

"There can be no happiness for me unless you share it. Oh, Crispin, what matters the past? If you love me as I love you there can be no gulf between us, now or ever."

"If I love you?" he repeated in a low voice. "You are dearer to me than life, or—God forgive me—than honour. I have no right to speak to you of love, I, an outlaw with neither home nor country, and in doing so I am false to the trust I accepted from your grandfather when he lay dying. It is not fitting that you should wed with such as I, when in a little you may make your choice among the noblest in England."

Gently Frances disengaged herself from his arms and turned away. For a space she stood with bowed head, and he watched her with eyes of pain and longing, cursing himself for a fool that he had cast away the priceless gift she would have bestowed upon him, even though he knew that in honour he could do nothing else.

At last she turned again to face him, leaning against the tree beneath which they stood, her hands behind her and her head tilted a little as she studied him with an expression he could not read.

"Save for my grandfather," she said musingly, "I have known only two men of noble birth. One would have forced me into marriage with him, and murdered my brother; the other, for his own selfish ends, did not scruple to lie concerning my relationship with him, and caused me much unhappiness thereby. If these be the nobles from whom you would have me choose a husband, then will I live and die a maid."

"These are but two," he replied slowly, "and you cannot damn all the gentlemen in England simply because your cousins are rogues. Some day you will meet a man worthy of you, whose birth and breeding match your own."

"Will I find one who, though I revile and insult him, will risk his life to serve me, asking nothing in return, as my pirate captain has done?" She smiled up at him lovingly, and put out her hands towards him. "Crispin, dear fool, you shall not break both our hearts for so slight a cause. I will not let you."

He took the outstretched hands in his own and looked down at her from his great height with troubled eyes.

"Love, it is for your sake that we must part. It is simple to plight troth here in the Indies; this is my world, and I have carved in it a place for myself, but when the time comes for you to return to England you will not wish to find yourself tied to a pirate. I could not go with you to Court."

"Then I would not wish to go, but why should you not return to England? Have you committed any crime worse than those of which your Captain Morgan was guilty? He was acquitted by the King himself, and given a knighthood and the Lieutenant-Governorship of Jamaica. What has happened once may well happen again."

He laughed ruefully.

"I am no Morgan, sweetheart. There is but one Welsh Harry."

She looked disbelieving, but did not dispute the point. Instead she said:

"Be that as it may, no-one in England would dare take you to task for these crimes which weigh so heavily upon you, when the King has shown such favour to your leader. A pardon at least will be forthcoming—you'll not deny that?"

He shook his head.

"A pardon, even from the King, cannot wipe out the past. Morgan wears now the uniform of Lieutenant-Governor, but he is still the man who put Panama and Porto Bello to the sword. I followed him then, and my hands, like his, are stained with blood. Think you your guardian, Lord Larchwood, would permit you to marry me?"

A hint of mischief crept into her smile.

"Would you have me believe that Captain Barbican cannot protect his own? I had another guardian once, and you stole me away from him, closely though he guarded me. But, if you wish, I will admit that to marry you would be an act of consummate folly. I will agree with all that you say, and confess that we are mad even to think of it. But folly is very sweet, and when was love ever wise?"

For a moment longer he regarded her, and then with sudden recklessness caught her to him.

"God knows I have no desire for such wisdom," he said in a low voice. "If you are content to link your fate with mine, we will be married at the first port we reach. What say you, my lady? Will you plight troth with a pirate?"

For answer she put her arms about his neck and raised her face to his, but even as their lips met the silence of the forest was shattered by the distant boom of a cannon. Startled, they stared at each other in blank inquiry, while the echoes of that ominous sound slowly died away, and a flock of birds circled up from the tree-tops, screaming noisy protest. Crispin was the first to speak.

"Another ship," he said, "and we have no guns. Come, we must return to the beach."

Her eyes searched his face.

"Does it mean danger?"

He smiled and shook his head.

"No, I think not. 'Tis only the Dons now whom we have to fear, and no Spanish ship would put in to Pirates' Island. 'Twill be some buccaneer craft, no doubt, and may mean an early escape from this place, and"—he raised her hand to his lips—"an early fulfilment of your promise."

So, secure in their new-found happiness and with no premonition of disaster, they went at leisurely pace towards the shore, and as they had penetrated some distance into the forest an appreciable time elapsed before they came again in sight of the sea. At length, however, they emerged into the little camp, and saw before them the sweep of silvery beach and the broad lagoon whereon a great ship rode at anchor, a glittering, sun-drenched background for the man who leaned upon a beribboned cane to watch them, with a pensive smile playing about his lips and his mis-shapen shadow etched sharply upon the white sand at his feet.

CHAPTER XVI

THE SENTENCE

AMID the fantastic splendours of the *Vampire's* great cabin, which both remembered so vividly and yet had thought never to see again, Captain Barbican and Lady Frances awaited whatever doom might be preparing for them. They were for the present alone, though outside the door a heavily-armed buccaneer was on guard, and Crispin himself had been deprived of his weapons. He stood now at one of the square windows astern, where the horn casement was set wide, and gazed blindly across the lagoon to the shore, thronged with the crews of the black frigate and the careened galleon.

The men of the *Santo Rosario* had made no protest at the summary carrying-off of their captain and his lady, though they had watched the procedure with some curiosity. Even had they resented it, however, there was nothing they could have done to prevent it, for the crew of the *Vampire* outnumbered them by more than three to one, and they had no guns to pit against the rows of cannon which grinned so wickedly from the black flank of Sarne's ship. Had they not been thus defenceless, Crispin reflected grimly, the frigate could never have entered the lagoon, for he would have had a battery commanding the channel through the reef.

Though he stood so still beside the window, that outward passivity was merely a cloak for the impotent anger which possessed him, anger against himself and his treacherous crew, against Gideon Crayle, but most of all against fate which had preserved them from the tempest only to cast them once more into the hunchback's power. But beneath the anger, like the still cold deeps of the sea untouched by the storm raging above, lay a fear greater than he had ever known. It was not for himself; death would be his portion, and he had faced that too often in the past to fear it now, but the thought of what might befall Frances was a torment sharper than any which the devilish ingenuity of the pirates might wreak upon his body. He stood with his back to the cabin, but he knew that she was huddled in the high-backed carven chair at the head of the table, and that the look of hopeless terror was in her eyes again. She had hardly spoken since that horrible moment when they had emerged from the forest to find Crayle waiting for them, but, white-faced and silent, had obeyed as though stunned the orders they had received to go aboard the *Vampire*. Jean-Pierre had escorted them thither, amiable as ever, but with a look in his dark eyes as they rested upon the girl which made Crispin's fingers itch to close about his throat.

He watched a boat put off from the shore towards the frigate, and as it drew nearer he saw that it contained, besides Sarne and Gideon Crayle, Jonathan and Lord Mountheath. It had covered more than half the distance before he realized that its coming meant the end of this brief period of privacy, and that the inevitable parting would be soon and probably for ever. He turned to face the room.

"They are coming," he said quietly. "Jonathan and Mountheath have been made prisoner."

She stared at him, her blue eyes dark with terror in a face so white that even the lips were drained of colour, and rising to her feet put out her hands towards him in a pitiful, imploring gesture. When he took her in his arms she clung to him in silence, hiding her face against his breast.

"Frances!" he said hoarsely, and then stopped, for there was suddenly nothing to say. Comfort and reassurance would be but empty lies, and she would know them for what they were, while for the rest his feelings were too deep for words. In the stillness the smallest sounds were audible, and they could hear the lap of the water against the frigate's hull, and the creak of rowlocks and splash of oars as the boat came steadily nearer. Presently it bumped against the ship's side, and, hearing its occupants coming aboard, they knew that the sands were running out.

"Crispin," Frances raised her head at last, and there was a steadfast purpose in her eyes, " 'tis death that comes, for me as well as for you. They may think to spare my life, but I swear that somehow I will find a way to follow you, before ——" She drew a shuddering breath and closed her eyes. "Oh, God, that I might die now, safe in your arms!"

Footsteps sounded, approaching the cabin. Crispin, his face as white, almost, as her own, bent his dark head to the kiss which must be their farewell, and it was upon that last, tragic embrace that Gideon Crayle looked as he entered. For a moment he checked, and an ugly expression flitted across his face. Then, advancing further, he spoke mockingly.

"You are somewhat too free of your caresses, my dear Frances. It is a fault you would do well to check."

He moved at leisurely pace to the chair she had recently vacated, and was followed into the cabin by his two new prisoners under the guard of Sarne and his French lieutenant. Hal and Jonathan were unbound, but the Viscount's sword had been taken from him. Gideon leaned back in his chair and regarded the captives with gentle satisfaction.

"I will not insult your intelligence," he announced, "by telling you how futile would be any attempt at resistance. I will merely point out that both Captain Sarne and Jean-Pierre are heavily armed, and that I"—he took a pistol from his pocket and laid it on the table before him—"am considered a fair marksman."

"You scoundrel!" The epithet burst from Mountheath's lips as though he could contain himself no longer. He took a pace forward, his comely young face flushed with anger. "Do you imagine that you could murder us, and go unpunished? You are not plotting in secret now, hiding your enmity beneath a mask of friendship. You have allied yourself openly with these cut-throats, and in the fullness of time you will go with them to the gallows."

"My dear Hal, you weary me! I can only suppose that you speak thoughtlessly, without having considered the situation. Reflect, I beg of you! All four of you set sail from Port Royal more than three months ago, and vanished from the eyes of men. It was naturally supposed that your ship had been lost in the tempest which followed your departure, and you are already presumed to be dead. Who, then, is to discover that you survived the storm by many weeks, and perished in quite a different fashion?"

Clearly this aspect of the matter had not occurred to the Viscount. He fell back a pace, biting his lip, and from red his face went white. Then, from the other side of the cabin, Crispin spoke with a note of mockery in his deep voice. He had led Frances to a chair and now stood beside her, her hand in his.

"Do you suppose that such a secret can be kept by close upon two hundred men? Not all the wealth of the Indies would be sufficient to buy their silence."

"It is by fear that I shall silence them, and not by bribes."

Crispin laughed shortly.

"Do you imagine that you can hold in subjection ten score of the Brethren of the Coast? You flatter yourself, Mr. Crayle."

"I am not so foolish, my dear Captain. There is one they fear as they will never fear me—your old friend and leader, Sir Henry Morgan. Your men do not love you, Barbican, but they would not have it come to his ears that they had delivered you to your death. Morgan's power is too great, and his reactions to the betrayal of a friend unpredictable in the extreme."

"Morgan is in London," said Crispin confidently, "and 'tis little aid he could be giving me, or harm he could be doing them, even if he were so minded."

Gideon's smile broadened. His aspect would have been benevolent but for the evil which lurked in his dark eyes.

"Your information is out of date, my dear sir. Morgan is in Port Royal, and waxes powerful there. He reached Jamaica less than two weeks after your abrupt departure thence." He laughed softly. "If you could have known that!"

Crispin stared in silence at the pale, too-handsome face, his own countenance schooled to an indifference he did not feel. So Harry Morgan was in the Indies! Morgan, with his far-reaching influence among the lawless sea-rovers backed now by the authority of a Royal commission. Under his protection Frances and Jonathan would have been safe even from Gideon Crayle, and they had missed him by so short a time. The bitterness of that knowledge was like salt upon an open wound.

"So you see, my friends," Gideon resumed after a moment, "all concerned in this business will be anxious to keep it secret. When the *Santo Rosario* puts to sea again it will be under a different name, and with such alterations made in her that it is unlikely that she will be recognized, for you may be sure that she will give Port Royal a wide berth. As far as it is known, she foundered in that convenient hurricane, and there is no reason why it should ever become known that she did not."

"What do you intend by us?" Hal spoke unsteadily, with none of his earlier bluster. "In God's name tell us, and have done."

"I intend to kill you, Hal," Gideon replied pleasantly. "I regret the necessity, of course, particularly in the case of my fair cousin yonder, but really I have no choice. You perceive, I hope, the deplorable consequences of unwarranted intrusion? Had matters been left in my hands only one life—Jonathan's—need have been sacrificed. Now all four of you must die." He sighed and shook his head, more, it seemed, in sorrow than in anger, and continued plaintively: "Why do so many seek to improve upon my plans, which are already beyond improvement? You are men of action, without whom, I confess, those plans might easily come to naught, but I am the wit and the brain behind you. Without me there would be no plans to execute."

A brief silence succeeded this extraordinary speech. Hal stared at Crayle with an expression of mingled horror and disgust, and Sarne grinned his appreciation of a rascality superior even to his own, but Jean-Pierre leaned against the forward bulkhead with a frown disfiguring his olive-tinted face. Clearly the hunchback's much-vaunted plans met with no approval from him, and from the manner in which his gaze constantly returned to Frances it was not difficult to guess the cause. But Crispin had grown suddenly still, as an idea took shape in his mind. Crayle spoke truth when he declared himself the spirit behind the present situation, for to ordinary pirates like Randolph Sarne three at least of the prisoners were worth more alive than dead, and Crispin had little doubt that were Crayle disposed of, he could strike a bargain with Sarne. The ransom would doubtless be extortionate, but no price would be too great if it extricated them from the trap into which they had fallen, and the combined wealth of Larchwood and Rotherdale must surely be equal to any demand made upon it.

He considered the odds arrayed against him calmly enough. Gideon's pistol lay before him on the table, and the two pirates were heavily armed, while he had not so much as a knife, but on the other hand they were lulled into a sense of security by the knowledge of their vastly superior strength. If he flung himself upon Crayle his fellow prisoners were unlikely to await idly the outcome of the struggle, and between them Hal and Jonathan might be able to hamper Sarne and his lieutenant for the short time it would take to choke the life out of the wistful-eyed devil at the table. What might follow then he had no means of knowing.

It was a fantastic scheme and held only the slightest hope of success, but anything was better than waiting quietly to be butchered. The distance between him and Gideon was only a yard or two, and the hunchback wholly unprepared. Crispin disengaged Frances's fingers from his own, gathered his muscles for the spring, and without warning launched himself across the intervening space. The chair went over with a crash, and Gideon sprawled upon the floor with the Captain's considerable weight on top of him, and the Captain's fingers like an iron band about his throat.

So unexpected was the attack that for an instant the other occupants of the cabin were held motionless by surprise. Then Sarne snatched a pistol from his belt, but before he could use it the Viscount flung himself upon him. He had no very clear idea of what was happening, but for all his jealousy of Captain Barbican he was ready to follow his lead in affairs of this kind, and yelled to Jonathan to tackle Jean-Pierre. Nothing loath, the little Marquis leapt upon the Frenchman with such force that both fell to the floor, overturning a small table and the carved coffer upon it. The lid of the casket flew open, and a motley collection of trinkets scattered across the floor at the feet of Lady Frances, who had risen in alarm. Looking down, she saw a small dagger in a jewelled sheath gleaming beside her foot, and, scarcely knowing what she did, she snatched it up and concealed it in the breast of her coat.

Jonathan was clinging gamely to Jean-Pierre, but slight though he was the young Frenchman possessed muscles of steel and broke free from the boy's grasp almost at once. Stumbling to his feet he cast a comprehensive glance round the cabin, saw that his captain was more than holding his own, and sprang to the assistance of Gideon Crayle. Gripping a pistol by its barrel, he struck a savage blow with the butt-end at the back of Crispin's head, a blow which stretched the buccaneer senseless upon the floor beside his intended victim.

Frances screamed, and flung herself on her knees beside Crispin as the door of the cabin burst open to reveal the varied collection of cut-throats who had been drawn thither by the sounds of strife. Captain Sarne, holding Mountheath in a cunning grip, spoke a sharp command, and in the space of a few minutes the three male prisoners were securely bound. Frances tried to protest when they laid violent hands upon the unconscious Crispin, but they flung her roughly aside and bound his arms behind him before placing him, at Gideon's command, in a chair at the opposite end of the table.

Between them, Sarne and Jean-Pierre had helped the hunchback to his feet and righted the overturned chair. The Frenchman had acted too quickly for Crispin to have inflicted any serious injury upon Crayle, but he was bruised and shaken, and there were purplish marks on his throat above the disordered lace. He touched them with unsteady fingers, and his face was diabolical in its white fury as he stared at the huddled figure of Captain Barbican. It kept even Sarne silent after he had dismissed his men, and held Frances motionless when every instinct was urging her to her lover's side. Some hellish scheme was brewing behind that livid mask, and in the stillness that followed the brief fight the hunchback's evil personality filled the cabin like a palpable thing.

But in spite of their fear of him they could not even begin to guess at the depths of the hatred raging in Gideon's breast, born of a bitter jealousy which had poisoned his whole life. They had no inkling of the torments endured daily by the proud and ambitious spirit imprisoned in his mis-shapen body. Contempt and revulsion had ever been his portion, from the day when Lord Henry Crayle, looking for the first time upon the pitifully deformed body of his infant son, had cursed both the child and the mother who had died in giving him birth. That attitude of his father's, persisting, had set the pattern of his childhood, and because Gideon possessed more than average intelligence he suffered accordingly. His own physical shortcomings made him passionately resentful of those with whom Nature had dealt more kindly, and from that resentment grew the desire to make his presence felt by those who despised him.

As he grew older the wish hardened into resolution, and with infinite patience he set about achieving his object. Power was what he coveted, and no crime was too horrible if it helped him to attain it, even the murder of his father being but a step nearer his goal. So long had he plotted, and brooded over his misfortunes, that his mind had grown as warped and twisted as his body, glorying in evil, and taking an unholy pleasure in the fear he inspired in those permitted to glimpse what lay beneath his outward charm of manner. By fear he had prevailed, holding even such cruel and ruthless criminals as Randolph Sarne in thrall, but one man he had never succeeded in bending to his will. At their first meeting Crispin Barbican had recognized him for what he was, but neither then nor upon any subsequent occasion had there been any indication that he feared him. He had thwarted Gideon at every turn, brought all his fine schemes to naught, and forced him to abandon concealment and ally himself openly with the pirates, but all this was little compared with his last offence.

That he should dare attack him barehanded, when Gideon had a pistol to hand and two armed men to protect him, argued a contempt which could not be endured. Crayle hated the buccaneer as he hated any man of great physical strength, and now that hatred had reached such a pitch that nothing, he felt, could ever satisfy his desire for revenge.

As he brooded savagely over the problem, the recollection of the scene he had witnessed as he entered the cabin flashed into his mind, and he realized that through Frances he could inflict upon Captain Barbican such suffering that even his hatred might be satisfied. As he considered its possibilities his enthusiasm for the plan increased, for he knew to his cost something of the agony inflicted by the subtle torments of the mind, and though he could—and would—break Barbican's body by torture, that alone was too crude and commonplace to satisfy him. Silently he contemplated the unconscious man, and a smile more dreadful than the erstwhile grimace of rage dawned upon his white face.

"Revive him," he said at length, and his usually musical voice was cracked and hoarse from the rough handling he had received. While the pirates moved to do his bidding he poured and drank a glass of wine, making no further remark until Captain Barbican groaned and opened his eyes. Then he waved the others away and so faced the buccaneer with only the length of the table between them.

When Crispin struggled painfully back to consciousness he was at first aware only of the fact that he was a helpless prisoner. Then as his head cleared and the mists dispersed from before his eyes he saw Crayle pondering him malevolently across the table, and knew that his mad scheme had failed.

"So! That is better," Gideon remarked pleasantly. "Captain Barbican, permit me to say that I am disappointed in you. I had judged you an intelligent man, but your recent conduct obliges me to alter my opinion. Even had you succeeded in murdering me your own death would have followed in a matter of minutes."

The grey eyes of the buccaneer considered him dispassionately, almost with contempt.

"Perhaps," he agreed levelly, "but at least I would have died knowing that I had rid the earth of a foulness which is an offence in the eyes of God and of man."

A spasm of rage contorted the hunchback's face.

"Now I know you for a fool," he retorted. "A wise man would keep silent, and not seek to provoke one who holds over him the power of life and death. A conciliatory manner would become you better."

"You confuse wisdom with cowardice, Mr. Crayle." Crispin shifted his head cautiously against the high back of the chair and studied Gideon sardonically from beneath lowered lids. "A natural enough mistake for you to make."

The stem of the wineglass snapped suddenly between Crayle's writhing fingers, spilling its contents across the table. Very deliberately he took out his handkerchief and wiped the wine and blood from his hand before replying.

"We shall see, my fine Captain," he said at length, "whether you crow as loudly when all is done. Somehow I take leave to doubt it. Sarne"—he turned to the pirate—"you have boasted often enough of your ingenuity as a torturer. Here, then, is to test your skill. You have told me of men who took hours, even days, to die, though with every breath they screamed for death to put an end to their suffering, but can you torture me a man so that he does not die? Can you bring him to the very brink of the Pit, and then drag him back to an earthly hell more horrible than the torments of the damned?" He did not pause for an answer to his questions. His voice rose and there was the light of madness in his eyes as he leaned across the table towards Crispin. "No, you shall not die, my friend! That were too easy and pleasant a road. You shall live, broken and maimed by the torture, but—you shall live. Can you conceive what it means to be as I am? 'Tis a hell on earth, and I have been thus all my life; but for you it will be a thousand times harder, for you are strong beyond the ordinary. A death in life, Captain Barbican! That is my sentence upon you!"

He dropped back into his chair, breathing heavily, his face damp with sweat, and for a space there was silence in the cabin, for his hearers, appalled by the inhuman savagery of his face and voice, remained motionless and dumb. Strangely enough, it was the girl who recovered first.

"No!" She dragged herself up from her chair and stumbled forward to lean upon the table midway between them. "Gideon, for the love of Heaven! Is it not enough that we must die? Will not the broad lands of Rotherdale content you?" She paused, searching his face for some sign of relenting. Finding none, she cast herself on her knees before him, pleading for her lover as she would never have done for herself. "Gideon, have mercy! You cannot do this dreadful thing! No man could be so cruel, so fiendishly cruel! Oh, merciful God!"

"I counsel you, my dear Frances, to save this fervour to plead for mercy upon your own account." He smiled terribly upon her, and in his voice was the threat of unspeakable things. "I promise you that you will stand in need of it."

Crispin's chair went over with a crash as, bound though he was, he heaved himself to his feet. Frances crouched still upon her knees, smitten into silence by the hunchback's words.

"You were foolish enough to flout me once, Frances," Gideon pursued amiably, "and to bring dishonour upon our name by fleeing with this adventurer, but in spite of that I am still prepared to marry you. When you are my wife you will learn to comport yourself becomingly, and one day I will permit you to meet again this gallant lover of yours." He laughed softly, evilly. "That would be amusing, I think."

"You lie!" Crispin said contemptuously. "You would never dare to marry her, since through her survival the truth of her brother's death would become known. If you wish to be Marquis of Rotherdale you must kill us all, and you know it."

"There is some truth in what you say," Gideon admitted frankly, "but I do not doubt that in time I shall discover some explanation which will satisfy the curious. You see, I am in no haste. We await here the arrival of our friends—did I mention that we had chosen this island as a rendezvous with another buccaneer craft?—and then we sail against the Spaniards on an enterprise which need not concern you, since you will take no part in it. Suffice it to say that there will be time and to spare to carry out my plans concerning you."

His brooding glance included them all in that last threat. In the background Hal and Jonathan stood silent, horrified at the turn events had taken; Frances still knelt before him, her face hidden in her hands; and Crispin, for all that his bearing was defiant yet, was white to the lips and there was agony in his eyes as they rested upon the girl. Gideon saw that his revenge was already beginning, and, smiling, delicately gave another turn of the screw.

"Cast the three of them into the hold, Sarne," he said, "so that they may have leisure to contemplate what the future holds for them. Her ladyship will remain here, to give us the pleasure of her society. See that a cabin is prepared for her."

Sarne nodded, and moved slowly to do his bidding, reluctant to set a term to a scene which had afforded him considerable amusement. A shout brought a couple of his men to the cabin, but as, in obedience to his commands, they were urging the captives towards the door, Frances awoke from the daze of horror which bound her and started to her feet.

"Take me, too, " she cried. "I'll accept no favours from this monster." She turned upon Sarne, holding out her hands in passionate entreaty. "If you have any spark of mercy in you, do not separate us now."

For an instant the pirate hesitated, looking inquiringly at Gideon. The hunchback sighed, and spoke with an affectation of weariness.

"It is my will that you remain here. You must learn obedience, Frances, and study to be a submissive wife. Take them away," he added to Sarne.

With a cry she flung her arms about Crispin and clung to him until Jean-Pierre dragged her, struggling, away. As he was thrust from the cabin Crispin heard her cry his name on such a note of despair that his heart turned cold. He stopped and half turned, straining furiously against his bonds, and saw her sink swooning in Jean-Pierre's arms, while in the background Gideon Crayle sat silent and fiendishly smiling. He glimpsed the expression on the Frenchman's face as he looked down at the girl, and then the door swung shut between them and he was left to the torment of his own dark thoughts.

CHAPTER XVII

FRANCES

WHEN Frances came out of her swoon she was lying on the cushioned locker below the stern windows, through which streamed the level beams of the westering sun, and save for Gideon the cabin was empty. She struggled into a sitting position and, leaning upon her hand, stared wordlessly at the hunchback, who still sat the table's head toying idly with a glass of wine.

"I am relieved to see you recovered, my dear," he remarked, and his tone made a mockery of the words. "This prolonged swoon was beginning to cause me some uneasiness."

She turned her head away, sickened by his hypocrisy, and he laughed quietly. Then, rising to his feet, he came to stand beside her.

"Why do you turn from me, my love?" he continued. "Is it because I am somewhat crooked of body? Do you yearn for your stalwart pirate lover? But wait, Frances, wait! When the good Sarne has completed his work upon the gallant Captain you will find the contrast between us less marked."

The words struck fresh terror into her heart. She perceived a sudden, sinister significance in the absence of Sarne and his associates, and struggled to her feet.

"You have not . . . they are not——?" She broke off, unable to voice her fears.

Gideon shook his head.

"No, my dear, not yet. There is a form of torture more subtle and deadly than mere physical pain, and he shall have full measure of it before he passes into Sarne's hands. He shall learn—you shall both learn—that I am not with impunity to be flouted."

Stung to brief defiance, she faced him boldly.

"Perhaps there is something that you have yet to learn, Gideon. Do you imagine that if I live I shall keep silent concerning what has passed? We shall not always be among outlaws; yours would be a barren victory if, succeeding to Rotherdale, you could not enjoy the fruits of your crime. One day we must return to England, and then, God aiding me, I will send you to the gallows."

He smiled, smoothing the lace over his long, white fingers.

"A wife, my dear Frances, may not give evidence against her husband. That is why from the first I determined to marry you."

"I will find a way," she retorted desperately. "It is not possible that any man should commit the crimes you contemplate, and escape punishment. Heaven itself would cry out against you."

He laughed.

"If you have put your trust in divine intervention to bring me to justice, my dear, you are like to be disappointed. It is said that the devil protects his own."

"No power of earth or hell will avail you once the law has

laid its hand upon you," she replied. " 'Tis said also that murder will out."

"My dear cousin," he said gently, "how little you know me. Murder, if carried out with sufficient ingenuity, need never be discovered."

He saw the bewildered horror in her eyes, and to show her how little he feared her threat, and how confident he was that she could not betray him, he added softly:

"How, think you, Frances, did my father die?"

She shrank back against the bulkhead, staring with dilated eyes.

"God in Heaven!" she whispered. "Your own father?"

"Yes, my own father," he repeated, and though his voice was quiet there was that in it which set her trembling. "Always I hated him, but as a child I feared him too. But I was patient, and the time came when he feared me in his turn. He coveted the marquisate, and was fool enough to think that I would help him to it. At first it pleased me to foster that belief, but he stood in my way, and when the time came I helped him to hell instead."

He paused, regarding her mockingly as, faint with horror, she sank down again upon the locker. After a little he continued:

"Now, my dear Frances, you share a secret known to no other living soul, but do not think to bring me to trial on that count. When my father died I was a hundred miles away, and had been for a week past, for there are weapons less crude than the knife or the pistol beloved of our pirate friends."

She heard his voice as from a great distance, through mounting waves of darkness. Evil though she had known him to be, she had not even guessed at the true extent of his villainy, and it was at that moment that she realized the true hopelessness of her position. He seemed to her omnipotent in his wickedness, and any effort at resistance a futile beating of her hands against an unyielding rock. She had prepared herself for death and he had given her her life, but from his hands life was the more dreadful gift. For a brief while her senses left her, and when she again became conscious of her surroundings she was no longer in the great cabin, but one of the smaller staterooms. She must have walked there, though she had no recollection of doing so, for Gideon was still beside her, a hand beneath her elbow. He guided her to a chair, and after a little the deadly faintness passed away.

"This is your cabin," he informed her then. "I do not intend to keep you prisoner, and you are free to use the great cabin and the poop-deck above. Have no fear of Sarne and his men. While I am here not one of them will dare to offer you insult. Here"—he crossed to a great chest and flung back the lid——"you will find clothes befitting your rank. They belonged to a Spanish lady who travelled in a galleon we took off the coast of Hispaniola. She has no need of them now."

"What—what became of her?" Frances asked faintly, and Gideon smiled.

"She died," he said, and there was a sinister meaning in the very brevity of the reply. "I will leave you now," he continued, "but presently I shall return to conduct you to supper in the great cabin. You will have changed your dress and will be ready to accompany me."

Frances shook her head and replied with an effort that she would prefer to remain in her cabin. Gideon came to her side, and his long, cruel fingers closed about her wrist.

"What you may or may not desire to do does not concern me," he said. "Henceforth you will obey me, implicitly and without question. If you do not, rest assured that I will find the means to make you."

For a long moment his gaze held hers, and something in those dark and brilliant eyes broke the last remnants of her will. She bowed her head.

"I will be ready," she whispered.

Satisfied, he turned to leave her, but at the door he paused and looked back.

"One last warning, my dear," he said. "You would do well to remember that aboard this ship I am your only sure protector, since I am the only man indifferent to your beauty. Let the contents of yonder chest serve as a reminder of what awaits you if any accident befalls me."

When the door had closed behind him Frances rose to her feet. Moving as one in a trance, she went to the chest and drew forth some of the rich garments it contained. Then, laying them aside, she slowly unbuttoned the coat of her worn and faded riding-habit, but as she did so something fell clattering to the floor and lay gleaming in the rapidly fading light. It was the jewelled dagger which she had picked up during the brief fight in the cabin, and which she had until now forgotten.

With a sob she snatched it up and drew it from the sheath, a slender blade shining and needle-sharp. Here, when all hope

168

seemed dead, was a way of escape placed almost miraculously in her hands, and she stared at it through a mist of thankful tears. Then, dropping to her knees, with closed eyes and her hands still clasped about the dagger's hilt, she murmured a heartfelt prayer of gratitude. Slowly she raised the weapon, and set its sharp point against her breast, but even as she nerved herself to drive it into her shrinking flesh her hand was stayed by a sudden doubt.

Had she the right to use this Heaven-sent weapon merely to secure her own freedom? If Gideon, coming to fetch her to supper, found only a lifeless corpse, would he not exact an even greater vengeance from the prisoners left to him? Crispin he had already condemned to the most hideous fate his fiendish cunning could devise, but there remained Jonathan, the beloved young brother, and Hal, who was in his present plight because of her.

Kneeling there in the gathering darkness Frances prayed for guidance, for the wit to form, and the courage to execute, some plan which would most avail them all. Upon her the burden had fallen, for she alone possessed a weapon and a measure of freedom. How, then, to use them?

For a moment she wondered whether she could bring herself to use the dagger upon Gideon when he returned. Were he removed, the pirates might well agree to ransom the prisoners, for she realized, as Crispin had realized earlier, that Sarne would have nothing to gain and much to lose by his captives' death. She recalled with a shudder the bold, dark eyes of Jean-Pierre, and Gideon's warning that aboard the *Vampire* he was her only sure protector, but it was not that which caused her to abandon the notion. She doubted whether she could bring herself to take a man's life, and if she made the attempt and failed they would be lost indeed.

No, better to conceal the dagger, feign obedience as Crayle demanded, and, while his suspicions were lulled by her apparent docility, seek an opportunity to thwart his evil plans. That such an opportunity would occur she was certain. The weapon had been placed in her hands for some better purpose than self-destruction, and might yet prove to be the salvation of them all.

Her resolve taken, she rose to her feet and kindled the lamp which hung from the ceiling. Then she laid aside the shabby riding-dress which she had worn for so long, and donned in its place one of the gowns from the chest, a typically Spanish garment of black velvet unrelieved by any touch of colour.

Finding an ivory comb to hand, she rearranged her hair, and cast over the red-gold curls a scarf of black lace, which could, if she chose, be used as a veil.

When Gideon returned to the cabin he found her sitting in an attitude of deepest dejection by the open port, oblivious of the starlit beauty of the purple tropic night. He raised his brows a trifle at the sombre tones of the costume she had chosen, but made no comment, merely commanding her to accompany him to the great cabin.

She rose obediently to her feet and placed her hand upon his proffered arm, and he smiled unpleasantly, accounting her spirit already crushed. So, with white, averted face and downcast eyes, Lady Frances moved away at the hunchback's side, leaving the jewelled dagger hidden amid folds of velvet and brocade in the carven chest.

CHAPTER XVIII

DISCORD AMONG ROGUES

RANDOLPH SARNE and Jean-Pierre awaited them in the great cabin, where lamplight shone golden over the table, and in shadowy corners gold and precious stones glimmered faintly. Frances looked neither to right nor left as Gideon led her to her chair, and when seated she kept her gaze resolutely lowered. At first the conversation was desultory, but it became more animated as they discussed the enterprise upon which they were bound when the awaited reinforcements arrived.

These, she learned, consisted of a buccaneer ship of twenty guns, named the *Venturer* and commanded by one Roger Shergall, and for a while the three oddly assorted confederates debated whether or not to delay long enough to add the *Santo Rosario*—now renamed the *Seagull*—to the fleet. The idea was finally abandoned owing to the galleon's lack of cannon, after they had also considered the advisability of refloating her and scuttling her at a suitable distance from the island.

"For," Sarne pointed out, "a ship supposedly sunk three

months ago is better at the bottom of the sea. Better and safer."

"You would need to sink her crew with her, my friend, to eliminate all risk," Gideon replied cynically. "No, let her go. Even if their fear of Morgan is not great enough to keep them silent, no-one would give credence to so wild a tale, and we shall not be returning to Port Royal. Henceforth the head-quarters of the *Vampire* will be at Tortuga."

Jean-Pierre frowned and shook his head.

"It does not please me, that!" he announced bluntly. "I do not like this running away from Harry Morgan. He is shrewd, that one! He will see that we avoid him, and he will ask him-self what it is that we fear. And when Morgan begins to ask such questions of himself, it is not good for us."

"Are you afraid of Morgan, Jean-Pierre?" Gideon asked gently.

"Afraid, no!" the Frenchman replied. "But I have for his wits a most profound respect. Why should we not return to Port Royal? Have we in all these weeks done anything which Morgan has not done? And he is now a knight and Lieutenant-Governor of Jamaica."

"And a friend of Crispin Barbican," Gideon added drily.

Jean-Pierre grinned.

"But does that concern us?" he said, with mock surprise. "The good Crispin's ship was lost in a great storm three months ago. Do we command the elements?"

A gleam of amused appreciation flickered for an instant in Gideon's eyes, but Sarne scowled and spoke with heavy sar-casm.

"No-one will wonder, I suppose, how her ladyship here happens to be safe and sound when the *Santo Rosario* was lost with all hands. Ye're a fool, Jean-Pierre!"

The smile did not leave his lieutenant's lips, but much of its amiability disappeared. Frances, listening intently now to the conversation, became aware of a certain tenseness in the at-mosphere.

"And will that question not be asked in Tortuga, and"— Jean-Pierre's glance flashed to Gideon—"in London? Of a certainty it will, and the story which will check curiosity in those places will serve also in Port Royal, *n'est-ce pas?*"

"Ye're mighty eager to return to Port Royal," said Sarne suspiciously. "Why?"

Jean-Pierre shrugged.

"Because I sailed long enough with Morgan to know that

where he is there also will be profit for such as we. What, will three years in London have changed that? Welsh Harry is a pirate, first, last and always, no matter what flag he flies or what coat he wears." He leaned back and lifted his glass, but over its rim his dark eyes regarded his companions with an expression Frances could not read. His next words gave her a clue. "Shergall will think as I do. He was one of Morgan's captains, and picks his men from those who sailed with the Admiral."

He tossed off the rest of his wine, leaving them to read into his words what threat or warning they chose. Gideon and Sarne exchanged glances. They were well aware that already there had been murmurs among the crew at the authority which Crayle had assumed, and at the meagre plunder which their three months' cruise had brought them. Jean-Pierre was popular, and Roger Shergall of the *Venturer* well-known and trusted among the Brethren. If it came to a test of strength matters might well go against the present leaders.

A brief silence followed the Frenchman's words. Frances looked from one to the other of her villainous companions, guessing enough of the discord among them to wonder whether it would present the opportunity she was seeking. Jean-Pierre refilled his glass, indifferent, apparently, to the effect of his veiled threat, and in the pale, cold eyes of Randolph Sarne a cruel anger awoke. He opened his lips to speak, but was checked by Gideon's uplifted hand.

"Let us suppose," said the hunchback gently, "that I have a plausible explanation of her ladyship's presence here. Have you any other reason, Jean-Pierre, apart from the hope of profit, for counseling a return to Jamaica?"

"Mais oui!" Jean-Pierre thrust aside his glass and leaned forward across the table. "I see it thus. When milady and her brother fled with Crispin Barbican, you desired to follow with all possible speed. Therefore you paid us well that you might sail in the swiftest ship in Port Royal, but, finding not those we seek, we sailed on about our usual business of harrying the Dons. No crime, that! Morgan was knighted for it. Then we find milady—how, I know not. That is for you, monsieur, to explain."

"It shall be explained," said Gideon quietly. "Go on."

"Why then, monsieur, the story of this so-miraculous rescue in time reaches Port Royal—and Sir Henry Morgan. But we do not return to Port Royal. We go to Tortuga. Will that

172

not give Sir Henry to think? Will he not ask himself why it is that you, an English marquis, return not to the English colony where your plantation lies, but go instead to what is little better than a pirate stronghold, and French to boot? *Du vrai, monsieur,* he will become suspicious, and when Morgan becomes suspicious——" He broke off to shrug eloquently, with outspread hands.

"There is much in what you say, Jean-Pierre," Gideon agreed slowly. He thoughtfully stroked his chin with his right hand, and the opal on his finger glowed sullenly in the lamplight. "We will give the matter our consideration."

"Consideration be damned!" said Sarne harshly. "I'll not sail my ship into Port Royal while Morgan is Lieutenant-Governor. 'Tis Tortuga for me."

"I said that we would consider it," Gideon repeated gently, and cast a warning glance at his henchman. "There is no need for haste, for 'twill be some time before we make port again. But, like Jean-Pierre, I respect the shrewdness of Sir Henry Morgan, and I have no wish to arouse his suspicions. Sooner or later I must return to Port Royal to settle my affairs."

They looked at him sharply. Sarne's sallow, hatchet face grew suspicious.

"What might you mean by that?" he asked.

Gideon regarded him with faint surprise.

"I mean that the sale of my plantation must be arranged. Did you suppose that with Rotherdale in my hands I should have any further interest in the Indies?"

"What of us?" demanded the pirate, and Crayle laughed.

"We shall part, I trust, with mutual expressions of goodwill," he said smoothly. "The *Vampire* shall be yours, Sarne. I shall make you a present of her, and ask no further share of her plunder. Then, with my charming bride—" he broke off to bow mockingly to Frances—"I shall return to England, as Marquis of Rotherdale. The New World has served my purpose in supplying me with the gold I needed to possess myself of the marquisate. Now I have no further interest in these barbarous islands."

"So ye'd desert us, would you?" Sarne leaned back in his chair and thrust his hands into his pockets. "Ye're very sure o' yourself to tell us that, Mr. Crayle—or very foolish. What's to prevent me making an end o' you, and being my own master again?"

"Nothing whatever," said Gideon, bored, "but I fail to see what you would gain by such a course, while you might one day be hard put to it to explain my death. As a cut-throat, Sarne, you are beyond compare, but you lack true wit. To murder me with no hope of profit to yourself would be the act of a fool."

He drew a jewelled box from his pocket and took snuff with a magnificent indifference to the pirate's reception of the insult. Sarne watched him for a moment, then slowly, almost furtively, his glance slid round to Frances and lingered there. He spoke conciliatingly.

"Aye, to be sure, I'd gain naught. We'll wait, then, to see what fortune sends us. As you say, there is no need for haste."

"Now you show wisdom," said Gideon pleasantly. "Remember, Sarne, it is no bad thing to have a friend powerful at Court, and I shall be powerful, never doubt it."

"I don't," said Sarne, and his wolf-grin flashed. "There's many will be dancing to a tune o' your piping when all's done."

Again he looked at Frances, and this time Gideon followed the direction of his glance. He smiled.

"Exactly," he said softly. "You perceive, my dear Sarne, that it is better to be my friend than my enemy. Frances!" The girl looked up with a start; Gideon thrust back his chair and rose to his feet, extending one slender hand imperatively. "Your persistent air of tragedy begins to weary me. Go to your cabin."

She uttered no word or protest at that summary dismissal, but rose in prompt obedience and followed him to the door. He opened it for her, but when she would have passed through he set a hand on her arm to detain her.

"You are discourteous, Frances," he said. "It is customary to bid the company good-night upon retiring."

This time a faint tinge of colour crept into her cheeks, but she turned submissively and curtsied.

"I bid you good-night, gentlemen," she said in a low voice.

Sarne continued to sprawl in his chair, hands in pockets, but Jean-Pierre came to his feet and bowed with a flourish.

"*A votre service*, milady," he said gallantly, ignoring his captain's derisive laugh.

Frances slept little that night, but lay staring into the darkness, seeking ever some means of escape. Though no scheme presented itself to her, she felt that she had at least acquired

174

one useful piece of knowledge in the discovery that her captors were beginning to quarrel among themselves. If with the arrival of the other ship the threatened mutiny did indeed materialize, she fancied that her greatest hope of freedom lay with those who shared Jean-Pierre's regard for Sir Henry Morgan. The events of the evening had showed her that nothing was to be gained by keeping close in her cabin, as she had intended, and she resolved to make full use of the freedom granted to her.

In accordance with this decision she sat next day upon the poop-deck, beneath an awning which Gideon had caused to be erected, for where material comforts were concerned it amused him to behave as though nothing were amiss between them. She was alone, and it was eloquent of the hunchback's power that she was able to sit thus solitary and unprotected aboard one of the most notorious pirate ships in the Caribbean.

Across the strip of sparkling water she could see the figures of men moving, ant-like, about the silvery beach. On the tree-crowned bluff which formed one of the sheltering arms of the harbour a dozen of the *Vampire's* cannon, dragged thither the previous day by sweating, cursing pirates, thrust their black muzzles over an improvised palisade, and ensured that no vessel could enter the lagoon unchallenged. A handful of buccaneers kept watch there, leaving their comrades free to occupy themselves as they chose, secure from attack.

Frances's gaze rested upon the clearing where stood the log cabin which had been her home for so many weeks, desolate now, for the tents beside it had been removed. Her thoughts travelled back to those few moments on the previous day when she had known complete happiness, but already that brief idyll was assuming the intangible quality of a dream, and only the hideous present was real. She closed her eyes against a sudden rush of tears, but they would not be checked and rolled helplessly down her pale cheeks. As she fumbled for her handkerchief her cousin's hateful, musical voice spoke softly beside her.

"I must beg you to desist, Frances. Nothing irritates me so greatly as a woman who weeps at every triviality. It is undignified and unbecoming."

She dashed the tears from her eyes and looked up at him as he stood beside her. A plumed hat shaded his face; he leaned upon a beribboned cane.

"I am going ashore," he announced. "You need not be un-

175

easy while I am gone. I have these curs well in hand." He took her hand and bore it, unresisting, to his lips. "For the present, my love, farewell."

She made no reply, and he laughed softly as he turned away. Clumsily he descended the companion and so passed out of her range of vision, and when she saw him again he was being rowed ashore. Randolph Sarne sat beside him in the boat, his rusty black coat contrasting sharply with Gideon's finery of crimson silk.

Frances rose to her feet. Now, if ever, was the chance she had been waiting for. If she could discover Crispin's prison and speak with him, they might be able to form some plan of escape. She did not know where to seek him, but she guessed that he would be imprisoned somewhere in the depths of the ship, and made her way cautiously below. She reached the gun-deck without incident, but as she hesitated there, uncertain which way to go, a step sounded behind her and she swung round to face Jean-Pierre.

He bowed with mock deference, but his white teeth flashed in a smile which held nothing of humility.

"A thousand pardons, milady," he said extravagantly, "but it is not permitted that you come here. I have orders to see that you do not leave your quarters."

Frances stood motionless, staring at him in dismay, a hand to her heart; Jean-Pierre stepped aside and with an airy gesture invited her to retrace her steps. In spite of his flamboyant courtesy she knew that if she refused he would carry her back by force, and so she submitted with what dignity she could muster, concealing her bitter disappointment.

Jean-Pierre escorted her to the great cabin, where she moved dejectedly to the chair at the head of the table and sank into it. He closed the door and leaned against it, watching her. She sat very still, her head against the emblazoned leather of the chair-back, her hands lying wearily along the ornately-carved arms, and at first she did not appear to notice his presence. Becoming aware of it at last, she said with a sigh:

"You need not stand guard over me, sir. I will undertake, if you wish, not to move from this room until my cousin returns."

He moved away from the door and strolled forward to perch on the table's edge, looking down at her. Her hands tightened a little on the arms of the chair, but she forced herself to meet his impudent gaze composedly.

"You were seeking the good Crispin, no?" he said interrogatively.

A weary smile that held no trace of mirth touched her lips.

"Who else should I be seeking, sir, aboard this ship, unless it were my brother or my cousin Mountheath, and they, I presume, are imprisoned with Crispin?"

He grinned, but vouchsafed no information on this score. Instead he said:

"But neither he nor they can aid you now, milady. You were wiser to seek a friend elsewhere."

Frances's heart began to beat faster. Perhaps fortune had not deserted them after all, if Jean-Pierre could be persuaded to help them. She said cautiously:

"Where then should I seek, for if Crispin cannot aid me no-one can? You would mock me, I think."

"Ah no, milady, *parole d'honneur!* I do not mock. I wish only to help you." He leaned forward and spoke almost in a whisper. "It may be that Monsieur Crayle is not as powerful as he imagines. He is not of the Brethren. There are those among us who ask ourselves why we should obey one who seeks to use us merely for his own ends."

She frowned.

"He pays you well, does he not?"

Jean-Pierre snapped his fingers contemptuously.

"With promises, no more! He said that he would take no share of the profits of our last voyage, or of this, and we agreed, for his share was ever the greatest. But there was no time to dispose of that last cargo before we left Port Royal, and since then we have taken but one ship. *En vérité,* milady, the men grow resentful, and now there is this matter of yourself and your brother and M. le Vicomte. It does not please them, that! If the truth of it becomes known, who will suffer? Not Monsieur Crayle. He is too clever, that one! He will find some way of casting the blame upon us."

She looked up and met his gaze squarely.

"Is it in your power to help us, Jean-Pierre? You would not find us ungrateful."

"It is possible, milady." He laughed softly as though at some pleasant thought, and fingered the gold ring in his ear. "One does not know yet how matters will fall out, but—it is possible."

"You await, perhaps, the coming of this other ship, whose captain was one of Sir Henry Morgan's men?" she prompted him, and he looked at her with mingled surprise and admiration.

"You have wit as well as beauty, milady. You were attentive last night, *n'est-ce pas,* although you sat so still and quiet? Yes, I await the coming of Shergall. I have sounded the men concerning a return to Jamaica, and I think that with the crew of the *Venturer* the odds would be in our favour."

"You mean mutiny?" Frances spoke breathlessly, for so much depended on his answer.

"A mutiny? I?" Jean-Pierre chose to be surprised. "But no, milady! We of the brotherhood choose our own captains, and if one does not satisfy us we choose another. We begin to be dissatisfied with Sarne. That is all."

She made an impatient movement, for she was in no mood for levity.

"Oh, call it what you will, so that you set us free! You will be well rewarded, I promise you. Were Gideon dead, my brother would regain his inheritance, and Lord Mountheath, too, is heir to a great fortune, and his father stands well with King Charles. Gideon will not reward you. He is more like to betray you to protect himself. Oh, I implore you to help us!"

In her eagerness and renewed hope her fear of him was for the moment forgotten. She leaned forward across the table, and even ventured to set a hand on his arm, her blue eyes raised beseechingly to his. Again he laughed, and his hand closed suddenly upon hers.

"But your brother and M. le Vicomte are prisoners," he pointed out, "and King Charles is far away. *Bien!* It is no matter. There is only one reward I desire, *ma belle.* Grant me that, and I will do as you ask."

She did not pretend to misunderstand him. A wave of crimson flooded her face, and she started to her feet, trying to withdraw her hand from his.

"No!" she whispered. "No, not that!"

He raised his brows.

"You prefer, then, to become the wife of Monsieur Crayle? *Ma foi, petite,* you do not flatter me!"

A sob broke from her lips and she turned her head away, covering her eyes with one hand. The other was still imprisoned in that of Jean-Pierre, and he looked down at it consideringly.

"So small a hand," he remarked, "to hold the lives of men."

Again she strove to withdraw it, and this time he let her go. She turned from him abruptly and went to stand by the stern-ports, staring out blindly across the lagoon. After a moment he followed her, and leaned against a bulkhead nearby, and though his eyes rested exultantly upon her he made no attempt to touch her. So certain was he of her ultimate surrender that he was prepared to practise restraint now.

Frances was scarcely aware of his nearness amid the chaos of her own confused thoughts. Her first horrified refusal of his proposal had been purely instinctive, and now she was wondering whether it had been justified. If she refused Jean-Pierre her last hope would be gone, for it was unlikely that aid would arrive from any other source, and she would be forced to marry Gideon Crayle, an unspeakable fate from which her mind recoiled in horror. It was true that she still had the dagger, but to take her own life and leave Crispin, Jonathan and Hal to face the hunchback's diabolical revenge would be the act of a coward. Were it not, perhaps, the finer course to purchase those three precious lives, even at the price demanded by Jean-Pierre?

She wrung her hands together in an agony of indecision. If they could know of it, what would be their choice for her? Little doubt of that, i'faith! They would have her take the one sure road of escape, with no further thought for them or the vengeance Gideon might exact, but that she could not do. Crayle's words of the previous day returned to her mind with terrifying clarity. 'Men who have taken hours, even days, to die, though with every breath they screamed for death.' No, she could not let them suffer so, when it lay in her power to prevent it.

"Oh, merciful God!" she said aloud. "Crispin, dear love, if 'twere done to save you, could you understand and forgive?"

The attentive Jean-Pierre raised a quizzical brow.

"Forgive you he might, milady," he said, "but of a certainty he would not forgive me. You have mistaken me, I think. We bargained for the lives of your brother and M. le Viscomte. Those only."

She stared at him in dismay.

"But Crispin——"

"Must die, milady. Oh, I regret it! I regret it deeply. I have for the good Crispin an admiration the most profound. But consider, *ma belle!* If he lives, and learns how his life was purchased, he will without doubt not rest until he has those so-strong hands about my throat. Am I a fool? *Mais non!* Your brother and milor' Mountheath, no more."

She turned upon him then, her eyes blazing scornfully in her white face.

"Then I refuse! Do you imagine that I will agree to your base demands if I am to be denied the power of saving the one dearest to me? Aye, the dearest, Jean-Pierre! Dearer to me by far than my brother, greatly though I love him. Get you hence, sir! Stir up your mutiny if you will, but if there is any mercy in earth or heaven both they and I will be dead before either you or Gideon prevail."

Patiently he listened to this outburst, nor made any attempt to speak until she had done. When she stood silent before him, with clenched hands and heaving bosom, he said quietly:

"Milady, you forget, I think, the fate which Monsieur Crayle has marked out for this man you so greatly love. He is not to die. He is to be given into the hands of Sarne—Sarne the Torturer. Have you ever heard of L'Ollonais, milady? He was the cruellest pirate who ever roamed the Caribbean, and 'twas with him that Sarne first sailed. He learned much from L'Ollonais. Your Crispin has great strength to endure the torture—death will not come to release him. And you, *ma chère?* You are to live also, as Mme. la Marquise. One day you are to meet again, for the amusement of Monsieur Crayle, who would make Crispin as he is himself. I offer you an escape from this. The lives of your brother and cousin, and a swift and easy death for him you love, instead of the living death of which Monsieur Crayle condemns him."

He paused, regarding her inquiringly. She had sunk down on to the locker, all her fine scorn dispelled by his words. Her face was a white mask of tragedy, with deeply-shadowed eyes.

"So!" he said at length. "I do not press for an answer now. You shall think on what I have said—no? Nothing can be done until the *Venturer* arrives." He bent forward, possessed himself of one of the limp hands which looked so frail and white against her black velvet gown, and carried it to his lips. "You know my terms, milady. The choice is yours. *Au revoir, ma belle.*"

He turned and went out of the cabin. As the door closed behind him Frances gave a low moan of despair and buried her face in her hands. The choice was hers, but which way to choose? Which was the greater, which the lesser, evil?

CHAPTER XIX

FURTHER EVIDENCE OF DISCORDANCY

MEANWHILE, ashore, Gideon Crayle sat in the pavilion on the edge of the forest which the men of the *Santo Rosario* had built for their comfort. This erection was no more than an ample roof of palm-fronds supported on rough-hewn timbers, which afforded welcome shade while standing open to every breeze, and it was the common gathering-place of the buccaneers. Here they ate and drank, gambled, sometimes fought and occasionally died, but at present its only occupants were the two men seated at a table at one end of the building.

Gideon sat at the table's head, an incongruous figure in his gold-laced crimson coat, a jewel glinting in the creamy lace at his throat, one hand toying idly with the glossy black curls of his periwig. Beside him sat Sarne, his arms folded across his chest and his chin sunk into his frayed linen collar. His gaunt face, framed in lank, iron-grey hair, was devoid of all expression, and his colourless eyes fixed morosely on the graceful lines of the *Vampire* as she rode at anchor a few hundred yards away.

The two had been fully occupied since coming ashore. The name of the *Santo Rosario* must be effaced, and replaced by that of the *Seagull*, and anything else which could connect her with the galleon commanded by Captain Barbican similarly disposed of. In spite of the excessive heat and his own deformity, which made exertion of any kind a burden, Gideon had personally supervised these very necessary precautions. It was this attention to the smallest details which had carried him thus far in safety along his evil road, and he had no intention of forsaking it now.

At last, however, he sat down with Captain Sarne in the pavilion to rest and to quench the thirst engendered by his labours, and while they took their ease there came to them a deputation from the crew of the galleon in the persons of three of her officers. It appeared that Captain Barbican's erstwhile followers, having discussed the matter among themselves the previous night, had conceived an earnest desire to join the enterprise upon which Shergall and Sarne were bound, having the hope of rich plunder therefrom.

Gideon received them pleasantly enough, but his hooded gaze rested speculatively upon Matt Briarly, who was one of the three. With his customary eye for detail the hunchback had taken the precaution of inquiring whether any of the crew were particularly loyal to Captain Barbican, and the mate had been the only man named.

"Be seated, gentlemen, I pray." Gideon gestured gracefully towards the chairs scattered about the table, and when all were seated addressed himself to Briarly. "You, I believe, are a friend of Captain Barbican."

If he had hoped to discompose the old buccaneer he was disappointed. Matt merely grinned.

"I'm friend to no man when his fortunes fail," he said easily. "My loyalty goes where the profit lies, and from what I hear it lies now with you."

Gideon smiled.

"You are wise, my friend," he said gently. "Captain Barbican is in no position to profit any man, least of all himself. You would be well advised to forget that you ever sailed with him."

"My memory's none of the best," Matt replied cheerfully. "As far as I can recall, the last time I saw Crispin Barbican was in Port Royal—eh, lads?"

With nods and winks his two companions signified their complete lack of interest in the fate of Captain Barbican. Gideon continued to regard Briarly narrowly for some seconds, but at length he nodded, satisfied.

"As to your desire to accompany us," he resumed, "nothing can be done until Captain Shergall arrives. For my part I know little of these matters, but the question shall be laid before him."

Briarly thanked him, but his two companions looked in some perplexity at Sarne, for since they knew nothing of Crayle they were surprised that the notorious pirate, who was known to impose upon his crew a discipline equal to that on any King's ship, should allow his authority to be usurped by this soft-voiced courtier.

The captain of the *Vampire*, however, was too deeply preoccupied to heed them, and had been so since the previous night. A queer twist of character had caused him to hoard, for his own gratification, treasures whose beauty pleased him, and now, as had happened often enough in his evil career, his gaze had alighted upon a thing of rare beauty, though this time it was no jewel or picture, but a living treasure of flesh and blood.

For the best part of a year, now, the beauty of Lady Frances had lingered in his memory, but, knowing her to be the cousin and future wife of Gideon Crayle, he had deemed her beyond his reach. Crayle's support, and the fortune he had amassed by its aid, were more to him than one woman, however beautiful, but now that support was to be withdrawn. Somewhat belatedly Captain Sarne realized that to the hunchback he was but a tool, to be cast aside when he had served his purpose, and the just resentment kindled by this cavalier treatment was added to the already violent turmoil of emotion inspired by the presence of Lady Frances.

Yet resentment had not wholly driven out fear. He could kill Gideon and possess himself of the girl, but all Port Royal knew that Crayle had sailed in the *Vampire*, and his disappearance would be difficult to explain. Nor was this the only danger attending such a course, for Sarne had a shrewd suspicion that Lady Frances might kill herself rather than submit to him.

All night he had wrestled with the thorny problem, but it was not until he sat in the pavilion on the beach that the obvious solution occurred to him. Her ladyship would resist any attempt at force, but might she not prove more amenable if he offered her the lives of her brother and cousin as the price of her surrender?

At first he intended no more than that, but as he dwelt upon the plan he perceived its tremendous possibilities, and so came to a momentous decision. He would offer her marriage, and then, with Crayle dead—a simple matter, that—he could sail back in triumph to Port Royal, the saviour of her ladyship and my lords Mountheath and Rotherdale from the evil machinations of Gideon Crayle. Glittering prospects opened before his dazzled eyes; he saw himself at Court, husband of the beautiful Lady Frances, outdoing even the odious Morgan in extravagant splendour, lavishing his ill-gotten riches in the brilliant, licentious society that revolved about King Charles.

For Captain Barbican he had only a passing thought, for his fellow pirate would be of no help to him in the new life he was so confidently planning, and might be expected to raise objections to her ladyship's marriage to Sarne. All things considered, Captain Sarne decided that it would be safer to kill him, though to gain favour with Frances he was prepared to forego the pleasure of torturing him first.

The matter of most immediate importance, however, was to contrive an interview with her ladyship. Captain Sarne pushed back his chair and rose to his feet.

"I must be going aboard again," he said abruptly. "Do you come with me, Mr. Crayle?"

Gideon raised his brows.

"I perceive no reason to do so," he replied. "We must of necessity spend much time aboard that accursed vessel, and for my part I find it more agreeable here. Sit down, man! There is no need for haste."

Sarne frowned, and, bending forward, spoke in a tone too low for their companions to hear.

"To tell truth," he lied readily, "I put little trust in Jean-Pierre. He is ripe for mutiny, and to leave him to incite the men to violence were the act of a fool. I'll be easier in my mind if I have him under my eye."

"As you please," Gideon replied carelessly, "though I think that you are unduly fearful. After all, Jean-Pierre is but mortal, and if he grows too troublesome there is an easy way to be rid of him."

An expression of real uneasiness crept into the pirate's eyes.

"Have a care, Mr. Crayle," he cautioned him. "He's popular wi' the men, and might do more harm dead than alive."

"May I ask, then, what course you intend to follow?"

"I've told you, Mr. Crayle. Give him no chance to stir up mutiny." He hesitated, and then added boldly: "You'd do well to set a watch on him yourself, since ye're trustful enough to leave him alone wi' her ladyship. He has an eye for a comely lass."

Gideon's heavy lids lifted, and his brilliant eyes looked coldly into Sarne's.

"My dear Sarne," he said in tones of profound boredom, "do not, I pray take me for a fool. We are in need, are we not, of a pretext to rid ourselves of Jean-Pierre?"

Sarne's jaw dropped.

"But devil take it, man, I thought you meant to marry her?"

Gideon sighed; the boredom in his voice deepened.

"Do you imagine that I cherish any romantic notions concerning her upon that account? Gad's life, I am not that young fool Mountheath! A' God's name, Sarne, take these vapours elsewhere, and cease plaguing me with them."

At any other time the pirate might have given rein to his resentment of such an insult, but now he was anxious to be off. He turned on his heel and strode towards the boat, shouting for the men who had manned the oars.

When he came aboard the *Vampire* one glance sufficed to show him that Lady Frances was no longer seated beneath the awning on the poop-deck. He summoned Jean-Pierre, sent him ashore on a trumped-up errand, and having removed the most likely source of interruption he went in search of her ladyship.

He found her in the great cabin, and so absorbed was she in her own unhappy thoughts that she did not hear the door open. He paused on the threshold to look at her, and his cold eyes quickened as they took in the beauty of the picture she made, seated still on the locker by the open windows, with the sunlight gleaming on her red-gold hair beneath the lace scarf and heightening the contrast between the whiteness of her skin and the sombre richness of the Spanish gown. He thought of the treasures he had gathered during his years of piracy, magnificent jewels and costly fabrics, and in imagination saw her wearing them, beauty enshrined in beauty.

He entered and closed the door, and the slight sound brought the girl's head round with a jerk, her eyes wide and apprehensive. Her face was white and drawn, and there were the marks of recent tears on her cheeks. The pirate moved forward to the table and stood there, leaning both hands on its polished surface and looking down at her with his usual profound gloom.

"You weep, my lady," he said abruptly. "Why?"

"Why?" she repeated. "Merciful Heaven! Do you need to ask? Those I love are threatened with torture and death, I am to be forced into marriage with their murderer, and you ask me why I weep! Do you look to find me merry?"

Ignoring this, he continued to regard her sombrely, diffident for perhaps the first time in his life. He was not accustomed to ask for the favours of any woman who pleased him, and, lacking the mocking gallantry of Jean-Pierre, he was at a loss how to proceed. At last, deeming directness the best approach, he said without preamble:

"It is in my power to free both you and them, Lady Frances. Crayle is as vulnerable to a knife-thrust as any man."

Frances had been gazing down at the end of her scarf, which she was pleating nervously between her fingers, but at that she looked up at him in blankest astonishment. After the veiled threats of the previous night, Jean-Pierre's defection had not greatly surprised her, but that Captain Sarne should be ready to desert Gideon was completely unexpected.

"What—what mean you?" she stammered, too startled to fence with him as she had fenced with Jean-Pierre.

"He deems himself safe because it is common knowledge in Port Royal that he sailed with me," replied the pirate, "and I may not say that he fell in battle since he is too weakly to fight. One may not murder noblemen with impunity. But he forgets that I hold prisoner the rightful Marquis, as well as yourself and Lord Mountheath. Three lives saved, and but one taken!" He grinned. "He sees no profit to me in murdering him, but he forgets that there is none in letting him live, now that he will protect me no longer."

Frances was puzzled. Did the pirate expect Jonathan or Hal to take Gideon's place as protector of his gang of cut-throats?

"Are you seeking another protector, Captain Sarne?" she asked. "My brother is but a child, and I fear that Lord Mountheath——"

Sarne shook his head.

"You mistake me, lass," he interrupted her. "I've a fancy to quit the brotherhood, for I've amassed a tidy fortune since I took command of the *Vampire*. 'Tis twenty years since I first went to sea, and for fifteen of 'em I've followed the black flag. A man's luck can't last for ever."

She thought now that she understood, and was relieved.

"Then 'tis a pardon you seek! No doubt my cousin Mountheath could procure one for you, for his father has some influence with the King." She leaned forward and spoke earnestly. "Last night, Captain Sarne, Gideon told you that it was well to have a friend at Court. Help us now, and you shall have three, for we shall be for ever in your debt."

He did not reply immediately, but continued to regard her with the curious lack of expression peculiar to him. At length he said:

"Perhaps I've a mind to go to Court myself."

"You would still need friends, sir," she replied, hoping that the dismay she felt was not apparent in her face. "I believe that it is not easy to enter Court circles without a noble patron."

"Maybe not." There was no change in the sallow face or

186

light-coloured eyes. "But 'twould be easier still wi' a noble wife."

For a moment she thought that she had not heard aright, and stared at him with disbelieving eyes and parted lips. Captain Sarne hastened to dispel any doubt from her mind.

" 'Tis marriage I'm offering you, Lady Frances," he said bluntly, "as the price of your brother's and cousin's lives. Say the word, and my fine Mr. Crayle goes over the side wi' a knife between his ribs."

Frances pressed her hands against her brow and strove to think clearly. The dissension among her rascally captors went even deeper than she had supposed, each being eager, for various reasons, to destroy the others, and it seemed that her own presence was the breath which had fanned these smouldering fires of treachery into flame. It would be a grim irony if in sparing her life Gideon had encompassed his own downfall, but she was doomed whichever of the rogues triumphed. No matter which way she turned, no road of escape offered.

Her prolonged silence caused Captain Sarne some misgivings. He sought about in his mind for a means of influencing her decision, and suddenly received what seemed to him an inspiration. Crossing to a cabinet which stood against the forward bulkhead, he unlocked a drawer and took out a small casket which he placed on the table. This, unlocked in its turn, yielded a magnificent necklace of pearls, the largest the size of a sparrow's egg and all perfect in tint and lustre. The pirate held up the splendid ornament and looked across at Frances.

"See here, lass," he said, "did you ever see the like o' this? Some o' the finest pearls ever to come out of Rio de la Hacha, fashioned into a necklace for a Castilian princess, only the galleon bearing 'em never reached Spain. Methinks they would become you better than any Spanish wench."

"They are very beautiful." Frances bestowed only a fleeting glance upon the pearls, for her mind was filled with a sudden fear. The pirate had made no mention of Crispin in the bargain he had proposed. "Captain Sarne, what of Crispin Barbican? Do you offer me his life also?"

"To hell wi' Barbican!" Sarne replied callously. "I'm not a fool, my girl, and I've no mind to be cuckolded by him."

A faint tinge of colour crept into the girl's wan cheeks, and she tilted her head proudly.

"If I should strike this bargain with you, Captain Sarne,"

187

she said coldly, "I should honour my marriage vows as though they were freely given. You gain nothing by insulting me."

Had she deliberately sought a way of increasing the pirate's eagerness she could not have chosen better. Before this unexpected show of spirit he became conciliatory.

"Why, lass, I meant no harm. See, here's an earnest o' my good faith." He dropped the pearls into her lap, where they shimmered with added lustre against her velvet skirts. "There's others, too, emeralds and diamonds and the like. I've been gathering 'em for many a year, but ecod, you're the first woman I've seen worthy o' wearing 'em."

"You flatter me, Captain Sarne, but I am not to be bribed with jewels." She picked up the creamy, iridescent rope and held it out to him. " 'Tis a man's life I ask, and naught else will content me."

He stared at her, momentarily at a loss. It had never occurred to him that the gems would fail to win her, for the pearls alone were worth a king's ransom, and he was prepared to cast at her feet the fruits of years of piracy. He was shrewd enough to realize that she meant what she said, and her uncompromising attitude merely rendered her the more desirable.

" 'Tis no small thing you ask," he complained at length. "You say I can trust you, but Barbican won't give you up—no man in his senses would—and whether or not I could trust him is a different matter."

Frances dropped the pearls, which he had neglected to take from her, into her lap again, and clasped her hands tightly together to stop their trembling. She was desperately afraid of this gloomy, cold-eyed man who could gloat with equal pleasure over his stolen treasures and the sufferings of his tortured victims, but he held Crispin's life in his hands, and for his sake she was prepared to continue this degrading bargaining.

"But if we swore never to meet again?" she suggested. "Oh, believe me, such a promise, once given, would be binding upon us both."

He gave his chilling laugh, that twisted his lips but did not touch his eyes.

"Barbican would never make such a promise."

"He might, if I asked it of him," she replied, and with the words all else was forgotten in an overwhelming desire to see Crispin again, if only for a moment. She looked beseechingly at the pirate.

"Let me see him, Captain Sarne," she pleaded. "If I may talk with him alone I can perhaps persuade him. Whatever befalls now we must part, and no fate could be more dreadful than that to which Gideon has condemned us."

Captain Sarne came to a sudden decision. If Crispin Barbican's life was the price she demanded, then he should live—until the ring was upon her finger.

"So be it, then," he said abruptly. "You shall see him, and if you can persuade such a promise from him he shall be spared. You had best come to him now, before Crayle comes aboard again. Nay, 'lass, keep the pearls," he added, as she held them out to him.

Frances shook her head.

"Do you wish to arouse Gideon's suspicions?" she retorted. "Take them, I pray."

He shrugged.

"Maybe 'tis better so," he agreed, and taking them from her dropped them into the casket again. "I'll give 'em to you for a wedding gift, my girl, and other gems besides." His eyes rested gloatingly upon her.

He led the way out of the cabin, and Frances followed with fast-beating heart. Down into the depths of the ship they went, where there was scarcely room to stand upright, and the light was dim and the air heavy with the stink of tar and bilge. Sarne paused at last before a low door and drew back the heavy bolts.

As the door creaked open Frances slipped past him and found herself in a low-roofed place of considerable size, dimly illuminated by light which filtered down from above. In the half-light a figure moved, her brother's voice cried her name, and next moment he was in her arms.

She held him close, but over his shoulder her eyes strove to pierce the gloom. Hal was beside her, clasping her unresponsive hand and stammering incoherent questions, but no tall figure moved in the dimness, and the voice she longed to hear was silent. With a sudden, dreadful fear clutching at her heart she released Jonathan and swung round to face the pirate captain.

"Where is he?" she demanded, her voice shrill with anxiety. "If you have lied to me——"

"Patience, Lady Frances, patience!" Sarne was lighting a lantern which he had taken from a hook on the wall. "Mr. Crayle would have it that he be imprisoned alone."

The lantern being satisfactorily kindled, he picked it up and

189

crossed to another door hidden in the shadows. The massive lock securing it he opened with a key which he took from his pocket, and dragging the door open he held the lantern high so that its beams illuminated the black and stifling hole beyond.

Captain Barbican, haggard and unshaven, was sitting with his back against the wall of a cell only a few feet square. As the door opened he got to his feet, flinging up an arm to shield his eyes from the sudden light, and a chain rattled as he moved. For an instant Frances remained motionless, staring with horror into that noisome prison, and then with a sob she started forward and flung her arms about him.

Captain Sarne regarded them morosely for a few seconds, and then hung the lantern on the wall and stepped back, but as he turned his glance fell upon Lord Mountheath. The Viscount was staring past him into the cell, his face livid and his underlip caught between his teeth, while murder looked out of his eyes. The pirate grinned, and, thrusting the door half shut with his foot, took his lordship persuasively by the arm.

"Let 'em be," he said. "I promised her ladyship a word alone wi' him, and ecod! it's not for you to be wagging your ears outside the door. You, too, my lad," he added to Jonathan. "Your sister'll not be wanting your company for a while."

He laughed hideously, and Hal, shaking off the detaining hand, strode to the far end of his prison and flung himself down on an empty cask, thrusting his hands deep into his pockets and staring moodily before him. Captain Sarne leaned against the wall and began to pick his teeth, while Jonathan, after hesitating for a moment midway between the two, sat down on the floor beside his cousin and, clasping his arms around his knees, regarded Sarne despondently, for his old admiration for the Brethren of the Coast was rapidly dispersing.

Within the cell Captain Barbican stood dazed and silent, with Frances's arms tight-clasped about his neck. He had put his own arms around her, clumsily because of the fetters on his wrists, but the surprise and wonder of her presence had for the moment deprived him of speech.

"Frances!" he murmured at last. "Beloved, how come you here?"

With an effort she fought back the tears which threatened to choke her, and steadied her voice sufficiently to answer.

"Captain Sarne brought me," she said. "Gideon has gone

ashore. Oh, Crispin, are you indeed safe? They have not . . . tortured you?"

He shook his head.

"No. Crayle is shrewd enough to know that the torment of the mind is sharper when there is no physical pain to dull a man's thoughts. Darkness and solitude breed nightmare visions that torture the very soul." His arms tightened about her, and there was that in his voice which told her something of the hell through which he had passed. "To lie helpless here, not knowing what had befallen you at the hands of these devils! God! I would rather they broke my body on the rack."

"Do not fear for me," she replied gently. "At present they treat me courteously enough, and if all else fails I have a sure road of escape." She told him of the dagger which she had picked up in the cabin the previous day.

"Thank God!" he said fervently when she had done. "Something, then, was achieved by that madness. But, Frances, why did Sarne bring you here? That was no part of Crayle's plan."

"It is of no importance," she lied hurriedly. "I had to see you, to tell you what I have learned. Crispin, they begin to quarrel among themselves. Jean-Pierre seeks to stir up mutiny, for he wishes to return to Port Royal, and Sarne, fearing Morgan, is for Tortuga. He, for his part, grows weary of being a tool in Gideon's hands, for Gideon says that now Rotherdale is within his grasp he will return to England and protect the pirates no longer."

Crispin frowned.

"He tells them that? God's death, has the man run mad?"

She shook her head.

"He believes that they fear him too much to harm him. It is known, you see, that he sailed in the *Vampire*, and if he does not return it will go hard with Captain Sarne. But Gideon forgets that in us Sarne has a shield against that danger. 'Tis in our power to send Gideon to the gallows, and Sarne knows it."

"In effect, only Crayle stands to profit by our deaths," said Crispin, "and were he dead we might strike a bargain with Sarne, since he gains nothing by murdering us."

"He knows that," she replied in a low voice, "and for that reason he is prepared to free us—at a price."

Something in the way she spoke stifled any relief he might have felt at these tidings, and in a voice which he hardly recognized as his own he heard himself ask:

"What price, Frances?"

She hesitated for a moment, and then set her hands on his shoulders and looked up into his face.

"Crispin," she said earnestly, "could we suffer any worse fate than that to which Gideon has condemned us? I would die sooner than marry him, and by God's mercy the means to do so has been placed in my hands, but how can I take that road of escape knowing what hell on earth he designs for you? Were it not better to live, if by living some purpose may be served?"

"Frances!" There was a sudden note of fear in his voice. "What are you trying to say?"

"That it is in my power to save us all, if you will but give me a certain promise. Captain Sarne offers me marriage as the price of our lives."

"What?" he exclaimed furiously. "He dares, that scoundrel out of hell——!"

"Oh, Crispin, take care!" Frances cast an apprehensive glance over her shoulder. "If he should hear you . . . ! Listen to me, dearest. He offered me at first the lives of Jonathan and Hal if I would wed him, for he dreams of outshining Morgan's glory at Court, and we are to be his key to the doors of London. When I demanded your life also he refused, knowing that I love you, but now he will set you free if we promise never to meet again." He opened his lips to protest, but she laid her hand across them and continued hurriedly: "Oh, 'tis hard, I know! I think my heart is like to break with the grief of it! But to know that you were alive and free, and Jonathan secure at last in possession of Rotherdale, would give me strength to endure."

He shook his head, and drew her hand down from his lips.

"Do you think that I would accept my freedom at such a price? That I would swear to put you out of my life knowing that you had sold yourself to that devil to save me? I would sooner die a thousand deaths, and Jonathan, child though he is, would rather see you dead by your own hand." He caught her to him, and laid his cheek against her hair. "Love, you know not what you would do! Sarne is a creature without pity and without honour. He would not keep faith with you, and God knows what you might suffer at his hands. Believe me, Frances, escape does not lie that way."

"Where, then, does it lie?" she sobbed. "Oh, I do not fear now for myself. There is a swift and easy way for me, but what of you? Gideon does not threaten idly! They will torture you!" She was weeping wildly; her hands clung to him. "Oh, Crispin, do not ask that of me! I cannot let you suffer if it is in my power to save you. I cannot, I cannot!"

"You must," he said sternly. "There is no torment which they can wreak upon my body that I would not endure a hundred times rather than know you sacrificed to that villain. Besides, we still live, and who knows what chance may occur to give us our freedom?" Knowing that they both were doomed, he yet contrived to force a measure of conviction into his voice. "You say that they begin to quarrel among themselves, and if it comes to open mutiny Crayle and Sarne may well be swept away."

She shook her head.

"Jean-Pierre would be leader then," she replied, "and he is less generous than Captain Sarne, for he would not spare your life." She read the dismayed question in his eyes, and sighed. "Oh, yes," she said wearily. "Jean-Pierre also seeks to bargain with me, though he does not offer me marriage."

There was a long moment of silence, and then Crispin spoke in a voice of subdued passion.

"God's death!" he said slowly. "To what insults I have exposed you! What malignant fate ever decreed that our paths should cross? When I chanced upon you that night in Bristol your grandfather welcomed me as a protector Heaven-sent to save you, but had he known the depths to which I was to drag you, he would have cursed me with his dying breath."

"Ah, no!" she protested. "Did you not save us then, and again in Jamaica, when all seemed lost? Perhaps you are right, and some miracle may occur to free us. If indeed they fight among themselves, and Jean-Pierre's faction prevails, perchance we could strike a bargain with this Captain Shergall, upon whose support he depends."

"Shergall?" Crispin broke in, and there was a new, compelling note in his voice. "Not Roger Shergall, of the *Venturer?*"

"Why—why, yes," she stammered. "That is the name of the man they await. Crispin, will he help us?"

"I do not know," Crispin replied slowly. "Much depends upon one thing."

"What thing, Crispin?"

"The question whether or not Roger Shergall is a man of his word." He took her hands in his and spoke swiftly, his voice subdued. "Listen, sweetheart! I knew Shergall when we sailed together under Morgan, and it chanced that at the sack of Porto Bello I saved his life. He swore then that if ever it

193

were in his power to perform a like service for me, I had but to remind him of that day. Now the time has come to put that to the test. When do they look for his coming?"

"At any time, I think. From what they said last night the appointed day of meeting is already past, for they looked to find him here before them."

"God send no harm has come to him," said Crispin fervently. "Somehow I must have speech with him, but how?" He paused, but presently continued, half to himself: "He will doubtless fire a salute when he reaches the island, and that will inform me of his coming. If I could break free then . . . ! Jonathan and Mountheath between them might break open the door of this place, but I should still be hampered by these damnable chains. God's light! What devil prompted them to put me in irons?"

"Is there no way of breaking them, Crispin?" she ventured, but he shook his head and lifted his fettered hands more fully into the light.

"I have tried," he said simply, and she saw that his wrists were raw and bleeding where the irons had bitten deep into flesh.

"Oh, my love!" Her voice broke, and taking the scarred hands in her own she laid her face against them, and he felt her tears upon his fingers. He looked down at the bright, bowed head, from which the lace scarf had fallen back, and realized suddenly that their chance of escape, if chance there were, rested solely in the small hands now clasping his own.

"Frances," he said gently, "I cannot break free from here— 'tis madness to think on it. It is you who must carry the tidings of our plight to Roger Shergall. If he is prepared to help us, tell him that his best chance of succeeding lies in supporting Jean-Pierre, for only thus can Sarne and Crayle be overthrown. But tell him also that he must protect you, for to that I charge him by memory of his old debt to me. Until Shergall's coming you must play off these rogues one against the other, and so gain time." He paused, his eyes searching her face. " 'Tis dangerous work, my heart, and you have no-one to turn to should matters go awry."

"I have a dagger," she replied resolutely, "and God knows I should not hesitate to use it, upon them or upon myself." Her eyes met his, and the faintest of smiles glimmered in them. "See into what a valiant-minded Amazon you have transformed a Puritan maid."

Footsteps sounded on the planks outside his prison, and the

faint, transient laughter fled from her face. She looked up at him piteously, and murmured his name.

"Courage, dear heart," he said softly. "When we meet again it will be within sight of freedom."

If we meet at all! he added in his heart, and read the same thought in her eyes. Neither would give it voice, but when they kissed, their lips clung as though this were indeed a last farewell.

When at length he put her from him and looked up, Sarne was standing in the doorway with Mountheath at his elbow. Not trusting himself to look the pirate in the face without striking him, Crispin addressed himself instead to the Viscount.

"Good-morrow, my lord." He spoke at random, conscious only of the fact that Frances was going from him into danger where he could not follow and protect her. "We are, I fear, companions in misfortune, even though divided by a door of solid English oak."

The Viscount stared at him, his face distorted by the jealousy which consumed him.

"There's more than a door divides us, you pirate dog!" he spat at him. " 'Tis my profound hope that before I die I may have the pleasure of hearing you scream beneath the torment."

Sarne gave his harsh bark of laughter, and beside him Crispin heard Frances catch her breath. His hand closed warningly upon hers, and he looked mockingly at his lordship.

"Faith, what a noble gentleman it is!" he marvelled. "Such fortitude to comfort and strengthen his cousins, and such courage to insult a man when there is no chance of a reckoning."

"Let be, let be!" Sarne broke in, with a grin. "Come, my lady, in a moment they will be at each other's throats." He reached up and took the lantern from its hook, and looked mockingly at Crispin. "I hope you've seen sense, Barbican, for both our sakes!"

He laid his hand familiarly on the girl's arm as he spoke, drawing her out of the cell, but Crispin leaned against the farther wall and folded his arms. He was not going to play into Sarne's hands now by any show of resentment, though the desire to drive his fist into the fellow's evil, leering face was so intense that the effort of conquering it brought the sweat to his brow.

Frances did not speak again, but she turned and smiled at

him in the moment before the door swung shut between them, and he forced himself to return the smile as though a lifetime of freedom and happiness lay before them. Both were too proud to reveal to others the anguish in their hearts.

But when the key had grated in the lock, and darkness enveloped him again, he slipped down once more into a sitting position and buried his face in his hands. He had known imprisonment before, in the fields of Barbados and the galleys of Spain, but not all those years of slavery had sapped his courage as had these few short hours of hell in that black corner of the *Vampire*'s hold. Even now he refused to let himself hope. The chance was so slight, the danger so great, and Frances must face it alone while he crouched here in the darkness, chained like a captive beast. No, hope was a torment more cunning than all the rest, for it gave a man strength to live through the long, haunted hours and not run mad. Better to think of his love as already dead, and safe alike from the mad vengeance of Gideon Crayle and the evil desires of his confederates; better to prepare himself for whatever hideous sufferings they chose to inflict upon him, and to pray for the courage to endure them, and for the peace of death when all was over. It was the counsel of despair, but in despair lay a certain calm.

CHAPTER XX

THE OFFICERS OF THE VENTURER

OUTSIDE Crispin's prison Frances turned once more to her brother, but Sarne broke in abruptly on her first words.

"No time to linger, Lady Frances. Your cousin may come aboard again at any time, and I've no wish to be found here."

She nodded, and drew the boy close to kiss him.

"Have courage, my dear," she whispered, under cover of the embrace. "Our case may not be as hopeless as it seems."

She saw the sudden question in his eyes, and frowned a

warning as she drew back. She did not so much as glance at the Viscount, but turning to the pirate said quietly:

"I am ready, Captain Sarne."

He had already extinguished the lantern and returned it to its place, but as she followed him to the door Hal started forward and caught her arm.

"Frances!" he exclaimed with mingled reproach and entreaty. "You cannot go like this, without a word. We may never meet again."

She shook off his detaining hand and looked up at him, and involuntarily he recoiled, for the blue eyes which could be so gentle were filled now with indescribable scorn and anger. Not a word did she speak, but she drew her skirts aside as from some contaminating presence as she swept past him and through the door which Sarne was holding open for her.

In silence and some haste the pirate conducted her once more to the great cabin, but once within that fantastic treasure-house he faced her grimly.

"Well?" he demanded. "Did he agree?"

Frances hesitated, clasping and unclasping her hands.

"No," she admitted reluctantly, "he would give me no promise." She took a pace forward, her eyes searching his gloomy, expressionless face. "But he will, I am sure of it! If only you will wait a little, Captain Sarne. Surely a few days are no great matter?"

He regarded her morosely.

"How long will Crayle wait? You try to grasp too much, my girl, and will end by losing all. If Barbican will not see sense there's an end to it, and he may rot in hell for all I care. I've humoured you long enough, and I'm not a patient man."

She perceived that only boldness would serve her now, and fought down a rising sense of panic. With an affectation of indifference she turned aside to study an exquisitely-wrought Madonna which stood on the cabinet nearby.

"Then I fear that you must learn patience, sir. Crispin Barbican's life is still the price I demand of you, and if you refuse to grant me that I'll have none of your bargain."

For a moment he stared at her, too surprised to speak, for never before had a woman dared to flout him in this fashion. When he had recovered his voice:

"D'ye dare defy me, you doxy?"

"I warned you, Captain Sarne, that you gain nothing by insulting me." With a slim forefinger she traced a fold of the

Madonna's jewelled robe, and glanced at him sidelong under her lashes. "What, do you suppose, would Gideon do if I told him of your proposal to me?"·

He laughed shortly.

"That threat will not serve, my girl. You fear Crayle more than you fear me, or you would not have listened to my offer in the first place."

"I listened because you held out a hope, however slight, of saving Crispin's life. Now you destroy that hope." She shrugged. "What matter then if Gideon learn of it?"

"What of your brother and Lord Mountheath?"

"My brother, sir, is a child, but he is also the Marquis of Rotherdale, and will, I doubt not, face death with courage. As for Lord Mountheath, he is a liar and a cheat, and has no longer any claim upon me."

For a space he stared at her in silence; then he said:

"Crayle does not intend to kill you, Lady Frances, or Barbican either. You heard what he said yesterday. Can you take that path when another offers?"

" 'Tis but a choice of two evils, Captain Sarne, and life is a burden which may be cast aside if it grows too heavy."

The meaning of this was unmistakable, and at this confirmation of his earlier fears his eyes narrowed in sudden alarm.

"You have not the means to kill yourself." He gripped her arm, swinging her round to face him. "Have you?"

She knew a moment's fear that he would guess at her possession of a weapon, but had the wit to cover her mistake. She looked at him scornfully.

"Fool, I have a dozen! May not silk or velvet be fashioned into a rope? Is there not water beneath the ship? I can take my own life whenever I choose, and you know it. Now do you agree to terms?"

He released her and stepped back, scowling.

"You think he will give you the promise?"

"I have that hope."

"I'll wait four-and-twenty hours, no longer, and if you seek to play me false, my girl, by God, you'll regret it! Barbican's not my only prisoner, and your young sprig of a brother might not face torture as bravely as a speedy death."

On that threat he left her, and Frances sank trembling into a chair and buried her face in her hands. She had gained at least a brief respite, but the danger was by no means over, for at any time Gideon might decide that he had delayed long enough and give the order which would doom Crispin to the torment and Jonathan to certain death; and Jean-Pierre would not wait for ever for an answer. If Roger Shergall did not come soon . . .

She slept ill that night, and rose next morning wan and heavy-eyed, to find the black frigate still riding alone on the sparkling waters of the lagoon. On the surface all seemed much as it had been the previous day. Gideon was urbanity itself, revelling in the power he so dearly loved, and if Captain Sarne seemed gloomy, that was his habitual aspect, but Jean-Pierre lacked his usual buoyant impudence and there was a faint frown between his brows. Frances guessed that he awaited the coming of the *Venturer* with an impatience wellnigh as great as her own.

As the long hours of the forenoon dragged past Frances sat beneath the awning on the frigate's high poop, her glance returning constantly to the headland where the buccaneers kept watch beside their improvised fort, for it was from them that the first word of the *Venturer's* approach would come. But the sun climbed slowly to the meridian, and no shout or salute of cannon-fire heralded the coming of another vessel, and by the time that they assembled for the midday meal Frances's nerves were strained to breaking-point.

With Gideon's watchful glance upon her she made a pretence of eating, though she felt that every mouthful must choke her. The twenty-four hours' grace granted her by Captain Sarne was almost over, and try as she would she could discover no way of obtaining a further delay. If Sarne took matters into his own hands and murdered Gideon, she would be lost indeed.

The meal seemed to drag on interminably, while Gideon discoursed charmingly on a variety of subjects with as much aplomb as though he sat in his own house in London. He seemed oblivious to the morose silence of his companions, and his beautiful, expressive voice flowed on and on, until Frances set her teeth and clenched her hands to keep from screaming aloud.

He was interrupted at last in no uncertain fashion. At no great distance a gun boomed, the sound echoing back from the wooded shore, and was followed by two pistol-shots fired in quick succession. Sarne thrust back his chair and rose to his feet.

" 'Tis the signal," he said. "That will be the *Venturer* at last."

He went quickly out of the cabin, and a brief silence followed his departure. Jean-Pierre had not moved. He sat sideways to the table, one hand buried in his pocket and the other twisting the stem of his wineglass, outwardly indifferent to the arrival of the man upon whom he had pinned all his hopes. Frances sat with bowed head, staring down at her hands clasped in her lap, fearful lest Gideon should observe the sudden tears of sheer relief which had started to her eyes. Crayle drank the last of his wine, set down the fragile glass, and dabbed his lips delicately with a laced handkerchief.

"Captain Shergall is tardy," he remarked. " 'Tis five days past the appointed time."

"The winds blow at no man's bidding, Monsieur," Jean-Pierre replied without looking up. "It is something that he arrives at all."

"Quite so, quite so." Gideon got up and went slowly to the door. There he paused and looked at her ladyship. "You will remain here, Frances," he said gently, and went out.

There was another pause; then Jean-Pierre, still without looking up, said softly:

"Shergall is here, milady. You have an answer for me—no?"

"I do not know." Frances rose to her feet and went to stand at the stern-windows, her back to the room. " 'Tis so evil a choice, so cruel! I do not know."

"You must decide quickly, milady. What is to be done must be done before we put to sea again, or not at all." His voice grew persuasive. "Come, *ma belle,* why do you hesitate? Think of those you love, whose only hope of escape lies in you. Will you send your brother to his death, and your lover to the torment, knowing that it is in your power to save them?"

"To save them, yes, but at what cost!" She swung round to face him, to make a last appeal which in her heart she knew to be useless. "Jean-Pierre, will you not be merciful? Ask anything—wealth, lands, honours—and it shall be yours. I swear it!"

He shook his head.

"When I want wealth, *ma chère,* I take it from the ships of Spain, and what are lands and honours to such as I? Come now, your answer! Does your way lie with me, or with Monsieur Crayle?"

"Or with Captain Sarne," she said quietly, and the words

200

brought him to his feet with an abruptness which sent his chair sliding across the floor.

"Sarne?" he repeated. "Mother of God! Does that black-hearted devil think to have you?"

"He offers me marriage," Frances replied steadily, "and the life of Captain Barbican."

"Marriage!" Jean-Pierre's fury was for an instant lost in amazement. "By all the saints! What maggot is now in his brain?"

"Captain Sarne is ambitious," she replied. "He would go to Court."

Jean-Pierre grinned.

"To outdo Morgan, *n'est-ce pas?* He hates Welsh Harry as much as he fears him. But me, I have no such ambition." He came round the table to her and gripped her by the shoulders, looking down at her intently. *"Ma petite,* it is not to be thought on. To be the wife of Sarne is no better than to be Mme. la Marquise. *Mon Dieu,* you do not know him!"

"He will set Crispin free," she said obstinately, "if we swear never to meet again, and to save him I would wed Satan himself."

"So!" He thrust her away, suddenly angry. "Do what you will, milady! But if Shergall supports me and we prevail, I shall be captain of the *Vampire,* and there will be no need to bargain with you. You shall come to me then, willing or no!"

On that he turned to leave her, and she was seized by sudden panic, for only through Jean-Pierre could she reach Roger Shergall, and only with the Frenchman's aid could Shergall hope to destroy Sarne and Gideon Crayle. She started forward and caught his arm.

"Jean-Pierre, wait! You do not understand."

He paused readily enough, regarding her questioningly, and she cast desperately about her mind for some way of conciliating him. Only one idea occurred to her, and though she shrank from it sheer desperation drove her on.

"You do not understand," she repeated, and moved a pace nearer. "If choose I must, surely you do not think that I would wed willingly with Captain Sarne?"

For one panic-stricken moment she feared that she had not deceived him. Then he laughed softly on a note of triumph, and she knew that her desperate gamble had succeeded; all that remained was to play the loathsome part convincingly.

"I fear him, Jean-Pierre, as greatly as I fear Gideon," she said plaintively, "but Crispin's life is at stake. Were it not for that"—she set her hands on his shoulders and even ventured to glance up fleetingly at his face—"were it not for that . . ." she repeated.

Suspicion lurked still in his dark eyes.

"And Crispin, milady? Do you no longer love him?"

She sighed, and turned her head away.

"Did I ever love him?" she said wretchedly. "I do not know. But save him I will, if 'tis in my power to do it. Gratitude, if nothing else, demands it of me." She pressed her hands against her brow, and her voice broke. "Oh, why will you not help me? If Captain Sarne can spare his life, why cannot you?"

"And if I did, *ma chère?* Would you not play me false, and return to him?"

She shook her head.

"Need you ask that? He is too proud to forgive. I will keep faith with you, Jean-Pierre."

He laughed again, exultantly, and caught her in his arms, but she held him off a moment longer.

"His life and freedom, Jean-Pierre? You swear it?"

"Aye, anything!" he said huskily. "Anything, *ma belle!*"

He kissed her then, and Frances suffered the embrace without protest. Neither she nor Jean-Pierre observed, beyond the half-open door, the gaunt, black-clad figure of Randolph Sarne standing shadowy amid the shadows. For a few seconds longer he watched them, his light, cruel eyes evilly narrowed, then he withdrew as silently as he had come. A minute passed, and then his approaching footsteps rang loudly on the wooden floor to warn them of his coming.

He entered the cabin briskly and addressed himself to Frances, ignoring his lieutenant, who was leaning unconcernedly against the table.

"My lady, Mr. Crayle commands you to go to your own cabin. At once."

She stared at him in sudden dismay, for it had not occurred to her that the arrival of Captain Shergall would mean any curtailment of her freedom. She glanced at Jean-Pierre, but he was refilling a glass and did not look at her.

Realizing that to protest would be worse than useless, she moved with outward docility to the door. Sarne followed her, and on the threshold of her own cabin she turned to face him.

"Sir?" she said, in tones of haughty inquiry.

The pirate grinned.

"Crayle's a cautious man, my lass. He wants you out o' sight when Shergall comes aboard, and he'll feel a deal safer wi' your door locked and the key in his pocket."

He took her arm and thrust her into the cabin, and a second later she heard the key turn in the lock. When his footsteps had receded again she flung herself down on the narrow bed and gave way to despair, for she knew that she would never reach Roger Shergall now. All her efforts, all that she had endured of shame and fear, had been in vain, and though she knew that Gideon could have no possible inkling of the truth, he had crushed her hopes as effectively as though he had known everything.

Meanwhile the *Venturer* came to her anchorage in the lagoon, and presently a boat bearing her captain bumped alongside the *Vampire*. Roger Shergall was a small, lean man with the wizened face, wide, thin-lipped mouth and mournful eyes of a monkey. He was dressed, after the fashion of the buccaneers, in a curious mixture of near-rags and tawdry finery, and armed with an immense cutlass which no-one who had not witnessed his deadly skill would have believed that he could wield.

He had been delayed, he told them, by the pursuit and capture of a Spanish ship whose cargo proved to consist largely of choice wines, and he suggested that to celebrate this victory and put the men in good heart for the proposed venture a generous proportion of this should be distributed among them forthwith. This being agreed, they came to the matter of the articles which must be signed between them, setting out according to custom the various shares which would fall to the officers and crews of the two ships, but as Shergall had come aboard the *Vampire* alone, save for the men who manned his boat, it was determined that he should return that evening with his two chief lieutenants to discuss this important matter. He then took his leave and returned to his own ship to order the disembarking of the captured wines.

Of all this Lady Frances knew nothing, and the first intimation she received that Shergall was no longer aboard came when Gideon himself released her from her cabin to join them at the evening meal. From the conversation which took place over this repast she learned that the captain and officers of the *Venturer* would be returning later that evening, but she had little hope of encountering them. Only a miracle, she felt, could avail her now.

The meal was almost over when Gideon addressed her for the first time. He was seated at the table's head, in the chair which should by right have been occupied by Captain Sarne, and his handsome face wore an expression of geniality even more marked than usual.

"Before you withdraw again to your cabin, my dear Frances," he said pleasantly, "I have something to say which should be of interest to you. For the past two days I have devoted considerable time to the fabrication of a suitable story to account for your survival of the wreck of the *Santo Rosario*—which, you will remember, was lost in a violent storm some three months ago—and I have at length evolved a tale which should satisfy even the most sceptical. It does not, I fear, present our good friend Captain Barbican in a very creditable light, but that, after all, will be the least of his sufferings."

He paused and took snuff from a jewelled box, his dark eyes fixed with evil amusement on the girl's face. White to the lips, she was staring at him with the terrified, despairing eyes of a hunted creature. Gideon smiled pensively, and continued:

"I do not think that I shall tell you yet what the explanation is, but I assure you that it is ingenious in the extreme, and remarkably affecting. You will receive a vast deal of sympathy, I make no doubt. But the point, my dear Frances, the point that I wish to make clear, is that there is no longer any necessity to delay. I may rid myself of my unwanted—er—guests whenever I choose."

Again he paused, and looked benevolently around the table. Frances sat motionless and stricken; Sarne and Jean-Pierre were, for their own reasons, hanging upon the hunchback's words.

"I have decided, however," Gideon resumed after a moment, "that the matter can well wait until we put to sea again. Greatly though it distresses me to deceive our esteemed friend Captain Shergall, his well-known attachment to Sir Henry Morgan renders it inadvisable to take him into our confidence." He sighed and shook his head. "A pity, this need for secrecy, a great pity! The reckless career of Captain Barbican, and its unfortunate ending, would have made such an amusing story. I should so much have enjoyed telling it. What, my love, you are not leaving us so soon?"

Frances had risen to her feet and with an inarticulate exclamation turned blindly towards the door. Two or three paces she took, and then without a sound she crumpled to the floor and lay still. Both Sarne and Jean-Pierre started to their feet, but Gideon merely turned in his chair and surveyed the slight, huddled figure dispassionately.

"How very affecting," he said coldly. "Her ladyship begins to learn, I think, the unwisdom of flouting me in any way. Yes, pick her up, Jean-Pierre. Captain Shergall may arrive at any time, and he could hardly fail to observe her there." He rose unhurriedly to his feet. "Pray do me the kindness of carrying her to her cabin."

The young Frenchman had dropped to one knee and raised Frances in his arms, and there was a scarcely perceptible pause before he rose obediently to his feet. Crayle preceded him to the girl's cabin and from the threshold watched him place her upon the bed. He spoke indifferently.

"We will leave her, Jean-Pierre, to recover her senses as best she may. Captain Shergall will be here soon, and as I have said, I do not wish him to learn yet of her presence here. Later, perhaps, but not yet."

Jean-Pierre went past him out of the cabin and paused to watch him lock the door and drop the key into his pocket. Then he followed him again towards the great cabin, but as they went he tripped, and stumbled heavily against the hunchback, to recover himself with a profuse apology. Crayle brushed this aside, and passed on in the direction of the deck.

The Frenchman watched him out of sight with a curious smile playing about his lips, and then he glanced down at his right hand. A key lay across the palm, for Jean-Pierre had been picking pockets before he reached his teens, and his fingers retained their old cunning. For a moment he contemplated his prize, and then he glanced over his shoulder at the door of her ladyship's cabin and laughed softly to himself. He tossed the key into the air, caught it, and slipped it into his pocket. Then he went into the great cabin, humming a tune beneath his breath.

Sarne was still there, lost in gloomy contemplation of one of the rare paintings which adorned the place, but he glanced round as his lieutenant entered and inquired the whereabouts of Mr. Crayle. Jean-Pierre shrugged expressively.

"He goes to await the arrival of Shergall," he said. "It would seem that he regards himself as commander of the *Vampire, n'est-ce pas?*"

He crossed to the stern-windows and rested a knee on the locker beneath them to look from the casement. The purple and silver of the tropic night was patched by the fires blazing in the buccaneer encampment, and the sound of discordant singing floated across the water. Jean-Pierre grinned.

"The men disport themselves," he remarked, "and Monsieur Crayle grows careless. He should recall that when the wine is in, truth will out. I do not think, my Captain, that his secret will remain so for long."

"Talking o' secrets," Sarne said slowly, "you were mighty close wi' her ladyship when I came upon you here today."

Jean-Pierre's eyes grew suddenly wary, but he shrugged and spoke naturally enough, without turning his head.

"She is sad, the poor little one, and very frightened, and I sought to comfort her. My heart is of a tenderness truly remarkable."

"It is, is it?" said Sarne ominously, and came softly across the room to stand beside him. "You'd not be plotting mutiny wi' Shergall, or scheming to have the wench for yourself? Ye lying, treacherous cur, did ye think to cozen Randolph Sarne?"

Jean-Pierre started to turn towards him, but before the movement was half completed Sarne's dagger, hard-driven, buried itself to the hilt in his side, and with a choking gasp he pitched forward on to the locker. Sarne caught him almost in the act of falling and tossed him up on to his shoulder. Then, with the intention of disposing of the Frenchman's body, he crossed to the door, but was checked on the threshold by the sound of approaching voices and footsteps. He heard the dulcet tones of Gideon Crayle and the harsher voice of Roger Shergall, and cursed as he realized that the captain of the *Venturer* must have come aboard without his knowledge. He thrust the body of Jean-Pierre into the shadows behind him, and swung round in the nick of time to face the newcomers.

Gideon and Shergall came first, and behind them were two dimly-seen figures whom he supposed to be the officers of the *Venturer*. In the ill-lit gangway he could see only that the foremost of them was a big man, solidly built and dressed with gaudy splendour, for between the wide-brimmed hat pulled low on his brow and the curling profusion of hair below it his features were indistinguishable. His companion, of sparer build and more soberly clad, preserved a similar anonymity.

Shergall greeted Sarne agreeably, and they all passed into the cabin, where Gideon, taking upon himself the office of host, begged them to be seated. No-one accepted the invitation, and he became aware of a somewhat odd silence. Looking about him, he discovered Captain Shergall leaning against the post of the half-open door with a curious expression on his simian countenance, while his two silent companions, their faces still shadowed by those broad hats, had advanced into the room. Gideon exchanged a puzzled glance with Captain Sarne.

"Is anything amiss, gentlemen?" he inquired, and it was the larger of the two strangers who replied.

"That is for you to say, Mr. Crayle," he said, and his voice had a faint, lifting lilt to it that was vaguely familiar. "There are a few questions, look you, that we are eager to have answered."

With the words he swept off the concealing hat, and so revealed a bold, strong face, long-nosed and somewhat fleshy, with a full-lipped mouth, and shrewd, almost cunning eyes under thin brows. An arrogant face which both Sarne and Crayle recognized, and at which they stared with incredulous dismay. The face of Sir Henry Morgan.

CHAPTER XXI

"WILL YOU BE FORSWORN?"

IN the stupefied silence which followed that dramatic unmasking Morgan tossed on to the table the hat which had served him so well, and regarded the discomfited plotters with a mocking, cat-like smile. Sarne stood just within the door, staring, with dropped jaw and starting eyes, at his old enemy, but though Gideon had lost colour and groped rather unsteadily for a chair, his recovery was quicker than the pirate's. Once seated, he turned his hooded gaze upon his formidable opponent and spoke in a voice which had lost none of its melodious calm.

"You must forgive us, Sir Henry, but we were unprepared for this honour. You are strangely furtive in your movements."

The cat-smile broadened. Sir Henry smoothed the fierce, upward curve of his moustache.

"It has never been my custom to give warning of my approach, Mr. Crayle. Or—I cry pardon—should I not say 'my Lord Rotherdale'?"

Gideon began to breathe more freely. Whatever the purpose of this visitation, it apparently had nothing to do with the prisoners, of whose presence Morgan was obviously unaware. Reflecting that he had been wiser than he had guessed in confining Frances to her cabin, he said with an appropriate air of melancholy:

"Indeed, Sir Henry, I fear that you are right. Diligently though we have searched, we can find no trace of the ship in which my unfortunate young relatives and their companions —God rest them—set sail from Port Royal. There can be little doubt that they perished in the storm which followed hard upon their departure."

"But what was the reason for that departure?" Sir Henry's companion broke in angrily. He, too, had cast off his disguise, revealing a pleasant, undistinguished face marred by lines of pride and self-indulgence, and now he strode forward to lean threateningly over the seated hunchback. "Aye," he repeated, "what drove them to such a desperate flight? What—or who —drove them to their death?"

"A moment, Lord Larchwood!" Morgan broke in, before Gideon could answer. "You agreed, did you not, to leave this matter to me?"

The Earl drew back, biting his lip, and Gideon looked up at Morgan.

"Tell me, Sir Henry," he said gently, "was it merely to question me concerning the fate of those unfortunate young people that you followed me here with such care and secrecy? If it was, may I venture to say that such precautions were scarcely needful, and even a trifle absurd?"

The Welshman pulled forward a chair and sat down. For a man of such violent passions he seemed singularly unmoved by Crayle's words.

"No, my lord, it was not. My business is with Sarne yonder, as you may suppose. 'Tis Lord Larchwood who is wishful to learn the truth of his son's death, and, knowing that you were aboard the *Vampire*, he chose to sail with me that he might meet with you the sooner. But I'll confess to a certain curiosity myself. You'll have heard, perhaps, that Crispin Barbican was my friend."

In the background Captain Sarne passed his tongue nervously over his lips. The glance which Morgan had bestowed upon him was in no way reassuring, and it seemed to him that there was an unspoken threat in his last words. Gideon, however, remained unperturbed.

"I shall, of course, be happy to share with his lordship what information I have concerning the tragedy, and I condole with him in his grievous loss. I, too, was bereaved."

Larchwood laughed shortly on a note of scorn.

"A bereavement, sir, which brought you a marquisate. Your grief does you infinite credit." His voice made an insult of the words, and Gideon turned a wistful gaze upon him.

"I remind myself, my lord, that Mountheath was your only son, and that it is grief which causes you to speak thus bitterly," he replied with gentle dignity, and added quietly: "Lady Frances was to have been my wife."

So well did he play his part that Larchwood was tricked into a muttered apology. Gideon accepted this magnanimously, and continued:

"You will understand, my lord, that I have little certain knowledge. That Lady Frances and her brother were carried off by Captain Barbican, and that Mountheath went with them, I know, and it is common knowledge that his ship was in no case to put to sea. That night there was a storm of extreme violence, and"—he sighed—"the unhappy conclusion is only too obvious."

The Earl made an impatient movement.

"All this, sir, we learned in Port Royal. What I desire to know is the reason for their flight. Do you tell me that Barbican carried off the boy and his sister against their will, and that my son aided him? Or do you suggest that Hal, too, was abducted?"

"My lords," said Morgan, breaking in again without ceremony, "these questions must for the present be set aside. What, is the King's business to wait upon private matters?" His menacing gaze shifted once more to Sarne. "You keep strange company, my lord Marquis. Dangerous company, egad! Yon rogue is going back to Port Royal in irons, bound for Gallows Point."

"Indeed?" Gideon spoke softly. "Upon what charge?"

"I am no lawyer, my lord," Sir Henry replied easily. "There will be evidence enough to hang him, no doubt. I wonder, now, what brought a gentleman like you into his company?"

Crayle shrugged.

"Surely, sir, the explanation is obvious? It was aboard the *Vampire* that my cousins and Lord Mountheath arrived at Port Royal last year, and 'twas Captain Sarne's lieutenant who saw them on the night they fled. I had need of a swift and powerful vessel, and the *Vampire* was ready to hand."

"A remarkable series of coincidences, my lord," said Larchwood with something of a sneer. "But you must have abandoned the search some time ago. Why did you continue to consort with these pirates?"

"My dear sir, I am not the commander of the ship. It was not Captain Sarne's wish to return to Jamaica, and I was obliged to wait upon his pleasure. Had I known, of course, that you were seeking me, I should have been less complaisant."

"To hell wi' that!" Sarne, flinging caution to the winds, strode forward to confront Morgan across the table. "So you'd drag me in irons to Gallows Point, ye renegade dog? You'd use the King's commission to settle old scores? But this time you've over-reached yourself! The *Vampire's* guns could blast that paltry hulk you sailed in clean out o' the water, and what's to prevent 'em doing it?"

Sir Henry laughed, and the sound was not reassuring. He settled his bulk more comfortably in the chair and looked up at the gaunt, sallow face of the pirate.

"I'll tell you what's to prevent it," he said. "Look you, Sarne, Harry Morgan's never yet walked into a trap he couldn't walk out of again when he chose, and on this occasion the snare is of my own setting. Ashore yonder they've been drinking these two hours and more, but whereas your men are now drunk, mine only appear so." He laughed. "A happy thought, that cargo of wines! As for the *Ventureer,* we used her to get past the battery on the bluff yonder, but you'll not be supposing me fool enough to venture here in no more strength than that. There's two ships of mine none so far off, but keeping the island 'twixt you and them." He chuckled again. "You should have used more caution, Sarne, than to join forces with one of my most loyal followers."

"The lousy traitor!" Sarne swung round upon Shergall, but was brought up short by the pistol of formidable proportions which had miraculously appeared in the smaller man's hand. Above that unwavering barrel Captain Shergall's mournful eyes met his steadily, and as he advanced Sarne was forced to retreat, until he all but fell over a chair. He dropped into it anyhow, and shot a desperate glance at his only hope of escape—Gideon Crayle.

The hunchback was leaning back in his chair, the tips of his unnaturally long, white fingers pressed lightly together and an expression of benign interest on his handsome face. Just for an instant his eyes met Sarne's in a glance which commanded him, as plainly as words could have done, to leave the whole affair in those same delicate hands, and though the pirate had no choice but to obey, he was by no means certain of the outcome. A single incautious word concerning the prisoners, coming to Morgan's ears from one of the drunken revellers ashore, would precipitate a disaster which not even Crayle could explain away. In his heart he cursed the tortuous schemes of vengeance which had led Gideon to delay their deaths, and, had the opportunity been suddenly given him, would readily have murdered all four of them to save his own neck.

Meanwhile, in the solitude of her cabin, Frances had come slowly out of her swoon knowing nothing of the powerful protector so close at hand. For a while she lay motionless in the darkness, trying to close her mind to the horror evoked by the memory of Gideon's words and the hopelessness of her own position. She had striven so hard to save them all, pitting her wits and her beauty against the evil desires of her captors, but now, in the very moment of success, she had to own herself defeated. Jonathan would be murdered, Crispin, whom she loved so dearly, broken and maimed by the torture, and she herself would become the prey of one or other of the pirates. Even the little dagger, which at first had seemed a sign from Heaven, was but another cruel trick of fate, useless unless it were to take her own life.

Despair claimed her for a time, but at length, out of despair, there grew a strong resolve. If she could not save those she loved, she could at least avenge them—that, perhaps, was the purpose for which the weapon had been placed in her hands.

She rose from the bed and fumbled with trembling fingers for flint and steel. When at last she had kindled the hanging lantern she turned to the chest and, spilling the costly garments heedlessly on to the floor, came at length upon the thing she sought. As she stood erect with the dagger in her hands the mirror showed her a face she scarcely recognized as her own, for though the tears were barely dry on the white cheeks there was a desperate purpose in eyes and lips. Her hands were steady enough now as she drew the weapon from its jewelled sheath and watched the light ripple along the bright blade. Her fear of Gideon was lost in a burning hatred, and she could contemplate quite calmly the thing she meant to do. Sooner or later he must come to release her, and that, God aiding her, should be his last action on earth.

At that moment the handle of the door turned.

Frances swung round, stifling a cry. Could it be that fate had brought Gideon to her at the one moment when she had nerved herself to kill him? She tossed the sheath back into the chest and faced the door resolutely, her left hand at her breast and her right, still gripping the dagger, hidden in the ample folds of her skirt.

A full minute crawled past before she heard the key turn in the lock, and a hand fumbled again at the door handle. The laboured movements, and a sound of heavy, difficult breathing which accompanied them, filled her with vague alarm, but she was wholly unprepared for the sight which met her eyes when at last the door swung open. Not Gideon but Jean-Pierre swayed on the threshold, clinging to the door-post for support. His face was ghastly, and his left hand pressed tight against his side, but between and over his fingers crept a slow, crimson stream which made a dark and ever-spreading stain on his gay, laced coat.

With a gasp of pity and dismay Frances started forward, the dagger slipping unheeded to the floor as she put out her hands to support him. His weight was too much for her and he sank to the ground, dragging her to her knees beside him, but she contrived to get her arm beneath his shoulders and raise him a little.

"Jean-Pierre!" she whispered. "Merciful God! Who has done this?"

"Sarne . . . damn him to hell!" he muttered painfully. "A coward's blow . . . he left me for dead . . . but I'll cheat him yet. Milady . . . Morgan . . . is here."

"Morgan here?" she repeated incredulously. "But how? Why?"

"For Sarne . . . the *Venturer* . . . Shergall betrayed us." The disjointed phrases, gasped out with such painful effort, brought conviction almost against her will, for she could not believe that such a miracle could come to pass when all hope seemed dead. Jean-Pierre shifted a little and a groan broke from his lips. "Go to him . . . he will . . . protect you."

"But you, Jean-Pierre," she was beginning, but he shook his head.

"Too late, *ma chère* . . . I am sped . . . but they shall go with me to hell." He tried to laugh, but choked in ghastly fashion. After a little he continued: "Sarne . . . shall not have you . . . nor shall Crayle. Crispin . . . your brother . . . in the hold. Morgan will . . . free them."

"I know," she whispered. "God bless you, Jean-Pierre."

A shadow of the old, mocking smile flickered across his face.

"A blessing, *ma belle?* You . . . know not what you say. The key . . . I stole it from Crayle. I . . . meant to break faith . . . with you." His head fell forward, and for a moment she thought him gone! Then with a supreme effort the heavy head was lifted again. "Tell them," he said more clearly, "who it was . . . who sent them . . . to the gallows."

He laughed, choked on a sudden rush of blood, and so died. When the brief struggle was over Frances lowered his head gently to the floor and remained for a few moments looking down at him, tears rising unbidden to her eyes. She knew that he had been prompted by no concern for her when he dragged himself with such agonized effort to release her, that his one thought had been to pull Sarne and Gideon Crayle down with him into oblivion, but the debt she owed him was not lessened for that reason. Kneeling there beside him, she murmured a brief prayer for this man who had died as he had lived, with laughter on his lips and thoughts of violence in his heart.

As she rose to her feet she felt a slight tug at her arm, as though the dead man sought to keep her at his side, and checked with a sudden thrill of horror. Then she saw that his hand had become entangled in the lace scarf about her shoulders, but, still in the grip of that unreasoning fear, she could not bring herself to unclasp the lifeless fingers. Flinging the scarf from her, she ran from the cabin without a backward glance.

The door of the great cabin was ajar, and within an unfamiliar, lilting voice was speaking, but its owner broke off to stare in blankest astonishment as her ladyship burst into the room. For an instant there was a silence so intense that it seemed almost tangible; then:

"As God's my life!" said the large gentleman emphatically. "Who the devil may you be, madam?"

Frances looked at him, and her last doubts were dispelled. That bold, arrogant face and commanding manner could belong to but one man.

"Sir Henry Morgan?" she said, half-questioningly, but did not pause for an answer. "Sir, I crave your protection for myself and for my friends. I am Frances Crayle."

Captain Sarne swore roundly, Sir Henry stared at Frances with eyes suddenly narrowed, and Gideon sat silent, his face inscrutable. The Earl started to his feet and spoke in a strangled voice.

"Frances Crayle?" he repeated. "You are Lady Frances Crayle?" He swung round to face Gideon. " 'Sdeath, sir! What villainy is here? Where is my son?"

"Aye," said Morgan softly, "tell us, my lord, how a lady presumably lost at sea comes to be aboard this ship."

"Madam," said the Earl abruptly to Frances, giving Gideon no chance to reply, "I am Larchwood. Where is my son?"

"Lord Larchwood?" she repeated, and stared at him, raising a hand to her brow. "How come you here? I thought——" She broke off and looked in growing perplexity from him to Morgan.

Sir Henry had risen to his feet, and now took her hand and bowed her gallantly to the chair beside his own.

"Now tell us, my lady," he said, resuming his own seat, "how came you aboard this ship, and where are your companions?"

"They——" Frances broke off and glanced uneasily at Gideon, for his utter lack of alarm had struck a sudden doubt into her mind. Why was he so calm, so unmoved by her unlooked-for appearance? She had expected to see him dismayed, furious, seeking a way of escape.

Meeting her gaze, Gideon spoke for the first time since she had entered the cabin.

"Tell them, my dear," he prompted her gently. "Let them hear from your own lips what has become of your brother and Mountheath and Captain Barbican."

Still she hesitated, and Morgan and the Earl exchanged puzzled glances. Larchwood spoke encouragingly.

"Come, my child, tell us. You have nothing to fear."

"They . . . they are prisoners aboard this ship," she faltered, but it was not the dramatic denunciation she had thought to make it. The hunchback's dark, unfathomable gaze still held hers, and the old fear of him returned with renewed force. "I, too, was imprisoned, but Jean-Pierre released me, and now lies dead. Captain Sarne killed him."

Gideon looked at the others. He raised his hands and let them fall again in a gesture of resignation.

"You see, gentlemen?" he said in a low voice. "You can all bear witness that Captain Sarne has not left this room since he entered it with us. Judge, then, the worth of whatever story this unfortunate lady may tell you."

"Good God!" exclaimed the Earl, staring at Frances. "What mean you, sir?"

"I think, my lord," Gideon replied sadly, "that you have already guessed the tragic secret which I had hoped to keep. Lady Frances has suffered greatly—too greatly. She is no longer sane."

The monstrous lie was spoken in tones of mingled grief and resignation, and Frances stared at him in horrified dismay. Was it possible that he expected so wild a tale to be believed? A glance at the faces of his hearers showed her doubt in their eyes, but it was doubt of her, and the realization brought her to her feet in quivering distress.

" 'Tis a lie!" she cried. "A vile lie! He knows that what I will tell can bring him to the gallows, and seeks to protect himself. Oh, you must believe me, you must!"

In her overwrought condition, with the horror of Jean-Pierre's violent death still upon her, she was fast becoming hysterical, and this lent colour to Gideon's words. He regarded her with some satisfaction, for with her blue eyes blazing in her white, tear-stained face, and her pallor heightened by her bright, disordered hair and sombre gown, she had a look of wildness which accorded well with what he had said of her. He read the growing doubt in Lord Larchwood's eyes, and though Morgan's countenance told him nothing the very fact that he did not attempt to question her spoke for itself.

"You must believe me!" Frances repeated desperately. "I can prove my words. I can lead you to their prison. My lord," she turned to the Earl, "your son is there, awaiting the death to which this villain has condemned him. Come with me now! Come, for the love of God!"

"Frances!" Gideon, deeming the moment apt, spoke in tones of gentle reproach. "My poor child, these are the wild fancies of a sick mind. Mountheath has been dead these many weeks, and you do but torture his father with false hopes." He came to her side and took her hand between his own, ignoring the way in which she shrank from him. "Come, my dear, let me take you back to your cabin."

"By your leave, sir." Morgan spoke with brisk authority. "Mad or sane, her ladyship will remain here until we have sifted this matter to the bottom. We await your explanation."

"So be it, then," Gideon agreed reluctantly. "It is a story which I had hoped never to tell, since to do so I must confess a sin of which I have since most bitterly repented, but matters have gone too far for anything but complete frankness to serve. First, however, I must disabuse your minds of any lingering hopes. Of those who sailed with Captain Barbican in the *Santo Rosario,* only Lady Frances still lives."

"He lies!" Frances broke in frantically. "The storm drove us here in a ship little better than a wreck, but not one life was lost. The *Santo Rosario* lies now upon the beach yonder." She flung out an arm in a wild gesture towards the stern windows. "Look, you may see her for yourselves."

Gideon sighed.

"That ship, gentlemen," he said, "is the *Seagull,* a buccaneering craft which put in here for careening a month ago. That you may verify—I do not ask you to accept my word that it is so."

"That, sir," said Morgan impatiently, "does not explain her ladyship's survival. No, madam, a moment, I pray." For Frances would have intervened. "We will hear your cousin, if you please."

Frances subsided into her chair, trying to calm her agitated thoughts, for she realized that to persist in her frantic denials was to play into Gideon's hands. She told herself that he could not prevail, that not even his cunning would avail him in the face of the evidence arrayed against him, but even as she comforted herself with this reflection she was conscious of a growing feeling that she was living through some ghastly nightmare from which there would be no awakening.

"To explain matters fully," Gideon was saying in a low voice, "it is necessary to go back to the time of her ladyship's betrothal to me, and I must confess, gentlemen, that she entered into that betrothal against her will. Her brother was ill, and I told her that unless she agreed to marry me he would not be permitted to recover. She believed me, and we were betrothed."

"Gad'slife, sir!" exclaimed Larchwood, as he paused. "You are infernally impudent, stap me if you are not! Lady Frances was to have wed my son."

The hunchback bowed his head.

"The reproach is deserved, my lord. What I did is beyond excuse or pardon, but what would you?" He flung out his hands, and bitterness and pain throbbed in his expressive voice. "Look well at me, gentlemen! Am I a figure to win a young girl's heart? And I loved her, loved her to distraction!" He turned to look at Frances, and face and voice softened to infinite tenderness. "I love her still," he added simply.

Bereft of speech by that colossal lie, Frances met his glance with one of mingled amazement and loathing. No whit perturbed, Gideon continued quietly:

"Although I had secured the promise of her ladyship's hand, her heart, as I well knew, was already in another's keeping. Ah, my lord," he added, turning to Larchwood, "when you planned the marriage of Lady Frances and your son you wrought more wisely than you knew. He loved her, and she him." He sighed heavily. "Would to God that I had never sought to come between them."

He paused, and the Earl, obviously much moved, covered his eyes with his hand. Morgan, however, with an elbow on the arm of his chair and his fingers caressing his moustache, looked thoughtfully from Crayle to Frances and back again.

"You are damnably slow, sir, in coming to the point of your story," he said brusquely. "We are not concerned, look you, with your past villainies and present repentance, but with the explanation of this lady's presence aboard this ship."

"Your pardon, Sir Henry." Gideon's cold civility seemed to rebuke the Welshman's rudeness. "I will endeavour to be brief. You will wonder, perhaps, why I did not marry her ladyship out of hand, but I wished to avoid any appearance of unseemly haste. Moreover, Jonathan was no better in health, and as time went by it became apparent that his illness was more serious than we had at first supposed. It was at this time that Captain Barbican returned to Jamaica.

"Now it appears that young Mountheath had certain suspicions, natural enough in the circumstances, concerning her ladyship's betrothal to me, and these he confided to Barbican. The buccaneer contrived to reach Lady Frances without my knowledge and so learned the truth, but though I knew nothing of this at the time I had reason to believe that some such attempt might be made and determined to delay my marriage no longer. This forced Mountheath's hand, and he resolved to carry Lady Frances off secretly on the eve of our wedding— with, of course, the assistance of Captain Barbican. This they achieved, and since she refused to be separated from her brother the sick boy went with them on their mad flight."

Again he paused, and this time no-one spoke. Frances, appalled by this skilful blending of truth and falsehood, wrenched her fascinated gaze from Gideon's face and looked anxiously at his other listeners. Morgan's expression she could not read, but Larchwood seemed already half convinced, and she saw with dismay that Sarne was grinning with frank amusement.

"Having made their escape from Port Royal," Crayle resumed after a moment, "the lovers may well have accounted their troubles at an end, but in this they were mistaken. Barbican, you see, cherished a violent and apparently hopeless passion for Lady Frances, and his readiness to assist the Viscount in his elopement was prompted by the desire to get her once more into his power. It is unlikely, I think, that any of his companions would ever have reached the English colony which was their goal."

"Continue, sir," said Morgan as Gideon paused, but his small, shrewd eyes were not upon Crayle. He was still watching Frances, who had risen protestingly to her feet. Sir Henry stretched out a hand that was half hidden in a fall of costly lace and drew her down again into her chair. "Well, sir, go on," he repeated impatiently. "Gad'slife, if this be brevity, may I be shielded from your notion of a lengthy tale."

"You desired an explanation, Sir Henry," Gideon replied with a hint of sharpness, "and it is necessary that I should make clear all the circumstances of my cousins' flight. Believe me, sir, the task affords me no gratification at all."

"Then a' God's name make an end of it," said Sir Henry unabashed. "Spare us any further conjectures upon what might have befallen them, and let us hear what did."

Crayle regarded him for a moment with faint hauteur, then, addressing himself somewhat pointedly to Lord Larchwood, he resumed his story.

"As you know," he said, "the *Santo Rosario* was overtaken by a violent storm, which in her unseaworthy condition, and manned as she was by a crew of rogues and poltroons, she failed to weather. When it became necessary to abandon the ship the crew tried to leave their Captain and his three companions to their fate, and it was only by dint of killing several of them that Mountheath and Barbican succeeded in placing her ladyship and her brother in one of the boats. Finding them so determined, the men drew off and made shift to escape as best they could, and, by accident or design, became separated from the boat bearing Mountheath and his companions, who, when dawn broke and the tempest subsided, found themselves alone.

"They made also a more tragic discovery, for little Jonathan was dead. Indeed, in his weak condition it was a miracle that he had survived for so long, but you may imagine the grief and bitter self-reproach which the discovery aroused in his sister.

"However, to make my story as brief as possible," he looked meaningly at Morgan, "I will spare you the details of their arrival at this island, which they accounted themselves fortunate in reaching. Here they found themselves amply supplied with food and water, and it seemed that it was merely a matter of time before they were rescued.

"This was not so. They had not been long upon the island before Barbican, himself a master of swordsmanship, provoked Mountheath into drawing steel upon him, with the deliberate intention of ridding himself of the last obstacle between himself and Lady Frances. That, my Lord Larchwood, is how your son met his death."

The Earl turned towards him a grey and stricken face.

"And Barbican?" he asked in a strangled voice. "By God, if the rogue still lives——"

"Rest you, my lord, the man is dead," Gideon replied calmly, and added: "There is little more to tell. A month ago the *Seagull* put in for careening, and Barbican, by means of his high reputation among the buccaneers, and his swordsmanship, which disposed of the previous captain, succeeded in placing himself in command of her. But for the chance which brought us here he might well have escaped and gone unpunished for his crimes."

" 'Tis false, every word of it!" Frances exclaimed brokenly. "They are alive, all three of them. Surely you can see that he is lying!"

Gideon sighed, as though these repeated accusations were growing wearisome.

"You are, of course, free to search the ship," he said sarcastically. "Perhaps it would be as well for her ladyship's peace of mind if you did so. In her affliction she finds it impossible to realize that they are indeed dead."

"Yet it occurs to me, sir," said Morgan, ignoring this suggestion, "that her ladyship must enjoy some periods of sanity, else you would not be so well informed upon events which occurred after the *Santo Rosario* left Port Royal."

"My dear Sir Henry," Gideon replied readily, "do not imagine that the story you have just heard came wholly from Lady Frances. From her I could glean only disjointed fragments of the truth, and a little I was told by the crew of the *Seagull*, but most of it Crispin Barbican was persuaded to confess—before we hanged him."

"Oh, so you hanged him?" said Sir Henry, mildly interested. "After he had been persuaded to confess?" He sat suddenly upright and there was a distinct menace in his next words. "Look you, sir, you take a deal too much upon yourself."

"Do I, Sir Henry?" The anger in Gideon's voice matched his own. "What of this unhappy lady? Can you not imagine what she must have suffered? Her brother dead, her lover murdered before her eyes, herself the helpless prey of a man as ruthless as Barbican? By God, sir, if the rogue could die a hundred deaths it would not avenge her wrongs!"

"My poor child!" Lord Larchwood came to Frances's side and took her hand in his; his voice shook. "I had hoped to call you daughter, but God has willed otherwise. You have no more to fear. You shall come home with me to England, and in time these terrible memories will fade and you will find a measure of peace."

"Sir," Frances turned towards him, placing a hand on his arm and speaking earnestly, "Hal is not dead. I saw and spoke with him only yesterday, and my brother and Crispin also. I can show you where they are imprisoned, if only you will come with me."

The Earl patted her hand and spoke soothingly, as though to a fretful child.

"I know, my dear, I know, but you must not trouble yourself now with such thoughts. Some day, when you are stronger, we shall speak of it again." He looked at his companions and shook his head. "Poor child. Poor child!"

Frances jerked her hand away and stared at him with something akin to horror in her eyes.

"You believe it!" she whispered. "You really believe that I am mad!" She broke off, pressing her hands to her head. "Merciful God, are you all bewitched? How can I convince you that I speak the truth? Will not one of you even look into

220

my cabin yonder? I tell you that Jean-Pierre lies there dead. Captain Sarne struck him down and left him for dead, but when he learned of your presence, Sir Henry, he dragged himself with his last strength to free me."

Morgan regarded her inscrutably.

"Would you have me believe, madam, that a man on the verge of death broke open a locked door to release you?"

"He had the key," she replied impatiently, and Gideon, clapping a hand to his pocket, exclaimed in well-feigned surprise.

"The key is indeed gone from my pocket," he said. "The light-fingered rogue must have stolen it for his own evil purposes." He swung round upon Sarne. "What do you know of this?"

The quick-witted ruffian seized upon his cue at once. To confess to one more murder could not greatly harm him, and he knew that his only hope of survival lay in Crayle. If the hunchback was defeated his own doom was sealed.

"I know nothing o' the key," he said sullenly, "but before you returned we quarrelled over the girl. Jean-Pierre drew a knife on me, but I was too quick for him, the mutinous dog. I thought he was dead, and cast him into the gangway yonder."

Gideon nodded.

"And he thought to be revenged upon us both by releasing Lady Frances, for he knew the sick fancies that trouble her concerning her companions. Yes, Sir Henry, no doubt you will find his body in her cabin."

With a sob Frances buried her face in her hands, struggling against a sensation of complete helplessness. For a moment she wondered desperately whether, by taking them unawares, she could reach the place of imprisonment and release Hal and Jonathan before she was caught, but she doubted whether she could find her way there in darkness and in haste.

"But if he had not released her," said Morgan suddenly, "what did you intend by her? You sought to keep her survival a secret even from her kinsman here. That seems strange to me, sir. Damnably strange, egad!"

"Lord Larchwood, sir, would have learned at a more fitting time of a matter which concerns no-one save her ladyship's family," Gideon replied sharply. "As for my intentions towards her, it was—and is—my hope that she will become my wife."

Frances looked up sharply, stung by that out of her daze of misery.

"Yes," she said brokenly, "you would marry me, would you not, to prevent me from denouncing you for the murderer that you are."

"But, my lady," said Morgan quickly, before Gideon could speak, "you insist that your three companions are alive. Your cousin is therefore no murderer."

She had no hope of being believed, and it was sheer defiance that made her fling her next accusation at Gideon.

"Is he not?" she retorted. "He murdered his own father because he stood in his way—yes, and boasted to me of the crime."

Lord Larchwood looked up sharply, and there was an infinitesimal pause before Morgan spoke again.

"Now that is a strange delusion, is it not?" he remarked. "What say you to that, sir?"

Gideon laughed lightly, though only he knew what an effort that laughter cost him. He had forgotten until that moment his reckless disclosure to Frances three days before.

"Merely, Sir Henry, that at the time of my father's death in London I was in Bristol, and also that were I indeed guilty of so foul a crime I would not boast of it to one who has no cause to wish me well."

"'Tis true, none the less," said Frances hopelessly, for she felt that the last wild challenge had finally convinced them of her madness. Her glance roved unhappily from one to the other, only seeking reassurance and finding none. At length it rested on the small, lean man who had been instrumental in bringing Morgan aboard, and who all this time had hovered like a silent, watchful shadow in the background. For a little she looked at him indifferently, and then her gaze quickened. She leaned forward.

"Captain Shergall," she said clearly, "when Crispin Barbican saved your life at Porto Bello you swore that if ever he stood in like danger you would aid him if it lay in your power." She paused, and knew from the sudden, tense silence that she had captured their attention. "Roger Shergall," she continued challengingly, "that danger threatens now, and only you can save him. Will you be forsworn?"

CHAPTER XXII

THE LIFTING OF THE SHADOW

IN the gloom of their prison Viscount Mountheath and the Marquis of Rotherdale sat in morose silence, each busy with his own thoughts. On a cask between them a lantern—unexpected and to them inexplicable generosity of Captain Sarne—shed its feeble light impartially over both, gleaming on the boy's bright hair and white, weary face and deepening the lines on the young man's brow and about his mouth which made him appear older than his three-and-twenty years. They had exchanged barely a dozen remarks since her ladyship's visit the previous day, for Jonathan, shocked and dismayed by his cousin's attitude towards Crispin, whose place in the Marquis's affections was second only to that occupied by Frances, was for once disinclined to talk, and Hal was still brooding savagely over her ladyship's mad preference for a pirate captain instead of his noble self.

So they sat until the sound of the bolts of their prison being drawn startled them into attention. They exchanged puzzled and somewhat apprehensive glances, for food had been brought to them some time earlier and they had expected no further attention until the following morning. An unlooked-for visit might well mean death for them, or—the thought flashed through Jonathan's mind—the start of the torture with which Gideon had threatened Crispin.

The door opened just enough for the figure of a man to slip through, though the lantern light did not reach far enough to show them whether he was friend or foe. The stealthy manner of his entrance, and the care with which he closed the door, argued a desire for secrecy which set their hearts beating wildly, and then, as he advanced into the circle of light, they recognized him as Matt Briarly, the mate of the *Santo Rosario*.

He was clad only in the loose, rawhide breeches favoured

by the buccaneers, and he dripped sea-water at every step. Jonathan was the first to recover from his surprise.

"Matt!" he exclaimed in a joyful whisper. "How did you get here? Why? Have you come to help us escape?"

"One thing at a time, my lord," Matt replied softly, "and for the love of God speak quietly. Where's Crispin?"

"Over here." Jonathan picked up the lantern and led the way to the inner cell. "But the door is locked."

"That's no more than I expected, lad," Briarly replied cheerfully, and drew a marline-spike from his belt. He inserted this between the door and the staple on which the lock was hung, and at the third or fourth attempt the staple came away with a sound of rending wood.

For a few breathless seconds they listened intently, but no alarm was given and they concluded that the noise had passed unnoticed. Matt dragged open the door and Crispin stumbled out, blinking in the sudden light.

"Plague on't, Matt. I had begun to doubt you," he greeted him. "Two days in that damned hell-hole would take the heart out of any man."

"Small use in freeing you wi' no refuge to fly to," Matt retorted. "Here, lad, let's have them irons off you." He produced a stout file and went vigorously to work, and Jonathan said incredulously:

"Did you know then, Crispin, that Matt would come?"

Captain Barbican smiled.

"I knew that he would if he still lived," he replied, "but I feared that Crayle would suspect him of being well-disposed towards us."

Matt chuckled.

"So he did at first," he said, "until I convinced him that I cared only to be filling my pockets. After that 'twas only a matter o' keeping my ears pricked to learn what was going on aboard this devil's craft. I could ha' had you out o' here ere this, had there been any hope o' you remaining free."

"What now, then?" Crispin asked quietly. "Shergall?"

The old buccaneer shook his head.

"Better'n that, lad," he replied. "Morgan! There's two ships flying English colours hove-to on t'other side o' the island, and who but Welsh Harry would venture to Pirates' Island in a King's ship?"

"Morgan!" Crispin repeated, and was silent for a little. At length he said: "He will be after Sarne, no doubt, and I'd stake my life Roger Shergall has some hand in the business. I thought it passing strange that he should join forces with Sarne." He looked sharply at Briarly. "You know how the land lies, Matt. What do you propose?"

"Arm ourselves first," Matt replied, "and then look for her ladyship. Crayle's keeping her locked in her cabin out o' Shergall's way—I had that from Jean-Pierre. Then try to get ashore. Shergall's aboard now, and his boat's left unguarded."

Crispin frowned.

"What chance have we of reaching the shore unobserved?"

"Fair enough," Matt replied with a shrug. "The crews are ashore and most of 'em dead drunk by now. There's no guard on the ships, but the men up on the bluff yonder might give the alarm."

" 'Tis a risk we must take," said Crispin firmly. "Once ashore we should be safe enough if we give the camp a wide berth, and if we can cross the island we can signal in some way to Morgan's ships. How did you learn of their presence, Matt?"

"By chance," Briarly replied. "I knew that Jean-Pierre was plotting mutiny, and I'd a notion we'd be well out of it until we knew which side had prevailed, and so I was looking for some place where we might lie hid for a while."

"I do not understand," said Hal, speaking for the first time, "why it is necessary for us to break free at all. If Sir Henry Morgan is here in force to arrest Sarne, why do we not await him here?"

"And provide yon crook-backed devil wi' hostages, so that he may bargain his way to freedom?" said Matt scornfully. "He's no fool, my lord, and he'd realize soon enough the value of his prisoners."

He prised open the link on which he had been working, the chains dropped to the floor, and Crispin stood free, though the iron manacles were still about his wrists. He stood up and stretched his arms to ease his cramped muscles, looking sardonically at the Viscount.

"Once again, my lord," he said, "it is necessary for us to set aside our differences in order to make an escape. I can, I suppose, depend upon you to follow me without question?"

"Of course," Hal replied stiffly. "There will be time enough to settle personal disputes when we are free of this coil."

"Then a' God's name let us delay no longer, and move softly as you value your lives. Come!"

He led the way out of their prison with Hal at his heels, Jonathan following and Matt bringing up in the rear. They encountered no-one, and having armed themselves from the ship's plentiful supply of weapons they crept stealthily aft, until, in a narrow gangway on to which the cabins opened, Crispin checked them suddenly with a whispered word. Ahead of them a door stood wide, and light streamed out to slash a bright pathway across the darkness.

Signing to them to remain where they were, Crispin crept forward until he could see into the lighted room, and then with a stifled exclamation he disappeared through the doorway. Alarmed by his bearing, his companions followed him, but were brought up short on the threshold by the scene which met their eyes.

Against the farther wall stood a carven chest from which rich, feminine attire had been dragged to trail in a mass of sombre colour on to the floor, showing only too plainly who had been the coccupant of the cabin. On top of the heap of silk and velvet lay an unsheathed dagger, its bright blade and jewelled hilt glittering in the light of the lantern which swung from the roof, and midway between the chest and the door Crispin was kneeling beside the body of Jean-Pierre. The Frenchman lay in a pool of blood, his ghastly face upturned and the fingers of his right hand clenched tight upon a scarf of black lace which they had last seen about the shoulders of Lady Frances. Crispin rose slowly to his feet and turned towards them a face as white, almost, as that of the dead man.

"We come too late," he said in a low voice. "This was her cabin." He paused to look round the small apartment, and his hand clenched tight upon the sword he held; then, "Get you to the boat," he added shortly.

"Good God!" exclaimed Hal. "You cannot leave the ship without making any attempt to discover what has become of her."

"You blind fool!" Crispin turned upon him savagely. "Can you not read the tale this room tells? This was her scarf, that her dagger." He pointed to it with his sword; his voice shook. "In the last extremity she meant to use it upon herself, yet there it lies, drawn, but with no stain upon it." He broke off and passed his free hand across his eyes. After a moment he added more calmly: "Matt, take them to the boat. Make your way to Morgan if you can, and tell him what has befallen here. I have a reckoning to demand of Gideon Crayle and his jackal, Sarne."

Matt's eyes were troubled.

" 'Tis certain death, lad."

"If I can send those two into hell before me I shall have lived long enough. Think you that life holds aught for me now but the hope of vengeance?" He set his hand on Briarly's shoulder and his face softened for an instant. "Carry the boy to safety, old friend, and in part at least the oath I swore to a dying man will be fulfilled."

Without waiting for an answer he stepped past them and went, with no further attempt at stealth, towards the great cabin. Matt looked after him and shook his head.

"Come on, lad," he said heavily, taking Jonathan's arm. "We can do naught to aid him. The whole pack of 'em will be upon us in a moment, and we may have to swim for it yet." He led the boy out of the cabin, leaving the Viscount to follow or not as he chose.

In the great cabin Frances had just made her impassioned appeal to Roger Shergall, and into the startled silence which succeeded it walked Captain Barbican, with death in his face and a naked sword in his hand. He strode into the cabin like an avenging spectre, but at sight of Morgan he stopped short in an amazement so great that even the thought of Frances was momentarily driven from his mind.

"Harry!" he exclaimed incredulously. "What miracle brings you here?"

"One of my own contriving," Morgan replied complacently and with no sign of surprise. "You come in a good hour, Crispin, to spare me the trouble of searching for you."

But the Captain's gaze had already passed beyond him to Frances, who had risen to her feet with a cry of joy and thankfulness. She ran to him, and he put his left arm around her—his right hand still held the drawn sword.

"Frances!" he said unsteadily. "Thank God that you have come to no harm! When I found you gone from your cabin I feared—" He broke off and his arm tightened about her.

Sir Henry chuckled.

"Time enough for dalliance when this affair is ended," he informed him. "What has become of your fellow-prisoners?"

Crispin glanced at him.

"They should be on their way to the shore by now," he replied. "There was a boat ready to hand."

Morgan nodded, and looked at Captain Shergall.

"Fetch them back, Roger," he ordered, "and give the lads the signal. We'll make an end here as quickly as may be."

Shergall went out, and Sir Henry transferred his attention to Gideon Crayle. The hunchback had neither moved nor

227

spoken since the appearance of Captain Barbican had brought
his elaborate edifice of falsehood tumbling about him, but in
his eyes was the bitter knowledge of ruin and defeat. Facing
him across the table, Randolph Sarne realized that he, too,
was lost, and submitted himself to his fate with the stoical resignation of his kind. He would mount the gallows cheerfully
enough, having made his peace with Heaven and assured of
forgiveness for his many sins—such was the simple faith of
the buccaneers.

But Crayle lacked even this slight consolation, for his trust
was in himself alone, and that faith had failed him at the last.
He had played for a great prize, but just when it seemed within his grasp the dice had fallen against him, and though he
might succeed in saving his neck, without the power for which
he had gambled life would be a hollow mockery. He had no
desire to live a broken man.

His gaze rested broodingly upon the man who, more than
any other, had brought about his downfall, and had he had a
pistol to hand Captain Barbican would have been doomed.
But, lulled to false security by the strength of his position,
Gideon had of late gone unarmed, and even vengeance was
denied him.

Lord Larchwood was staring at the Captain with perplexity
and some dismay. Morgan's words had informed him of the
identity of this tall, grim-faced stranger, but so greatly had
Gideon's story wrought upon him that he was not yet certain
whether or not he was looking upon his son's murderer. The
joy with which Lady Frances had greeted the buccaneer
should have convinced him that Crayle had been lying, but it
merely added to his mental confusion.

To relieve his most pressing anxiety there came the sound
of hurrying footsteps, and Mountheath himself burst into the
cabin with Jonathan and Matt Briarly at his heels. Shergall
had found them still aboard the *Vampire*, engaged in a violent
dispute arising out of Hal's determination not to leave the
ship without more certain knowledge of her ladyship's fate,
and Matt's equally strong resolve to place the young Marquis
in safety with all possible speed.

Morgan waited patiently while the Earl embraced his son
and his youthful kinsman, noting meanwhile with grim
amusement the darkling glance which the Viscount cast upon
Frances and Crispin. When he judged that the greetings had
lasted long enough, Sir Henry brought them to an end with a
brisk reminder that a good deal remained to be explained.

"As for you, Mr. Crayle," he continued, "you will consider yourself my prisoner. I am placing you under arrest."

Gideon made a gesture of resignation.

"I have no choice, it seems," he replied insolently, "but may I know upon what charge you hold me? You would appear to have a wide choice."

"One will suffice," Morgan replied uncompromisingly. "Murder—or, to be more particular, parricide."

"Indeed?" Gideon raised his brows. "Her ladyship's word against mine? You surprise me, Sir Henry."

Morgan smiled his catlike smile.

"You will be more surprised anon," he promised him. "My Lord Larchwood, inform Mr. Crayle of the mission which brought you to Jamaica."

"Willingly," the Earl replied promptly, and turned to Gideon. "Some time after your father's death there came to light a paper signed by him in which he confessed to causing the death of his brother Richard, and made certain accusations against you concerning your intentions towards your cousins. He stated also that he feared for his own life at your hands, since he, too, stood between you and the marquisate, and you were skilled in the study of poisons. He so ordered matters that this paper should be discovered only in the event of his death, and in the fullness of time it came to pass as he had planned."

He paused, but Gideon made no comment. He sat very still, his long fingers clenched so tightly upon the arms of his chair that the knuckles shone like polished marble. After a moment the Earl continued:

"This remarkable document, being placed before the King, occasioned His Majesty some perplexity. He could not ignore it, and yet it could not be taken as absolute proof of your guilt since it was known that you and your father had quarrelled bitterly upon that very subject. Lord Henry had known that he was suspected of instigating the murder of his unfortunate brother, and rumour had it that he had taken his own life to escape the consequences of his crime. Finally it was decided that I, being closely concerned in the matter, should travel to Jamaica, whence my son had sent me word that you had taken charge of your cousins, and endeavour to learn from your treatment of them whether or not there was any truth in Lord Henry's accusations. Tonight, Mr. Crayle, that question has been answered."

For some moments after Lord Larchwood ceased speaking

there was a profound silence, for the thought of the dead man who had reached out from the grave to bring justice upon the son who had murdered him cast a chill over them all. It was Gideon who broke the silence at last, broke it with a mirthless laugh.

"Gad'slife!" he said callously. "I did not suppose that the old fool had wit enough for such a plot. Wherever I might have looked for betrayal, 'twas not there."

"You admit it, then?" said Larchwood, half incredulously. "You confess to the murder of your father?"

Gideon shrugged.

"Why not?" he said indifferently. "If you fail to prove me guilty of that you will break me upon some other charge. Yes, I killed him. He died by poison, swiftly but, I trust, most painfully." His hands clenched again upon the arms of his chair, and into his voice crept the terrible note of hatred that Frances had heard when he spoke of Lord Henry's death. " 'Twas a poor enough revenge for all that I suffered at his hands when I was a child. Was it through any fault of mine that I was born thus mis-shapen? My father never forgave me for it, as I never forgave him for the slights he put upon me, though I thought the debt paid when I made his crimes known and sent him to rot in hell. Oh, damnable irony that his should be the hand to drag me down!"

He seemed scarcely aware of his companions as he spoke, for his features were distorted and his eyes blazing with insane hatred. So for a moment, and then the satanic fury faded from his face, the clenched hands relaxed, and the heavy lids dropped once more over the evil, tormented eyes. Incredibly he laughed, softly and with wicked amusement.

"Egad, we are an estimable family, are we not? My uncle a traitor, my father guilty of a brother's blood, and I of my father's, while Frances, for all her sweet face and saintly air, is the paramour of a pirate. I wonder what vice time will reveal in Jonathan?"

Crispin, wasting no time on words, moved purposefully forward in a way that boded Crayle no good, but Morgan had risen to his feet and his bulky person was interposed as if by chance between them. The impatient oath which rose to Crispin's lips was checked as he met the elder man's compelling glance, and it was left to Mountheath to voice a protest.

"Liar!" he exclaimed furiously, and had his father not clutched his arm he would have struck Crayle across his pale and smiling face. "Keep your foul tongue and fouler thoughts from her! She is innocent—I would stake my life on't!"

"My dear Hal," Gideon protested, "such faith is touching, upon my soul it is, but somewhat rash under the circumstances. One can only suppose that you are deliberately blinding yourself to the obvious truth."

" 'Tis a lie!" Hal was almost stuttering with rage. "A vile lie—!"

"Is it?" said Gideon gently. "Then why does she not deny it? Why does the gallant Captain not spring to the defence of maligned beauty?"

"Aye." Larchwood released his son and turned with sudden suspicion to Crispin. "Have you nothing to say, sir?"

"I have, my lord." Crispin was keeping a rigid hold upon his temper, but not all his efforts could drive the scorn and anger from his voice. "In lending even a moment's credence to such a slur upon her ladyship you dishonour both yourself and her. Lady Frances is my promised wife."

This announcement was received in startled silence, for not even Hal had supposed that they were already betrothed. Again it was Gideon who recovered first.

"I should have guessed that, of course," he remarked pensively. "Not only is she beautiful, but when Jonathan inherits Rotherdale she will be a great heiress. Captain Barbican, I salute you."

"Frances!" Hal turned to her incredulously. "It cannot be true! You cannot have been mad enough to promise yourself to this adventurer!"

Frances drew herself up proudly. A tinge of colour had crept into her wan cheeks, but she placed her hand in Crispin's and faced them all composedly.

"I have plighted troth with the man I love," she said quietly, "and I care not whether he be prince or pirate. My hand is mine to bestow where I choose, and"—she turned to smile to Crispin—"I have chosen."

Gideon laughed softly.

"Another _mésalliance_ contemplated," he remarked. "A year ago 'twas Hal's play-actress, now 'tis a pirate. B'gad, Larchwood, our young kinsfolk are singularly misguided in their affections!"

Stung by this reminder of his plans for the future of Hal and Frances, the Earl frowned ominously upon her ladyship.

"So you have chosen!" he repeated. "Bold words, madam!

But I would remind you that I am your guardian, and have some voice in the bestowal of your hand. It would ill become me to countenance your marriage to a man of low birth and no fortune."

"My Lord Larchwood," Crispin broke in firmly, "I am aware of your authority over Lady Frances, and in all humility I ask you for her hand in marriage. I am not a poor man, and as for my degree, I am of gentle, though not of noble, birth. My brother is Sir Oliver Barbican of Kings Lovat in Gloucestershire, and for the rest Sir Henry Morgan will vouch for me. We have been friends these many years."

"So pleads the suitor," said Gideon, as though to himself. "This is the swashbuckling Captain in a new rôle."

"And if I refuse?" Larchwood demanded coldly. "What then, Captain Barbican?"

"Then I shall regret it, my lord," Crispin replied quietly, "but I shall wed her in spite of you. She is mine, and not all the guardians in the world shall take her from me."

"And there speaks the pirate." Gideon's voice was malicious. "Methought this sudden humility would be of short duration. Hal, my friend, you are sped. While he lives he will yield her to no man."

His words had a disastrous effect on the Viscount. Already racked by the jealousy which had tormented him for months, and which during his recent captivity had become his paramount emotion, he had been goaded beyond endurance by the hunchback's repeated jibes. At his side swung still the sword filched from the *Vampire's* armoury, and at Crayle's final taunt he cast discretion aside and, dragging it from its sheath, flung himself upon the unarmed and unprepared buccaneer.

"Then if he'll not yield her living," he exclaimed furiously, "let him die and be damned!"

It was fortunate for Crispin that almost the width of the cabin was between them, for had they been closer he would have had no hope of escaping that murderous thrust. As it was he sprang aside, missing death by inches, and snatched up the rapier which he had cast aside on discovering Morgan's presence. Like Mountheath, he was now in a towering rage, and engaged the Viscount with every intention of killing him.

So quickly had the thing happened that even Morgan was taken unawares, and so furiously were they fighting that in the cramped and overcrowded cabin he dared not intervene. For a few seconds he watched intently, his small, shrewd eyes following every movement of the flickering blades, and he cursed beneath his breath. He had seen Captain Barbican fight before, and he knew that against him Lord Mountheath had no hope of prevailing, or even of defending himself for more than a few minutes.

Crispin was pressing the Viscount hard. It would be only a matter of moments now, for the younger man's defence was already faltering. He had fought before, but never under such conditions and never against such a swordsman as the buccaneer. He saw death leering upon him, read it in the pitiless grey eyes beyond the flashing swords, and suddenly life seemed a very precious thing, even life without Lady Frances. Too late he regretted the unbridled jealousy which had led him to attack Captain Barbican.

He fell back a pace, and Crispin, following, had a sudden glimpse of Gideon Crayle, who had not moved from his seat beside the table. The hunchback sat in his favourite attitude, with the tips of his long, white fingers pressed lightly together and a smile of wicked satisfaction on his pale face, and suddenly several things were made clear to Crispin. He realized that Gideon had deliberately provoked this quarrel, that even in the hour of his defeat he was scheming to drag his enemies down with him. If Hal were killed so soon after being restored to his father, Larchwood would not let his death go unavenged. He would demand nothing less than the life of the man who had killed his son, and though Crayle was himself doomed he would have the satisfaction of knowing that he had blasted the lives of those who had brought about his downfall. This, then, was the reason behind the urgent warning in Henry Morgan's eyes as he stepped between his friend and Gideon a short while ago.

All this flashed through Crispin's mind in the space of a heartbeat, and at the same moment his sword beat Mountheath's weapon aside and leapt on unhindered to his throat. Someone gave an audible gasp of horror and Gideon's pale smile broadened, but the bright blade checked with its point almost touching the lace beneath Hal's chin.

So for a moment they stood motionless, the Viscount backed against a chair, his face deathly pale and beaded with sweat, Crispin grim as fate, and the slim blade glittering between them. The onlookers held their breath, afraid to speak or move lest they precipitate a tragedy. At length Hal's courage broke beneath the strain of that silence, with the dark face watching him inscrutably across the keen death that hovered at his throat.

"Make an end, damn you!" he gasped. "In God's name make an end!"

Very slowly Captain Barbican lowered his sword until the point rested upon the floor. He shook his head.

"No, my lord," he said quietly. "We'll not give Mr. Crayle the satisfaction of seeing us destroy each other in the hour of our deliverance."

Hal gaped at him, not understanding and scarcely daring to believe that he had escaped, but Sir Henry Morgan took the point at once.

"Thanks be to God you've seen sense at last!" he said shortly. "I feared you'd never realize that yon smooth-tongued devil was making fools of the pair of you. Now let us make an end of this affair! The lads will be aboard by now and the ship in our hands." He chuckled. " 'Twill be a rude awakening for those rascals ashore when they find the *Vampire* captured and their leaders dead or prisoner without a shot being fired. You"—he turned to Matt Briarly—"go summon me men to make these two rogues fast. We'll put them where they can do no further harm." Matt went out and Morgan looked at Larchwood. "You are satisfied, my lord?"

The Earl inclined his head.

"Perfectly, Sir Henry. Crayle must, of course, be sent to England to stand his trial, but there is now no doubt of his ultimate condemnation."

Gideon had not spoken since Hal's attack upon Captain Barbican, and now sat with an elbow on the arm of his chair and his right hand pressed in a curious gesture against his lips. At the Earl's words he looked up, his face even more pallid than usual and his dark eyes brilliant and mocking.

"I shall never be condemned," he said, "because I shall never be brought to trial. Fools! Did you suppose that I had never envisaged this danger? That I would submit me meekly to being carried back to England to become a galanty-show for the rabble of London? Look now upon this ring!" He thrust out his right hand, on the third finger of which he invariably wore the antique opal. "It came out of Italy, and I have worn it night and day these seven years. 'Twas my last defence, and it has served my purpose."

Staring upon that slender white hand emerging from its cloud of lace, they saw that the gem had risen from its setting like the lid of a box, revealing a tiny cavity beneath. Gideon laughed at the dismayed comprehension in their faces.

"Aye, poison!" he flung at them. "I could not use a sword, so I found me a more subtle weapon. Would to God, Crispin Barbican, I had used it upon you the night we met in Port Royal!"

The last words were spoken in a choking whisper, and he clutched at the lace at his throat as though he would tear it off. He tried to rise to his feet, but pitched forward and fell writhing to the floor. His last moments were not pleasant to watch, but the poison was as swift as it was violent and the end came mercifully soon. When it was over and he lay still at last, there was something oddly pathetic in the huddled, clumsy body, and the ravaged features from which all semblance of beauty had disappeared.

"Poor devil!" said Crispin quietly at length, and Frances, who had been crouching in a chair with her hands covering her face, looked up at him wonderingly.

"You can forgive him?" she whispered.

Crispin shook his head.

"Forgive him, for all that he made you suffer? No, but who can say that, with that cross to bear"—he pointed with his sword to the mis-shapen body—"he would have been otherwise? It is not for us to judge him."

The door opened to admit Roger Shergall, with Matt and two more sturdy fellows at his heels. The little man came in briskly, with the air of one who has successfully carried out an important task, but he stopped short with an oath at sight of Crayle's body. Morgan, who had watched with unmoved countenance the whole tragedy, spoke calmly:

"All is well, Roger?"

"Aye, the ship is in our hands." Shergall's eyes were still upon Gideon. "What happened here?"

"Poison," said Sir Henry briefly. "In the ring he wore, carried to cheat the gallows. Have him carried hence, and bestow Sarne in some secure place. You found Jean-Pierre?"

Captain Shergall nodded.

"In my lady's cabin, as she said, and blood in the gangway between that door and this. Little doubt how he met his death."

In accordance with Sir Henry's instructions the corpse was borne away, and in its wake went Randolph Sarne, a prisoner in the ship he had commanded for so long. The *Vampire* would sail no more with the black flag flying; the Lieutenant-Governor of Jamaica had taken her as a prize of war, and when next she put out from Port Royal it would be under the command of one of those trusty captains of whose loyalty Sir Henry was certain. The sometime admiral of the black could find a ready use for a vessel of the frigate's quality.

"So ends a strange business," he remarked now on a note of satisfaction. "There's a deal more still to be explained, stap me if there's not, but one thing at least is certain. There's no more to be feared from that ill-formed villain. You may rest easy at last, my Lord Rotherdale, and so may your lady sister." He turned to her as he spoke, with a resumption of his air of gallantry. "Madam, in a few hours it will be possible for you to go aboard my own ship, for it's not likely that you'll wish to make the journey back to Port Royal in this craft, not likely at all. I'll see to't, madam, as soon as may be."

Frances tried to thank him becomingly, but to her own ears her voice had a curious, faraway sound, and her surroundings were beginning to assume an air of unreality. She knew that he spoke no more than the truth, that Gideon was dead and they had nothing more to fear, but her mind refused to accept the fact. The danger had been so great, and had threatened for so long, that she could not yet realize that it existed no longer. She knew that she should feel relief at their escape, but was conscious only of an overwhelming weariness.

It was, of course, the inevitable reaction from the strain of the past few days, and the culminating horror of this dreadful night when she had seen two men die violently and had herself come near to taking a man's life. Never, afterwards, could she recall with any clarity the events immediately following the death of Gideon Crayle, though she had a hazy memory of being carried in Crispin's arms to a boat which took them both, with Jonathan, Hal and Lord Larchwood, to the larger of the two English ships which had appeared during the night. There for two days she kept to her cabin, seeing no one but her brother, and so she knew nothing of the steps taken by Sir Henry to deal with the mob of cut-throats whom he had so cunningly made prisoner.

Great was the consternation among that ruffianly throng when with the dawn their carousal came to an end, and those among them who were still capable of coherent thought beheld the two unknown and heavily-armed ships which had apparently materialized out of thin air while they had been at their revels. But it was nothing to the dismay which visited them when a boat put off from the *Vampire* and, presently reaching the shore, disgorged a large and gaudy gentleman whom they had no difficulty in recognizing as Sir Henry Morgan.

Most of them were, at least, conscious by this time, the sleepers having been roused by their more hard-headed comrades to behold the singular spectacle of two ships which had miraculously become four, a phenomenon which could not possibly be attributed to that excellent Spanish wine with which they had made so disastrously free. Sir Henry walked through their ranks as calmly as though he trod his own quarter-deck until he reached a slight eminence, where he stood to regard them disparagingly before addressing them.

He spoke briefly and to the point, informing them that the *Vampire* was now in his hands, Sarne a prisoner, Crayle and Jean-Pierre dead. For the rest, he was disposed to be lenient. Those among them who were prepared to forsake their present evil trade, blandly announced the greatest buccaneer of them all, might return with him to Port Royal and there devote themselves to some more peaceable occupation. The rest would be left on the island with the careened galleon, and when they had succeeded in rendering her once more seaworthy they could sail her to hell or anywhere else they pleased, provided that it was not within the reach of the Lieutenant-Governor of Jamaica. Thus spoke Sir Henry, with sardonic glance, and a mocking curl to his heavy lips, and when he had done he betook himself once more to his ship and left Captain Shergall to deal with the discomfited pirates. Twenty-four hours later the four ships weighed anchor and set a course for Jamaica.

They had been a day and a night at sea, and Pirates' Island was but a memory, when Lady Frances ventured once more from her cabin. Escorted by my lord her brother, she came, a little timidly, to the poop-deck, where Captian Barbican was standing with Lord Larchwood and Sir Henry Morgan. The Viscount, Jonathan informed his sister, was keeping close in his cabin and sulking to his heart's content.

Crispin came forward eagerly to greet her and bore her hand to his lips, looking down at her the while with an expression in his grey eyes which brought the colour to her face. Lord Larchwood saluted her cheek and expressed a hope that she found herself recovered, and Sir Henry, with a magnificent bow, led her to a day-bed beneath an awning, which, he said, he had had placed there for her comfort when she should find herself well enough to join them.

She found his gallantry a little overpowering, but thanked him with a shy smile and sat down with the Earl at her side. Sir Henry engaged her in conversation in which Crispin joined, and they did not notice Lord Larchwood's silence.

His lordship, in fact, was wondering how best to broach a delicate subject, a matter which he heartily wished had been settled when it was first mentioned three nights ago. He was a proud man and hated anything which savoured of retreat, but upon mature consideration, and closer acquaintance with Captain Barbican, he had realized the folly of persisting in his objection to Frances's marriage to the buccaneer. He could, of course, forbid the match and force her to wed the Viscount, but it seemed highly probable that the unwilling bride would be carried off by her pirate captain before ever such a knot could be tied, or, if that did not succeed, that she would be a widow almost as soon as she was a wife. No, it would be better and safer for Hal to look elsewhere for a bride. There was, in England, a sixteen-year-old heiress who in birth and fortune, if not in beauty, was the equal of Lady Frances, and whose father had already made tentative inquiries concerning the Earl's matrimonial plans for his son. So decided Lord Larchwood, but there seemed no way of making his decision known and at the same time retaining his dignity.

In the end his dilemma was resolved by Sir Henry, who had no delicacy whatsoever and was curious to know how the affair would end. The simplest way of satisfying that curiosity was obviously a direct question; he asked it.

"Come, my lord," he said jovially, turning to the taciturn peer, "this is no time for silence. Tell us rather what you intend by her ladyship here and my good friend Crispin Barbican. Will you give your consent to the match, or must he carry her off by force?"

Frances blushed, but Crispin met the earl's eyes calmly enough.

"Aye, my lord," he said quietly, "tell us that, I pray. The time has come, I think, for us to arrive at an understanding."

Larchwood frowned and pursed his lips.

"Very well, Captain Barbican," he said reluctantly, "I will tell you. It is not what I had hoped for my ward, but since her grandfather thought so highly of you, and did not hesitate to entrust her to you then, I will offer no opposition to your marriage, provided—and this I insist upon—you abandon the trade of piracy and follow some lawful calling."

Sir Henry loosed a great guffaw of laughter.

"Softly, my lord, softly!" he said, before Crispin could reply. "He followed me through every Spanish stronghold from Puerto Principe to Panama, and since His Majesty was pleased to acquit me of any nefarious intent it follows that Crispin is blameless. For the rest, I'll stand surety for him, for I have need of such men in Jamaica if we are to prevail against the Dons." He laughed again, as though at some secret jest. "Aye, I'll be his surety!"

"One thing more," said the Earl, acknowledging Sir Henry's assurance with a somewhat frosty smile, but determined to do the thing handsomely since he was committed to it. "There is now in Jamaica a plantation lacking a master. Jonathan is Crayle's only kin and the estate will come to him, but it is my intention to make of it Lady Frances's marriage portion." He rose to his feet and smiled complacently upon them both. "No, do not thank me! It is, I think, an admirable solution. Now, Sir Henry, if you will be good enough to step aside with me, there is a small matter connected with Crayle's death which I should like to discuss with you."

Morgan chuckled.

"Aye, to be sure!" he agreed readily, and turned to Frances. "I cry pardon, madam, but your ladyship will understand that affairs of moment must be dealt with. Affairs of great moment, I assure you."

He bowed over her hand, clapped Crispin on the shoulder, and winked significantly at the Earl. Lord Larchwood, though deploring such vulgarity in one who held the important office of Lieutenant-Governor, permitted himself a slight smile in return, for he was feeling very pleased with himself. The matter of the plantation, he felt, had been a stroke of genius, for it would ensure that Lady Frances and her husband remained in the Indies, and there would be no opportunity for Lord Mountheath to compare the blue-eyed beauty he had lost with the plain but well-dowered damsel of his father's choosing. Nor would there be any necessity for the Earl of Larchwood to acknowledge a swashbuckling pirate captain as the husband of his ward. It was, as he had said, an admirable solution.

He moved away with Sir Henry, and Frances and Crispin found themselves alone, for Jonathan had long since wandered off towards the forecastle and the very unsuitable company to be found there. For a space they regarded each other in silence, half afraid of the great good fortune which had come so suddenly upon them. The crooked shadow which for so long had darkened their lives was gone for ever, and before them lay peace and security and the hope of happiness.

Captain Barbican dropped to one knee beside the couch, and, careless of any who might be watching, took his lady in his arms.

"Sweetheart," he said unsteadily, "it seems that after all you are to be given in marriage to a respectable planter. Thus does your noble guardian resolve all difficulties, for what matters the past when the future is ours?"

She smiled at him, and laid one small hand against his bronzed cheek.

"It matters not at all," she replied softly, "save that in the past I learned to love—and will always love—a pirate."